Praise for Edward Sklepowich's Mysteries of Venice:

LIQUID DESIRES

"A BOOK THAT FANS
OF THE SERIES WILL NOT WANT TO MISS…
Sklepowich creates a picture of Venice
that one can almost walk into…
The plot has twists more intricate than the path
through the Contessa's garden maze"

Mystery News

DEATH IN A SERENE CITY

"DAZZLING…TANTALIZING…
AN ELEGANT INTRICATE NOVEL"

Kirkus Reviews

"A THOROUGHLY CIVILIZED MYSTERY…
WITH A NICE MACABRE TOUCH"

The New York Times Book Review

FAREWELL TO THE FLESH

"AMBITIOUS AND SUCCESSFUL…
Sklepowich once again shows a fine feel for Venice."

Chicago Tribune

"Sklepowich paints a fascinating portrait of that
most exotic of Italian cities at its most exotic time"

Library Journal

Other Avon Books by
Edward Sklepowich

FAREWELL TO THE FLESH
DEATH IN A SERENE CITY

LIQUID DESIRES

EDWARD SKLEPOWICH

AVON BOOKS NEW YORK

AVON BOOKS
A division of
The Hearst Corporation
1350 Avenue of the Americas
New York, New York 10019

Copyright © 1993 by Edward Sklepowich
Published by arrangement with William Morrow and Company, Inc.
Library of Congress Catalog Card Number: 92-21981
ISBN: 0-380-72150-3

First Avon Books Printing: July 1994

AVON TRADEMARK REG. U.S. PAT. OFF. AND IN OTHER COUNTRIES, MARCA REGISTRADA, HECHO EN U.S.A.

Printed in U.S.A.

RA 10 9 8 7 6 5 4 3 2 1

The one-line statements in Liquid Desires *are the "Truisms" of language artist Jenny Holzer,* whose Venice Installation *was the official United States exhibit at* La Biennale/XLIV esposizione internazionale d'arte, *1990.*

. . . to lose myself in the luminous and Venetian corpuscles of my Gala's glorious body.
                                                    —*Salvador Dalí*

LIQUID
DESIRES

Venice Melting

FORGET ABOUT VENICE sinking into the sea. Its fate this late July seemed to be to melt into the lagoon.

When Urbino Macintyre boarded the vaporetto two days ago to escape to the Lido, he had felt as if he were abandoning some vast diorama by Salvador Dalí.

Call it *The Persistence of Summer*, with the fabled stones of the city unstable and liquid, its winged lions reflected in golden pools of their own melting, the tower of the Moor clock dissolving into blues and bronzes, and the snowy domes of the Church of the Salute diminishing down into the Grand Canal like mammoth scoops of vanilla ice cream.

Even here on the veranda of the Grand Hotel des Bains with the Adriatic only two hundred feet away and a Campari soda within much easier reach, Urbino felt stifled this afternoon. If New Orleans had ever been this bad, memory mercifully failed him. Thoughts of New Orleans bringing, however, an unwelcome reminder of the imminent visit of his former brother-in-law, Eugene Hennepin, Urbino occupied his mind by reviewing the little drama he had been innocently caught up in yesterday afternoon at the Biennale modern art exhibit in the Giardini Pubblici, the Public Gardens.

It was his second visit to this year's exposition. He had
been approaching the Italy Pavilion to take another look at the
paintings by a group of Italian artists when a figure had stormed
down the steps of the building and rushed past him. He could
see that it was a woman, but caught only the briefest glimpse of
a frightened, pale face behind large dark glasses. A plain brown
scarf covered the woman's hair and she grasped a knife close
to her side. Urbino moved instinctively away from the woman,
as did the other people around him, as she went through the
exit and became lost in the crowd. Several men ran after her
from the Italy Pavilion, one of them a guard with his eyes
streaming with tears.

When Urbino went into the building a few minutes later,
he learned what had happened. The woman had slashed a
controversial painting, *Nude in a Funeral Gondola,* by the Venetian artist Bruno Novembrini.

Against a background of a flooded Piazza San Marco, a
beautiful nude woman with luminous, pearl-colored skin,
bright green eyes, and a body less voluptuous than nubile was
reclining seductively in a funeral gondola. She wore only emer-
ald earrings, a thin gold bracelet, and a rose-colored Oriental
turban that lent a glow to her face, longish neck, and breasts.
She stared directly and provocatively at the viewer, one slim-
fingered hand nestled between her legs like Titian's Naked
Venus. The gondola, a deep shade of ebony, was draped in
thick black material and overflowing with flowers and wreaths.
At its prow was the Angel of Death with a torch. Another angel,
this one bearded like a biblical patriarch, and a lion weeping
into a black handkerchief hovered over the woman.

The attendants at the Italy Pavilion told Urbino that the
vandal, whom no one recognized, had gone directly to the painting, slashed it in one swift motion, and then escaped after spray-
ing a chemical substance at the two guards who tried to seize her.

Urbino now opened today's *Il Gazzettino,* where he found an
account of the attack. The woman had not been apprehended.
Massimo Zuin, the artist's Venetian dealer, said that the damage
to the painting had not yet been assessed.

Urbino's good friend the Contessa da Capo-Zendrini, sum-
mering in her villa up in Asolo, would be amused to hear about
the attack. She was sure to say that it was only what all this
modern art deserved, and especially this particular painting, a

reproduction of which she had seen in *Corriere della Sera*. The Contessa's comments on the Biennale were themselves as sharp as any knife brandished by a vandal could ever be. They hadn't become blunted since Urbino had first heard them at a Biennale reception ten years ago when he first met her.

During the previous Biennale, however, the modern art show had taken its revenge against her. It happened at the United States Pavilion at the exhibit of Jenny Holzer, an American artist who uses words as her medium and who won that year's coveted Golden Lion Award. The Contessa almost collapsed, so disagreeably affected had she been by the moving electronic lines of Holzer's text flashing ideological messages, pop psychology, and "mock clichés," as the artist herself called them, in five languages on the walls of a mausoleum-like room. One after another they had assaulted the Contessa:

A MAN CAN'T KNOW WHAT IT'S LIKE TO BE A WOMAN
ABUSE OF POWER COMES AS NO SURPRISE
EXPIRING FOR LOVE IS BEAUTIFUL BUT STUPID
AN ELITE IS INEVITABLE
HIDING YOUR MOTIVES IS DESPICABLE
KILLING IS UNAVOIDABLE BUT IS NOTHING TO BE
   PROUD OF
ROMANTIC LOVE WAS INVENTED TO MANIPULATE
   WOMEN
FATHERS OFTEN USE TOO MUCH FORCE
MOTHERS SHOULDN'T MAKE TOO MANY SACRIFICES
PRIVATE PROPERTY CREATED CRIME
ALL THINGS ARE DELICATELY INTERCONNECTED
MURDER HAS ITS SEXUAL SIDE
CHILDREN ARE THE MOST CRUEL OF ALL
I WILL KILL YOU FOR WHAT YOU MIGHT DO
DEATH CAME AND HE LOOKED LIKE A RAT WITH CLAWS
EVEN YOUR FAMILY CAN BETRAY YOU
MEN AREN'T MONOGAMOUS BY NATURE

Similar phrases had also been carved on the stone benches and in the marble floor tiles of the other rooms of the exhibit and had been printed on T-shirts, hats, posters, and billboards. They had been inescapable, even on the Venice water buses and in taxis across the lagoon in Mestre, but it was their electronic version at the United States Pavilion that had done the Contessa in.

She had reached for Urbino's shoulder and had him guide her to fresh air and sunlight, and then to a soothing *coppa* of gelato at the Caffè Paradiso outside the Biennale gates.

"I felt like that poor woman who went mad in the Marabar Caves in Forster's novel," she had said as she proceeded to spoon in her pistachio gelato. "My temples are still throbbing."

This year the Contessa was risking nothing. She was remaining cool and unruffled in her self-contained Villa La Muta in the hill town of Asolo not far from Venice. She vowed not to go anywhere near the Biennale grounds until every last piece of dubious art was crated back to where it should have stayed.

Continuing to page through the newspaper, Urbino came across a follow-up on a case that had shocked the city last week. A fifteen-year-old girl named Nicolina Ricci had been raped and murdered on one of the hottest days of the summer. Her parents, returning from an outing to the eastern shore of Lago di Garda, had found her naked body in her bedroom. The public had been spared none of the grisly details, including bloodstained bedsheets, multiple knife wounds, and the clump of hair gripped in one of Nicolina's hands. Today's paper reported that a forty-four-year-old man and close friend of the family, who lived alone in the same building, had confessed to the murder. Sexual obsession and the sultry sirocco, he said, had driven him mad.

Venice was a relatively quiet town, violence usually erupting on the mainland, but this summer had already seen Nicolina Ricci's vicious murder, the slashing of the painting at the modern art show, and several muggings of tourists in the less frequented alleys.

Urbino closed the paper. He looked off at the Adriatic, where the gray forms of ships were like ghosts on the horizon. A small plane droned over the water, and Vespas and bicycles passed along the Lungomare Marconi beyond the hedges of the hotel. A couple in a bicycle shay pedaled by, shaded beneath the floral canopy, and waved to him. An old man in a flat cap was crying *"Fragole fresche!"* outside the gates of the hotel. Urbino slipped off the veranda to buy a small box of the fresh strawberries and sat eating them as he mulled over what to do next.

Perhaps he would go down to the private strip of beach, take a swim, and then rest in one of the cabanas—just as he hoped to do tomorrow and the day after.

Urbino felt more than a little hedonistic in his *dolce far niente* existence at the Grand Hotel des Bains. Yet, although he might be "doing sweet nothing" here on the Lido, things hadn't been any better back at the Palazzo Uccello, where he had been trying to decide on his next biographical project and steeling himself for his ex–brother-in-law Eugene's visit.

Urbino was about to get up and go to his room to change his clothes for the beach when a welcome, familiar voice greeting one of the staff floated up to him from the brick pavement below the veranda. It was the Contessa da Capo-Zendrini. As she came slowly up the shell-shaped stone stairs, Urbino went over to her.

"Barbara, whatever are you doing here?"

The Contessa turned with a smile of mild exasperation on her attractive face. She wore a blue-and-green Fortuny dress that had once belonged to her mother and a pert straw hat. A furled green parasol was under her arm.

"To rescue you from all these purple hydrangeas and fronds and take you back to Asolo with me—and not just for my garden party tomorrow but for the rest of the summer. Don't tell me that you haven't the time! Look at the way you're languishing here like Aschenbach in your cream-colored suit! I know how you can allow yourself to sink indecently into summer. I insist that you do it up in Asolo."

Urbino kissed her cheek. It was pleasantly cool.

"Milo's waiting with the boat. You can go right home to pack and to get Serena, if you like." Serena was the cat Urbino had rescued on a wet November day in the Giardini Pubblici where the Biennale was held. "The car's at the Piazzale Roma."

"I can only come for the weekend, Barbara."

"Don't tell me you prefer a hotel to La Muta."

The Contessa looked around the veranda, where guests were absorbed in nothing more strenuous than their own sedentary pleasures. She wrinkled her nose, as if the Grand Hotel were a mere pensione with smelly drains and an obligatory breakfast of burned coffee and damp crackers.

"Have you forgotten that my ex–brother-in-law Eugene is coming up from Florence on Monday?"

"Can't you think of a less unwieldy way of referring to the poor man?" she reprimanded him as she sat down. "It's been ages since you were married to his sister."

"But that's the way I think of him."

"I'm afraid it means you haven't yet let go, *caro*, but I've never been one for psychologizing." She put her parasol on an empty wicker chair. "I'll have a *Coppa Fornarina*," she said, naming her favorite macaroon-and-cherry-garnished gelato she always ordered at Florian's. "They do have them here, don't they?"

"I'm sure they can make one, Barbara."

After ordering the Contessa's ice cream concoction and another Campari soda for himself—this time bolstered with some white wine—Urbino asked her how things were in Asolo.

"If you came more often than once or twice a month you wouldn't have to ask! Bands of teenagers have been running around pulling up plants and breaking windows. It makes me almost happy not to have had any children. They'd be going through the difficult years now."

Urbino let the Contessa's exaggeration pass. If she and Alvise had had children, even the youngest would have long passed through its difficult years. The Contessa must be approaching sixty, but suspicion was the closest he would come to truth until her seventy-fifth birthday when she promised a revelation. Urbino, twenty years her junior, felt that she was entitled to her vanity, especially since she looked a good ten years younger than sixty.

"I hope you appreciate my taking time out from all the preparations for the garden party to coax you into the hills of Asolo, *caro*. By the way, I broke down and extended a neighborly invitation to that retired American actress you've been wanting to meet—the one who's always parading around in pants and a turban and probably just waiting to break out in a leopard print and boa! *I've* never heard of her," the Contessa said a little too lightly, "but Silvestro has told me all about her."

Silvestro Occhipinti was the eighty-year-old longtime friend of the Contessa's dead husband, Alvise. In need of money, he rented out his villa to foreigners—currently the retired actress Madge Lennox—while living in several rooms in the center of Asolo.

"This impertinent person in pants is my last attempt to try

to persuade you gently to grace us all with your presence. I know you don't like *les grandes fêtes*, my dear, but this is my very own. If you refuse again, I'm prepared to have Milo strong-arm you."

The waiter brought the gelato and the Campari soda. For a few minutes the Contessa enjoyed her *coppa* in self-indulgent silence before filling him in on the gossip in Asolo. The most interesting was the story of a young American man who had been trying to gain devious access to Freya Stark, the well-known British traveler and writer, who had made Asolo her home for decades. The Contessa somehow held Urbino, as both a biographer and an American, responsible for the intrusion of his countryman.

The Contessa turned silent again and ate the rest of her *coppa* with the restrained enthusiasm of a well-bred child.

"You look as if you could use a pick-me-up yourself," she said when she finished. "Why don't we order you some gelato? Alcohol is going to debilitate you in this heat."

"Would you like another *coppa* yourself, Barbara?"

"Most definitely not."

But despite the Contessa's refusal Urbino knew she was tempted, the only thing holding her back being not satiation or the fear of gaining weight—something she seemed to be bless-edly immune to—but the embarrassment of being seen to in-dulge in two *coppe* in a row. She would be more than willing, however, to have her seconds somewhere else.

"An even better remedy than gelato for your haggard look, *caro*, would be La Muta," the Contessa persisted. "The fresh air will do wonders for you! I'll take better care of you than they do here—and it won't cost you a single, solitary lira. You *are* coming back with me, aren't you?" There was a plaintive look on her face. "It's just that I miss you so abominably. Doesn't my coming here all the way from Asolo on one of the hottest days of the summer prove that?"

"I've missed you, too, Barbara. Of course I'll come."

"Do you think I'll get to meet this ex–brother-in-law of yours, or are you going to keep him a big, dark secret like so many other things in your past?"

"You'll meet him. You might even like him better than me."

"An impossibility of the most impossible kind, *caro*—even if your Eugene is handsomer and younger than you are. I'm yours forever, a fate I haven't chosen. But I do hope he has some tales—or would he call them 'yarns'?—to tell of the days when your hair was as bright as Huckleberry Finn's and you hadn't yet become jaded!" She reached for her parasol. "Finish your drink and let's make a gracious but quick exit. I'll be walking in the garden while you arrange things. We might even have time for a real *Coppa Fornarina* at Florian's before we leave. This one"—she nodded down at the empty goblet—"left a lot to be desired."

Making no comment, Urbino signaled for the waiter.

PART ONE

Death on the Grand Canal

1

"Now, isn't this just what you needed?" the Contessa said softly
to Urbino as she seemed to glide past him the next afternoon to
greet a newly arrived guest in the gardens behind Villa La Muta.

Urbino smiled. The Contessa's "this" included not just the
sixteenth-century villa and its gardens with their grassy par-
terres and laurel-shaded dolphin fountain, the hidden, apparently random water sprays triggered by secret sources, the herb
and medicinal plant beds famous centuries earlier, and the maze
and the *giardino segreto* where they often shared tea and drinks.
It also embraced the view across the wide Trevisan plain to the
Alpine foothills, the walled, arcaded town above them with its
castle and citadel, and the lambent air playing over the hills—
everything, in fact, down to the brilliantly plumed parrot in the
brass cage under the pergola which kept saying *"Ciao!"* in a
distinctly clear and welcoming voice.

The Contessa's guests were gathered in decorous groups
on the various levels of the gardens. A string quartet played
Vivaldi, competing with the rustle of the wind and the singing
of the birds. The whole golden scene, suffused with an air of
dalliance and genteel conversation, was evocative of Watteau

and delicately burdened with that faint suggestion of the melancholy and the transitory so often found in his compositions.

The da Capo-Zendrini family had chosen its retreat well. Instead of following in the footsteps—or rather the boat wakes—of other eighteenth-century Venetians who had made their summer *villeggiature* on the banks of the now brackish Brenta Canal between Venice and Padua, the da Capo-Zendrinis had gone to the hill town of Asolo, twenty-five miles northwest of Venice, where they had taken over La Muta, designed by Palladio's follower Scamozzi. The British, who regularly descended on the area for villa tours, often mistook La Muta for one of Palladio's own buildings.

The woman Urbino was talking with now said that she had once made the same mistake. She wasn't British, however. She was the retired American actress the Contessa had mentioned yesterday on the Lido—the woman renting Silvestro Occhipinti's villa farther up the hill toward town.

Although the Contessa claimed never to have heard of her, Urbino certainly had. Madge Lennox had made a respectable reputation for herself in a dozen American films, playing primarily independent-minded women, and had lived in an air of notoriety because of her rumored interest in both sexes. Known as "the woman whom Garbo and Huston had loved," she had moved to Europe in the early sixties, after a dearth of roles in the States, and had appeared in Franco-Italian productions until her retirement fifteen years ago.

A tall woman with high cheekbones and skin that had avoided the sun and sought out the best of plastic surgeons, Madge Lennox looked much younger than her seventy years. A broad-brimmed hat shaded a face whose makeup was close to dead white, giving her aging beauty a timeless, even sexless look. She had a pair of large sunglasses that she kept putting on and taking off, drawing attention to both her large dark eyes and shapely hands. Her hair was completely covered beneath the hat by a deep-pink scarf. She wore ecru silk trousers and a man-tailored peach jacket. From the way she was holding her head and looking up at him, Urbino knew that she didn't want his scrutiny and judgment, however, unless they were benevolent. She wanted to be seen as she saw herself on her best days. If he showed that he saw her this way she would treat him with special kindness and care.

"When I saw the villa ten years ago," she was explaining in her lovely, exquisitely controlled voice, "I was certain it was by Palladio. Do you know something of its history?"

Urbino accommodated Madge Lennox by beginning with the villa's name—*La Muta*, or "The Mute Woman"—telling her how it came from a seventeenth-century woman who had retired to Asolo after witnessing a murder in Florence and who had never spoken again in public. The Contessa had been disquieted by this somewhat Gothic association. After several unsuccessful attempts to establish a new name—among them *La Barbara*—she had eventually found a way around the problem by commissioning a copy of Raphael's painting of a gentlewoman, known as *La Muta*. The painting now hung prominently on the stone staircase in the front hall.

"Yes, I've seen it," Madge Lennox said. "Wasn't the original stolen?"

"Back in seventy-five. The art police came and examined the Contessa's copy."

"I've heard the Conte da Capo-Zendrini was flattered that they bothered to come here to look at it," Lennox said in her soft, clear voice, showing that she knew something about *La Muta*—or at least the Conte—herself. "He was an unusual man. The people here still hold him in high regard."

"I never met him. He died before I met the Contessa."

"Oh, I see." She seemed vaguely disappointed. She searched his face with her bold, black eyes. "I was wondering, Mr. Macintyre," she said, slipping her sunglasses back on and smiling at him, "if you wouldn't mind venturing into the maze with me. I must say you're most appropriately dressed for that kind of thing."

Lennox's dark eyes ran over Urbino's boater, red bow tie, blazer, and flannels. The Contessa had pronounced him perfectly "delightful," but Urbino wasn't so sure himself.

"I regret to say that I don't know my way through," Urbino said, "but there are covered signs you can lift whenever you're lost."

"But that's no fun! I'd prefer being lost completely or being led through by someone who knows his own way." She took a sip of her punch. "Do you live here, too? I've seen you at the Caffè Centrale with the Contessa."

"No. I live in Venice, but I come here often."

"Oh, you must be the American friend with the palazzo that I heard someone in town talking about!"

"I suppose so. I inherited a small building through my mother. She was American but her family was Italian. Venice has been my home for more than ten years now."

"How interesting! I've never had the courage to live completely as an expatriate myself—to cut all the ties that bind me to home. I admire you, but isn't there a danger you're going to lose touch—with your past, your origins, I mean? Or have I read too many Henry James novels? To live in Venice all the time!" Madge Lennox shook her head slowly. " 'Venice the impossible' is how I think of it, especially during this time of the year. It's a smelly, slippery trap ready to catch you one way or another! Just look at that poor girl who was raped and murdered! You can't convince me that it had nothing to do with all the heat and madness in Venice this summer. I was there last week for two days, and it was more than enough! I got caught in the middle of a sweaty mob pushing and shoving for a view of the Bridge of Sighs. I almost passed out. 'The living are just the dead on holiday.' That's what Maeterlinck—an impossible dramatist—said, and he could have been describing Venice in high season. But Asolo!" she came close to sighing. "I've been here since April and I don't ever want to leave."

At this point they were joined by Silvestro Occhipinti, a bald, birdlike man who had had the ill fortune to outlive most of his family and friends, among them the Contessa's husband. He was all turned out in a white suit and cravat.

"I hope you never do leave, my dear," Occhipinti said in accented English in a high-pitched, reedy voice. "Villa Pippa is yours for as long as you like. 'God's in his heaven—all's right with the world!' I couldn't be more pleased!"

Occhipinti often sprinkled his conversation with quotations from Robert Browning, who had lived in Asolo with his wife on what was now the Via Browning, where Occhipinti had his own rooms. Sometimes the quotations were apt, at other times inappropriate or enigmatic. What they always were, however, was precise, age having done nothing to dim the memory of the old friend of Alvise da Capo-Zendrini.

"I'll have to leave in October as I've told you, Signor Occhipinti. The affairs of the world call me, I'm afraid."

Occhipinti frowned. Looking up at the woman with his round

little eyes from behind thick spectacles, he said, " 'Where the apple reddens never pry, lest we lose our Edens, Eve and I.' "

Madge Lennox, like the cited apple of Eden, somehow managed to redden beneath her heavy makeup. Her color deepened when Occhipinti added, "Perhaps you are planning to return to films. Wouldn't that be a happy day! How I remember you in *Dark Lady*! My heart was in your hands. But that was long ago. You've had a great career. Perhaps Signor Macintyre will write a book about you."

"You're a writer, Mr. Macintyre?" the actress said, turning to Urbino with evident relief.

"A biographer. I write about people who have some connection with Venice. Not complete biographies but only their lives in relationship to the city."

"He's written one on Robert Browning! 'What of soul was left, I wonder, when the kissing had to stop'!"

"You must know Venice like the back of your hand, Mr. Macintyre. You probably found me foolish, running on the way I was. Why don't you stop by Villa Pippa sometime? I have an open mind. I would love to love Venice."

Occhipinti nodded as if he knew exactly what she meant and recited, with a thin-lipped smile, " 'Dear dead women, with such hair, too—what's become of all the gold used to hang and brush their bosoms? I feel chilly and grown old.' "

Madge Lennox's brows knitted in perplexity and annoyance.

"Consider it an open invitation, Mr. Macintyre," she said, holding her head a little higher. "I'm leaving Wednesday for a few days in Milan. Anytime before or after that would be fine."

Urbino said he would stop by. Excusing himself, he went over to the Contessa who was near the blue and white marquee.

"How are things going, Barbara?"

"Swimmingly!"

The Contessa's eyes were shining with pleasure. Dressed in flowing fawn and cream with a wide-brimmed hat slightly angled on her head, she looked especially attractive this afternoon.

"So you've finally made the desired acquaintance of La Lennox. What do you think of her? No, you don't have to say! I can see that you like her. Beware! She's an actress down to her fingertips." Just in case Urbino might have interpreted this

as a compliment, she added, "Not that *I* have ever even heard
of anything the woman has done. I notice that she decided
against a turban today. But excuse me, *caro,* I see that the
Rienzis would like to make their usual early exit."

After the Contessa left, Urbino made his way up to the
terrace near the conservatory to chat with Tommaso Beni, the
landscape architect who had designed the maze. Beni soon got
on one of his hobbyhorses—the eighteenth-century landscape
gardener Capability Brown—and Urbino made the appropriate
responses as he surveyed the party.

His eye was caught by a woman about twenty-five coming
through the frescoed atrium from the front of the house. The
Contessa's Doberman, Catullus, was striding beside her. Gervasio, the majordomo, was behind her, keeping pace with a man
and placing a hand on his shoulder. The man—small, wiry, and
unattractive to the point of homeliness—stopped and called
something to the woman. She continued walking. Gervasio hurried after her.

Here were two people Urbino didn't recognize. Catullus,
however—usually feisty with strangers—was acting as if he
knew the young woman or, uncharacteristic of him, had immediately taken to her. There was something vaguely familiar
about her, but Urbino doubted that he had ever seen her before.
He would have remembered.

Slim, with a slightly elongated neck and abundant auburn
hair that drifted behind her like a thick cloud, she had a Pre-
Raphaelite look that Urbino found attractive. Her features
weren't perfect but they were close to it. Urbino had a good
opportunity to take them in as the young woman passed beneath the terrace and turned her face up toward him. Deep-
green eyes and generously curved lips were what immediately
struck him and he knew he would find it impossible soon to
forget them—along with her hair, bronze and gold in the sun
and slightly wild.

But something seemed to be missing from the eyes. He
didn't expect to find recognition there or interest or even curiosity, but he did expect something. Oddly blank, they gave her
striking face a lifeless look. Yet, as she strode across the par-
terre, oblivious of the other guests, there was force, even violence, in her movements. Heads turned, but no one seemed to
recognize her.

The auburn-haired woman went directly to the box garden
enclosed by the stone pergola where the Contessa was now
talking with Occhipinti. She stood in front of them for a few
moments, Catullus docile at her side like a unicorn in medieval
paintings of the Virgin. Gervasio went over to the Contessa
and bent close to her ear. The Contessa shook her head, and
Gervasio left. He rejoined the ugly man, who was still standing
at the end of the atrium, and led him to the front of the house.

Occhipinti peered through his spectacles at the young
woman, who was now saying something to the Contessa. An
angry look transformed Occhipinti's features. The woman was
smiling and had an unmistakable expression of triumph on her
face.

But the Contessa's expression spoke the loudest. It was as
if something had collapsed inside her and she was doing all she
could to put the best face on it. Her attempts at concealment
might have fooled almost anyone but not Urbino. She was in
distress. Urbino was already making his way down the terrace
steps before the Contessa looked at him across the heads of her
guests with what was a silent cry for help.

Urbino was at her side in time to hear the Burne-Jones
woman say in low, soft Italian, "Yes, Contessa, I'm your daughter." She paused, looking briefly at Urbino with her green eyes.
"Or I should say that I'm your husband Alvise's daughter.
Didn't he ever tell you?"

She reached down to pat Catullus on the head. The dog
seemed in ecstasy.

2

URBINO AND THE young woman were waiting for the Contessa
in the *salotto verde*. Catullus lay on the Aubusson, his eyes following the woman as she ran her slim hand along the carved and
gilded Brustolon and Corradini furniture and glanced at the
pastels and miniatures by Rosalba Carriera.

"I know I upset the Contessa," she said in Italian in a voice that seemed to come from a long way off. "I'm sorry. It's a terrible thing when someone you love and trust betrays you. Your soul shrivels up. Do you think hers is all shriveled now? But the Conte Alvise da Capo-Zendrini *was* my father. Don't you think I look like him?"

She turned more directly toward Urbino. On closer view her jaw was far from as square nor were her lips as wide as one of Burne-Jones's languid maidens, but there was nonetheless a resemblance to the painter's women, perhaps mainly in the abundance of auburn hair. Was this why she had seemed familiar earlier?

"Well, signore, do I look like him or not?"

Urbino had never known Alvise, but photographs, portraits, and reputation told him that he had been blue-eyed and handsome in his first and second youths. Urbino could trace no resemblance between him and this young woman, but perhaps he might have if he had known Alvise in the flesh.

The woman smiled, the smile never quite reaching her green eyes. Perspiration beaded her forehead.

"Never mind. I wouldn't want you to risk endangering your relationship with the Contessa. My name is Flavia. And you are—?"

"Urbino Macintyre."

"Of course. I've heard of you. The American. Older women are a European tradition, yes? Is that why you came to Italy?"

Flavia laughed. Once again Urbino was struck by how aloof her eyes were from any humor. Flavia took in his blazer and flannels and bow tie, the boater now in his hands. Urbino had always found people like her disconcerting—people who might burst out and say whatever might be in their heads with little regard for the consequences.

As they waited for the Contessa, Flavia spoke to Catullus in soothing tones that made the Doberman look even more devotedly at his new—or possibly his old?—friend.

When the Contessa joined them, Flavia introduced herself, giving only her first name as she had a few minutes before to Urbino.

"Please sit down, my dear."

"No, thank you, Contessa. I won't be staying long. I can see that I've upset you and that isn't my intention."

Flavia was scrutinizing the Contessa's face and seemed to get some satisfaction from the bewildered look touched with pique that she found there.

"But surely, signorina, you don't intend to descend on me like this and then just sweep away again. Of course I'm upset at what you said!" the Contessa said with passion, almost turning candor into a pose now that she realized she hadn't succeeded in concealing her feelings. "And in such a manner—in front of my guests! Whatever do you mean by it?"

Two spots of color, almost as bright as anything artifice could have painted, appeared on the Contessa's cheeks. She looked quickly at Urbino and then away again. It was almost as if she were embarrassed at being put in this situation, at having to say such things. But a second later Urbino revised his impression. It wasn't so much embarrassment the Contessa seemed to be feeling, an embarrassment that sent the blood to her cheeks and put a tremor in her voice. It was something much colder. It was fear.

"I mean nothing by it, except that it's the truth. I want nothing from you." Flavia seemed to reconsider this, for she added, "Nothing but a photograph of my father." She paused before adding, "Your husband, Alvise."

Flavia was walking back and forth slowly until she reached a formerly overlooked easel portrait in a corner. It was of Alvise, from around the time of his marriage. Flavia stared at it for a few moments and gave a little sigh before turning back to the Contessa.

"My father was such a handsome man."

Without missing a beat, the Contessa said, "That is my husband, the Conte Alvise Severino Falier da Capo-Zendrini," wrapping Alvise's indisputable relationship to her, his names, and his title around her like a protective cloak.

Flavia turned from the portrait and picked up one of the hand-painted ceramic *fischietti* from the marble ormolu-mounted table. The whistle she was holding was in the shape of a sea horse. She seemed about to put it to her lips but returned it to the table with the other bird and animal whistles, and smiled. There was something actressy and calculated in her movements.

"My father—I mean the man who *says* he's my father—the man who *believes* he is," she finally clarified with a trace of the violence that had been in her stride earlier, "would love your little collection here. Lorenzo collects things, too. He has a whole room filled with photographs and portraits of my mother." Her face darkened as if at an unpleasant memory. "She was very beautiful, my mother, and Lorenzo always insisted on having her portrait painted and her picture taken. Perhaps one of her portraits ended up here at your villa, Contessa."

Flavia looked around the room as if in search of a portrait of her mother that she had overlooked.

"My dear Signorina—Flavia," the Contessa added almost reluctantly, "you are being insufferable. I'm afraid I'm going to have to—"

"Ask me to leave?" the woman completed the Contessa's sentence. "But I said I couldn't stay long in any case. You do have time to look at this photograph of me, though."

Flavia reached into the pocket of her dress and took out a small, black-and-white photo, ragged around the edges. She handed it to the Contessa, who looked at it and gave it to Urbino. A pretty girl about ten smiled out at him.

"Yes, that's me, a long time ago," Flavia said. Her voice had an echo of a dead girl's voice. She took the photograph back and returned it to her pocket.

She moved toward the door, pausing to dip her hand in an *acquasantiera* filled with holy water. She didn't so much bless herself, however, as rub her forehead with the water as if she were feverish. In fact, she did look flushed, no longer as infuriatingly aloof as before. Her green eyes now glittered. The dead, lifeless look had been replaced with something close to passion.

"Remember, Contessa, I would like a photograph of my father! I will be in touch with you about it!" She pushed her auburn hair away from her face. "I must have one from you—only from you! Good afternoon."

Before the Contessa could say anything, Flavia hurried out into the hall. Catullus started to follow her.

"Catullus!" the Contessa called in a peremptory tone.

The dog paused and seemed to consider two desires—to follow the departing woman or to obey his mistress. After what seemed inordinately long seconds of indecisiveness, Catullus turned around and came to the Contessa's side. The Contessa, her face now etched with all the years of the decade she could usually deny having lived, breathed a sigh of relief completely disproportionate to the smallness of this victory over the beauti-

ful young woman who had shattered the Watteau of her garden
party.

3

IT WAS SUNDAY. Urbino and the Contessa were sitting on the
terrace of the Caffè Centrale in the main square of Asolo. Usually they were content to enjoy the idyllic scene in Piazza Gari-
baldi—the liquid music of the fifteenth-century winged-lion
fountain, the profusion of bright flowers hanging from the
arcade windows, the arrival and departure of the jitney buses
from the bottom of the hill, the people strolling on the pink
and yellow marble pavements, and the view of the golden-
stoned castle and the green hills beyond.

Today, however, not even the charms of this town so beloved by Browning that he had named his last volume of poems
after it could soothe them, especially not the Contessa. To an
even less discerning and affectionate eye than Urbino's own,
she was very troubled.

"Even its name mocks me today," she said wearily, staring
with sleep-deprived eyes at the arcade opposite. The seafoam
of her dress, usually a flattering shade for her, this afternoon
drained her of color. Urbino knew what she meant. The town
in whose rose gardens Giorgione had lingered with his lute and
where the Venetian Queen of Cyprus had held fabled court had
bequeathed its name to a verb. Pietro Bembo, the Renaissance
humanist who had used Asolo as the setting for his dialogues
on love, had coined the verb *asolare* to describe spending one's
time in pleasurable inactivity.

One of the Contessa's favorite phrases during her summers
here was *Asolo in Asolo*, whose meaning lost its wit when translated into any other language as "I'm doing sweet nothing in
Asolo."

"I won't have a peaceful moment until this is resolved,
Urbino," she said, abandoning her spoon beside her barely

touched *Coppa Tartufo* and absently fingering her strand of freshwater pearls. "I'm devastated. She's not playing a prank, I assure you. She meant everything she was saying. I could see it in her eyes."

Because Urbino had been struck with just how little Flavia's eyes had seemed to reveal—unless it was their very vacuousness that had been so voluble—he found the Contessa's comment puzzling.

"Oh, I don't mean that I believe she was telling the truth— I have absolutely no reason to believe that—absolutely none," she emphasized, not meeting his eye. "But she was convinced of what she said."

"The best way to convince someone else of your lies is to believe them yourself," he said, feeling foolish even before the words were out of his mouth.

The Contessa managed a wry smile.

"I don't have the energy or the desire to try to figure out if that's a platitude or a profundity, *caro*, but I accept the intended consolation. Perhaps our Flavia is herself not aware of her own intentions."

"She said she only wants a picture of Alvise."

"Don't play the role of the *naïf*, Urbino. It doesn't really suit you—or maybe it suits you all too well! But you're wrong. She wants more than a picture. She must be thinking of lire— unless she just wants to smash Alvise's—and my—reputations out of pure maliciousness. I've already put my solicitor here on alert. He says to do nothing, of course, and I've advised him to do the same. In any case, to give her a picture would be to give her everything, don't you think? It would be the great acknowledgment, the painful admission. It would be admitting that she was right. I can't even say that I ever suspected such a thing, that I even considered it a possibility. Perhaps *I'm* the one who's naïve—who's been naïve for the past twenty or more years. I'm sure this Flavia isn't much over twenty-five. That would make it about nine years after we were married."

The Contessa narrowed her eyes as she apparently tried to remember the period in question, then shook her head and picked up her spoon, only to put it down again.

"It would have been around the time of the maze. Alvise never really wanted one. I should have respected his wishes."

As if this might be the original sin for which she was now suffering, she sighed deeply.

"Of course, if there's anything in all this," she said in a low voice, as if speaking only to herself, "it could have begun before then, long before then."

Urbino didn't interrupt the Contessa's thoughts, but plucked and ate the grapes in his iced bowl and absently watched the people descending from the jitney bus. Among them was a smiling, broad-faced man who for a few startling moments Urbino thought he recognized. But the man's loud German spoken to a stout woman behind him dispelled the unexpected possibility that his ex–brother-in-law Eugene had somehow found his way at not the best of moments to Urbino's retreat in Asolo.

"I can't go on like this," the Contessa said. "I *refuse* to! I must know."

Silvestro Occhipinti's thin, reedy voice sounded in Urbino's ears from yesterday—the birdlike man's quotation from his beloved Browning about the danger of losing our Edens by prying where the apple reddens. The Contessa was obviously not going to be satisfied until she had pried in the orchard of her own past with Alvise. But after the satisfaction of that would come—what? Urbino shared the fear on his friend's face.

"You can help me, *caro*. You can find out if this young woman could conceivably be telling the truth. If she is, I owe her something more than only the picture she says she wants. And if she isn't—oh, if she isn't, Urbino, I'll never stop thanking you!"

But what might he get instead of gratitude if he had to tell her that Flavia *was* Alvise's daughter?

"I *must* know, *caro*," the Contessa said again, this time reaching out to press his hand gently as if he were the one in need of consolation. "Don't be afraid just because I am. It will be your chance to live out one of your fantasies," she said, her face lightening as she gave him a little smile. " 'The knight in shining armor' rescuing a lady in distress. And whatever you end up finding out, there's going to be a lady grateful for a rescue, isn't there? You can't lose. Don't you see that? It's a mission made in heaven!"

"I can see that I'm in a difficult position."

"Because you think you have no choice? You can always say no."

"And forever be made to regret it."

"So you're going to help me! You can't hide anything from me, you see, no matter how hard you might try. And I know what *I* have to do. I'm going to have to tell you all about Alvise and me again, not just what I already have, but other things. It's not that I've intentionally held anything back from you— not the way *you* have, you sly thing!—but that I've kept much of it to myself. It's not quite the same, *caro*, so don't give me that look!"

As far as Urbino knew, he was giving her no look except one of sincere interest. He had always wondered about the Contessa's marriage, had always felt that there was something that he didn't understand even though he knew so much about it. Perhaps he was going to learn what it was now. Yet he felt uneasy. This wasn't quite the way he wanted to find out, not when so much was at stake for the Contessa and so much was expected of him. As a biographer, he was wary of any strong personal involvement that made him reluctant to discover unpleasant truths or eager to find their opposite.

"I assure you that I won't hold you responsible for anything I might end up regretting I've told you—or anything that you dig up in your inimitable way. But before I begin I'm going to need a fresh *coppa*," she said, looking down at her almost completely melted gelato.

After ordering another *Coppa Tartufo* and a Campari soda for himself, Urbino waited for the Contessa to begin, but first she ate her gelato slowly and silently, as if fortifying herself for a difficult ordeal.

4

"WHEN I CAME to Venice from London to study music at the conservatory," she began, "I was just a green girl, hard though it might be for you to believe now. I thought I was the most sophisticated little thing who had ever come along. I fought like a tigress with my parents to go to Italy. They finally relented only because I agreed to stay with their friends the Wilverlys and because the director of the conservatory promised to take special care of me. Even my sister Patricia tried to keep me from going, saying all sorts of terrible things would happen. But I was determined. Venice was going to be my adventure. So I came here, and as it turned out, I never really went back, not to live. Once I left, I left for good.

"As you know, I studied voice and piano at the Palazzo Pisani," she went on. "I was one of those hopeful girls you can hear when you're walking past or sitting in Campo Morosini, one of the ones whose soprano trills never quite reach high C. I was better at piano. In fact, it was my piano-playing that brought Alvise and me together. It was at the Wilverlys'. I was practicing the barcarolle from *I Quattro Rusteghi* by Wolf-Ferrari who used to be director of the conservatory."

The Contessa had charmed a small group several years ago at the Ca' da Capo-Zendrini playing her rendition of the barcarolle intermezzo. At the time, however, she had said nothing about its association with Alvise.

"It caught Alvise's ear. He had always loved the piece, he said, because it captures the movement of a gondola so well. The windows of the *salone* were open that particular evening. After I finished the barcarolle, the doorbell rang. I went down and found a handsome man standing there with a girl around my age. He was about forty, with black hair, light Venetian skin, and blue eyes. At first I thought he might be the girl's father but I soon realized he wasn't by the way she looked at him. He gave me a boyish smile and apologized for disturbing me but said, in grammatical English with only a slight accent, that he had to know who was playing the barcarolle so divinely. He and the young lady had been passing by and he had been startled to hear it for the second time that day. Surely I had been playing it at the conservatory that morning? My touch was unmistakable, he said. By this time the girl was getting impatient. I thought that she might not understand English so I said something to her in Italian. She answered in English in a haughty way. They didn't stay long after that, but he gave me his card before they left. I was upset when I realized that I hadn't told

him what my name was—and by that I knew that I was interested in him. It wasn't until I read his card that I saw that he
was a count. He had introduced himself as simply Alvise da
Capo-Zendrini."

A soft look had come over the Contessa's face as she recounted her first meeting with her future husband. Urbino
believed that the seeds of the destruction of a relationship might
be found in the circumstances of its origin. If this was true,
then what might the Contessa's romantic little story reveal
so far?

What the Contessa had to face presently, now that the
young woman had intruded into her life, was a possibly dark
side to the romance of her marriage. But here on the terrace
of the Caffè Centrale, even though she must be fully aware of
where reminiscence might eventually lead her—and Urbino in
her wake—she was slightly flushed with the pleasure of remem-
brance.

It was a long time since Urbino had reminisced in this way
about his own first meeting with Evangeline. Would he too feel
a similar pleasure? Eugene's arrival tomorrow might give him
a chance to find out—or make it difficult for him to continue
to evade thoughts of his marriage.

Any kind of evasion seemed far from the Contessa's intentions, however, as she continued after taking a sip of her mineral
water.

"I wanted to see him again, but I wasn't about to ring him
or pay him a call. I did go to see where he lived, though—and
was disturbed to find it one of the biggest, if not the best kept,
palazzi on the Grand Canal. I was prepared for a penurious
Italian count marrying a young woman with enough money to
keep them both comfortable, though not luxurious—oh! my
imagination was racing even after only our brief encounter. It
was the stuff of the novels I couldn't get enough of. It was what
my parents feared would happen to me. But a count who lived
in a real palazzo, no matter how much in need of repair, was
something else entirely! I was convinced I'd never see him
again. But he knew where to find me, and he did," she said with
a smile of satisfaction.

"The Wilverlys'?"

"No, the conservatory. A few days later I had just finished
vocalizing in the drawing room when who came in but Alvise!

He was dressed impeccably in a beige linen suit and was carrying a rose. He handed it to me and asked if I would join him for coffee. We went to Caffè Paolin and I ordered pistachio ice cream. It never tasted so good!

"That was the first of many meetings. Alvise did things the proper way, however. He soon came to the Wilverlys' when they were at home. It caused quite a stir. 'Do you know who he is, Barbara? He's the best catch in Venice, one of the best in Italy. Three generations of women have been trying to get him to marry—but he's old enough to be your father!' I suppose it was true—he was forty-one—and I—I was much younger, but I never thought of him in that way. We seemed almost the same age. I was mature for my years, and he was young for his. We met in the middle.

"We went all around Venice together. My studies suffered, but I was learning so much else that it didn't matter. I don't mean what you might be thinking, *caro*—I mean things about Venice, things I never would have learned if left on my own. Alvise seemed to know everything about it, as you would expect someone who said he could trace his family history back to the eighth century. On New Year's Eve he asked me to marry him and I said yes. I didn't learn until later that he had been considering marrying the girl who was with him when he rang the Wilverlys' bell. I met her several times when Alvise and I were going about Venice, and she was as cold as ice. She started to go out with Silvestro but soon despaired of ever getting him to the altar. He was even older than Alvise and a confirmed bachelor. She'd still be waiting. As it was, she didn't marry until about ten years after we did."

She took a sip of her mineral water.

"I was warned by Patricia, warned by my parents and friends, but I didn't listen. I was certain there was no first Contessa lurking in the attic of the Ca' da Capo-Zendrini, nothing but a lot of furniture, paintings, and clothing. And so, as Jane Eyre said, 'Reader'—or 'Listener' I should say—'I married him.' And I never regretted it. Oh, we had our disagreements. I don't want to give the impression that we lived in a Venetian version of Cloud-Cuckoo-Land. The most difficult time was about ten years after we married, not long before the flood. The doctors in Geneva told us that I would never be able to conceive. It was a blow even though we had suspected it by then. That was the lowest point in our marriage. Alvise was wonderful. He said it really didn't matter, that he was only concerned about me, that he knew how much I wanted to have a child.

"I threw myself into getting the La Muta garden back to the way it once had been and planning a maze. Alvise wasn't as enthusiastic about it all, although he never came right out and said so. He must have thought all this business with the garden was a form of therapy for me, as I suppose it was, and for that he was grateful.

"I went to England in July with Tommaso Beni"—Beni was the landscape architect who had been at her party yesterday— "to show him the English mazes. I was determined to have a Victorian puzzle maze. Tommaso threw himself into the project. He studied the mazes at Hampton Court, Breamore House, Somerlyton Hall—all the famous ones and quite a few of the ones most people haven't heard of. Tommaso was taking photographs, sketching, poring through garden and estate books the entire time.

"I don't think Alvise was very happy about the idea of Tommaso and me being together even though he trusted me. Alvise didn't want to stay at La Muta while I was away, so he and Silvestro went to Silvestro's villa on Lago di Garda. Alvise and I would talk several times a week on the phone. He was noncommittal, not giving me many details.

"While I was away I got two strange phone calls. One was from Silvestro. Alvise was lost without me, he said, and when was I planning to put the poor man out of his misery? The other call was from Oriana." Oriana Borelli was a friend of the Contessa's who lived in Venice on the Island of Giudecca. "Oriana said that as a friend she advised me to come back immediately. When I asked her what she meant, she paused and said that people were talking, 'people who mattered,' she emphasized. You can imagine how puzzled I was. Oriana worrying about what people thought, when she and Filippo conduct their extramarital affairs like an opera buffa! But I assumed she was concerned about my reputation even if she never seemed to be about hers. I left England within forty-eight hours. Tommaso stayed on for another week.

"Alvise came back from Lago di Garda and hardly ever

mentioned my trip to England with Tommaso. He had a gift waiting for me—the nymph that's now at the center of the maze." Her face clouded. "Not having children puts a tremendous strain on a relationship when the two people want to have them, but I never felt that Alvise blamed me."

"Surely it wasn't a question of blame."

"You know what I mean. He never made me feel that it was because of me that he—that *we*," she emphasized, "were being denied something. But I've felt it as just that, *caro*—a denial, a deprivation. I thought it would get better as the years went by but it's become worse since Alvise died."

Urbino had always believed that the Contessa's not having children had been the only real deficiency in her otherwise idyllic marriage, one that she and Alvise had adjusted to down through the years. But now Flavia had come into the picture— had, in fact, rudely intruded herself into it. How drastic an adjustment might the Contessa have to make in the way she viewed her marriage?

The Contessa was nearing the end of her story, speaking more quickly, as if eager to get her part over with so that Urbino could begin his.

"After that low point, we seemed to grow even closer. For a while, though, I couldn't help but have negative feelings about the maze, but when I thought of the nymph, I saw the maze as almost symbolic of what we had gone through—a difficult time that was now behind us. I've never had any reason to think differently."

The Contessa's unspoken words—"until now"—hung over them as they sat there on the terrace of the Caffè Centrale. Neither of them said anything. They watched the scene in front of them, so different from the hurly-burly of high-season Venice to which Urbino would be returning this evening. The Contessa absently greeted an acquaintance as the woman walked past the winged-lion fountain.

"So that's the story, *caro*. Make what you can of it. I'm no fool and I don't expect you to pretend to be one—for my sake or anyone else's. This young lady was obviously born around the time of the maze. Find out what you can, but be discreet. I'd prefer not to give you a list of Alvise's friends and business acquaintances unless it becomes absolutely necessary. And forget about what's left of his family. That's all I need! Oriana might be of help, though. We knew her and Filippo from the start. But you might not have to talk with anyone but Silvestro."

"But wouldn't he be inclined to protect Alvise?"

The Contessa's wounded look made Urbino realize anew how difficult and delicate this was all going to be.

"Yes, he would, but he's grown especially fond of me, sometimes I think too fond. He may very well feel that he owes me the truth whatever it is."

But if Occhipinti was so fond of the Contessa, what if the truth were a painful one? Perhaps the best and only way for Occhipinti to reconcile the dual claims of his old, dead friend and of the widow he had come to care so much about would be to protect them both by blithely and benevolently lying. And how would he take to Urbino's poking around in not only the da Capo-Zendrinis' past but his own as well?

Urbino hadn't even begun his inquiry yet into the possible truth behind Flavia's claim, but he could already see what was in store for him.

5

AN HOUR LATER Urbino was approaching Occhipinti's building on the Via Browning, when he saw the elderly man, a straw hat perched on his bald head, walking toward him under the arcade. There was a briskness in his stride that belied his years. His cocker spaniel, Pompilia, named after a character in Browning's *The Ring and the Book*, was at his side on a leash.

"Ah, it's you, Signor Macintyre." The birdlike man's high-pitched voice expressed surprise, as if it were unusual to see someone you knew in a small town the size of Asolo. "Out for a stroll?"

"Actually I wanted to see you, Signor Occhipinti."

Even though Urbino had met Occhipinti on many occasions, they remained formal with each other. The man seemed in many ways from another era. It wasn't just his age or his preference for Browning, that consummately Victorian poet, but something that seemed to go to the core of this eccentric little man.

"Please come up then," Occhipinti said, continuing in English.

He unfastened Pompilia's leash. The cocker spaniel was the latest of the dogs his sister had bought him so that people wouldn't think he was talking to himself when he went out on his walks.

Urbino followed Occhipinti and Pompilia up the dark stairs to the second-floor apartment where the man had moved fifteen years ago when he began to lease his Villa Pippa. The fact that the apartment was in the building next to the one where Browning had lived was its main attraction for him.

Occhipinti's *salotto* was crammed with Browning memorabilia. An entire wall behind a heavily upholstered chair was filled with English and Italian editions of Browning's poetry and correspondence, and biographies and critical studies of the poet. Another wall was given over to framed photographs of the poet, his home here in Asolo, the Ca' Rezzonico in Venice where he had died, and his grave at Westminster. Also displayed were an original letter from Browning to his solicitor and a program of *The Barretts of Wimpole Street* from a long-ago London production. On shelves and little tables were various objects—among them a fountain pen, a page cutter, and a chipped plaster Tower of Pisa that had supposedly once been the possessions of the poet. Occhipinti had a larger collection of Browning memorabilia than the local museum. On the sofa was an embroidered silk pillow with the lines: "Open my heart and you will see/'Graved inside of it 'Italy.' "

"Please sit down, Signor Macintyre." Occhipinti took his own place in the chair in front of the books. "What was it that you wanted to see me about?"

Urbino sat down on the sofa next to Pompilia.

"It's the Contessa who sent me, Signor Occhipinti."

"Ah, yes, our beautiful Barbara. It was a lovely party yesterday, wasn't it? 'Summer redundant, blueness abundant' and all in the Contessa's incomparable gardens."

Occhipinti's tiny round eyes twinkled behind his even rounder, rimless spectacles.

"Yes, it was lovely," Urbino agreed, "but not completely carefree for Barbara."

"One's parties never are. I remember when my sister and I used to give parties at Villa Pippa. She had to have at least two glasses of Prosecco before they began. But I've never found that to be the case with *la bella* Barbara. She's always the soul of serenity."

"It doesn't mean that she's never troubled. And she was troubled yesterday. You were there when the young woman came up to her under the pergola."

"How could I forget? 'A face to lose youth for, to occupy age with the dream of, meet death with'! Not only beautiful but familiar. The kind of face one seems to have seen before—perhaps in one's dreams. *La bellezza* is always both familiar and strange, don't you think, Signor Macintyre?"

"And you heard what the young woman said, didn't you, Signor Occhipinti?" Urbino asked, perhaps too abruptly, not wanting to encourage the old man's tendency to ramble, however poetically.

"Yes, I heard. 'Any nose may ravage with impunity a rose,'" he recited, nodding his little head slowly, "but the ear is forced to hear what it would prefer not to. That is how it was yesterday afternoon."

"Do you think there's any truth in what the woman said?"

Occhipinti threw back his little head and let out a sharp peal of laughter.

"So that is why Barbara sent you! She wants me to set your mind at ease! How foolish of her to give it a thought! The young woman is beautiful, but she was speaking nonsense." He seemed to think for a moment before adding, "That is why I wish I had heard nothing. To upset the beautiful Barbara with such silliness! Alvise was the most faithful, devoted man."

"Barbara is asking for your help, Signor Occhipinti. She's very upset—what woman wouldn't be?—but she needs to know the truth, and she's counting on you to help her."

"I can only help her by telling the truth. The young woman has a father like us all, but he wasn't Alvise da Capo-Zendrini!" Pompilia, drifting off to sleep, perked up and looked at her master. "How do I know Barbara sent you here to ask these questions? I know you ask questions all the time! That's your job, isn't it?" He gestured at the wall of books. "Like some of these writers with all those crazy ideas about Browning! I can hardly read some of the things they say! Lies! Good people should be protected from such things once they're gone. But excuse me. I know you're her good friend, too. Unfortunately, though, we can't always protect the people we love from the cruelty of others, can we?"

"Is that what you think? That this young woman was being cruel?"

"Cruel or mischievous! Sometimes it's the same thing to these young people today." Occhipinti stood up. "I'd like a glass of wine. Would you join me?"

Occhipinti got them two glasses of white wine. After they had taken a few sips, Occhipinti, staring at the embroidered pillow next to Urbino on the sofa, said in a disembodied voice, " 'Flower o' the broom, take away love, and our earth is a tomb.' Alvise loved Barbara, loved her until the day he died. Their marriage was the best, my friend! This doesn't mean that they didn't have their little problems, their sorrows—what is life without them?—but their life together was—was just like the Brownings'!"

Occhipinti, having uttered this superlative, sat back and nodded with satisfaction. Urbino regretted having to act as devil's advocate, but he wasn't going to get anywhere unless he did.

"You mentioned 'sorrows.' What sorrows were you referring to?"

Suspicion gleamed in Occhipinti's round eyes.

"Are you still so young, Signor Macintyre, that you don't think of death—the 'pale priest of the mute people,' as Browning called him? Death is surely the greatest sorrow. 'Death stepped tacitly and took them where they never see the sun.' "

"But before Alvise's death were there any lesser sorrows?"

" 'Lesser sorrows'? Perhaps, but married people keep many sorrows to themselves. But they had the usual ones."

"Like what?"

Impatience hardened the man's birdlike face.

"Just what you would expect! They didn't have any children, did they?" Occhipinti seemed upset at having said this. "That's all there was to it. They faced what they had to face and went on with their life. There might have been talk but that doesn't mean there was any truth to it."

"When was there talk?"

"I don't remember exactly. Sometime before the flood."

The flood Occhipinti was referring to was the one of November 1966 that had ravaged Venice and Florence.

"That must have been about the time the maze was being built at La Muta. When Barbara and Tommaso Beni went to England together."

" 'First of the first, such I pronounce her, then as now perfect in whiteness'! What are you suggesting? I said that there was no truth to any of that talk!"

"And what about Alvise during the same time?"

"He was with me at Lago di Garda. He was sad—what man wouldn't be? He wanted a child, and the wife he loved wasn't there with him." Might this be the strongest criticism Occhipinti would ever give of the Contessa? "Our friends were staying all around Lago di Garda but he hardly showed any interest in seeing them."

"Barbara says that you phoned her when she was in England and asked her to come home."

Occhipinti seemed surprised.

"Yes, I phoned her," Occhipinti admitted, "but Alvise didn't ask me to." He immediately seemed to realize that this didn't put his friend in the best light, for he added, only making it worse, "He didn't want me to." Then, in evident exasperation, he said, "He didn't know I called! I thought it would be best for poor Alvise—so sad and lonely—if Barbara came back to La Muta as soon as possible. Alvise was only with me at Lago di Garda because he didn't want to be alone at La Muta. Don't think that he was happy to be free. Yes, he was handsome, and women were always trying to get his attention, but he was faithful to Barbara." Anger mottled his face. "And this beautiful young woman yesterday! She should know better than to say such things. It's not just Barbara we have to think about, but it's Alvise's memory—his reputation! 'We that had loved him so, followed him, honored him, made him our pattern to live and to die!' "

Occhipinti then reminisced about his and Alvise's youth between the two world wars, revealing just how deep the bonds

of friendship and loyalty had been between the two men long
before the Contessa came into the picture.

6

EUGENE HENNEPIN, URBINO's former brother-in-law, was a stout,
balding man in his early forties who had made millions of dollars in sugar cane. Back in Louisiana he was known as the "Sugar
Cane Prince" only because his father, Emile, was still very much
alive and indisputably the "King." When he descended from
the train on Monday morning, Urbino was relieved not to see
him accompanied by Evangeline, who used to be known, before
her married days, as the "Princess."

Before Urbino mentioned Evangeline, Eugene said, "Evie's
in Florence, but we'll talk about her later"—an assurance that
made Urbino uneasy. Was Eugene going to try, once again, to
effect a reconciliation? Eugene had always tried to be a peace-
maker between Urbino and Evangeline and between Urbino
and the Hennepin family. But none of his strenuous efforts
had been able to help save a marriage that, though well-inten-
tioned, had been a mismatch from the start.

"A gondola, that's what I want," Eugene said within the
first hour of his arrival. "Put it on that lake behind the old
house—wouldn't *that* be fine!"

And so here Urbino and Eugene were at the *squero* on the
Rio di San Trovaso, one of the few boatyards where gondolas
were made to order. The fact that the gondola maker frequently
had to repeat Urbino's translation had nothing to do with the
quality of Urbino's Italian but everything to do with what Eugene was saying.

"Red, white, and blue?"

"Like the American flag," Urbino said unnecessarily.

"Tell him I want room for an outboard motor—and one
of these doohickeys on it, too." He jabbed a stubby finger at an

illustration ripped from a book, indicating the enclosed cabin, or *felze*, that used to be part of the gondola. "I want stars on it—white ones on a blue background."

Urbino duly translated all this. The gondola maker raised his eyes to the old wooden balcony covered with geraniums that looked down on the beached gondolas.

"Tell him I'll pay extra if he can have it done so Evangeline and I can bring it back in a few weeks."

"*Impossibile!*" the man said.

Eugene had no trouble understanding this expletive.

"Why's he bein' so difficult?" Eugene mopped his brow with his handkerchief. "He should be able to knock off two or three of these things a week! He's got a pretty shabby outfit here. His competitors must be gettin' all the business."

Urbino explained again that the Squero di San Trovaso was the best in Venice.

"They make only three or four a year."

"A *year!*" Eugene shouted so loudly that the gondola maker cringed. "What kind of a way to run a business is that? This guy probably has something else goin' for him." Eugene looked at the man with a mixture of pity and contempt. "Tell him I want to be next on the list."

As it turned out, Eugene had to settle for a four-month wait before his gondola could be shipped. When Urbino started to translate the man's explanation about the two hundred and eighty pieces of mahogany, cherry, elm, and five other kinds of wood that had to be specially chosen and carved, Eugene waved his hand and said to tell him to stop making excuses. As long as the thing was in Louisiana by Christmas, he would be satisfied, but why it took so long to make a simple little boat like that was beyond him.

After leaving the *squero*, Urbino and Eugene walked along the crowded Zattere embankment, a favorite promenade for Venetians, even during winter since it faced south. On the other side of the canal was the Island of Giudecca, which only a week ago had been connected to the Zattere by a temporary pontoon bridge in celebration of the Feast of the Redeemer. This floating bridge allowed Venetians to make their annual pilgrimage across the Giudecca Canal to the Palladian Church of the Redeemer, which had been built to thank the Lord for delivering Venice from the plague in the sixteenth century. The feast was one of fireworks and mulberry eating and bathing at the Lido at dawn. Urbino loved it, but the Contessa avoided it like the plague itself.

Urbino slowed his usually brisk pace for Eugene, who was feeling the effects of the heat and dabbing his forehead and the back of his neck with a handkerchief. Ahead was Ristorante Da Gianni. It might be a good idea for them to lunch there at an umbrellaed table on the terrace.

"I still don't understand why you don't have a gondola of your own," Eugene said, eyeing one of the coffinlike boats gliding by. "What's the point of livin' in Venice if you don't? I know you can't be hurtin' much for money. You inherited the place here, sold the house on Prytania, got all your momma and poppa's money when they died in that car crash, plus have bucks from your books—and I know you never had to give Evie a penny. So why not invest in a gondola?" Eugene pressed, once again accenting the word heavily on the second syllable instead of the first. "Does that Countess friend of yours have one?"

"The last person to have her own was Peggy Guggenheim."

"That's the lady I was readin' about on the train. She led quite a merry life! Had a pile of money—one of those rich Guggenheims. Bought a picture a day, didn't she?"

"Right," Urbino said. "During the Second World War— Kandinsky, Klee, Dalí, Miró—all the modern masters. She eventually brought her collection here to Venice. It's open to the public at her palazzo."

"Quite a woman!" Eugene said with such enthusiasm that Urbino wondered if he were commenting on Peggy Guggenheim's scandalous life or her commitment to modern art. Eugene went on to say that he would like to do just what Guggenheim had done while he was here in Venice—buy something "arty" every day. He made it clear that he expected Urbino's help. "I've already bought something today and I've only been here a few hours. We won't have to worry until tomorrow."

Urbino was happy to hear it. He was even less prepared to entertain Eugene than he had been before Flavia showed up at the Contessa's garden party. He was much too preoccupied with what he had learned from the Contessa and Occhipinti and with trying to understand why the young woman had seemed familiar. Hadn't Occhipinti said the same thing? Urbino planned to see Oriana Borelli later today. He glanced across the canal to the Island of Giudecca where Oriana and Filippo lived.

"And you'll have to take me to this Guggenheim gal's palace," Eugene was now saying, "and I want to go to that big art show. They had a piece in the *Times-Picayune* about it a few weeks back. Then there's that island of glass—what's it called?— I hear I can find a nice big chandelier there. And the place where those little old ladies make lace. Remember, Urbino, I'm not goin' to be here much more than a week. There's all the other things I gotta see."

Urbino inwardly groaned as they sat at a table on the Da Gianni raft terrace. Eugene examined the gray-haired waiter balancing a tray of ice cream sodas and mineral water.

"This country's got the *oldest* waiters I've seen anywhere. Is it something Italians do when they retire? I have to admit they're pretty spry, though. Maybe they take blackstrap molasses! Hennepin might be able to do a big deal with the Italians."

During lunch, as Eugene complained about the problems he and Evangeline had encountered in Rome and Florence, where "we didn't have anyone to guide us around, of course," Urbino's mind drifted back to Flavia. He was beginning to understand why she had looked familiar. Surely he had seen her before, hadn't he? And the Contessa would have, too, if she hadn't kept herself disdainful up in Asolo, removed from the kind of art that Eugene's admired Peggy Guggenheim had bought up as if it were so many pieces of candy.

7

"A PILE OF JUNK!" Eugene said contemptuously as he surveyed the arrangement of gray rocks, worn army boots, and rusted rifles and sabers. "I wouldn't give a cent for any of it! Who are they tryin' to kid?"

Urbino and Eugene were at the Biennale exhibition. So far, his ex–brother-in-law's responses were, in spirit if not in language, so close to the Contessa's that Urbino was beginning to think the two were destined to become fast friends.

"It's not *this* kind of stuff I'm interested in bringin' back. Not by a long shot! I want some pretty stuff."

Eugene, eager to return to the air-conditioned Danieli, could have quit now without a regret, but Urbino persuaded him to go to one more pavilion.

It was the Italy Pavilion, set back against the Giardini Canal. Urbino left Eugene in one of the front rooms while he sought out the paintings of Bruno Novembrini. He didn't go directly to the empty space on the wall where one painting was missing, but moved slowly from painting to painting. Most of them were Venetian scenes in which the standard tourist images of the city—gondolas, the Bridge of Sighs, the Basilica, the Doge's Palace, Piazza San Marco—were fantastically juxtaposed or were floating or sailing as if in a dream or hallucination.

Immediately before the empty space was a large canvas with a naked man and woman embracing as marble eagles and columns melted around them, the liquid flowing into a golden river in the foreground. *Let Rome in Tiber Melt,* it was called, the quotation identifying the passionate couple as Shakespeare's Antony and Cleopatra.

Next to this painting in the empty space was a hand-lettered sign:

NUDE IN A FUNERAL GONDOLA has temporarily been removed from exhibition. It is hoped that it will be exhibited again before the end of the Biennale.

Urbino had just finished reading the sign when a man behind him said, "It should be back soon. It wasn't as damaged as we thought at first."

The speaker was a man in his sixties of medium height with long gray hair and beard and a prominent nose. He was dressed in a subdued charcoal-gray suit given a calculated touch of color by a loosely folded blood-red pocket square. Urbino recognized Massimo Zuin, a prominent art dealer and owner of a gallery in the arty Dorsoduro quarter.

"Signor Zuin, I'm Urbino Macintyre. Perhaps you can help me. I'd like to see a reproduction of *Nude in a Funeral Gondola.* You're Bruno Novembrini's dealer, aren't you?"

Zuin said he was and told Urbino to wait while he got a catalog. Eugene sauntered into the room and went over to look at a painting of a funeral of gondolas going up the Grand Canal carrying pieces of Venetian monuments. Zuin returned with the catalog.

"You'll find a color reproduction of the painting here," he said in his courteous but patronizing voice, opening the catalog and handing it to Urbino.

The painting was as Urbino remembered it. Floating in a flooded Piazza San Marco, with the Basilica in the background, was a funeral gondola, an even deeper shade of black than the customary color. Hovering in the left-hand corner, as if they might have detached themselves from the facade of the Basilica, were a lion weeping into a black handkerchief and a bearded angel. Both were looking at the figure reclining in the gondola—a beautiful nude woman, her hair obscured in an Oriental turban and her bright green, eerily vacant eyes looking directly at the viewer.

Urbino now had no doubt that underneath that turban must be Titian hair and that the model was the young woman who had exploded her bombshell under the Contessa's pergola on Saturday afternoon.

"I was particularly struck with it the other times I was here," Urbino said. "As a matter of fact, the last time I saw it was minutes after it was slashed."

Zuin's face hardened almost imperceptibly.

"It's a pity. These crazy feminists! It must have had something to do with that girl murdered near here. Some woman blaming the sexual attack on art, most likely. Once the painting is repaired, no one should be able to notice the damage. There was only one tear. I'm sure we can agree on a fair price if you're interested in it."

"Right now I'd like to know about the model."

More surprise than disappointment showed on Zuin's face. He scratched the long gray hair at the nape of his neck.

"The model? Bruno only used her the one time."

"Do you know what her name is?"

"If I did, Signor Macintyre, I couldn't give you that information."

"But you *do* know who she is?" The art dealer didn't answer.

"Perhaps Novembrini wouldn't mind telling me. Do you have his number?"

It occurred to Urbino that Zuin might be no more inclined to give him Novembrini's phone number than the name of the model, but Zuin surprised him by smiling and saying, "I'll give it to you only because it's listed in the phone directory. Surely you understand that art dealers have a responsibility to protect their artists in whatever way they can. *And* our own interests. I wouldn't be quite so willing to give you Bruno's number if I thought the two of you might strike a private deal between you."

With a cool smile, Zuin took out a fountain pen, wrote a phone number on the front of the catalog, and handed the catalog to Urbino.

Eugene joined them. Urbino made the introductions and told Eugene that Zuin was the dealer for the painter whose work was in the room.

"So you work for this November fellow! Wonderful!"

"I do," Zuin said in English. "Are you interested in contemporary Italian painting?"

"Is that what this is? I know what I like and I like this stuff here. Is any of it for sale?"

Zuin's face brightened.

"Most of it. Are you interested in any in particular?"

"That one." Eugene pointed to the painting of the gondolas transporting pieces of Venice up the Grand Canal. "Has anyone grabbed it up yet?"

"Not yet, but you'll have to wait until the end of September when the Biennale closes."

"No problem. I've got to wait until almost Christmas for a gondola!" Eugene turned to Urbino. "We're one day ahead of ourselves now! I'm determined to buy something every day," he explained to the puzzled Zuin, "something nice like this November's paintings. I've already bought a gondola at a run-down boatyard. By the way, I guess we should talk about money. How much you askin'? You don't have to decide right away. You can give me a call at the Danieli Hotel—is that how you pronounce it, Urbino? I'm stayin' there instead of that tiny little palace Urbino has. It's in such a pokey part of town. I like to be where the action is."

Zuin suggested that the two of them talk about the painting

in the morning at his Dorsoduro shop. After leaving the Biennale, Urbino and Eugene had a drink at the Danieli bar before Urbino went to the Island of Giudecca to visit Oriana Borelli.

8

THE LIVING ROOM of the Ca' Borelli was so austere that it was almost like a slap in Urbino's face.

Just about the only things in the large white room that could possibly be a focus of Urbino's attention—that is, other than the histrionic Oriana in her Versace outfit—were the massive lightwood bookcase with its six halogen lamps, a Barovier-Toso vase filled with dried brown flowers, and the neo-Biedermeier sofa on which its owner was now sprawled. The Contessa's flamboyant friend looked a little exhausted. She must be recovering from one of her strenuous marital infidelities.

"Poor Barbara! I wish I had been there." Oriana said. "But it's all nonsense—*assolutamente*! As far as that phone call was concerned, I was worried about what people were saying about Barbara—not about Alvise. Yes, there was talk, and some people were even saying that if the *bell'*Alvise wandered a bit it would only serve Barbara right. But Alvise was the most faithful husband I've ever come across."

Oriana looked at him unblinkingly through her large Laura Biagiotti sunglasses, which she wore indoors and out from May until October. She was speaking from a vast experience of other women's husbands who had been unfaithful with her and about one—her own—whose infidelities came close to matching hers.

"Barbara knows I was attracted to Alvise—both before and after they got married. It was no secret, darling! I'm a woman, aren't I? And he was so handsome, so gentle—and devoted to Barbara. Never showed me any interest except a friendly one! In any case I would have restrained myself for Barbara's sake," she assured him. "She's my one, dear friend, and I'd never do anything to hurt her. How absolutely terrible it would be if I knew that Alvise had had an affair with another woman! What would I do then, I ask you? Even if Barbara says she wants to know the truth, how could I be the one she hears it from?" She shook her light blond head firmly. "She's asking you to do something *molta delicata*! But I'm not so sure if you should have agreed! I'll tell you one thing. *If* Alvise had been unfaithful to her, Barbara would never have found out—absolutely never! He would not have left anything behind to incriminate himself. He never would have wanted to hurt her. If he knew something like this was happening now—"

As to what Alvise would have done, Oriana didn't say. She left it to Urbino's—and perhaps even her own—imagination.

"Someone must have been telling this girl stories. Barbara has enemies here. She's had them from the first and she'll have them until the day she dies—may it be many, many years from now."

"Enemies, Oriana? Who?"

"Barbara's right! Sometimes you are so absolutely American! Hasn't Italy done you any good? Of course the poor dear has enemies. We *all* have enemies—even innocent little you! I wouldn't be at all surprised if it was one of Barbara's enemies who put the girl up to it."

"Do you know of any in particular?"

" 'In particular,' Urbino! You are amusing. As if dear Barbara doesn't know herself. But if it embarrasses you too much to ask her, I'd suggest her archenemy, Violetta Volpi."

"Violetta Volpi? I don't believe Barbara has ever mentioned her."

"Her maiden name was Grespi. I don't know her well but I think she has a sister. A branch of the Grespi family are *comaschi*—silk manufacturers—in Como."

Urbino shook his head. The name Violetta Grespi meant as little to him as Violetta Volpi.

"She's led a pampered life," Oriana went on, as if pampering were something alien to her. "A nurse who looked after Filippo knew her. She's a painter now. She was on the point of marrying Alvise when Barbara came along. Violetta Volpi never seems to have forgotten how 'the Englishwoman almost ruined her life,' as the nurse said she used to say, but perhaps Barbara would like to forget it."

9

"I MOST CERTAINLY *have* mentioned her!" the Contessa said when Urbino phoned her that evening from the Palazzo Uccello. "I mentioned her as recently as yesterday at the Caffè Centrale! You're not going to be any help to me if you don't pay more attention."

"As I remember, Barbara, you mentioned a woman who was with Alvise when he rang the Wilverlys' bell. Was it this Violetta Grespi—or Volpi as she's now called?"

"Exactly, *caro*. And perhaps you'll also remember that she tried to latch on to Silvestro afterward. She was eager to make a good marriage—and she did. A respectable man with a respectable income. Bernardo Volpi owns an import-export business in Mestre. He's almost an invalid these days—his heart or his liver, I'm not sure. You have to understand that I don't court information about Violetta Volpi—any more than I go out of my way to be told what nasty things she might be saying about me. To be honest, though, I'd like to believe that it's Violetta Volpi or someone like her who's behind this. I'm far less frightened of any lies that this Flavia person might be telling than I am of it all turning out to be the truth. I know you don't like to hear that, *caro*—not when I've asked you to get at the bottom of this—but I assure you again that no matter how afraid I am of the truth, I have to know it. Don't hide anything from me. Don't protect me. Just be gentle."

Her voice had been gradually getting softer but when, after a brief pause, she spoke again, it had a harsh, sarcastic edge.

"Violetta Volpi is an *artiste*." It was a word the Contessa reserved for only the least talented and the most pretentious. "I mention this only as a warning."

Urbino next called Bruno Novembrini.

"Ah, yes, Signor Macintyre. Massimo said I might expect a

call from you." Novembrini's voice was low and smooth. "He tells me that you're interested in one of my paintings."

Surely Zuin would have been more specific than that.

"I am, but not in buying it. I'd like some information about the model you used."

"You would?" There was an almost total lack of surprise in Novembrini's question. "In that case I don't think we should discuss it over the phone. Why don't you meet me at Massimo's gallery tomorrow morning at ten. Massimo said that a relative of yours would be stopping by then."

10

EUGENE WAS IN an exuberant mood the next morning despite the heat as the crowded vaporetto went up the Grand Canal between rows of palazzi and under a sky as gray as lead. His exuberance, however, had nothing to do with the scene around them. Urbino kept pointing out buildings as they stood in the front of the boat, but Eugene only nodded and inevitably returned to his preferred topic of conversation since leaving the Danieli.

"I like that Zuin," he said for what must have been the fifth time. "Not one for piddlin'. Called me up right before you came—wanted to be sure it was still a convenient time for me to stop by. Very accommodatin'—the most accommodatin' man in his line I've ever come across," he added, giving the impression of a long and rich experience with art dealers. "Says he's got some mighty fine stuff at his shop—big things—and he won't even charge for shippin'!"

"It might not be a good idea to seem too eager, Eugene."

" 'Cause he might take advantage of me? You know there's nobody on either side of the big lake that can do that to Eugene Lee Hennepin! I know you want to help me out—Europe and this place bein' your turf—but let's face it. You have no more business sense than Evie. Good thing you never agreed to join our family business. Between you and Evie you would have run us into the ground!" He gave Urbino a quick sideways glance. "Evie isn't so happy these days, Urbino."

Eugene waited. Urbino had no choice but to ask him why.

"Seems like her marriage to Reid is over and done with! That's what comes from marryin' a cousin from the Delisle side of the family. The only good Delisles are the women, like our Momma. Could I ask you a personal question, Urbino?" Not waiting for an answer, Eugene went right on, "Could you love another man's child?"

Urbino stared at Eugene in disbelief.

"Damn hot in this city of yours!" Eugene said quickly. "Even worse than back home! And I keep gettin' these glimmers in my eyes and feelin' unsteady on my feet as if I'm on a ship!" Eugene applied his handkerchief to his flushed face while looking surreptitiously at Urbino. "Don't look at me like that! You know what I mean! Could you love Evie and Reid's little Randall like your own?"

"Whatever are you talking about, Eugene?"

"I know I'm bein' premature and jumpin' the gun, but let bygones be bygones. It's been *years* since you've even seen one another. She's as fresh as ever, and you haven't changed all that much," he added with less conviction, squinting at Urbino. "The reason I mention little Randall is that Evie would never remarry under any other circumstances. And you wouldn't be reminded of Reid. Little Randall looks a lot more like me, poor kid, than Reid—or even Evie! Funny how genes work out, isn't it? So what do you say, Urbino?"

The only comfort Urbino got was knowing that Evangeline couldn't possibly be behind all this.

"Evie still thinks about you," Eugene went on. "Mentions your name all the time. Has a soft spot in her heart, she does. Drives old Reid up the wall."

Evangeline's pretty oval face swam before Urbino's eyes. He hadn't seen her in ten years, and that had been only briefly on a visit to New Orleans to see his great-aunts. Evangeline had looked just as lovely as ever. She had been with her parents and her father's two brothers—in other words, very much within the deep bosom of the Hennepin family from which Urbino had tried to help her escape. Back when they had first met, Evangeline had wanted and needed Urbino as a counterweight to the Hennepins, but ultimately she had been too much of one not to leave him standing alone against the family.

Pushing away thoughts of Evangeline, Urbino tried to deflect Eugene's attention to the Palazzo Dario with its multicolored marble facade. Eugene suspiciously eyed the building, whose outside walls inclined to the left at a noticeable angle.

"Looks like it's ready to fall over, like half this town! Don't know how you stand it. Is it always so jam-packed? Just look at all the people! I'm surprised the whole place doesn't just sink plumb out of sight! But I'm not so sure all this would bother Evie one little—"

"That building there," Urbino said, indicating a large, low white building with gold-and-white-striped wooden poles in front of a water terrace where people were lounging, "is the Palazzo Guggenheim."

Urbino hoped that the interest Eugene had expressed yesterday in Peggy Guggenheim would get him off the topic of Evangeline.

"Nothing much to the top of it," Eugene said in a disappointed tone. "Matter of fact, looks like the whole damn top was sliced right off."

"That's because it was never finished. It's called the 'Unfinished Palace.' It would have been the biggest palazzo on the Grand Canal."

"What happened? Run out of money?"

"That's one story. Another one is that the family who owned that palazzo"—he pointed to the Palazzo Grande on the other side of the Grand Canal—"objected. They didn't want their view of the lagoon taken away."

Eugene looked skeptical.

"Must have been the money. Would have cost a bundle even in those days. How much did Guggenheim fork over?"

"Sixty thousand dollars."

"A steal!"

"That was back in 1948 though."

As the boat went under the Accademia Bridge and approached the vaporetto station where a crowd was waiting, Eugene looked as if he were doing some mental calculations.

"Even back then, it was a steal." He nodded in satisfaction.
"Now *there* was a businesswoman—even if she *did* get a palace
without a top floor."

11

THE FRONT ROOM of Zuin's gallery in a little courtyard behind
the Accademia was filled with objects from the sixteenth to the
nineteenth centuries, among them Victorian photogravures of
Venice, statuary and sculpture, and period furniture.

"Do you think these are fancy enough for May-Foy, Urbino?" Eugene asked as he peered at two eighteenth-century
gilded chairs with a carved doge's hat decorating the backrests.
"You know how picayunish she can be."

May-Foy—actually Ma Foi—was Eugene's wife back in
Louisiana. Thinking of May-Foy's ornate sitting room in which
she spent almost all her waking hours, Urbino, who was examining a sixteenth-century glass reliquary inset with jewels, assured
Eugene that the Brustolons would do.

"I don't know, though," Eugene said, shaking his head.
"Seems kind of funny to bring chairs back from Italy."

Zuin, today sporting a lavender pocket square, led them
into the first of the other two rooms. Eugene smiled in satisfaction.

"Look at all these paintings! Some of them are so big!"

The walls were covered with Venetian scenes, several portraits, and more than enough abstract and expressionist works
to keep the Contessa complaining for hours. A good-looking
man of medium height dressed in black came walking toward
them.

"You must be Urbino Macintyre," he said in accented English, his voice smooth, taking Urbino's hand. "I didn't recognize your name when we talked on the phone but I've seen you
around town. I'm Bruno Novembrini."

Novembrini was tall and dark, with short-cropped hair

graying at the temples and deep-set eyes in a bony, handsome face. From the biography in the catalog Zuin had given him, Urbino knew that Novembrini was forty-two and a native of Venice. He had a degree in economics from Ca' Foscari, the local university, but had been "devoted to art since Peggy Guggenheim had met him as a teenager and showed him her private collection." Knowing Peggy Guggenheim's somewhat scandalous reputation, Urbino couldn't help wondering exactly what Novembrini's association with the woman had been.

"So you're the one who did all that stuff we saw yesterday!" Eugene said. "I bought one of them. I hope Zuin here doesn't hold back on any of the lire with you. Just jokin', Zuin. I'm sure you're on the up-and-up."

Novembrini smiled.

"I trust Massimo completely—and so can you. Is your name Macintyre, too?"

"Hennepin—Eugene Hennepin. Urbino and me aren't related, except through marriage." Eugene gave Urbino a knowing look. "I don't want to hurt your feelings, Mr. Novembrini—am I pronouncin' it right?—but I'm not here to get another one of your paintings. Variety is what I want. You see, I plan to buy something nice every day, like that Guggenheim lady from the palace with the top sliced off."

Novembrini's surprise was so mild that either he was an accomplished actor or Zuin had already told him about Eugene's quota.

"Look here, Urbino, what do you think of this? It isn't anything like Mr. Novembrini's stuff."

It was a portrait of a girl of thirteen or fourteen with brown eyes and a pale face. She was sitting on the side of a rock near a pool of water and was carrying an armful of flowers. The execution was simple but there was something haunting about it, mainly, Urbino felt, because of the melancholy expression in the girl's eyes.

"Real pretty," Eugene went on. "May-Foy loves flowers, and she's nuts about pictures of girls. You know what she thinks of that *Pink Lady* she has. What's this one called?"

"The artist didn't name it," Zuin said, "but I call her 'Young Ophelia,' for obvious reasons."

Eugene squinted at the portrait. Urbino explained about Ophelia's mad scene with flowers and her death by drowning.

"I wish you hadn't told me that. Kind of takes away from the picture. But why don't you just run along, Urbino? Don't worry about me. Mr. Zuin and I know exactly where we stand with each other, don't we, Mr. Zuin? We don't need you standin' around and gawkin' at us."

Zuin added nothing but Urbino was sure that he agreed.

12

URBINO AND NOVEMBRINI were sitting at an outdoor café next to the Accademia Bridge. From their vantage point they could take in the boats going up and down the Grand Canal and the people thronging the wooden bridge for a view. The sky was still leaden and the air oppressive. Novembrini sat with a pensive expression on his bony face and a cigarette in his hand. Urbino wondered how anyone could smoke in this heat.

"So you'd like to know the name of the model for *Nude in a Funeral Gondola*," he said after draining his espresso in one swallow. He took a last drag of his cigarette, stubbed it out, and flicked it into the Grand Canal. He smiled. "It'll be washed out by the tide, Macintyre. About my model, I'm sure you understand that I have a responsibility to protect her from unwelcome attention."

"I do. She came to a party in Asolo last weekend at the villa of my friend, the Contessa da Capo-Zendrini." Novembrini gave no sign that he recognized the name. "She left hurriedly and the Contessa would like to contact her."

A smile curved one side of the artist's broad, sensuous mouth.

"The Contessa doesn't know who her own guest was? What about you?" he asked.

"She looked familiar. I realized yesterday that she was probably the model in your painting. I know her first name." Urbino hoped that the woman had given her real one. "Flavia."

Novembrini raised an eyebrow.

"But she didn't mention her last name? Obviously that's the way she wanted it. Flavia must have her reasons."

Urbino decided on a different tack.

"Are you afraid of her getting more attention than she's had already? I mean because the painting was slashed?"

"Yes, there's that."

"The woman who slashed the painting got away, didn't she? I was at the Biennale when it happened. She pushed past me and escaped into the crowd."

Novembrini looked at him sharply just as Urbino had expected him to.

"Massimo told me you saw her. The painting wasn't damaged much. It all happened very fast. The guards couldn't do anything. She sprayed them with a chemical. I don't know whether she was a feminist or an art critic—maybe both!" he added with a strained laugh.

"I may be wrong, Signor Novembrini, but I think that you *do* know. It was Flavia, wasn't it? Flavia in dark glasses and a scarf. When I saw her at the Contessa da Capo-Zendrini's, she looked familiar mainly because of your painting, but it was also because of the glimpse I had of her. I realize that now."

"Is that why you're asking all these questions? You come to me with some story about a party up in Asolo and all along you just want to get Flavia in trouble—*and* me, too!"

"I'm not free to tell you why I'm interested in Flavia, but it has nothing to do with the slashing. And I have no intention of informing the authorities, although surely someone else recognized her."

Novembrini shook his head.

"As I said, it happened very fast, and, as you yourself saw, her hair and her eyes were covered. But of course I knew it was Flavia."

"What about Zuin?"

"He wasn't there, and I didn't tell him it was Flavia. He has mixed feelings about her," he added with a laugh.

"What's her last name?"

"Brollo."

The name meant nothing to Urbino but perhaps it would to the Contessa.

"Is she from Venice?"

"Yes, from San Polo. Flavia's mother is dead, and her father lives in the San Polo house with his sister, but Flavia prefers to stay in a pensione near here—the Casa Trieste. She says she's in search of the ideal home, although what she sees in the Casa Trieste is beyond me. It's a rattrap run by a guy called Ladislao Mirko, a drug addict just like his father was, but Flavia won't listen to a word against him. Listen! I don't want her to know that I've told you any of this—or even that we've spoken. We've had a stormy relationship. I wouldn't want to make it any worse." The fear and uneasiness were back in his deep-set eyes. "She's been upset enough lately, as you can tell from what she did at the Italy Pavilion. She was friends with that girl murdered on Sant'Elena. It hit her pretty hard. I'm sure it had a lot to do with slashing my painting."

"What do you know about her father?"

There was no hesitation in Novembrini's response.

"Very little, considering Flavia and I have been so close. He's a pianist. His family used to own one of those petrochemical plants in Marghera that spew their filth into the air. He still has a lot of his money invested in petrochemicals. Flavia hates that—says he's helping to pollute Old Mother Earth and destroy our museum city here! Flavia refuses to take any money from him."

"Have you ever met him?"

"No. Flavia's made it obvious that she wants me to steer clear of him. But I thought it was Flavia you were interested in? Listen, Macintyre, if you say anything to the police about Flavia doing the slashing, I'll deny it."

A few moments later a small, dark-haired young woman came up to their table and asked Novembrini if she could speak to him. Novembrini was about to get up and draw the young woman aside, but Urbino said that he had to be leaving. As Urbino walked over the Accademia Bridge, he saw the woman start to lift her face to Novembrini's, but the artist said something to her and she put her head down.

13

HALF AN HOUR later Urbino walked into a little square near Campo Santa Margherita. Lines of laundry crisscrossed the square and plastic bags of refuse hung from the doorknobs of the buildings. A cat sat in a corner beneath a street shrine of the Blessed Virgin, eyeing a pigeon making its way over the uneven paving stones.

The Casa Trieste looked little different from the other flaking buildings around it except for a small wooden sign announcing its name above its bell. Many of these inexpensive lodging houses were scattered throughout the city. They fell somewhere between *pensioni*, with their obligatory breakfast, and youth hostels.

Urbino pushed the bell several times before the lock was released. He went in. Disinfectant was heavy on the dead air. A dark wooden staircase rose in front of him.

"Upstairs," said a man's nasal voice in Italian.

A figure detached itself from the darkness. The man was in his early thirties, of less than average height, and extremely thin. Large, lusterless eyes watched Urbino's ascent as thin fingers reached up to tug down a black knit skullcap. The nostrils of his nose were large. Urbino immediately recognized him as the man with Flavia Brollo on Saturday afternoon. He didn't seem to recognize Urbino.

"May I help you?"

"I'd like to speak to Signorina Flavia Brollo."

Something flashed in the man's dull eyes, but still not recognition. Urbino had the impression the man was either drugged or drunk. He seemed a little unsteady on his feet. Novembrini had said that he took drugs.

"She's not here."

"When will she be back?"

"She didn't tell me. She comes and she goes."

"Is she back in Asolo?"

The man looked at Urbino more sharply. He sniffled and ran a finger under his red nose.

"I don't know her business, signore! And if I did, I wouldn't tell a stranger! It isn't easy having a *pensione*," he whined. "Just this week a woman comes in and wants a room. I ask for her *carta d'identità*. Later, she says, and goes to her room. She takes a bath. Then what does she do? She leaves! How can I pay my bills with guests like that?"

"Is that the kind of guest Signorina Brollo is?"

The man seemed confused. Before he could answer, a woman with a Neapolitan accent came down the hall to retrieve something from the *pensione*'s safe. After he gave it to her, he turned back to Urbino and, sniffling again, said, "Signorina Brollo is my friend. I don't consider her a guest. Good day, signore."

As Urbino was leaving, a small, fair-haired woman in her fifties was ringing the bell. She slipped in before the door closed, looking at Urbino sideways with pale blue, bloodshot eyes. The sweet odor of anisette wafted behind her.

In the *campo* Urbino stopped an elderly man letting himself into his apartment.

"The *padrone*? Ladislao Mirko—a strange name, yes? He and his family came here from Trieste years ago. He's on his own now. He's going to lose that place one of these days. Money problems—always looking for *la grana*!"

The man rubbed his thumb and first finger together.

"Have you noticed a very attractive young woman with auburn hair coming and going to the Casa Trieste?"

The man broke into a big smile.

"Have I! She's a beauty! Mirko is always sniffing after her like a dog. Half the boys and men in the neighborhood would like to get at her."

Urbino thanked him and started off in the direction of the Danieli to have lunch with Eugene.

14

BUT EUGENE HAD left a message saying that he had gone to Murano with Zuin to visit the glass showrooms.

Outside the Danieli, Urbino joined the press surging along the sun-beaten Riva degli Schiavoni toward the Piazza. An occasional breeze from the lagoon blew hot and humid against Urbino's sweating face, and he felt assaulted by the smell and the noise of the crowd. Urbino always warned friends and relatives against coming to Venice during the summer. It was impossible. Tourists, ravenous for their promised portion of Venice, overran the city like an invading army, pointing cameras like guns and mounting attacks on the sights with a ferocity that had little to do with genuine interest and appreciation.

As Urbino inched his way past a group shoving each other for a glimpse of the Bridge of Sighs, he remembered what Madge Lennox had said about these tourists being like the dead on holiday. She was right. Delirium and desperation were adding their burden to the already thick, almost unbreathable air.

A group of street musicians were performing under the pillar of St. Mark. Their folk song, vaguely familiar to Urbino, emanated in a melancholy stream from a wooden flute, bagpipes, and a drum and cymbals worked with a foot pedal. Letting the swarm of people pass around him, Urbino stopped to listen and then dropped a ten-thousand-lira note into the proffered hat of one of the performers.

The man, unshaven and snaggly-toothed, smiled at him and said in a thick Neapolitan accent, "May you be as far from death as you are from poverty, signore."

In Piazza San Marco long queues inched toward the Basilica and the Campanile. Hundreds of weary heads were craned toward the Torre dell'Orologio—the clock tower—waiting for the bronze Moors to strike the hour. On the Lido last week Urbino had fantasized about the clock tower melting down into the Piazza like a Dalí painting, but now its brick and blue tile were hard-edged in the glare of the sunshine.

People crowded under the arcades, sat and sprawled on the steps and against the columns, and danced and milled in the large open space of the Piazza as the orchestras outside Florian's and Quadri's played Broadway show tunes. This was not for him, Urbino decided. Turning his back on the Piazza, he made his slow way through the clogged arteries surrounding the historic heart of the city until he reached the quieter alleys and squares and could breathe a sigh of relief. Soon he would be back at the Palazzo Uccello, which even in high season was blessedly remote from all the hubbub, a comfortable ark within the greater ark that was Venice. Behind its walls he could remain apart from what the Contessa called the "faceless hordes of high season," yet close enough to the flow of life not to feel isolated. The result was that he felt snug, if also a little self-satisfied, in his solitude.

A long time ago he had read a French novel about a neurotic *fin de siècle* aristocrat who retired to his mansion outside Paris to lead a self-contained, eccentric life of the mind and senses. Urbino liked to think that he was doing something similar at the Palazzo Uccello although he shared very little of the hero's decadent sensibility. But like that aristocratic hero he, too, preferred to distance himself somewhat from vulgar reality. Yet, ironically, Urbino was often in quest of this same "vulgar reality" in his investigations and in his *Venetian Lives*. He told himself, however, that this wasn't perhaps inconsistent at all, since the end result of both endeavors was the kind of order that he craved.

Back at the Palazzo Uccello, Urbino called the Contessa and told her about the artist Bruno Novembrini and Ladislao Mirko, the *padrone* of the Casa Trieste.

"You've learned quite a bit already, *caro*! Now we at least know her last name. Brollo, Brollo. The name doesn't quite mean anything to me, and yet—" She broke off, ostensibly to search the corners of her mind for some association. "I'm being teased. I seem to have heard the name before."

"It isn't all that unusual."

Then Urbino told her that Flavia's father was a pianist.

"That could be it," the Contessa said. "I could have heard his name at the conservatory. He might even have been one of the teachers. I'll go through my bits and pieces from those days. You know, Urbino, I'm even more apprehensive now than I was before. If this Flavia Brollo could bring herself to slash the painting the way she did, who knows what she might be capable of? You said that Novembrini seemed afraid for himself. He's probably afraid she'll come at *him* with a knife next time! Do you think they're having an affair?"

"Either they're having one—or it's over. That might be the reason she slashed the painting. An attractive young woman joined him at the café when I was leaving. Maybe it's his new girlfriend."

"Now I have something to tell you, *caro*," the Contessa said with a little thrill of excitement in her voice. "I'm seeing the young lady in question tomorrow. She called and said that she would like to see me at Florian's."

"Florian's?"

"It surprised me, too, but now that you've told me about how violent she can be, I'm almost glad it won't be here. Somewhere public might be better—or should I say 'safer'? But then again you couldn't find a more public place than the Italy Pavilion, could you? That's why I'm glad you'll be with me."

"It might be better to see her alone."

"But then I wouldn't be able to see her at all. Signorina Brollo insists on you. She said to be sure that my good-looking young friend was there, too. I've added the 'good-looking,' *caro*. Call me unredeemably prejudiced, but as for the rest—yes, she insists."

"But why?"

"It's obvious, isn't it?" The Contessa paused dramatically. "She's afraid of being alone with *me*! That's why she chose Florian's. You may think you're a master of concealment, Urbino, but one thing you can't hide is how much your heart goes out to women in distress. She knows she can count on you to keep me in line. Thursday at four."

15

THE EXPRESSION THAT Urbino found on the Contessa's face on Thursday afternoon when he slipped into the chair across from her revealed all the irritation she felt about the way the Chinese salon at Caffè Florian had been invaded. The doors between the salon and the arcade, usually closed so that the only access to the room was through the café itself, were thrown open. What in other seasons was the Contessa's vantage point from which she could peer into the square from behind a shield of dark wood and glass was now itself in the midst of activity.

Tourists intruded their heads to take in the salon's paintings under glass, its *amorino* lamps, marble tables, and banquettes. Others wandered through the eighteenth-century salons as if they were rooms in a gallery, peering curiously up at the ceiling with its strips of dark wood and floral paintings, at the parquet floors and mirrors, and at the Oriental frescoes under glass. Photograph takers backed into the Contessa and Urbino's table to get a good shot. Waiters bustled to the tables in the square and under the arcade, getting each other's attention with kissing noises.

Florian's orchestra, on its stage in front of the arcade, played one Broadway show song after another.

" 'Frogs and lice,' " the Contessa suddenly said.

"What was that, Barbara?"

"It just popped into my head." Her face had a slight flush of embarrassment, and she rearranged the lace handkerchief in the pocket of her Valentino linen suit. "Last week I was reading a collection of letters by one of my countrywomen, Lady Montagu. It seems that she felt the same way about the crowds in Venice as I do—and that was two hundred and fifty years ago! *Plus ça change, plus c'est la même chose!* She said they tormented her 'as the frogs and lice did the palace of the Pharaoh.' A rather apt image, even if she was talking about her own fellow Englishmen. You have to admit she had a point, *caro*. My own not so original image is that it's like a circle of Dante's Inferno."

"A circle reserved for whom, Barbara? For those who have sinned against charity by not wanting to have their fellow men around them?"

The Contessa gave a sigh of pure exasperation.

"Don't get democratic on me, Urbino. You hate this just as much as I do—maybe even more! After all, *I* wasn't the one who decided to sequester himself away in a remote Venetian palazzo in his prime. *I* married into Venice."

This particular distinction didn't seem to give her any satisfaction this afternoon, however, and she was silent while Urbino ordered his Campari soda. Urbino didn't interrupt her thoughts, but gave his attention to the swirling scene only a few feet away.

"At least the orchestra could play Strauss or Offenbach!" the Contessa said finally when Urbino was enjoying the first sip of his drink. "And our Signorina Brollo is atrociously late. I've already had a *Coppa Fornarina*."

She was now working on a plate of petits fours accompanied by tea—uniced, and made from the first-flush Jasmine brought over every month by Mauro, her majordomo at the Ca' da Capo.

"It's not much past four, Barbara."

"It's almost twenty past! Oh well, considering how the girl has acted already I suppose I can't expect punctuality, can I?"

Two young men with short blond haircuts strolled past under the arcade, their chests bare. Swollen money bags were belted around their waists, and hanging from their back pockets were their T-shirts.

"Can't these people keep their clothes on? And look at those obscene pouches!" the Contessa said. She looked away from the two men only to see a young man and woman embracing against a column. Once again she sighed. "What did Yeats complain about? 'The young in one another's arms,' wasn't it? Oh, it's in the air here—in the Italian air!"

She appeared to ponder this for a few moments.

"Italians! Sometimes I think most of them live only for the sake of physical beauty," she said, apparently giving Urbino the fruit of her brief reflection. "I know it's a ridiculous exaggeration, but there's more than a little truth in it. Italy is such a difficult country when you see your own beauty, however great or small, slipping away. The Italians!" But this time she said it with a sadder inflection. "There are moments when I've felt like crying when I see a beautiful young woman pausing to look at herself in a mirror or a shop window. I can't help but wonder what Flavia Brollo's mother looked like. She must have been beautiful."

She looked impatiently out into the crowd.

"Wherever is that girl! It's so insufferably hot in here!" She opened her lace fan and waved it vigorously back and forth, succeeding only in making herself hotter, Urbino was sure. "She'll probably torture me more now by never even coming! I—"

The Contessa was staring at the door into the next salon where Flavia Brollo was standing. She was wearing a simple shift dress in the shade of green preferred by Italians—the same shade as in the national flag. It brought out the green of her eyes, which were not at all as blank as they had been in Asolo. In fact, they were shining brightly.

"Contessa," Flavia Brollo said with an attempt at a warm smile. "And Signor Macintyre."

Urbino got up and held out a chair for her.

"I would like to speak in English, if you please," she said somewhat tentatively as she sat down. "To show you that I want to be honest." She smiled again. "It is very hard not to tell the truth in a different language."

This, Urbino perceived, was a somewhat different Flavia from the one who had intruded on the Contessa's garden party on Saturday. She was just as assured, certainly, but she seemed less anxious and more inclined to please, to put them both at their ease. Perhaps the difference was because she had already made her great revelation.

"No, thank you," Flavia said when Urbino asked her if she wanted anything, pushing back her auburn hair in what must be an habitual gesture.

"I hope you've come here to give us an explanation, Signorina Brollo," the Contessa said without any preliminary, snapping her fan closed.

"So you know my legal name." Flavia shrugged. "It does not matter."

"But it *does* matter," the Contessa insisted. "Surely you have nothing to do with my husband."

"I am sorry, Contessa, but the Conte da Capo-Zendrini *was* my father. Soon you will believe me. You will have no choice."

Flavia Brollo tilted back her chin and stared at the Contessa with her green eyes.

"Why do you say that he was your father, Signorina Brollo?" Urbino asked before the Contessa could respond to the young woman's challenge.

"I prefer it if you call me simply 'Flavia.' I hate the name of Brollo!" Anger animated her face, but she gained control of herself a few moments later. "I say that the Conte was my father because he *was*! I know!"

"Isn't your father a pianist?" Urbino pursued.

"Him! He is the man who *says* he is my father but I know he does not believe it. He *cannot* believe it!" Her green eyes flashed with a cold fire. "You have a photograph of my father for me, Contessa?"

The Contessa took a deep breath.

"My dear Signorina Brollo, I have no intention of humoring you so that you will go away and leave me in peace."

"You're being foolish, Contessa!" Flavia Brollo said, now speaking in Italian. "The Conte da Capo-Zendrini might have loved you. I don't know anything about that. You seem like a good woman. But he also betrayed you. He loved my mother. You're making a mistake! Can't you see that! Something terrible happens when people don't listen! When they refuse to believe what they know must be true!" She stood up, knocking her chair over and bumping against a waiter who was going out with a full tray of drinks. The fire in her green eyes was no longer cold, but burning. "Proof!" she shouted. "I'll bring you proof, one way or another, I promise you! Then you'll know that the Conte da Capo-Zendrini was my father! You'll believe me. You *must* believe me," she said desperately.

Her raised voice had brought the maître d', who now stood in the doorway. The Contessa caught his eye and shook her head slightly. He moved to one side as Flavia Brollo stormed out of the Chinese salon to the foyer, her auburn hair flying behind her. She went to the guest book, picked up the pen, and wrote in the book. After she hurried out into the Piazza, Urbino went over to see what she had written. An angry-looking script read "Flavia da Capo-Zendrini."

16

"Do YOU THINK she actually *does* have proof?" the Contessa asked Urbino several hours later as they were dining at Al Graspo de Ua near the Rialto Bridge. It was one of the Contessa's favorite restaurants, but she had hardly touched any of her dishes. Even the gelato in front of her now was melting. "If she does, it changes everything, doesn't it? For one thing, it means you're off the hook, *caro*." She managed a weak smile. "You won't have to worry about being the one to bring my whole world crashing down around me."

The Contessa looked up at the overhead beams, as if she expected the crash to begin imminently. She spent so long gazing upward before going on that Urbino thought she might be trying to read the Venetian sayings on the beams.

"I tell you, Urbino," she said, bringing her eyes back to his, "I tell you as surely as I'm sitting here that I'm up to it. If this young woman has proof, let her show it to me, and if it's *real* proof," she said redundantly but not passionlessly, "I'll accept it. Whatever else can I do? I'll stand by her for Alvise's sake. But I can't imagine her having any proof that won't bear some discreet checking into. I'm not about to swallow things down whole! So you'll have your onerous little task to do, after all. If you don't, there would be only one reason why. It would mean that her proof was as obvious as the nose on my face—and that's one thing I just couldn't bear!"

Almost involuntarily, Urbino glanced at the Contessa's patrician nose. It was one of her best features. She held her head higher when she noticed the direction of his glance.

" 'Ocular proof,' you mean," Urbino said, wondering if the Contessa's reference to noses had made him think of eyes.

"Why does that sound familiar to me?"

"Because it's what Othello says to Iago—to give him 'ocular proof' of Desdemona's infidelity."

"As I recall," the Contessa said dryly, "that play didn't end happily for anyone. Let's hope we have a better resolution to my own little Venetian drama!"

The Contessa had aimed for a light note but it failed. The anxious look on her face told Urbino how much she knew she had to fear. He was sure that all the way back to La Muta she would be able to think of nothing else but Flavia Brollo's "proof."

That night a violent thunderstorm shook Venice. About midnight, after the height of the storm, the Contessa called Urbino from Asolo.

"I'm sorry for calling you at this hour, *caro,* but I can't get to sleep. Tell me it's going to be all right. Tell me that Flavia Brollo is either silly or malicious. Tell me—"

She didn't go on but apologized again and hung up. Urbino knew that he would have trouble sleeping himself. He went to the study, put Mahler's Third Symphony on the player, and, with Serena in his lap, tried to lose himself in the gossipy pages of Peggy Guggenheim's memoirs.

17

WHILE URBINO AND the Contessa waited for Flavia Brollo to contact her again, Urbino devoted himself to Eugene.

His ex–brother–in–law had found a chandelier to his taste on Murano—"big, all different colors, with pagodas and dolphins" was his enthusiastic description. He had also decided on the painting of the melancholy girl with flowers at Zuin's gallery. Having made these purchases, along with the gondola and Novembrini's painting, he was now ready for some sightseeing.

And so, in the enervating heat of a sirocco, Urbino and Eugene made their rounds of the sights along with hordes of tourists. The Bridge of Sighs was pronounced "dirty gray" and the Basilica San Marco "a cave dark enough for bats." The canals were as smelly as "a low-tide bayou," the *calli* "too narrow to even change your mind in," and the dank, low-ceilinged dungeons of the Doge's Palace "probably no worse than half the parlors in the city." Only when Eugene was looking at Tintoretto's *Paradiso* in the Doge's Palace did he seem to find something commensurate with his taste.

"The largest painting in the world!" he exclaimed. "Must be at least twenty-five yards long and a good seven wide! Look at all them angels and saints and whatnots around Jesus and His Momma. I reckon there must be about a thousand."

Unfortunately, it was all a disappointment for Eugene after he had seen paradise. Even a gondola ride up the Grand Canal and along the back waterways on Saturday afternoon with a mercifully silent gondolier couldn't spark his interest. He was manifestly unimpressed with it all, and barely condescended to give a glance at anything—not at the Rialto Bridge or the palazzi or the silent, secret squares. He did, however, find some amusement in the plaque adorning the side of the Ca' Rezzonico. On it were written the lines from Browning that were embroidered on Occhipinti's pillow:

> Open my heart and you will see
> 'Graved inside of it, "Italy."

Eugene joked that this might be a good epitaph for Urbino himself, now that he had turned his heart against his own country.

"Just like that Guggenheim gal! Say! How about havin' this fellow drop us at her building with the top missin'?"

Pleased to have Eugene show an interest in something, Urbino had the gondolier deliver them to an embankment near the Palazzo Guggenheim.

Urbino and Eugene first wandered through the small garden at the back of the museum. A tour guide was animatedly speaking to his small group in front of the huge, thronelike stone seat that Peggy Guggenheim had loved to pose on. Urbino pointed out the pieces of sculpture scattered throughout the garden to Eugene, among them one by Giacometti, but Eugene wasn't paying any attention. He was listening to the tour guide's story of the notorious Marchesa Casati, who had owned the palazzo before Peggy Guggenheim.

"The Marchesa, known as the Medusa of the great hotels, kept leopards and panthers here. She let them range around freely, from what I understand, and loved to wear a live boa constrictor around her shoulders. One of her last parties, after which she had to flee Venice in disgrace, was given in Piazza San Marco. Handsome young men holding flaming torches stood on columns placed throughout the Piazza. They wore absolutely nothing except golden paint." The tour guide paused, assessing the reaction of his listeners, before going on. "Unfortunately, one of them suffocated to death under the paint. Years later, Peggy Guggenheim bought the palazzo for sixty thousand dollars."

Eugene gave a broad smile.

"I'm sure she gave plenty of wild parties of her own! Why, look here, Urbino," he said, pointing to an engraved marble sign against the wall: HERE LIE MY BELOVED BABIES. Eugene shook his head. "She certainly had a passel of kids! And look at these names! White Angel. Hong Kong. Madame Butterfly. She *was* a strange woman. Is your Countess anything like her?"

Urbino assured him that the Contessa wasn't and explained that the names were those of Peggy Guggenheim's dogs.

"Too bad the gal passed on, Urbino. She sounds mighty interestin'. Let's go inside and take a look at those paintings she bought every day."

But once inside the gallery, he seemed bewildered and was perhaps reconsidering his high evaluation of the woman who had bought all this abstract and Surrealist art.

"She must have known what she was doin' but I can't make head nor tail out of these things, Urbino! Just look at this contraption here!" He pointed to a Giacometti bronze on a block. "*Woman with Her Throat Cut*! Can you believe that one! Looks like a lobster split open. Reminds me of that girl I heard about at the hotel—the one stabbed to death. And why is this one called *Sad Young Man on a Train*? Do you see any train? I don't even see a man! At least I could make out all those eyes in the painting in the other room that had 'eyes' in the title."

Appreciation of the taste of his new heroine was proving

difficult for the poor man, and perhaps no more difficult than
when they were looking at the Surrealist paintings.

"*The Robing of the Bride*?" Eugene stared at Max Ernst's
painting. A naked woman, barely covered by a bright red cape
and a hood of feathers, was flanked by a bizarre birdlike crea-
ture with a spear, another naked woman, and a pygmy figure
with four breasts, a protruding belly, and a penis. "Am I missin'
something, Urbino? I just don't get it."

Urbino, not feeling up to an explanation of Surrealism,
mumbled something about fantasy and the dreamworld. It was
to Eugene's credit that he didn't even pretend to understand.

"And look at this one," Eugene said. "It's called *The Birth
of Liquid Desires*. Looks more like the *death* of something to me!"

It was by Salvador Dalí. A bearded nude man, with a
woman's breasts and a prominent erection draped by a scarf,
grabbed a young woman in a white gown. The woman's head
was a burst of colorful flowers, with random petals falling to
the ground. Behind them loomed a weirdly shaped rock with a
womblike opening in which another man, wearing nothing but
a sock, his back turned to the viewer and the couple, was bending down and reaching a hand into a pool of water. Kneeling
behind the rock was another pale woman, her face turned aside
and shielded with one hand as she poured liquid into a bowl in
which the bearded man's foot was standing.

Eugene kept staring at the Dalí until he finally pronounced
that he liked it.

"Can't figure out why, though. It has something to do with
water, right? That must be it. Or it could have something to do
with money, too, couldn't it? You know, liquid cash. Isn't that
a safe up there in the corner?" He scrutinized the painting for
a few more moments. "Lookee here! That man's all ready and
rarin' to go, ain't he? What they don't put in paintings! Wonder
how much Peggy paid for it?" Eugene asked, obviously feeling
closer to Miss Guggenheim now that he was seeing her house
and belongings. "Probably a lot less than Zuin soaked me for
the girl with the flowers."

Eugene gave one last look at the Dalí before they left the
room.

"I really like that *Liquid* picture," he said."You don't think
it could be for sale, do you, Urbino?"

"Definitely not, but they probably have a postcard reproduction at the desk."

"Guess that'll have to do," Eugene said in a disappointed
tone, but then he laughed. "Maybe I'll send one off to May-Foy
and tell her I bought the real thing. Wouldn't that be a hoot!"

They went out to the terrace on the Grand Canal. The two
stone benches were occupied and people were sitting on the
stone balustrade. For a few moments Urbino and Eugene stood
there looking out at the heat-shimmering Grand Canal with its
water traffic and the palazzi on the other side.

"Look at this, Urbino!" Eugene said in a stage whisper.
"Just like the old fellow in the *Liquid* picture."

Urbino knew exactly what he was referring to. It was *The
Angel of the Citadel*, Marino Marini's metal sculpture of a horse
and rider—or rather one particular detail of the rider whose
head was thrown back and arms outstretched as if in ecstasy.
The detail was there for anyone on the terrace or passing on
the Grand Canal to see—namely, the rider's erect penis. Peggy
Guggenheim used to unscrew the penis whenever nuns or sensi-
tive visitors came to the palazzo.

"What a woman!" Eugene said, shaking his head slowly in
bemused admiration. "I'm beginning to see why you like this
watery town. It certainly seems to attract an unusual crowd. Are
you sure your Countess friend—"

But Eugene didn't finish. A woman's scream shot through
the air. Several people were pointing through the wrought-iron
grille gate that separated the terrace from the Grand Canal.

Floating face downward between two of the gold-and-
white-striped wooden *pali*, or mooring poles, was a body, its
arms trailing down into the water. Shrouded in green material,
the body was rocked by the wake of a vaporetto moving up the
Grand Canal. Long hair fanned out in the water—long hair
whose color was evident only where it broke the surface of the
water and caught the rays of the late-afternoon sun. It was a
Titian auburn.

A museum official hurried from the palazzo past Marini's
tumescent rider. Two men dressed in work clothes came out
seconds later, climbed into one of the boats moored against the
posts, and reached down to grab hold of the body. Straining,
they lifted it over the side of the boat, water streaming from it.

As they brought the body into the boat, the face turned toward Urbino.

Although bloated and misshapen, the face was still recognizable enough for Urbino to realize that Flavia Brollo's days of being an object of desire—but not of mystification—were now over forever.

PART TWO

The Sun in Its Casket

1

ON SUNDAY AFTERNOON, twenty-four hours later, Urbino and the Contessa were slowly walking through the puzzle maze at La Muta, trying to make some sense of the death of Flavia Brollo. Urbino, along with Eugene, had arrived earlier in the day to help ease the Contessa through the shock and confusion.

That morning's *Gazzettino* had carried a piece on Flavia Brollo's death:

BODY OF WOMAN FOUND IN THE GRAND CANAL

The body of a woman, Flavia Brollo, 26, of this city, was found floating in front of the water steps of the Palazzo Venier dei Leoni ("the Palazzo Guggenheim") late yesterday afternoon.

A group of people, who were at the Palazzo Guggenheim to see its renowned collection of modern art, noticed the young woman's body from the water terrace.

Death was apparently from drowning. This morning Professore Renzo Zavarella, appointed expert of the office of the substitute prosecutor, Maurizio Agostini, will perform the autopsy on San Michele. The police are making inquiries into the last hours of the life of Signorina Brollo.

Signorina Brollo was the daughter of Lorenzo Brollo of the San Polo quarter, and the late Regina Grespi Brollo. Signor Brollo is a pianist and founding member of La Serenissima Orchestra. The Brollo family is the former owner of Riva Petrochemicals in Marghera.

Although the article made no mention of foul play, Urbino couldn't rid himself of the fear that this was what they might be dealing with. Who knew what dirty waters Flavia had stirred up after she rushed from Florian's to get proof that Lorenzo Brollo wasn't her father?

Yesterday Urbino had given a statement at the Venice Questura to Commissario Francesco Gemelli of the *Pubblica Sicurezza* with whom he had a somewhat adversarial relationship. They had worked together, unofficially, in the past, not so much with the police chief's approval as by his sufferance. Gemelli had been less than pleased to learn that Urbino and the Contessa had been acquainted with the dead woman and that Urbino suspected murder. Urbino had told him about Flavia's intrusion at the Contessa's villa last Saturday, the blowup at Florian's on Thursday afternoon, Flavia's link to Bruno Novembrini, and her lodging at the Casa Trieste.

"A delicate situation for your Contessa to be in," Gemelli had said. "Shortly after a public threat to the reputation of the Conte and Contessa da Capo-Zendrini, the young woman is found floating in the Grand Canal. You say you think foul play might be involved. Well, we'll have to see, won't we? By 'we' I mean the police, the medical examiner, and the prosecutor. It might be much better if you and the Contessa da Capo-Zendrini prayed that Flavia Brollo died any way other than by foul play, although a judgment of death by suicide could do its own kind of damage to the Contessa's peace of mind and reputation." Gemelli had given his supercilious smile. "We'll proceed with our inquiry and wait for Zavarella's report. Nothing is likely to slip by him."

When the Contessa had read the article in the *Gazzettino*,

she was stunned, as Urbino knew she would be, to find the Grespi name surfacing. Grespi was the maiden name of Violetta Volpi, the woman who the Contessa's friend Oriana Borelli had said bore a long-standing grudge against the Contessa. Urbino had given Oriana a call, asking her to try to get information from her husband Filippo's old nurse. Oriana had told him last week at the Ca' Borelli that the nurse knew Violetta Volpi. Since his arrival, Urbino and the Contessa had stayed close to La Muta in anticipation of Oriana's response, venturing this afternoon only as far as the maze to take advantage of the fresh, cool air blowing across the Dolomites.

Although the Contessa, dressed in flattering apricot charmeuse, was leaning on Urbino's arm and seemed to be paying little attention to their meanderings, it was she who was leading him. Despite Urbino's many negotiations of the maze's devious twists and turns and cul-de-sacs with the Contessa—and once, completely alone, on an interminable summer afternoon when he had been too proud to uncover the signs—he had never learned the route. Trying a trick he had read about, he had kept his left hand in constant contact with the hedge wall, but it had done no good. The Contessa's maze was much more complicated than that. Now, as on other occasions, Urbino was content to have her lead the way. His only responsibility was to carry the wicker hamper with their late-afternoon snack.

"If you think my problems are over now, you're sadly mistaken, *caro*," she said, looking straight ahead along the line of neatly clipped yews. "However Flavia died—suicide, accident, or God forbid! murder—I feel responsible. How can I not? One minute she's all wrought up and desperate for me to accept that Alvise is her father, and the next she's dead. All night I've been tortured thinking about her and worrying about myself, and about what it means to me now that she's dead. The burden hasn't been doubled. It's been tripled, quadrupled! I don't know if I can bear it."

Despite her distress, however, the Contessa didn't hesitate when they reached a junction but went to the left and almost immediately to the right. All they could see above the hedges were the upper stories of La Muta, the clear blue sky, and the top of the viewing tower in the center.

The Contessa stopped and looked at Urbino.

"She *can't* have been Alvise's daughter! I've searched

through all my records from my conservatory days, but I didn't find the Brollo name anywhere. And as for Violetta Grespi—or Violetta Volpi as she is now—I'm almost convinced she must be related in some way to Flavia Brollo's mother. Sharing the Grespi name would be too much of a coincidence. Well, whether she's related to Flavia Brollo's mother or not, Violetta Volpi could give me back my peace of mind. Of course, if she *does* say that Alvise was Flavia's father, how will I know whether she's being spiteful by lying or being spiteful by telling the truth? Oh, it's impossible!"

"The truth is what you want, Barbara, no matter what it is."

Urbino didn't toss this out lightly. The Contessa was a highly moral though not at all moralistic woman. She prided herself on doing what was right and facing things squarely.

"And don't worry. We'll recognize the truth when we hear it," Urbino assured her with more conviction than he felt as they resumed their slow pace. "What's much more important is how Flavia died. If she committed suicide, it's going to be a hard blow. There's going to be regret and guilt. But if Flavia was murdered, it's not going to be any better—"

" 'Better'!" the Contessa repeated. "They're equal evils as far as I'm concerned."

"But if she was murdered, Barbara, it could have been because of Alvise in some way, and we *have* to know." The Contessa's gray eyes widened in fear. Urbino squeezed her arm gently. "But things should be clearer tomorrow after Zavarella hands in his report."

They were on a long, curving stretch now with several alternate passages to their right but the Contessa ignored them.

"I'm depending on you more than ever before. Do what you have to do. After poor Flavia's outburst at Florian's, there's no way that her accusation about Alvise is going to be kept a secret. It might even be better this way. It won't seem as if I have anything to hide. People might be more willing to tell you the truth—and if there *is* a relationship between her death and Alvise you'll be in the best position to find out and help the police. You've proven so good at it in the past," the Contessa added, giving him a brave little smile.

They had reached a spiral junction, one of several in the maze. The Contessa came to a halt, but not because she had lost her way and was tempted to read one of the covered signs that said LIFT IF LOST in three languages. She was looking at Urbino in dismay.

"Am I being a fool? Should I just let it go? Fidelity leaves nothing behind but a clean sheet—a clean *page*," she corrected herself quickly, "but infidelity—betrayal—that's something else entirely, isn't it? A person can always find proof of that—or something that looks enough like it. I have to keep my two feet squarely on the ground. If I don't I'm lost, absolutely lost!"

She looked around her with a slightly bewildered expression, as if illustrating just how lost she could become. As if to compensate, she turned down one of the paths with an almost aggressive quickening of her stride.

"But now that poor Flavia is dead—possibly murdered—there's no way that Alvise and I aren't going to be dragged into things whether I want it or not. There's absolutely no way I *can* let it go, is there, *caro*?"

They were such good and close friends that their silences were almost as communicative as their conversations. The Contessa leaned more heavily on Urbino as the minutes passed, but she continued along the gravel path without the slightest hesitation. After more twists and turns, the marble bench at the center appeared. Behind it were rose bushes, the viewing tower, and a classical statue of a nymph—Alvise's gift to his wife during the summer of the maze.

As Urbino sat next to the Contessa on the bench and opened the hamper with the sandwiches, chilled wine, and mineral water, a shout floated down to them from the tower.

"Hey, you two! I'm up here!"

It was Eugene, whom they assumed hadn't yet returned from his trip into town. Urbino and the Contessa looked up at the tower. Eugene's round, flushed face smiled down at them.

"It took you two a mighty long time to get through! I was watchin' you all the way. Mind if I join you?"

"Please do, Mr. Hennepin. We're having a little repast."

" 'Repast'! I love the way you Countesses talk. I'll be down in a jiff."

His head disappeared. Footsteps clattered down the staircase.

"I like your ex–brother-in-law, *caro*. He's so—so"—she

searched for a word to do the man justice—"so *primitif*, in the
best sense. He doesn't seem to think before he speaks. It's absolutely delightful! I find him charming."

"Charming?"

"Are you jealous? Or are you worried that this charming
man is going to tell me all the secrets about you and Evangeline
that you've hugged so close all these years? Don't begrudge me
what little pleasure I can find right now!"

Eugene burst through the Gothic-arched opening.

"Sorry to barge in on your little 'repast' like this, Countess,
but I wouldn't want you to think I was spyin' on you from up
there."

"Please call me Barbara."

"How about Countess Barbara? You can call me Eugene.
You've got a mighty fine contraption here—and thank the Lord
you had the good sense to put up those signs. They should have
them in Venice instead of the ones pointin' in two different
directions with the same name! I walked through lickety-split.
You were just pokin' along. Why, thank you, Urbino, don't
mind if I do have a bit of wine, but I'll hold back on a sandwich.
Now you two just pretend I'm not here and go right on with
your confab. I won't pay you no mind."

But no sooner did he say this than he reached into his
pocket and took out a list on which he had written everything
he had bought so far in Venice. For the next hour, there at the
center of the maze, he solicited the Contessa's advice about
what other things he should invest in. The Contessa gave every
appearance of being interested.

2

DURING DINNER A large unoccupied part of the Contessa was
waiting for Oriana's call. So conversationally expansive, however, was Eugene that an observer less attuned to the Contessa

than Urbino might have thought that her attention was completely captivated.

"Urbino was always a mite strange," Eugene was saying now as he sat in full possession of a Louis Quinze armchair in the *salotto verde*. "How could he help it? No brothers and sisters, and only a meager sprinklin' of great-aunts and cousins in the whole wide world! Practically an orphan even before his poor momma and poppa were killed in the car crash. You'd think someone with hardly any kin would want a passel of kids of his own, but Evangeline and him, they never had none. You might have had a son, Urbino. Maybe he would have grown up to work in the Hennepin business even if you never wanted to, not that I ever faulted you. You know I was on your side."

Urbino, who had never regretted being the only child of two only children and who had never wanted to be part of a large, potentially smothering family, said nothing.

"Your sister has a lovely name, Eugene," the Contessa said, giving Urbino a secret little smile from the Brustolon sofa. Behind her on the wall was her collection of eighteenth- and nineteenth-century fans from Venice, Spain, France, and England, which, for Urbino, always seemed to whisper back the questionable conversations they had masked in a long-gone era.

"We call her Evie most times," Eugene said proudly, "but Urbino always called her Evangeline."

"I believe she's remarried since she and Urbino divorced, hasn't she?"

"Married to our cousin Reid—our *second* cousin," he emphasized, "but things don't look too good for them now. Evie's cuttin' loose. Says it'll be better for little Randall in the long run."

"Little Randall?"

"Evie and Reid's son—nearin' on ten, he is. Evie misses him something terrible. She still has a few more things she wants to do here"—he looked meaningfully at Urbino—"but she'll be happy enough to head on back home if the plane'll take all the duds she's been buyin'!"

"Do you mean your sister is here in Venice, Eugene? Urbino didn't tell me that."

"No, not here in Venice, Countess Barbara. She's hangin' around Florence, goin' to all the museums and buyin' up half the town. She'd *like* to come to Venice, but we'll have to see about that. I'm givin' her a call tomorrow."

"Please tell your sister Evangeline that if she does decide to come, I'd be happy to show her around. It would be delightful to do the museums and shops with her. Just say that I'm a good friend of Urbino—unless she wouldn't think that was a favorable recommendation."

The Contessa laughed lightly and even, Urbino was not a little surprised to see, nervously.

"What I meant was that, since she and Urbino are divorced, she might—"

"Oh, she doesn't have anything against Urbino! She only says the nicest things about him. Sometimes I try to get her to say something bad, just for a hoot. I'll say something like, 'Well, Evie, what do you think Urbino is up to in that palace of his over in Venice? Whyever did he sell that big place on Prytania and want to live in a tiny run-down building?' And to think it's called a palace! Why it's called a palace is beyond me. But when I saw your palace on the Grand Canal, Countess Barbara, Urbino said it was only called a house! Everything seems upside down in Venice!"

Urbino, who had been feeling increasingly uncomfortable, started to explain again why the Ca' da Capo-Zendrini was referred to as a "casa" in Venetian usage instead of a "palazzo." Eugene and the Contessa listened patiently, but they seemed to consider his explanation a somewhat unwelcome digression from a much more interesting topic.

"So, Eugene, how does Evangeline respond when you say such things about Urbino?"

"Oh, she defends him, Countess Barbara. Yes, she certainly does." Eugene nodded his head vigorously. "She says that he was always a reserved kind of guy. It was one of the things that took her fancy. 'He don't mind bein' by himself, Genie. He likes his peace and quiet there. Venice is the perfect place for him— all that water and fog.' Wait until I tell her that we found a body floatin' in the Grand Canal and that Urbino knew the girl! That'll shoot to smithereens her idea that it's peaceful and quiet here. From what I hear tell there've been a good number of bodies around ever since Urbino turned his back on his own country."

Eugene laughed, then took a sip of his scotch.

When the telephone sounded from across the hall, the Contessa glanced nervously at Urbino. Rosa, the Contessa's maid, came in.

"It's Signor Occhipinti, Contessa."

A look of disappointment, then one of relief, passed in rapid succession over the Contessa's face.

"Countess Barbara's real nice," Eugene said when she left. "Nothing airish and biggity about her at all. And she's a good looker for someone her age. I noticed you kind of squirmin' before. If you don't want me sayin' anything about you and Evie, I'll keep my trap shut."

Urbino, knowing that putting a gag on Eugene was impossible, told him that he didn't have any secrets from the Contessa.

"A new one on me, Urbino—you not havin' secrets! Your mouth has always been shut tight! I don't even think Evie was able to pry any secrets from you, though she pretends she did just to keep me wonderin'."

Fortunately Evangeline, even though she shared a lot of qualities with her brother, was far less garrulous and a lot more discreet.

"I can tell that Countess Barbara is curious about you. You must be keepin' her pretty hungry. Maybe I should—"

What Eugene was threatening—or offering—was lost when he cut himself off as the Contessa reappeared.

"Silvestro will be stopping by. He seems upset about something. He just got back from Venice. He was there for a few days on business at the Ca' Rezzonico. Milo's gone to collect him with the car."

"I've been meanin' to ask you, Countess Barbara. It's obvious that you're not hurtin' for money, if you don't mind my sayin' so. You got this big spread here and that huge marble palace in Venice. Then there's the Bentley and, from what Urbino tells me, a motorboat, but why didn't you ever get around to buyin' yourself a fancy gondola?"

Urbino enjoyed the momentarily helpless look on the Contessa's face. Perhaps she was beginning to see that even if Eugene was, in his fashion, "charming," he could also be more than a little disconcerting.

"Quite frankly, Eugene, I would love to have one."

"What's holdin' you back?"

"Well, it's just that going around in a gondola, pleasurable

though it would be, might be considered rather affected. It
would seem—"

"Ha! Ha! You surprise me, Countess Barbara! A fine
woman like you concerned with what the neighbors think! Well,
as the Good Book says, I'm a stranger in a strange land here.
I'm sure you know what you're talkin' about. But you aren't
even Italian yourself! You're a foreigner like that Guggenheim
gal—and *she* had a gondola. *She* didn't care what the neighbors
thought!"

"No, she certainly didn't," the Contessa agreed. She poured
out more tea for herself. "Eugene, I wonder if you have a
photograph of your sister Evangeline."

"I certainly do. I got pictures of just about all the Hennepins—at least the immediate family, and that's close to a double
dozen."

Eugene reached into the breast pocket of his jacket and
took out a thick wallet. Opening it, he extracted a photograph
from one of numerous plastic envelopes.

"Here's our Evie, Countess Barbara."

The Contessa took the photograph. It was Evangeline's
engagement photograph that had appeared in the *Times-Picayune* more than fifteen years ago.

"Why she's absolutely exquisite. What beautiful dark hair—
and such beautiful eyes. What color are they?"

"Light green, almost like a cat's, and skin like magnolia.
Everybody used to say she looked just like Scarlett O'Hara—
and Evie wasn't one to disagree. That picture's a tad old, but
she doesn't look much different now. She's the kind of woman
who's agin' right well—just like yourself, Countess Barbara,
though Evie's a whole lot younger."

The Contessa looked up from the photograph at Urbino.
He hoped she couldn't see the smile he was trying to curb.

"But Evie *has* changed," Eugene went on. He looked directly at Urbino as he explained. "Not physically, but she's
changed—yes, she certainly has. Evie's become a sweet, lovin',
stable woman."

The Contessa exchanged a quick glance with Urbino. Was
she thinking of the antonyms to Eugene's "sweet, lovin', and
stable," or was she only now beginning to realize what might be
behind Eugene's praise of his sister?

"Well, Eugene, you just tell this lovely young woman that she's welcome here or at the Ca' da Capo whenever she decides to come," the Contessa said, handing back the photograph. "You can tell her that I'm your new friend."

"Oh, she already knows who *you* are, Countess Barbara! Urbino's great-aunts told her years ago that he was fast friends with an honest-to-goodness Countess!"

"I'm happy to hear that, Eugene," the Contessa said, although her expression clearly showed less pleasure than bemusement. She reached over and patted Urbino's hand. "How sweet to let me indulge my understandable curiosity with your charming ex–brother-in-law, Urbino. You see, Eugene, you're the first person from Urbino's past I've ever met."

" 'Past'?" Eugene frowned with evident displeasure. "I don't think of myself as bein' part of his *past,* ma'am. You don't know nothin' about us Hennepins—and you don't know nothin' about *Southerners*—if you think that just because the water's gone down the river it's still not flowin' as strongly as it ever did! Urbino might be holed up in his poor excuse of a palace but he can't escape."

Eugene was prevented from going into more detail by the ringing of the telephone. This time it was for Urbino. The Contessa looked at him anxiously as he left the *salotto*.

"Urbino!" Oriana Borelli said huskily over the line. "I thought it best to ask for you. How's Barbara holding up? I'm afraid I have bad news. Filippo's old nurse, Graziella Gnocato, told me that Regina Grespi Brollo and Violetta Volpi *were* sisters. It came as a surprise to me, but neither Barbara nor I knew Regina Grespi. She was away from Venice a lot, staying in sanatariums around Milan and in Switzerland. Graziella looked after Regina for periods of time after Regina married—in fact, one of them was right before she died. It seems that Regina got all the beauty in the family—something I'm sure Violetta resented, not being anywhere near a beauty—but not much of the luck. She ended up drowning herself at Lago di Garda about ten years ago. Graziella is an invalid now herself, living in a dismal flat in Santa Marta, poor thing, and looked after by her niece. Tell Barbara I'm devastated that there's this connection between the dead girl and herself, but maybe it's not as bad as it looks. I've got to run."

When Urbino went back to the *salotto*, the Contessa turned worried eyes to him. Eugene was in the middle of lamenting that he hadn't found very much to buy in Asolo in his brief foray into town before dinner except for villas.

"I got to admit I was tempted. Kind of shocked me at first when I saw all those millions of lire, but it doesn't amount to all that much when you figure it out with your calculator. You never know, Countess! I might end up bein' your neighbor one of these days—here or maybe even in Venice. Then there would be at least one neighbor you wouldn't have to be afraid of! Excuse me, Urbino, I guess I mean two!"

For the next quarter hour, Eugene regaled them with his impressions of life in Italy, at the top of the list being the constant ringing of church bells and the shocking quickness with which Italians belted back their morning coffees while standing up at bars. All the while the Contessa wore an interested expression on her face that didn't deceive Urbino. She was thinking of nothing but the phone call.

"And then there's this 'passage' thing," Eugene was saying when they heard footsteps approaching along the hall.

"The *passeggiata*," Urbino corrected almost reflexively.

"That's it. One minute there's hardly a soul anywhere. But you just turn your back and the next minute the street is just swarmin' with people—men, women, children, little bambinos, grandparents—all dressed up in their best duds, huggin' and kissin' and talkin' as if they haven't seen each other in years—and it happens every single day like clockwork! Then they disappear as fast as they came out. And as for that wind from hell—what's it called, Urbino? The sambuco?—Why, I could barely move nary a muscle in my body! But I pressed on. I wasn't goin' to let a wind come between me and my sight-seein'!"

Silvestro Occhipinti appeared in the doorway just as Eugene was finishing. When Eugene saw him, Eugene leaned forward to Urbino and said in a stage whisper, "Well, what do you know. I saw this same bald little fellow in town today, draggin' along a cocker spaniel. Talkin' two-forty when he wasn't sneezin' away, but I'm not sure if he was talkin' to the dog or to himself. Most of it was in Italian, but I did hear him say something about God bein' in heaven."

Occhipinti looked at Eugene with a frown on his birdlike face.

"Browning, signore, the best poet after Dante!" Occhipinti insisted in his high-pitched voice.

Eugene stood up and put out his hand.

"Pleased to meet you, Signor Browning. My name's Hennepin—Eugene Hennepin."

3

THE CONTESSA QUICKLY straightened out the confusion. After Urbino poured wine for Occhipinti, she maneuvered the little man into reluctant conversation with Eugene, who, for simplicity's sake, was introduced as Urbino's "American friend." While the two new acquaintances were talking—or, rather, while Eugene was going on about his custom-made gondola and Occhipinti was darting little looks at the Contessa—Urbino told her about Oriana's call.

The Contessa went white under her carefully applied makeup and started to twist her Florentine gold wedding band. When she realized what she was doing, she forced her hands down into her lap.

She was about to say something when Occhipinti turned away from the still-speaking Eugene and said, "Yes, Violetta Volpi. I'm sorry to interrupt, but I heard you mention her name, Signor Macintyre. She's one reason why I had to come tonight, Barbara. The girl they found in the Grand Canal—her mother's maiden name was Grespi. That was Violetta Volpi's maiden name. *You* remember Violetta. 'Balls and masks begun at midnight, burning ever to midday'—Violetta Grespi was at them all, and for a while she took me with her. And isn't Flavia the name of the girl who came here last week, the one you were asking me about, Signor Macintyre?"

Urbino said it was and that it appeared that Violetta Grespi Volpi was her maternal aunt. Occhipinti's small, round eyes widened and his thin-lipped mouth made a perfect pantomime of surprise.

"Now isn't that something! Who would have thought it!"

"What else did you have to tell Barbara, Signor Occhipinti?" Urbino asked.

Alvise's faithful old friend looked uneasily in Eugene's direction. The Contessa told him he was free to speak.

"If you say so, Barbara dear. Do you remember what I said to you last week, Signor Macintyre, about this Flavia Brollo—although we didn't know what her last name was then?" He didn't wait for Urbino to answer, but went on energetically, the light glancing off his bald head. " 'A face to lose youth for,' I said, 'to occupy age with the dream of, meet death with'! Do you remember? And I also said she looked familiar."

Urbino nodded.

"Well, I've remembered why she looked familiar and wanted to tell you." Occhipinti seemed seized by an eagerness to be of help. He was breathing quickly. "It was because of my villa, La Pippa, you see! I've seen the girl with the actress who's renting it. She might even have been staying with La Lennox!"

Here was an additional connection between Occhipinti and the dead woman. Not only had he kept company with Flavia's aunt Violetta right after the Contessa and the Conte were married, but also Flavia had struck up a friendship with the very person who was renting Occhipinti's villa. If all this was merely coincidence, Urbino sensed that it was a coincidence that seemed to make Occhipinti uncomfortable. The little man had hurried over to the Contessa's villa fresh from his return from Venice to tell them about having seen Flavia with Madge Lennox.

Eugene, quite understandably, looked eager for an explanation to all the confusing things he was hearing, but this time it wasn't forthcoming from Occhipinti—nor from Urbino or the Contessa, both of whom were waiting for Occhipinti to go on. It was obvious he hadn't yet finished.

"But don't worry, Barbara," Occhipinti said, looking at her earnestly through his thick spectacles. "This Flavia Brollo is dead. She won't bother you anymore."

"But it's *not* over yet, Silvestro. It's not going to be over until I know the truth about Alvise."

The old man's face clouded.

"Let him rest in peace. The truth! Our Alvise was the best of men." Occhipinti's high-pitched voice was filled with conviction. " 'Where my heart lies, let my brain lie also'—it's advice you should listen to."

"The young woman's mother—Violetta's sister—drowned in Lago di Garda, Signor Occhipinti," Urbino said. "Barbara didn't know Violetta Grespi very well. She didn't even know she had a sister, let alone one who had killed herself. You had a villa on Lago di Garda years ago. Do you remember anything about the death of Violetta's sister?"

Occhipinti closed his eyes, lifted his head back, and opened his mouth wide. Urbino found it a rather peculiar prelude to whatever he was about to reveal about the death of Regina Brollo, but then the man sneezed—not once, but several times.

"Excuse me. Nothing worse than a summer cold. I must have got it from a woman in my building. Wouldn't it be fitting if I ended up dying from a cold the way Browning did? Ha, ha! But I shouldn't tempt fate, should I, by saying such things, even if there are much worse ways to meet the 'pale priest.' No, Signor Macintyre, I'm afraid I don't remember anything about any drowning. I didn't even know myself that Violetta had lost her sister. We didn't keep in close contact at all. I know she has a reputation as an artist now. I've even seen some of her paintings. Not to my taste." He paused before going on. "I never really liked her very much, Barbara. She used to say such bad things about you. I know how upset you were about what that silly girl said last week but it's all nonsense. I'm sure that Violetta Grespi—I mean Violetta Volpi—put her up to it."

"I'm hoping Urbino can see her and straighten things out."

"But I can pay her a visit, Barbara."

"No, thank you, Silvestro."

The little man seemed crestfallen, even upset.

"Urbino has the advantage of not knowing Violetta Volpi," the Contessa explained in an attempt to assuage the man's apparently wounded feelings. "It might make things easier."

"He didn't know Alvise either, did he?" Occhipinti said. "No, he didn't, so how can he know how you and I feel about this girl's accusation?"

The Contessa didn't seem to have the energy or inclination to pursue things any further. Eugene was still waiting for an explanation, but the Contessa deftly introduced a less disturbing topic that she knew would engage Alvise's old friend and Urbino's ex–brother-in-law.

"Mr. Hennepin was saying before you came, Silvestro, that he's interested in villas. He was looking at the notices at the real estate bureau."

But before Occhipinti would allow himself to rise to the bait, he stared at Barbara and, putting as much urgency as he could into his reedy voice, said, " 'Let who lied be left lie!' "

But hadn't Occhipinti come to La Muta precisely not to let things lie? Urbino asked himself. It didn't quite make sense. And who was the birdlike man referring to? Flavia Brollo, her mother, Regina, or possibly even Alvise? The puzzled look on the Contessa's face seemed to indicate that she was just as uncertain as Urbino was himself.

4

NOT UNTIL MUCH later that night, after Occhipinti had left and Eugene had gone up to his room, were Urbino and the Contessa able to talk alone together in the *salotto verde*. The Contessa had agreed to a glass of Remy Martin and was sitting once again on the Brustolon sofa, peering down into the wide glass.

"What possible relationship could there have been between that actress Lennox and Flavia Brollo?" she asked with a touch of petulance, raising her gray eyes to Urbino's face. "I know what kind of reputation she has," she added.

What Urbino knew she was really asking, however, was what connection there might have been between Lennox and Flavia Brollo's descent on her garden party.

"And then there's what the old nurse said about Flavia's mother," the Contessa went on. "Lago di Garda was where Alvise spent his time with Silvestro while I was in England looking at mazes. Perhaps this Regina Brollo was accustomed to spending her summers there the way other Venetians are.

It's something you'll have to look into, too. You *will* tell me the truth, won't you? Whatever it is?"

"Whatever you hear from me will always be the truth."

"I hope you won't be tempted to break your promise. I could never forgive you—or, even more, myself for putting you in that position."

The Contessa's face clouded and for a moment Urbino thought she was about to cry.

"I'm so absolutely blue, *caro*! When I force myself not to think of Alvise and me, I start thinking of poor Flavia."

The Contessa fell silent for several minutes. Urbino didn't interrupt her reverie. She was obviously trying to come to terms with a great many painful things. He had no doubt, however, that the Contessa's moral strength, coupled with her intelligence and feeling heart, wouldn't let her down. They were the very things that would help her get through this crisis—along with his own efforts and support, of course.

"Flavia was a victim, one way or the other, wasn't she, even if she wasn't murdered?" the Contessa said, looking directly at Urbino. "Either she was teeming with lies—or she was let down horribly by Alvise, and now me."

The Contessa considered her own culpability for several silent moments. Once again Urbino said nothing, but waited for her to work things through as much as she could at this point.

"If Alvise *was* her father," she eventually went on, "then Alvise and I have failed her. And if she made it all up, for whatever inscrutable reason, what does it say about her? About her life? Her relationship with her real father? I know you've thought of all these things, too, Urbino, and I beg you: Don't be so concerned about my feelings that you try to spare me any pain."

What the Contessa was saying and what her frightened eyes implored seemed so opposed that Urbino, for the rest of that night until he finally escaped into sleep, couldn't even begin to sort it out.

5

IT WAS THE next afternoon. The Sant'Anna Cemetery, on the gently rolling hills below the walls of Asolo, at first seemed empty of anyone living except two attendants raking the gravel paths on the lowest terrace. But then Urbino saw Madge Lennox. The tall, androgynous woman was standing at the grave of Eleonora Duse, the actress who had rivaled Sarah Bernhardt at the turn of the century. The grave, on one of the highest tiers, was set off by low bushes and cypress trees.

Urbino often came here to the Sant'Anna Cemetery. One of his interests—or his "eccentricities," as the Contessa preferred to call them—was visiting cemeteries, something he had shared with Evangeline. In this, as in other things, he admitted to being something of a sentimentalist. Wherever he was, if he had time he would seek out the main cemetery and wander among the graves, read the inscriptions, and chat with the caretakers. What was morbid to the Contessa, who despised any *memento mori*, consoled him. He took pleasure from seeing the graves that hadn't been forgotten, the fresh jars of flowers, the recently tended flowerbeds, the notes left for the weather to obliterate. He tried not to concentrate on the greater number of neglected plots.

Urbino approached Madge Lennox. The seventy-year-old actress was wearing a cerise scarf that concealed her hair, a broad-brimmed hat, and billowing crimson-colored pants and top. She was looking down at the gravestone. There was something almost marmoreal about her stiff pose—even her pale, taut face—that made her seem very much at home among all the marble of the cemetery. But then her head suddenly snapped up and she stared through her large sunglasses at Urbino.

"I didn't mean to startle you, Miss Lennox, but your maid at Villa Pippa said that you might be here. I'm Urbino Macintyre. We met at the Contessa da Capo-Zendrini's garden party." The actress nodded in recognition. Urbino walked the rest of the distance to join her by Eleonora Duse's grave. "I come here often, too. She has a splendid spot."

"She does, doesn't she?" Madge Lennox agreed in her low, exquisitely controlled voice.

She adjusted her hat—different from the one she had worn to the Contessa's party—and smiled at Urbino. Once again, as he had been last week, he was struck by the almost sexless, ageless beauty of her white, high-cheekboned face. Everything about her seemed studied and restrained, something that Urbino found both appealing and yet strangely disconcerting. She reminded him of someone, and it troubled him that he couldn't remember who, for he vaguely sensed that the association wasn't entirely pleasant.

Madge Lennox bent down to rearrange a jar of small yellow flowers. "Perhaps you can help me decide," she said without looking up yet somehow making him feel bathed in her approval. "Do you think Eleonora's spot is more like a secluded balcony or a small stage?"

"Either comparison would suit the final resting place of an actress, don't you think? And a balcony can also be a stage, of course. *Romeo and Juliet*."

"Well answered! And Eleonora played Juliet many times, on one memorable occasion in Verona itself. She was one of the few actresses who's ever played the role when she was the right age for it." She straightened up and laughed. "I played her when I had just turned thirty. But you're here to ask me about Flavia Brollo, aren't you? Signor Occhipinti must have told you that he saw us together. By the way, please call me Madge, especially since I want to call you Urbino." She gave the "U" of his name the correct Italian sound. "Such an unusual name for an American."

When Urbino didn't satisfy her implied question, she smiled, revealing even, remarkably white teeth and very few lines for someone her age.

"Yes, I knew Flavia, but I didn't think it was my place to tell the Contessa that I did."

Madge Lennox's surface was so fine and polished, and she seemed so complacent, that Urbino felt the need to shock her.

"It's possible that Flavia was murdered, you know."

"But that's preposterous!" She appeared more angry than shocked. "The paper said nothing about murder. Is that what the police think?"

"They're looking into all possibilities, of course. They'll know more after the autopsy."

"But you're already convinced, aren't you? Or trying to make me believe you are."

Lennox took off her sunglasses and put them in her pants pocket. Her eyes were dark and bold, and they searched his face.

Urbino sensed that Lennox was trying to absorb the idea that Flavia might have been murdered. A conflict—or a good semblance of one—was evident in the actress's high-cheekboned face.

"Murder," she said in her soft voice. "It doesn't seem possible. But wouldn't this best be left to the police if *they* share your—your suspicion? That's all it is, isn't it? A suspicion? At any rate, I doubt if I can be of any help."

She wasn't reluctant to give him information, however. As they walked from the cemetery and up the hill in the direction of town, she told him how Flavia used to drop by the villa from time to time and would sometimes spend the night. Lennox had a room set aside for her for whenever she stayed.

"Flavia liked to get away from all the commotion of Venice—the things that you and I talked about at the Contessa's party. I would leave her to herself. I never bothered her. We understood each other. She said she felt safe and secure here in Asolo."

"Safe and secure," Urbino repeated. "Was she afraid of something?"

"I'm sure it was just a manner of speaking."

"Where did you meet her?"

"In the cemetery. Don't look so surprised, Urbino," she said, taking obvious pleasure in slowly drawing out the syllables of his name. "*We* met there, didn't we? Flavia had a devotion to Duse, you see. She was standing by the grave very much the way you found me. We talked for a while, then I invited her up to La Pippa for a drink. She came back the next week and we eventually became more friendly. It was in early June."

They passed a small Franciscan church and continued on toward the main road. Cicadas creaked from the adjacent grass and vineyards. In the distance, villas looked like jewels in the velvet green of the surrounding hills.

"Flavia was like a 'melodious apparition,'" Madge Lennox went on. "That's from the inscription on Duse's house in town. It suited Flavia with that face of hers and those melancholy green eyes! Those eyes always showed so much—or so very little," she added, making Urbino think of the blank look in Flavia's eyes at the Contessa's garden party. "I called her 'Principessa Flavia' after the character Madeleine Carroll played in *The Prisoner of Zenda* back in the thirties. She might have made a good film actress. She said she had been in some minor theatrical productions."

Urbino and Madge Lennox reached the main road and turned up the hill toward town. The road was flanked by villas and smaller private residences.

"Did Flavia tell you why she was in Asolo?"

"All she would say at first was that she was here to visit Eleonora's grave, but it didn't take me long to realize that she was interested in the Contessa. What did she look like? Did I think she was attractive? What kind of woman was she? What was Villa La Muta like? Did I know anything about the Contessa's husband? I'm afraid I couldn't give her much information about anything. I hardly knew the Contessa and what little I knew I learned from Signor Occhipinti, my maid, or people from town who don't mind gossiping with a *straniera*."

Urbino remembered that at the Contessa's garden party Madge Lennox had broached the topic of Alvise with him. Could she have been hoping for information she could pass on to her occasional houseguest?

A Dalmatian behind the fence of one of the villas started barking loudly as they passed. Madge Lennox said a few soothing words in Italian and the animal settled down. Urbino was reminded of how the Contessa's Doberman, Catullus, had behaved with Flavia.

As if in response to Urbino's unspoken thought, Madge Lennox said, "Flavia and I shared a way with dogs. She used to go down to the gates of the Contessa's villa and talk with her dog. She said they became good friends."

"Didn't you find Flavia's interest in the Contessa unusual?" Urbino asked as they walked along the fence of the villa, followed docilely now by the Dalmatian.

"Of course I did, even more so when I saw some of the things in her scrapbook."

Madge Lennox's white face was a mask that showed neither embarrassment nor uneasiness.

"She kept a scrapbook?"

"Yes, since she was just a girl. I think she held on to it for sentimental reasons, the way one does with these things. She asked me to add my autograph to some others. It seemed a typical scrapbook. Programs and tickets, newspaper clippings, photographs, and several pages of autographs. There were a lot of clippings from the Venice newspaper about the Contessa and her husband, some of them with photographs, and one of Signor Occhipinti. I found those clippings a bit strange but didn't give them much thought. Anyway, almost at the same time that I knew Flavia had this—this fantasy about the Conte being her father, the Contessa knew it, too," Lennox went on quickly in her low voice. "Flavia told me the morning of the garden party. She begged me to take her with me but I refused. When I saw her go up to the Contessa, I knew what she must be saying. And later at La Pippa she told me."

The sorrow that seemed to touch Madge Lennox's face momentarily confused Urbino. It was the appropriate response, albeit somewhat belated in their discussion of Flavia, but Urbino couldn't help wondering how authentic and heartfelt it actually was.

With this thought came the realization of whom Madge Lennox reminded him. Urbino was carried back to his hours as a fifteen-year-old wheeling a retired actress around the Garden District at the request of his parish priest. He had been enchanted by her stories and warmed by her gratitude. For him she had been a magical presence, one of the charismatic older women of his life, but he had always wondered how much he could believe or trust a person so much of whose life had been artifice. Lennox was about the age of the actress, but Urbino was almost a quarter century older than he had been then. But it didn't matter. He felt the same as he had during that unending summer in New Orleans.

The sorrow on Lennox's face—true or feigned—faded as she greeted a carabinieri officer swaggering out of the door of the local headquarters, but it was soon back in place. She went on with her story as they continued up the hill in the heat.

"We were together one more time before she died. Wednesday morning here in Asolo, then later on the train to Venice." This was the day before Urbino and the Contessa had met Flavia at Florian's. "She seemed more excited and nervous than usual. She kept talking about that murdered girl in Venice. You don't think that man who murdered the girl could have—? But no, of course not. He was in custody before Flavia died. Anyway, Flavia knew the girl and wasn't able to get her out of her mind. She seemed to become more obsessed about things after the girl was murdered. It was frightening to see her in the grip of something that wasn't quite in her control. That last time I saw her she kept saying over and over again, 'I'll make the Contessa believe me. I will!' We both took the train to Venice an hour later. She went on and on about the poor girl and the Contessa all the way. I said good-bye to her at the train station and continued on to Milan. I never saw her after that."

"Did she ever talk about her family?"

Madge Lennox looked at Urbino without breaking her stride. There was a slight hesitation in her eyes as if she were considering something—or perhaps trying to give him the impression she was. He sensed that she was not just uncertain but even a little afraid, but once again he wondered how much he could trust his own judgment about the behavior of someone whose life was based on artifice.

"Rarely. When she did, she would refer to 'my mother and Lorenzo'—never her mother and father. 'Lorenzo il Magnifico,' she used to say scornfully. Sometimes when she would see an older man, she'd say, 'He's just like Lorenzo!' or 'There goes another Magnifico!' " She looked at Urbino as if assessing his response to what she was telling him. "She said it the first time she saw Signor Occhipinti walking his dog past the villa. It seemed so inappropriate for the little man that I laughed. She had only good things to say about her mother, though. She idealized her."

"Did she ever mention someone named Violetta Volpi? Or Violetta Grespi?"

"No, but the name is somehow familiar."

"It was mentioned in Flavia's obituary."

Madge Lennox nodded slowly.

They had reached a small café with tables set up outside. The road turned up to the right, where it passed the Villa

Cipriani Hotel before entering the walls of the town. Just inside the walls was Eleonora Duse's house with the inscription to the *melodiosa apparizione* that Madge Lennox had mentioned.

"I think I'll only go this far today," the actress said, stopping. She looked a little weary and perspiration beaded her forehead. "Why don't we rest and have a drink?"

They sat at one of the outdoor tables and ordered Proseccos.

"Did Flavia ever say anything that might indicate she was afraid of someone? Someone who might have meant her harm?"

"Someone who might have murdered her, according to your theory? I'm sorry, Urbino, but I can't believe that Flavia was murdered. An accident, yes—even suicide. I can't imagine anyone wanting to harm a hair on her head." The steady look Madge Lennox gave Urbino didn't convince him that she was telling the complete truth. Once again he detected a slight uneasiness as she raised the glass to her lips and took a sip. "She *was* acting strangely last week, but who would have thought—?" She shook her head. "I think you should just give your energies to putting the Contessa's mind at ease about her husband. Murder strikes me as so—so preposterous."

And frightening, Urbino added silently for her.

Madge Lennox stood up, slipping her sunglasses back on now that their talk was over. It was as if she had wanted Urbino to see her eyes and judge how little she had to hide. Over Urbino's protests she dropped several lira notes on the table.

"Please give my regards to the Contessa and thank her again for a perfectly wonderful afternoon last week."

Urbino watched Madge Lennox walk back down the hill. She had told him quite a few things about Flavia, but could he believe them all? And why did he have the impression that she hadn't told him everything that she could have? Maybe it was the residue of his experience with the actress he had wheeled around the Garden District so many years ago. The woman had ended up complaining to the priest that Urbino with all his questions had intruded on her, even though she had basked in his attention and encouraged him. To this day he wasn't sure whether he had misread the actress, been intentionally misled by her, or been lied to, for some obscure reason, by the priest himself.

It wasn't unlike his feeling now as he watched Madge Lennox stride down the hill, determination in her shoulders.

6

THE CONTESSA, HAVING extricated herself from her duties as hostess to Eugene by foisting him off on Occhipinti, was free for some conversation with Urbino on the terrace of the Caffè Centrale later that afternoon.

"I wonder what Eleonora Duse would think if she knew she had become a sundae?" the Contessa asked as she paused briefly in the middle of her decorous assault.

It was a question that required no response, all the more so because it was far from the first time the Contessa had posed it. Urbino could hardly remember an occasion when she had ordered this particular concoction of vanilla ice cream, strawberries, blue liqueur, and cream and *not* asked it.

"I would love to see the scrapbook that Flavia kept," she said, having reached the bottom of her goblet. "It's frightening to know she kept clippings about Alvise and me."

"And she was gathering information about you and Alvise here in Asolo."

"And in Venice she had Violetta Volpi! Oh, the lies that woman was likely to have told her!" The Contessa put down her spoon and took a sip of mineral water. "I wouldn't be surprised if Lennox knew Violetta Volpi. She says she never heard Flavia mention her, but I don't believe it any more than that she's told you everything important. She wrapped you around her little finger, didn't she? I know how you are with these women."

"You're wrong. She didn't charm me at all," he defended himself. "And what do you mean by 'these women'? American women? Retired actresses? *Older* women?"

"Watch yourself! Suffice it to say that I know you have a

great desire to please—especially women of a certain kind—
but more specific than that I don't care to be. It will have to
remain within that large dim realm of things two people know
very well about each other but never have to be specific about."

Urbino could usually distinguish among the Contessa's various forms of banter, and this afternoon it was banter that
covered anxiety. If he needed any more proof, he was soon
provided with it when she ordered another *Coppa Duse*.

"I have to see Violetta Volpi," Urbino said after the waiter
left. "She's the key to this whole thing—certainly to Alvise and
maybe even to Flavia's murder."

" 'Flavia's murder'!" The Contessa shook her head slowly
from side to side. "I do hope you're wrong about that, but if
you're not, I pray that it has nothing to do with Alvise."

Urbino, not wanting to give the Contessa false hope, said
nothing.

The waiter set down the Contessa's second *Coppa Duse*. She
removed the crowning cookie and ate it. Before attacking the
rest she said, "Commissario Gemelli should have the autopsy
report tomorrow, shouldn't he? Give him a call. I pulled a few
strings this morning to get him to be more cooperative than
usual, although I have a feeling he's warmed to you a bit over
the years."

The Contessa looked across the square and waved.

"I'm afraid our little tête-à-tête is about to end. Here come
your ex–brother-in-law and Silvestro." The Contessa started to
speak more quickly. "I haven't had a chance to tell you how
much I've been learning from Eugene about your past. Is it true
that you rescued Evangeline from the clutches of a malevolent
man?"

"That's more than an exaggeration. It makes me wonder
exactly what he's been telling you."

"So what's the truth?"

"I've already told you. I met Evangeline when she had just
broken up with someone who hadn't treated her well. I consoled
her, and we became very close."

"Now that's the most detached response I've ever heard,
even from you! I assume, *caro*, that you mean you both fell
in love—you notice I don't say 'madly'—and eventually got
married! And all because of your propensity to rescue damsels
in distress!"

A cloud seemed to come over the Contessa's levity. Perhaps she was remembering, as Urbino was, that she had said something similar to this, here on the terrace of the Caffè Centrale after Flavia's descent on her garden party.

"I hear her uncle, a bishop, performed the ceremony," the Contessa went on, recovering herself, "and that you refused to have your father-in-law set you up in a charming house in the French Quarter or some such place and that—"

The Contessa, obviously enjoying finally being privy to things about Urbino that he had either glossed over or not mentioned at all, didn't have the chance to tell him what else she had heard, for Eugene and Occhipinti had reached the terrace. Eugene was glowing.

"Sylvester told me he had some items at his villa he was willin' to part with for the right person"—Eugene smiled amiably down at Occhipinti—"so we stopped by. Interestin' woman he has stayin' there. Couldn't figure out exactly how old she was. Probably somewhere in your ballpark, Countess Barbara. His villa isn't as big as yours by a long shot, but it's crammed to the gills. I bought a marble statue of a—what did you call him, Sylvester?"

"A *bravo* who was in the service of our family many, many years ago."

The old man's voice was slightly hoarse and he had a feverish look. He took off his straw hat and used it as a fan before putting it back on his bald head.

"He looks real fierce. I also bought one of the wood angels he has hangin' on the wall, so I might not have to do any more buyin' until right before I leave."

"Silvestro! Not those lovely eighteenth-century angels over the door to the library!"

"I took only *one* of them, ma'am. There's no need to get so agitated. Sylvester doesn't seem to mind, do you?"

Occhipinti shrugged.

"I'm 'guiltless forever, like a tree that buds and blooms, nor seeks to know the law by which it prospers so.'"

"'Prospers,' is right!" Eugene said. "You can be sure I paid him a pretty penny for it, Countess Barbara."

Eugene and Occhipinti sat down and ordered drinks. As the Contessa was finishing her sundae, she asked Eugene if he would like to stay a few days longer at La Muta.

"Just the two of us, Eugene, and no one else. Oh, don't give me that hurt look, Silvestro. You'd be better off far away from Eugene and me and everyone if I can judge by your peaked look. Bed rest is what you need. And that will leave dear Eugene and me all alone to our own devices, won't it, my dear? We'll continue our little chat about Urbino. He's kept me mercilessly starved for information."

The Contessa, as if to illustrate the extent of her famine, avidly took up the last spoonful of gelato.

7

THE NEXT MORNING, back in Venice, Urbino called Commissario Gemelli about the autopsy report. The Commissario seemed to be in the cooperative, albeit begrudging, mood that the Contessa had predicted.

"Flavia Brollo was alive when she fell into the Grand Canal," Gemelli said. "If she hadn't been, her tissues wouldn't have had any of those algae in them. Not the kind that scummed up all the Adriatic beaches a few summers ago. I forget what they're called." There was a rustle of paper, then Gemelli said, "Diatoms. She had been dead for at least thirty-six hours. That puts her death at no later than about midnight Thursday."

This was just eight hours after Urbino and the Contessa had seen her at Florian's.

"I could go on," Gemelli continued. "Froth at the nostrils, the skin on her hands and feet as wrinkled as a washerwoman's, terrible bloating from the heat, loss of tissue from the tips of some of her fingers and her nose, presumably by water rats, and so forth—but the point is that she drowned, all right."

"She drowned, but that doesn't mean that foul play couldn't have been involved. What else did Zavarella find?"

Gemelli gave an impatient sigh. Once again Urbino heard the rustle of paper as Gemelli continued, "No trace of semen in any of the body orifices, no sign of recent sexual activity and she wasn't pregnant, no blunt trauma or wounds except ones consistent with hitting herself against stones or being abraded by the junk on the bottom of the Grand Canal, some slivers from the Palazzo Guggenheim mooring poles embedded in her skin. The tide must have dragged her—that and the action of the vaporetti and other water traffic."

"Couldn't the wounds have been caused by something other than by hitting herself or abrasion? If the body was as messed up as the report says because of submersion in the water and being dragged around, how can Zavarella be sure none of the wounds was caused by a blow *before* she went in the water?"

"There *are* two wounds on the front of her head that, in other circumstances, might indicate foul play. And several teeth were knocked out. But Zavarella says that the wounds and the missing teeth are consistent with trauma after death."

Urbino detected a slightly dubious note in Gemelli's voice.

"And there are other things in the report that make it probable that foul play wasn't involved."

"What?"

"A half-empty bottle of an antidepressant was found in her room back at the Casa Trieste. Zavarella says the drug is controversial, especially in the States. It's supposed to cure depression but some researchers say it can make the depression worse. It's been linked with suicide and violence in general. From what Zavarella said, people taking it can be preoccupied with death and self-destruction. The toxicology report will probably turn up a high concentration of the drug—and maybe even some others—in Flavia Brollo's body."

"But even if it does, it wouldn't be proof of suicide or accident, would it?" Urbino insisted. "When it comes to drowning, it's difficult to distinguish cases of suicide, accident, or murder."

"So now you're a medical expert, Macintyre?"

"Couldn't she have been knocked unconscious with a brick or a piece of wood before she drowned?" Urbino asked, ignoring Gemelli's sarcasm. "Were her fingernails checked for any tissue not her own?"

"Zavarella found none under her fingernails."

"But the report says that the tips of some of her fingers were eaten by water rats. That could have destroyed any evidence of tissue under the nails, too, couldn't it? If—"

"Just listen to you, Macintyre! 'Could have'! 'If'! Maybe we should get rid of Zavarella and hire you or some card reader! We have medical examiners for a very good reason—to give us their expert opinion, and that's what Zavarella has done. He sees no sign of foul play but plenty of indications of suicide. There's the antidepressant, and both you and the Contessa said that she seemed unstable. Our preliminary investigation indicates that she was pretty upset on Thursday evening, the last time anyone saw her alive."

Something had occurred to Urbino when Gemelli mentioned the antidepressant again.

"What does the doctor who prescribed the drug have to say? Does he think that Flavia Brollo was suicidal?"

"The bottle had no label on it. Her family and what friends we've contacted have no idea who she might have gone to for the prescription. Of course, the doctor could read about her death in the paper and come forward, but until he does, there's not much we can do on that angle. And not much that we *should* do unless the substitute prosecutor gives us the go-ahead. I just don't understand you!"

Gemelli had been holding back his impatience, and now he let it go.

"Would you and the Contessa da Capo-Zendrini feel better if this woman had been murdered like Nicolina Ricci in Sant'Elena? The fact that Flavia Brollo knew the murdered girl and was upset makes a death by suicide even more likely. Thank God the Ricci case is sewn up with a confession and the perpetrator is in custody or you'd be telling me that we had a serial killer on the loose! I've already got a call from the mayor who doesn't want all this blown out of proportion, especially during high season. Flavia Brollo's father is respected here in Venice, and so is her aunt, the artist. They are good solid citizens. The *vice-questore* agrees with the mayor. No, Macintyre, the substitute prosecutor is unlikely to move that an inquiry is warranted in the death of Flavia Brollo, and I agree with him. There's no case to answer. If you or the Contessa have any complaints or doubts—if either of you is *disappointed*—go and bother Maurizio Agostini, but I warn you: Substitute prosecutors are even less patient than commissarios of police. Maybe you think if you poke around yourself, you'll be able to prove us all wrong and deliver a murderer to the steps of the Questura! You'll just be wasting your time and not earning anyone's good will. Good day, Macintyre."

After his conversation with Gemelli, Urbino went over what he had just learned from him.

Suicide didn't ring true—even given the medical evidence and what Madge Lennox had told Urbino about Flavia's melancholy and nervousness and the urgency that had gripped her after the murder of Nicolina Ricci. Even when Urbino threw into the balance the tragic death of Flavia's mother and a rejected, unloved—perhaps unloving—father, he still found himself resisting the idea of suicide.

Urbino kept coming back to the wounds to Flavia's head. They could have been caused by someone wielding a heavy object of some kind. All that was necessary was for Flavia to have been knocked unconscious—perhaps only severely stunned—and then pushed into the Grand Canal. Maybe even her teeth had been knocked out in a struggle. And who was to say that hair or skin tissue of the murderer wouldn't have been found under her fingernails if she hadn't been in the water so long?

As far as the pills found at the Casa Trieste were concerned, Urbino would wait for the toxicology report before he speculated about them.

But he couldn't keep his mind away from why Flavia might have been murdered. Flavia had stormed out of Florian's to get proof that Lorenzo wasn't her father and that Alvise was. She had seemed confident about finding it. Searching for that proof—or finally finding it—could have led to her murder.

It was because of this possibility that Urbino couldn't let things lie where they were. Perhaps the substitute prosecutor would decide that there was a case to answer after all, despite Gemelli's skepticism. But even if he didn't, Urbino was determined to conduct his own investigation into Flavia's parentage and into what he strongly suspected was murder, not suicide.

Someone could have silenced Flavia to protect himself. And who was to say that the silencing was over? Whoever murdered Flavia might strike again to prevent the secret from ever coming out. This person would breathe a little easier if Flavia's death ended up not being treated as a homicide. Perhaps this could work to Urbino's advantage.

Urbino searched out the address of Bernardo and Violetta

Volpi from the Venice phone directory and set out for the Ca'
Volpi. Venetian addresses being as confusing as they were, he
knew only that it was somewhere in the San Marco quarter.
After following house numbers for almost half an hour with no
success, Urbino stopped at a café in Campo Morosini. When he
asked the barman if he knew where the Ca' Volpi was, he was
directed toward a *calle* near the Accademia Bridge. The Ca'
Volpi was one of the palazzi on the Grand Canal.

8

AFTER GIVING HIS card to the Volpis' maid, Urbino waited in a
sunny *sala* perched above the Grand Canal. Reflections from
the canal played in patterns on the frescoed ceiling, where a
fan added its quiet sound to the chug and throb of the water
traffic. The room, stylishly but minimally furnished, was hung
with the paintings of Violetta Volpi, the aunt of Flavia Brollo.

Over the sofa, covered in an antique Rubelli print, was a
portrait of a girl with flowers. It was almost a replica of the
painting Eugene had bought from Zuin except that the eyes of
this girl were green, not brown, and the hair was a bright red.

On an easel next to a wooden chair was a painting of a
naked, prepubescent girl tensely posed on a shadowed bed.
Over a trestle table hung a large canvas of a group of women
on the Accademia Bridge. The waters of the Grand Canal were
choppy and lightning zigzagged in the right-hand corner above
a dome of the Salute. All the women were wearing long dark
gowns, had faces without features, and had their hands clapped
over their ears.

Most of the other pictures contained these same wide-eyed,
haunted-looking women and emphasized moonlight, night-
time, and water.

Urbino was unprepared for these paintings, so much like
those of Edvard Munch. He had been too quick to place Violetta
Volpi in a category. When he heard that she was a painter, he

had expected watercolors or aquatints of Venice, the conventionally pretty kind that artists offered for sale along the Molo in front of the Giardinetti Reali. He hadn't expected these violent, even tragic canvases that had love and death as their themes.

The maid led Urbino down a flight of stairs to a hall flanked by large Venetian *torchères*. At the end of the hall she threw open a door and announced his name. Urbino stepped into a large, sunshine-filled room smelling of turpentine and linseed oil. The maid closed the door after her.

The room was obviously Violetta Volpi's studio. Canvases were turned to the wall, paraphernalia was scattered about, and brushes and rubber gloves hung above a sink. A beringed, berobed, and mascaraed woman was kneeling on a clear space on the floor. She was in the first stages of stretching a frame.

"Good afternoon, Signor Macintyre," she said in a deep, throaty voice, looking up at Urbino. "I'm Violetta Volpi."

Urbino was no more prepared for the woman than he had been for her art. "Sensuality" was the word that immediately came into his mind as he gazed at Violetta Volpi. It was there in her not unpleasantly coarse features, her full body that the robe only partly concealed, her easy smile that seemed to take pleasure in showing an appealing gap between her two front teeth, and the remarkably dark irises of her light green eyes. It was even there in the musky odor that mixed with the aroma of her perfume.

"That's my husband, Bernardo."

She nodded toward a man around seventy-five sitting in a chair in the sunshine of a garden. Behind him was bougainvillaea and ivy, a pergola of vines, and a white stone wall, beyond which sparkled the waters of the Grand Canal.

The contrast between Bernardo Volpi and his wife could hardly have been greater. He had a fragile-looking face, and beneath his parchment-colored skin the contours of his skull were visible. Dressed in a beige Prince of Wales linen jacket and linen trousers, with an ascot around his neck, Bernardo Volpi sat immobile and gave no sign of greeting.

Violetta started to cut the canvas around the stretching frame with a knife, her bracelets jangling. A beam of sunlight from the open door struck red highlights in her graying brown hair.

"Please sit down, Signor Macintyre. You won't mind if I

continue with this? It's important that I throw myself into my work. All I can think about is my niece."

Violetta was speaking in Italian even though, according to the Contessa, she knew English—or had known it thirty years ago.

Urbino sat on a small sofa against the wall.

"But I'm not going to get any respite from thoughts of Flavia with you, am I, Signor Macintyre? You're here about her, aren't you?"

Violetta Volpi, tucking her paint-spattered robe around her more tightly to get it out of the way, stared at him. Urbino saw grief written in her face but, as he continued to look at her, it was as if she banished the grief by an act of will. Her strong features exerted their influence and once again Urbino felt the power of her sensuality. He remembered what Occhipinti had said the other night at the Contessa's villa about Violetta having been at all of the balls in her youth. Seeing her now Urbino didn't doubt it.

Violetta bent over and continued to cut the canvas.

"I'm afraid you're right, Signora Volpi. I *am* here about Flavia—more precisely about Flavia and the Contessa da Capo-Zendrini."

"But surely that goes without saying! I've been expecting either you or the Contessa ever since Flavia told me she paid the Contessa a visit. It's all pure and simple nonsense!" she said dismissively in her throaty voice. "When Flavia told me that she had mentioned this business of Alvise da Capo-Zendrini being her father to the Contessa, I was appalled, and, I admit, I felt a little responsible. After her mother—my sister—died, I looked after her, gave her what advice and help I could. Bernardo was a second father to her. We've never been blessed with children, and what time I could spare from my Bernardo and my art, I gave to her. She was certainly getting nothing from her *other* aunt."

She finished cutting the canvas and dropped the knife on the floor.

"Her other aunt?"

"No relation to me, thank God! Annabella Brollo, her father's sister." Violetta almost sniffed with disapproval as she put the stretching frame to one side and started to shave down the knots and slub threads of the canvas with a large pumice. "I wouldn't be surprised if Flavia got her crazy idea about Alvise from Annabella. Poor, poor Alvise," she added in an affectionately commiserate tone. "He was a good man. He deserved better."

The ambiguity of this comment would in no way please the Contessa.

"But Annabella! She did everything she could to turn Flavia against me—and against her own mother! Always scheming behind the scenes! All she cares about is her brother and that jungle of flowers she grows up on their *altana*."

"But surely she wouldn't have led Flavia to believe that her brother wasn't Flavia's father, would she? Not if she cares so much for him."

Violetta Volpi rubbed with the pumice at a recalcitrant imperfection in the canvas before answering. Urbino suspected that Violetta's activity was a way of not giving him a clear view of her face.

"Who knows?" Violetta said. "Maybe she was trying to poison Lorenzo's mind against my sister. He was devoted to Regina. He still is." She looked over at Bernardo, who was still sitting silently in the garden. "Two sisters got two good husbands. Annabella never married. *That's* the source of her problems. She's all twisted up and resentful. You can see it in her face. She might be trying to drive her brother crazy for some reason by spreading a story like that. Didn't that happen in a play by Ibsen?"

"I believe it was Strindberg. But isn't that a bit far-fetched? Perhaps Annabella knows something you don't."

Violetta Volpi stopped rubbing and stiffened.

"If I believed that, I'd slit my wrists! Annabella has always lived in a dreamworld. The happiest day of her life was when my sister died. She just moved right in with Lorenzo and hasn't moved out since! No, she couldn't know anything about my sister that I don't."

Although Urbino had gone to see Violetta Volpi in quest of information, he was somewhat surprised at her willingness to give it out.

"Did your sister know Alvise da Capo-Zendrini?"

"Hardly. He was *my* friend until he married. Even after that, I saw him from time to time because of Silvestro Occhipinti."

Violetta Volpi's brow was beaded with perspiration. She put down the pumice and ran the back of her hand across her forehead.

"I'm sorry, Bernardo dear," she said, looking at her husband and pushing back her hair. The man had said nothing although he was close enough to hear their conversation. "I know you don't want me to go on." She turned her face to Urbino fully now and smiled, once again unabashedly revealing the space between her teeth. "My husband doesn't like me to criticize others, Signor Macintyre. Such high morals in the world of business is one of life's mysteries! And he's been extremely upset since Flavia died. Ever since Saturday, he doesn't want to go anywhere near our water gate." She lowered her husky voice. "You can see the Palazzo Guggenheim from there."

She returned to the piece of cut canvas, picking up a hammer lying beside some nails on the floor.

"Of course, the Contessa needs to have her mind put at ease. Such a terrible shock to the system to be told that your dead husband might have been unfaithful—and with such a beautiful woman, too."

Violetta Volpi hammered a nail through the canvas and wood in the middle of one of the horizontal pieces of the stretching frame. She did the same on the opposite side.

"My brother-in-law treated Flavia like a princess! All this foolishness about Alvise and Regina has come close to breaking his heart—all the more so since it was Flavia who brought up the whole silly thing years ago."

Urbino found this a strange way for Violetta Volpi to describe her niece's belief that Alvise da Capo-Zendrini had been her father. The almost offhand, cold manner in which she referred to Flavia seemed not only inappropriate but also inconsistent with the grief Urbino had glimpsed on her face earlier. Someone listening to their conversation would find it hard to believe that she had just lost a niece in such tragic circumstances.

"But where did she get this idea?" Urbino asked. "You call it silly but it was obviously anything but silly to her. She believed it. It had to come from somewhere."

"I honestly don't know. I've asked myself a hundred times and I've never come up with an answer."

"Did you ever ask your niece?"

Violetta shot a dark look at Urbino.

"Of course! This was my sister she was talking about, and a man I had a high regard for! But no, Flavia would never tell me where she got her idea. She would just say she got it from the best source possible."

"Which would be either your sister or Alvise, wouldn't it?"

"Are you asking me or telling me? It wasn't my sister *or* Alvise because there was no truth to it. I tell you I don't know *where* she got her crazy idea from!"

She pulled the canvas taut with a bit more force than was necessary and hammered nails in, alternately, on each side of the stretching frame.

Perhaps having reconsidered her outburst, Violetta looked at Urbino again with her bright smile.

"Believe me, Signor Macintyre, I have no idea. And I don't think that my niece had any firm grasp on things. She had a lot of strange fantasies. Sometimes I used to worry that she might have inherited her mother's illness. My sister Regina might have had almost everything—certainly beauty and intelligence—but she was most sadly disturbed." Violetta gave the euphemism an ominous emphasis and shook her head slowly. "As for me, I'm no beauty, as you can see, but I got most of the strength in the family—and the talent."

Urbino detected a mixture of pride and resentment in the comment.

"When was the last time you saw your niece alive?"

The question sounded abrupt even to Urbino's own ears. When Violetta looked at him there wasn't even a trace of her former smile. Her lips were set in a straight line.

"I find that a most peculiar question, Signor Macintyre. I've already spoken with the police. Are you suggesting I need an alibi? It's not as if my niece had been murdered!" She gave a hollow laugh. Urbino was about to tell her that he did, indeed, suspect murder, but she rushed on to say in her throaty voice, "Suicide is horrible enough, maybe even worse! It leaves everyone feeling so guilty, so powerless. I know I didn't have anything to do with what happened to her—nothing at all—but yet—" The grief slipped back into place for a few moments before it was once again banished. "She must have been disoriented from that drug they found in her room at the pensione. Flavia was a good swimmer, you see, although she refused to swim after my sister drowned. The drug must have totally confused her, might have even destroyed her instinct to stay afloat."

When Urbino left Violetta and Bernardo Volpi shortly afterward, he tried to sort out what he had learned. Violetta had denied any liaison between her sister and Alvise and claimed not to know where Flavia had got the idea that Alvise was her father. But why had she been willing to give him the information she had? To end any further speculation about her sister? To protect her niece? But she hadn't gone out of her way to give a good picture of Flavia, suggesting that she might have been almost as emotionally disturbed as Regina. And the controlled coolness in her manner toward her niece disturbed Urbino. But then he remembered the unmistakable look of grief that had come and gone several times.

Urbino didn't in any way believe that Violetta Volpi had been completely frank. She was withholding information—and, it seemed, concealing her real feelings over the death of her niece. The question was, why. Could it have something to do with whatever resentment and envy she still might feel for her sister?

The Contessa might be able to help him. He needed to know more about whom Flavia had seen the night she died. Violetta Volpi had avoided telling him when she had last seen her niece, but she had told the police. The Contessa had a friend attached to the Questura whom she had contacted recently to help smooth things between Urbino and Commissario Gemelli over the autopsy. She would have to give Corrado Scarpa another call.

9

"I DON'T BELIEVE a syllable of what she told you!" the Contessa's usually dulcet voice crackled over the telephone line an hour later. "She must know why Flavia thought Alvise was her father.

No, I don't trust her. She's still seething with resentment after all these years."

The Contessa's lack of logic on this point might have amused Urbino under other circumstances.

"Wouldn't it make more sense for her to feed your fear that Alvise *was* Flavia's daughter?" Urbino asked her. "Wouldn't she have greater satisfaction in doing that?"

"The woman is devious. She might not want to admit that her own sister had a relationship with a man she had wanted to marry herself. We can't see *what* she's up to. She may be trying to lull me so that the blow will be even heavier when it comes. She's planning some embarrassing way for it all to crash down on me. No, Urbino, I don't trust Violetta Volpi any more than I ever trusted Violetta Grespi! Even if she's *not* lying, how can we assume she would know about something her sister was determined to keep secret from her? Any way you look at it, we can't put much trust in what Violetta Volpi has to say."

Urbino mentioned Corrado Scarpa, asking the Contessa to give her friend a call and find out about Flavia's last night. They then discussed what they knew so far about Flavia Brollo's life and death but came to no conclusions. The only thing they both agreed on was that they weren't being told the whole truth by anyone so far—except, the Contessa was quick to assure him, Occhipinti. Urbino said nothing in response to this.

It was almost with an audible sigh of relief that the Contessa changed the topic to Eugene, who had stayed in Asolo at Villa La Muta.

"By the way, *caro,* your former brother-in-law may be a little upset with me since I've had to refuse his very generous offers for my fan collection, determined as he is to bring it back for his wife. The dear man seems driven to appropriate as much of Italy as he can. He's asked me to look around for another doge's ring like the gold and lapis lazuli one I gave you. He's one of the most acquisitive—and *in*quisitive—persons I've ever met."

"I'm sure you outdo him in inquisitiveness, Barbara. Weren't the Sisters at Saint Brigid's a Dominican order and didn't the Dominicans run the whole Spanish Inquisition? Eugene has probably had question after question volleyed at him. He's being made to sing for his supper, I'm sure."

"Urbino! I've never volleyed a question at a person in my

life! You've brought all this on yourself, at any rate. Your reticence has created an insatiable curiosity, and if Eugene wants to feed it, then who I am to stop him? We've had some interesting talks since you've left, you can be sure. I can't wait to hear what else he has to say, but first I'll call Corrado. Until later, *caro*."

10

TEN MINUTES LATER Urbino, in both a restless and contemplative mood, took a walk. He first went into the northern part of the Cannaregio where many of the buildings were flaking from age, dampness, and the cancerous exhalations of mainland industries like Riva Petrochemicals, which the Brollo family used to own. This was mainly a workingman's part of town, and seldom visited by tourists except those seeking out the Church of the Madonna dell'Orto or those who had strayed from the Ghetto.

Laughter and cooking odors drifted down to Urbino as he passed beneath the open windows of the houses, making him feel even more alone and excluded as he pursued his thoughts.

Who might have killed Flavia? And why? Urbino asked himself. And what, if anything, did her death have to do with the Conte da Capo-Zendrini? He hoped that the Contessa would be able to get information from Corrado Scarpa. He needed to know more about Flavia's last night.

Where had she met her death? Had it been in a deserted area on the Grand Canal or one of the many small canals that fed into it? The tide would have been strong enough to drag her body into the Grand Canal and eventually to the Palazzo Guggenheim, where it had surfaced. She might even have drowned right at the Palazzo Guggenheim itself.

Seeing two teenagers kissing in a doorway made Urbino wonder what romance Flavia had had in her life. What had her relationship been with Bruno Novembrini, who had painted the nude portrait of her? Flavia had been stunning. She must have had her choice of men. Ladislao Mirko, who ran the pensione where Flavia had stayed, said that they were only friends, but how did he really feel about her?

And what about Madge Lennox, the actress who "had been loved by Garbo and Huston"? Had Lennox been anything more to Flavia than just a surrogate mother? She had said that Flavia felt safe and secure whenever she stayed with her at Villa Pippa. Safe and secure from what? From Mirko? Her family? Life in general?

Violetta Volpi had assured Urbino that there had never been anything between her sister and Alvise, but if Regina Brollo had shared Violetta's sensuality, who was to say what might have happened between Alvise and her under the right— or the wrong—circumstances?

Urbino realized that the thrust of almost all these ruminations was sex. Flavia's life and death, in fact, seemed saturated with sexuality. Not only had she been an object of desire but also there was her erotic portrait, the rape and murder of her friend Nicolina Ricci, the possibility of her mother's adultery, and even the surfacing of her body under the metal gaze of *The Angel of the Citadel,* the Guggenheim's tumescent horseman.

What had Occhipinti said about Flavia the day after she showed up at the Contessa's garden party? It was from Browning: "A face to lose youth for, to occupy age with the dream of, meet death with."

"A face to meet death with." But that face didn't seem to have given Flavia herself the kind of solace Occhipinti meant. Quite the opposite. It could have been her face—and her body—that led her to her death.

Urbino reached a boat landing with a view of the lagoon. Out in the smooth, gray waters floated Murano and the brick-walled, cypress-clad cemetery island of San Michele where Flavia's body had undergone an autopsy. Was her body still there? The papers had said nothing about a funeral. As Urbino turned away from the lagoon to continue his walk, not wanting to return to the Palazzo Uccello yet, he decided to call Lorenzo Brollo about the funeral arrangements. It might give him an opportunity to ask the man other questions.

Urbino walked along, mulling over all the unanswered questions about Flavia. As they multiplied in his mind so did the crowds, so that by the time he was crossing over the Rialto

Bridge to the other side of the Grand Canal the swirl of tourists
around him approximated the state of his mind. He bought a
bunch of grapes from one of the vegetable stands. The clerk
washed them off for him, and Urbino plucked at them as he
walked deeper into the maze that was the San Polo quarter. It
was the area where Lorenzo Brollo lived.

Urbino stopped in a bar and looked through the phone
directory for the address of the Palazzo Brollo. The barman
told him that he would find the building in a *campo* not far from
the Church of San Giacomo dell'Orio. Novembrini had said that
Flavia had spent little time in the San Polo house, staying instead
with Ladislao Mirko in the Casa Trieste.

The Palazzo Brollo was a tall, narrow building covered with
uneven, pinkish-gray stucco. A small stone and iron balcony
with pots of plants protruded from the *piano nobile*. A wicker
basket, to be lowered for newspapers or bread or whatever the
occupants of the house didn't care to descend for, hung a few
feet over the balcony railings from a thick rope. All the shutters
were closed even though the *campo* was sunless and empty of
people except for Urbino and a few local residents who paid no
attention to him as they went about their business.

Black crepe encircled a death notice on the front door of
the building. In stark letters beneath a not-too-recent black-
and-white photograph of a smiling Flavia it said:

Saturday, 25 July
Returned to the House of the Father
The good soul of
FLAVIA MARIA REGINA BROLLO
26 years old
We announce this with profound sorrow, the father
Lorenzo Brollo and the aunts Annabella Brollo and
Violetta Grespi Volpi

The date was that of the discovery of Flavia's body, not her
probable day of death sometime on Thursday night.

Urbino pushed the brass bell. He waited several minutes
and pushed it again, but there was no response this time either.
Looking up again at the somewhat forbidding building, he
started back to the Palazzo Uccello.

Urbino's nerves must have been a little on edge because

after a few minutes he felt that someone was following him. It was such an uncharacteristic way to feel that he took special notice of it. Footsteps belonging to no one visible kept pace behind him and at times seemed to come from directly ahead. When he stopped, so it seemed did the footsteps, and no one appeared. He was in the network of alleys that twisted between San Giacomo dell'Orio and Campo San Polo, one of the more labyrinthine parts of the city that was dark and dank even at midday, like now. Someone who knew the city better than you could easily outwit you and be following you one minute and waiting for you around a blind corner the next. Urbino knew his way, but he wasn't invulnerable. He reminded himself of the rash of muggings in this very area.

But if he was being followed, it might not even be by a mugger. It might be by someone who wanted to frighten him away from asking any more questions about Flavia.

Urbino quickened his stride and felt better once he became part of the *corso della gente* that flowed, eddied, and became periodically dammed at intersections and on the steps of the Rialto Bridge. He didn't feel completely secure, however, until the door of the Palazzo Uccello was closed firmly behind him. He was sweating, and it wasn't only because of the heat.

The phone started ringing as he went up the staircase. When he picked it up, an unfamiliar male voice asked in precise British English, "Am I speaking to Signor Urbino Macintyre? Yes?" The voice was well modulated and commanding despite its lowness. "This is Lorenzo Brollo. Would it be possible for us to have a talk?"

Urbino could hardly have been more surprised. He was also a little uneasy. Had Brollo seen him outside the Palazzo Brollo? Could Brollo himself—or someone Brollo knew—have been following him?

"A talk?"

This was exactly what Urbino wanted, but he was so taken off guard that all he could do was repeat what Brollo had said.

"Exactly, Signor Macintyre. Tomorrow morning at eleven?"

Brollo didn't wait for Urbino to say he could make it. He just hung up—and, Urbino couldn't help but notice, without giving his address.

Urbino changed his shirt, which was damp with perspira-

tion, and then sat in the study with Serena on his lap. He tried
to make some sense of Brollo's call. The man's voice echoed in
Urbino's mind. It was the kind of voice that would brook little
resistance. It belonged to a man accustomed to having his way.
And he was having it with Urbino, wasn't he? Urbino was going
to see Brollo at Brollo's request and at a time the man himself
had decided on. It didn't make Urbino feel comfortable at all.

Puzzling over Brollo's possible motivations for setting an
appointment for tomorrow morning, Urbino went down to a
room on the *piano terreno* that was bare except for a large table
and various chemicals and implements. This was where he occasionally restored oil paintings, something he had learned to do
in preparation for a biography on a Venetian family of restor-
ers. He had become competent at restoration, and it both
soothed and gratified him to bring even a small patch of canvas
back to its original freshness.

Last month the Contessa had given him a portrait by Bartolomeo Veneto that had hung in a room now being done over
at the Ca' da Capo-Zendrini. It was an engagement portrait in
semiprofile of a young lady of Cremona painted in 1542. She
was dressed in a red velvet dress with puffy sleeves and an
embroidered top, a large, padded turban, pearl eardrops, a
necklace of amber beads, and delicate leather gloves with reversed cuffs.

He had already gone over it with cotton swabs dampened
with saliva and mineral spirit and was in the process of removing
the old yellow varnish with poultices, leaving only a thin layer
of the original varnish. He was now working on one of the
long corkscrew curls from her temple to her chin. He cleaned
carefully and methodically, marveling, as he always did, to see
the original colors coming out.

As he worked, he couldn't get Lorenzo Brollo's unexpected
phone call out of his mind. Violetta must have told Brollo about
Urbino's visit earlier that day. How close was the relationship
between Violetta and Brollo? Italians usually didn't distinguish
between blood relatives and in-laws. Violetta had praised Brollo,
saying he had treated Flavia like a princess, but she certainly
hadn't had any good words to spare for Brollo's sister. What
was her name? Annabella. The sister with the passion for flowers, the unmarried sister who had devoted her life to her
brother ever since his wife, Regina, died. Violetta had said that

she wouldn't be surprised if Annabella were the source of the story about Alvise. Annabella, she said, had done everything she could to turn Flavia against Violetta and against her own mother. But Violetta could very well be trying to turn Urbino against Annabella, even before he met her.

Brollo's call had to be related to his visit to Violetta. Perhaps Violetta and he were acting in concert in some way—Violetta to protect her sister's reputation and Brollo to save face. The voice that had come so imperiously over the telephone belonged to a man who wanted to be in control of appearances.

Urbino continued to work on the corkscrew curl. The color of the Cremonese lady's hair was only slightly darker than Flavia's had been, and the turban on her head, although much larger and ornate, reminded him of the one Flavia wore in *Nude in a Funeral Gondola*. He stared at the lady's face, and for several moments it became Flavia's, strangely serene and yet just as strangely imploring.

Before he saw Brollo tomorrow morning, he should go back to the Casa Trieste and ask Ladislao Mirko some more questions. Maybe he could find out why Flavia had preferred to stay there instead of her own home, and could get some insight into the relationship between her and Mirko. He should also see Bruno Novembrini again. Urbino had to go to Brollo's armed with more information about Flavia than he already had. Neither Mirko nor Novembrini had been eager to talk about Flavia last week, but now, with Flavia dead, they might be in a different frame of mind.

Urbino looked at his watch. It was almost three. He could be on the other side of the Grand Canal at the Casa Trieste to see Ladislao Mirko in less than an hour.

Before he left for the Casa Trieste, however, he called Bruno Novembrini and told him he had some questions about Flavia Brollo. Novembrini asked him to hold for a few moments. Urbino could hear a muffled conversation on the other end. When Novembrini came back on the line, he said in his deep voice, "Massimo seems to think it might be a good idea if I talked to you about Flavia. Maybe he's afraid if I hold things in I'll get blocked and then where will much of his income go?" Novembrini laughed, but Urbino felt it was less for Urbino's hearing than Massimo Zuin's. "Shall we say seven-thirty in Campo Santa Margherita?" Novembrini named a café.

11

As URBINO WENT up the dark staircase of the Casa Trieste, Ladislao Mirko, wearing his black skullcap, peered down at him. The thin, homely man was paler than he had been last week, and the two gaping holes that were his nostrils seemed even larger. A scratch marred his cheek and there were dark rings beneath his dull, lifeless eyes.

"Hello, Signor Macintyre," Mirko said in his nasal voice. "Flavia told me who you must be. She said I should be nice to you."

Sniffling as if from a cold, Mirko led him along the upper hall to a dark, windowless room filled with a few pieces of furniture. A calendar and a map of Venice were tacked on the walls. At the back of the room a large wooden table, with a tabby cat curled up on it, faced the door. Behind the table was a curtain on a runner, drawn partway and revealing the edge of a stove.

"Sit down," Mirko said, going behind the desk.

Mirko gave off a rancid odor. Urbino couldn't tell if it was his breath or his body—or both. Whatever it was, Urbino wished he weren't in such close quarters with him.

"You know Flavia Brollo is dead, don't you?" Urbino asked him, sitting down on the sofa.

"Yes, I know she's dead," Mirko said, touching the end of his nose with several fingers.

"When was the last time you saw her?"

Mirko had just said that Flavia had told him to be "nice" to Urbino. Urbino hoped that this meant that he would get some answers from him.

"Last Thursday night about seven-thirty," Mirko said without any hesitation.

Commissario Gemelli had said that Flavia had been dead

by no later than midnight Thursday. Mirko was giving Urbino the first piece of information he had about where Flavia had been the night she died. He hoped that the Contessa was having success with Corrado Scarpa. Urbino desperately needed a full chronology of Flavia's last night.

"Wednesday, when she came back from Asolo," Mirko continued in his nasal voice, "I told her that a man with an American accent was asking about her. She said it must be you, the Contessa da Capo-Zendrini's friend, and that I should tell you the truth if you ever asked me anything again. Flavia loved the truth. She hated secrets."

"You were with Flavia at the Contessa's villa in Asolo."

Urbino still wasn't sure whether Mirko recognized him from that afternoon.

"Yes. We were good friends—for fifteen years!" The whine was back in his voice. "That's a long time! We looked after each other, like brother and sister." He took out a handkerchief and wiped his nose. "I tried to convince her not to go, I really did, but once she got an idea in her head, you couldn't stop her. She wanted to tell the Contessa that the Conte was her father."

Mirko scooped up the cat, pulled the table drawer open, and took out a small metal object. He held the cat tightly in his lap as it squirmed and cried. Pushing the pad of one of the cat's paws to extend its claws, Mirko started to trim the claws with a clipper.

"You have to do this every so often," Mirko explained with a little laugh, "or else something like this happens."

He indicated the scratch on his cheek.

"I know," Urbino said. "I have a cat myself and quite a few scratches." He watched Mirko trim the cat's claws for a few moments and then said, "But why did Flavia think the Conte da Capo-Zendrini was her father?"

Violetta Volpi claimed not to know where the idea had come from—unless, she said, from Annabella. But perhaps Mirko, who had been Flavia's friend for fifteen years, was in a better position to know. There were many things that one would share with a close friend but never with a relative.

Mirko smiled at Urbino, revealing several missing side teeth. "You won't believe me when I tell you." He paused, clearly savoring Urbino's anticipation. "It was Flavia's own mother who told her. It's the truth! Flavia told me."

Mirko continued to clip the cat's claws. His own nails, broken and encrusted with grime, could have used some attention themselves.

"Yes, that's what Flavia said, and she never lied to me. She said that her mother had been driven into another man's arms by Lorenzo and his scheming sister. She told me two or three years after we got to know each other. She said she trusted me enough to tell me."

Urbino wondered if it was the memory of Flavia's trust that made Mirko furrow his brow the way he now did. The cat howled and tried to escape, but Mirko got a firmer grip and started on another paw.

"And there's something else," Mirko said, not looking up at Urbino. "An argument Flavia and I overheard the summer her mother died. I was visiting Flavia at the villa they were renting on Lago di Garda even though Lorenzo wasn't keen on Flavia hanging around older guys—or any guys at all. She was fourteen. Flavia and I were walking past her mother's bedroom when we heard Lorenzo, Flavia's mother, and her Zia Violetta arguing. Violetta shouted to Lorenzo, 'Flavia's *not* your daughter! You know it's true. Why don't you admit it!' Then we heard her saying something about the Conte da Capo-Zendrini. There was a slap and Violetta started to cry. Flavia's mother was crying, too, and called out Lorenzo's name, kind of shocked. Lorenzo told Violetta to leave them alone. Flavia and I got out of there fast. Her Zia Annabella was coming up the stairs. After that time at Lago di Garda Flavia would ask me to go over the argument again and again, to tell her what I remembered, and she would always nod her head. 'He's not my father,' she would say. 'I always knew he wasn't.' Oh, there's little doubt that the Contessa's husband was Flavia's father. Even so, I told her not to go to see the Contessa. I was afraid of what the Contessa might do to her—and to me."

When Flavia had given Mirko permission to tell Urbino the truth—if, in fact, she had—had she meant he should confide all this? Urbino asked himself. And did it make sense that Flavia would have gone in search of "proof" that Alvise da Capo-Zendrini was her father if she had learned it from her mother?

Perhaps, however, Flavia needed something more tangible than the word of a dead woman. She might have been seeking out a living witness. But what about Mirko himself? He might have been the "proof" she had gone out to get.

Something else puzzled Urbino. If Flavia had believed for over ten years that the Conte da Capo-Zendrini was her father, why had she only started to act on it recently?

"When you saw Flavia on Thursday night, did she say anything about having some kind of proof that the Conte da Capo-Zendrini was her father?"

Mirko looked up, his dull eyes returning Urbino's gaze for a few moments.

"She had her mother's word. She believed that more than anything else. And there was what we heard at Lago di Garda."

"On Thursday evening did she ask you to tell the Contessa da Capo-Zendrini what you both had heard at Lago di Garda?"

"She said that I might have to. Flavia was very upset that evening. After about ten or fifteen minutes she rushed out to see her Zia Violetta. I never saw her again."

"But didn't you wonder where she was when you didn't see her for several days? And especially when she was so upset? She stayed here with you most of the time."

"Not *with* me, but in the pensione," Mirko corrected, sniffling and touching his nose. "Sometimes she'd go off for days—even weeks. She'd spend them with an American woman in Asolo or with that pompous artist Novembrini. She liked to say that her home was everywhere and nowhere."

"So Flavia had her own room here," Urbino said, looking pointedly at the drawn curtain. "But you don't have many rooms to rent out, do you? It must have cut into your profits to have Flavia take up one of the rooms—unless she paid you, of course."

"She never gave me any money, and I didn't want any! Money had nothing to do with our friendship."

"Maybe you got the price of the room from her in some other way," Urbino risked saying.

"Listen to me!" Mirko said angrily. "Flavia and I were only friends—like brother and sister, as I said! All I ever wanted from her was her friendship!"

"It's just that I need to know as much about Flavia as I

can. Not only for the Contessa da Capo-Zendrini's sake but for Flavia's, too. Hasn't it occurred to you that she might have been murdered? She drowned, but there were wounds on her forehead. She might have been hit first."

Mirko's fear was as palpable as his odor.

"Murdered! Where did you get a crazy idea like that! Who would want to murder Flavia? Everybody loved her." Fear still showed on Mirko's face as he shook his head. "You're wrong. Flavia talked about suicide so much it scared me. She was fascinated with it." Mirko was talking more quickly now. "Probably because her mother killed herself, right? Don't they say that children usually end up doing the same thing? After her mother killed herself Flavia used to say that her mother was at peace. It would sometimes pop into my head that she might do the same thing—yes, even last week when she left so upset. But what could I do?"

Mirko released the cat and watched it as it ran from the room. When Mirko met Urbino's eyes, the fearful look was still there but also something else, something very much like guilt. Was Mirko considering his own culpability if his friend of more than fifteen years had killed herself and he hadn't been in a position to help her?

"What do you know about the medication that was found among Flavia's things?"

"What do you mean?"

"Did you ever see her take it?"

"Many times. She said it helped her be happier."

"What doctor prescribed it for her?"

"I didn't know *everything* about Flavia! Maybe she didn't want anyone to know who the doctor was. Maybe that was why there was no label on the bottle."

"So you know there wasn't any label?"

"Of course. I saw that bottle plenty of times. And others just like it," he quickly added.

"Did you ever ask her why there was no label?"

"What's going on here? The police took that bottle and that's that. Those pills show that Flavia wasn't on an even keel, don't they? Why worry about the label?"

"Because without the label we can't be sure whether she was really taking them, can we?"

"She was taking them all right! I think we've finished,

Macintyre. Flavia told me to be nice to you but maybe she didn't know that you weren't nice yourself, and would be saying bad things about her. You and the Contessa da Capo-Zendrini just want to make Flavia seem unreliable, now that she's dead and can't defend herself! You have no regard for the dead! I think it's—it's despicable!"

As Mirko got angrier and angrier, Urbino found something forced in it, as if the man were giving a performance or saying these things because he thought they were expected of him. Mirko took a deep breath and seemed about to go on in the same vein, perhaps at an even higher volume, but instead he remained silent, rubbing his nose again. It was as if he had decided, for whatever reason, that it would be better if he wasn't so passionate in Flavia's defense—better, instead, if he continued to do what Flavia had asked him to do and tell the truth. A doubt remained in Urbino's mind, however. How could he know whether Flavia had said this to Mirko at all?

"I didn't mean to get so worked up, Signor Macintyre," Mirko said, shrugging his thin shoulders. "But it's been hard on me. I cared about Flavia."

"I understand," Urbino said. "That's why I'm sure you want to know exactly how she died. We might not realize it but we always feel better when we know the truth about these things, even when it's a hard truth."

"You're right," Mirko responded flatly. "I suppose that means you have more questions."

"Just a few. Is there anyone still at the pensione who might have had any contact with Flavia last week? Anyone who might have seen her on the last night she came here?"

"No."

"Flavia kept a scrapbook," Urbino said, hoping that Madge Lennox had told him the truth about it.

Mirko didn't seem surprised.

"I have it. Don't tell Lorenzo, but I kept a few of her things. The scrapbook, a few books, and an old robe I like. They were special to Flavia and they make me feel close to her. Want to see the scrapbook and the books?"

Mirko opened the table drawer and took out two paper-bound books and a large album with a dark blue cover. He was now being as cooperative as possible, it seemed.

Urbino took the album and paged through it quickly as

Mirko observed him nervously. The scrapbook was almost completely filled with newspaper clippings, postcards, and other memorabilia.

"Would you mind if I took this for a day or two?"

Mirko was still looking down at the album.

"I—I'd rather you didn't."

Urbino was puzzled at this apparent change in Mirko. If he hadn't wanted Urbino to look at it, why had he volunteered to show it to him? Mirko was a difficult man to read. Was there craft behind what he was doing or was he making things up as he went along? What roles, if any, were grief over Flavia and love for her playing in all this?

Taking back the scrapbook, Mirko handed the two books to Urbino. One was an Italian biography of Eleonora Duse and the other a catalog of the Peggy Guggenheim Collection. Urbino fanned the pages of the biography. Nothing was between the pages.

He turned to the Guggenheim catalog. On the cover was a photograph of the terrace of the Palazzo Guggenheim. Marino Marini's tumescent horseman—although the state of his arousal couldn't be seen from the angle of the shot—gazed out at the Grand Canal through the wrought-iron gates. One of the mooring poles against which Flavia's body had surfaced three days ago was visible.

Urbino opened the booklet. On the flyleaf was the inscription:

> To my favorite niece on her twenty-first birthday. Does it make any difference that you're also my only one?
>   Love,
>   Zia Violetta

Urbino riffled through the catalog. He had his own copy at the Palazzo Uccello. There were English and Italian forewords about the collection, followed by color illustrations of most of the museum's works. The binding was loose and several pages slid out and fell to the floor. Urbino picked up the pages and started to rearrange them in their proper sequence. He soon noticed that one leaf of the book was missing, comprising pages 71 and 72, opposite sides of the same sheet. He handed the

books back to Mirko, who stared fixedly at the cover photograph
of the catalog.

"I'm sorry, Signor Macintyre," Mirko said with a touch of
impatience, "but I have to go to the Questura now to bring over
the registration slips."

Urbino thanked Mirko for his help and left. As he walked
slowly in the direction of Campo Santa Margherita, Urbino
started to play over his conversation with Mirko. Could Regina
Brollo actually have told her daughter that Alvise da Capo-
Zendrini was her father? Had she been telling the truth? If not,
then why did Regina Brollo fill her daughter's mind with such
a monstrous lie?

But how much of what Ladislao Mirko told him could he
believe? Mirko hadn't acted in a completely consistent way. He
had some of the signs of cocaine addiction—the reddened nose,
the sniffles, the dull eyes, even a slight confusion at times. And
then there was the scratch on his cheek that he had made a
point of saying the cat had done. Urbino's investigation was
going to be very tricky because of his close relationship with the
Contessa, but he would have to be careful to keep an open
mind. Perhaps—

Urbino's thoughts were interrupted by quick footsteps behind him and the calling of his name. He turned. It was Mirko,
his homely face now flushed. He was carrying two objects under
his arm. One was the large envelope for the Questura. The
other was Flavia's scrapbook.

"Here," Mirko said, thrusting the scrapbook at Urbino.
"Flavia wouldn't mind. She liked you. I know she didn't know
you but—but Flavia could tell about a man. If he could be
trusted. She always trusted me," Mirko emphasized.

Surprised but pleased at this sudden reversal of Mirko's
decision, Urbino thanked him and said he would return the
scrapbook as soon as he finished going through it. Mirko, without saying good-bye, hurried ahead into the *calle*.

12

URBINO, WITH TWO hours before his appointment with Novembrini in Campo Santa Margherita, decided to go back to the Palazzo Uccello and see what he could learn from Flavia's scrapbook. He was still puzzled why Mirko had changed his mind about giving it to him. What had gone through the man's mind in those minutes after Urbino had left him? Was it possible that he had removed something from the scrapbook?

Unlike earlier that day when he had returned home from the Palazzo Brollo, Urbino departed from the direct route. He wanted to avoid the crowds clogging the main *calli*, making it almost impossible to squeeze through. Spirits were high and the alleys echoed loudly with enthusiastic voices. The crowds became thinner and the sounds more muted, however, as he went through a network of alleys that groped and twisted their way toward the Grand Canal. They were a tourist's nightmare. Unless you knew exactly where you were going, you could easily get turned completely around and end up far from your desired destination—or find yourself, an hour later, back at your starting point.

Urbino knew the city so well that he didn't have to pay particular attention to his route. This was fortunate since his mind was filled with just about everything but the scene in front of him. For a brief moment Urbino remembered how he had felt vaguely menaced and stalked on his earlier walk. It now embarrassed him that he had become a victim of one of the city's familiar tricks.

Urbino thought about what he had learned. Mirko said that Flavia had been at the Casa Trieste until seven-thirty and then, angry, had left to see Violetta Volpi. Fifteen minutes on foot would have brought her to the Ca' Volpi on the other side of the Grand Canal. If she had taken the *traghetto* across the canal by the Ca' Rezzonico, she could have been there even quicker, for the gondola ferry would have deposited her only a short distance from the Ca' Volpi. Venice was a small town, only about twice the size of Central Park in New York City.

But had Flavia gone to the Ca' Volpi directly? Had she stopped to see someone on the way? Urbino hoped that Corrado Scarpa would be able to give the Contessa the information they needed about the chronology of Flavia's last night.

Urbino turned down a usually deserted *calle* near San Gia-como dell'Orio that was a shortcut for those who knew their way. Wooden planks were set down on the paving stones to make the alley negotiable for *acqua alta*. As could so often happen in Venice, even on the driest of days, an oppressive damp-ness dropped down over Urbino like a heavy cloak. He took several deep breaths but the thick air didn't satisfy him.

A few seconds later Urbino heard footsteps behind him on the plank but paid them no mind. Just someone else who knew his way through these back alleys, someone else just as eager to get through and out into more breathable air.

Then a man appeared in front of Urbino. He wore a dark cap low on his forehead. Urbino felt a rapid surge of apprehen-sion. Something about the man's wary, catlike stride and ap-praising look made Urbino sense that he was not just going to pass him by. Urbino tried to draw more air into his lungs. He almost felt as if he were drowning.

Urbino turned to retrace his way, but now another man was standing a few feet away, blocking Urbino's path. He was over six feet tall and very broad. If Urbino hadn't been so concerned—if he hadn't still been struggling for breath—he would have laughed because this man, too, wore a dark cap identical to the other's. In a quick, hot flash of fear, Urbino realized he was about to be mugged.

What happened next happened very quickly. The man behind Urbino was upon him, holding him around the neck and putting a hand over his mouth. Urbino couldn't move. What little air he had been taking into his lungs was now cut off completely. The other mugger rushed up and reached into his pockets, extracting his wallet and his keys.

Urbino clasped Flavia's scrapbook closer. The man holding him in a viselike grip said in unpolished Italian whose regional

accent Urbino couldn't place, "Get the damn book." The man
going through his pockets reached for the scrapbook. It was
soon in his hands.

"That's it," the mugger holding Urbino said. "Let's go!"

He pushed Urbino to the pavement and his cohort, with a
strange, scraping laugh, threw the keys down into Urbino's face.
Urbino instinctively closed his eyes and the keys struck him in
the left eye. He heard the two men hurry off in the direction
Urbino had come from.

It took him a minute or two to get to his feet. He braced
himself against the side of one of the buildings, the bricks slippery to his touch. His head was swimming and his left eye was
throbbing. He put his hand up to touch his eye. He took his
hand away and looked at it in the dimness of the narrow alley.
There was no blood.

Urbino got enough breath to shout for help. He hurried
in the direction he had heard his two muggers run. A middle-
aged man and his wife were farther up the alley, toward San
Giacomo dell'Orio. They said that two men had rushed by them
a minute or two before but they weren't sure which way they
had gone. Urbino went as far as the quiet Campo San Giacomo
dell'Orio. He saw no trace of the two men. If they knew the
city as well as he did, they would be camouflaged by a crowd
by now.

Angry and still a little fearful, Urbino went to a nearby
trattoria and called the police.

13

WHEN URBINO JOINED Bruno Novembrini at the café in Campo
Santa Margherita, his bloodshot and swollen left eye required
an explanation. He quickly described the mugging and the theft
of his wallet, but didn't say anything about the scrapbook. He
had never been mugged before and he was still shaken by the
experience. Could the two muggers have been trailing him since

earlier in the day? Had they seen him standing outside the Palazzo Brollo and then followed him later to the Casa Trieste?

Urbino had filled out several forms for the police, but the police seemed almost resigned. Another mugging to add to the string of others this summer. Urbino had tried to convince them that this mugging, however, might not be part of the pattern, but what did he have as proof except his own suspicion?

Urbino was just as distraught at the loss of the album as he was by having been physically attacked—perhaps even more. The police were alerting sweepers and trash collectors, since the muggers might have tossed away the scrapbook if it was worthless to them. But this was too much to hope for. Urbino was afraid the muggers hadn't just been after his wallet but rather the scrapbook. The man restricting him had been determined that his accomplice take it.

Urbino ended up being fifteen minutes late for his appointment with Novembrini at seven-thirty. Campo Santa Margherita, which the area's residents used as an extension of their homes, especially during the *passeggiata* that so amused Eugene, was filled with locals. Its comfortable, unpretentious rhythm helped soothe Urbino somewhat as he sat across from Bruno Novembrini at the outdoor café.

Novembrini's handsome, bony face was heavily lined with fatigue this early evening, giving him an even more rakish look, especially with the dark shadow of his beard gleaming in places with spikes of gray. Urbino could easily imagine Novembrini as a model for those darkly handsome, vaguely sinister men whom virginal heroines fall in love with in bodice-ripper romances. Almost invariably this kind of man ended up being—in fiction, at least—well intentioned. What had Flavia's relationship been with the older Novembrini? Had she found the glowering artist abusive or kindly intentioned in the end? And just how virginal and vulnerable had she actually been? If appearances meant anything, she hadn't been virginal at all; yet Urbino knew only too well that appearances often were the very greatest deceivers.

"I'd like to get this over with," Novembrini said in his low, mellifluous voice. "I'm doing this at Massimo Zuin's urging. He thinks it might help me to talk about Flavia with someone who—who wasn't involved in any way with her. I've been keeping a lot to myself and he thinks it's taking its toll. But first you should tell me exactly why you want to know more about Flavia. Is it really because of the Contessa da Capo-Zendrini, as you said when we talked before?"

Novembrini opened a sketchbook and took a pencil from his pocket.

"Would you mind if I sketched you while we're talking? It helps my thoughts along."

Urbino explained why he needed to know more about Flavia. He told Novembrini how she had insisted that the Conte da Capo-Zendrini was her father and how Urbino suspected that her death not only had something to do with her accusation but wasn't suicide at all, let alone an accident.

Novembrini just listened, squinting against the smoke from the cigarette in the corner of his mouth. He busied himself with his pencil, looking back and forth between Urbino's face and the sketchbook. He took the cigarette from his mouth and put it on the edge of the table.

"Murder? Would it shock you if I said I wish I could believe it?" Novembrini said. "Maybe then I wouldn't feel guilty about her having committed suicide. But suicide or not, it's her father and her father's sister who should feel the most guilty. Flavia never felt loved by either of them. She said that Lorenzo resented her after her mother's death. But this is the first I've ever heard of anything about the Conte da Capo-Zendrini—or any other man. She never said anything like that to me."

Novembrini frowned. Did it bother him that Flavia hadn't told him about the Conte da Capo-Zendrini? The artist studied Urbino's face for several moments, but didn't return right away to his sketch. A burning odor hit Urbino's nostrils. Novembrini reached down for his cigarette, which had scorched the tablecloth, and took a long drag, trying, not very hard, to blow the smoke away from Urbino.

"I honestly don't know anything about it," Novembrini said, looking down at the sketch again and making a few strokes.

"How long did you know Flavia?"

"Almost two years. I met her at Zuin's. She came in with her aunt—not Lorenzo's sister but her mother's, Violetta Volpi. She's a painter, most of it imitation Munch. She's envious of me, although she should just turn a cold eye on her own work to see why she never even made it as far as the Aperto."

The Aperto, an exhibit devoted to up and coming artists, was mounted every Biennale at the rope works near the Arsenal.

"Massimo carries her work. Your relative bought one—a portrait of a girl standing by a pool of water. Violetta painted a whole series like that. Flavia didn't like any of them. They reminded her of her mother's death. To give Violetta credit, though, she was devoted to Flavia. Although Flavia sometimes said that Violetta might have resented her mother a little— because her mother was so beautiful and Violetta knew Lorenzo first—she never doubted her love. And if Flavia needed anything she needed love—deep love—not just affection, and certainly not just sex." Novembrini paused before saying, "I tried to be the kind of man she seemed to need. I loved her but I must have failed her somehow. She used to say that she trusted me a long time before she loved me. I've thought about that a lot since she died. I think that for her, trust was just about everything. If I ever violated her trust, I knew that she would be destroyed—and I never did."

Where, Urbino asked himself, did the dark-haired young woman he had seen with Novembrini at the café before Flavia had died and whose show of affection Novembrini had checked fit into this picture?

"So why did she slash the painting?"

Novembrini, who should have expected the question, seemed surprised. He put down the sketch pad.

"I said that I never violated her trust, but that's not the same as her thinking I had. About two weeks ago she started accusing me of seeing someone else and saying that I had been lying to her. A friend of hers put the idea in her head. Ladislao Mirko, the weird guy who runs the pensione I mentioned when we first talked. I never took to him. He's a real loser."

"What do you know about him?"

"Not all that much. Just what Flavia and—and one or two of her friends told me about him."

"What friends?"

"I don't remember their names now. Just friends."

"What did they say?"

"That Mirko and his mother and father drifted in from Trieste about fifteen years ago. His mother ran off a few years later and his father eventually ended up overdosing on drugs or drinking himself to death. Obviously these things run in families. Mirko's pathetic. All he probably ever thinks about is where he's going to get his next hit." Novembrini inhaled deeply on the cigarette. "He was jealous of Flavia and me. Can't blame him. Just look at him—ugly and emaciated! I couldn't say the slightest thing against him to Flavia, though. She was loyal to him, and she believed she had no reason to question his own loyalty. I said to her once that Mirko wanted nothing more than to get his hands all over her. She slapped me. 'Sex has nothing to do with Mirko and me,' she said. But I had my doubts—I mean, where *he* was concerned. He was just burning to be more than friends with her."

Obviously no love was lost between Novembrini and Mirko.

" 'Beauty and the Beast,' I used to call them to myself," Novembrini went on. "I envisioned a painting on the subject, using them both as models but, needless to say, I never mentioned it to Flavia."

Novembrini finished his wine and poured more into his glass and Urbino's from the carafe.

"But we're getting off the point, aren't we? I don't know anything about Flavia's mother and the Conte da Capo-Zendrini. Why she would have told you and the Contessa—and even Ladislao Mirko—and not me, I don't know. She made it very clear to me, though, that she hated Brollo."

Novembrini looked off into the thinning crowd in Campo Santa Margherita.

"What did she say about him?"

"Oh, she didn't mince any words. She despised him. When I asked her why, she would just refuse to say. I assumed it was because of how he might have treated her mother, because Flavia had only good things to say about her."

"Can't you remember anything specific about what she said about Brollo?"

"That's just it. She never was specific. I just knew she hated him. I did get the impression, though, that she was holding back when she talked about him, as if she were afraid of what she might say—or even do—if she let herself go. She was capable of sudden, violent emotions."

"Do you mean something other than slashing the painting?"

Novembrini spent a few minutes working on the sketch before answering.

"I'll tell you something only because maybe it will help you see why I'm afraid that she committed suicide. A couple of times when she was spending the night, she became hysterical. All I did was look at her in a way that let her know what was on my mind—which wasn't just to turn out the lights and go to sleep. When I went closer to her to try to calm her, she slapped me and either ran from the apartment or locked herself in the bathroom for hours. She never wanted to talk about why she reacted the way she did. Most other times we had no problems when it came to sex."

"What state of mind was Flavia in when you saw her last?"

"You're not fooling me, Macintyre! What you really want to know is when I last saw Flavia. Well, it was a good week before she died, right after the slashing. I told her that I wouldn't tell anyone that she had done it but that she should consider getting some help. She just laughed as if it were a joke, but I was serious. Her mother wasn't all that emotionally balanced."

"Was Flavia taking any medication?"

"I doubt it. She made a big fuss about taking aspirin and she hardly ever touched alcohol."

"Did she ever mention a doctor she might have been going to?"

"Flavia hated doctors. She would have had to be dying to let one come near her."

Novembrini's dark, deep-set eyes seemed touched by sadness and regret. He drained his glass and stood up.

"I have to be getting back. Zuin and I are having dinner with a buyer. Take this." Novembrini ripped off the sketch he had been doing of Urbino and handed it to him. "You'll have to forgive me. I got carried away by your nose. I made it a bit more prominent than it actually is," he said with a smile.

"Before you go, could you tell me if you know anything about a scrapbook Flavia kept?"

"A scrapbook? She never mentioned she had one. Good day!"

Novembrini strode off into the *campo* in the direction of San Pantalon.

Urbino looked at Novembrini's sketch. It was a good likeness, capturing Urbino's sharp features and even the bruise under his eye, but Novembrini was right about the nose. The sketch looked not a little like Pinocchio after a few of his lies.

Urbino went into the café and called the police. No, he was told, they hadn't found the muggers and the scrapbook hadn't turned up. The officer assured him that he would be notified as soon as they learned anything and that the scrapbook would be returned to him immediately, if it were found.

Urbino rang off, not feeling in any way encouraged. He was afraid Flavia's scrapbook, along with whatever vital information it might contain, was lost to him forever.

As he was walking back to the Palazzo Uccello, he paused in the middle of a small bridge over a side canal. He stood there musing for several minutes, enjoying the relative calm and quiet and watching two young boys play by the canal bank with their dog.

He thought about what he had learned from Bruno Novembrini about Flavia—how she had felt unloved by both Lorenzo and Lorenzo's sister, how Lorenzo had resented her after her mother's death, how she had apparently loved and admired Violetta Volpi, her mother's sister. There seemed no doubt in Novembrini's mind that his former girlfriend had hated Lorenzo, but yet she had never given him any indication that she thought Lorenzo wasn't her father or had ever said anything about the Conte da Capo-Zendrini. Had she been afraid to tell Novembrini? And what about Flavia's hysterical reaction to the looks Novembrini gave her—looks that indicated he wanted to have sex with her? Once again Urbino wondered about the possible role of the dark-haired young woman.

Urbino felt he had learned a lot from Novembrini, but he wasn't clear as to what it might all mean. And neither was he satisfied that Novembrini had been completely honest, that he hadn't held back something vital. The artist had had a strange relationship with his model, but was it a relationship that could have ended in his murdering her? Novembrini claimed not to have seen her for a week before her death but perhaps he had—on the night she died.

Last week at the café by the Accademia Bridge, Novembrini had seemed afraid of giving Urbino any information about Flavia. Should Urbino assume he was any the less afraid now that she was dead? Perhaps Novembrini was only feeding him the information he wanted him to know for his own reasons.

Urbino was pulled away from his speculations by the sight of a man crossing another bridge about thirty meters farther along the same canal. He was small, wore a straw hat, and walked with quick steps behind a group of tourists.

"Signor Occhipinti!" Urbino called.

The man halted momentarily and light reflected off the surface of his spectacles. Then the man quickened his pace and went down the steps of the bridge and disappeared down a *calle*.

14

BACK AT THE Palazzo Uccello, Urbino opened the glass doors of one of the bookcases in the library and took out his copy of the catalog of the Peggy Guggenheim Collection. He turned to pages 71 and 72.

On one side of the page was a color reproduction of Yves Tanguy's *The Sun in Its Casket*—or, as it was more correctly but less disturbingly translated, *The Sun in Its Jewel Case*. One of the words of the painting's original French title described a small jewel coffer or "casket," but most Americans thought it meant a coffin. The Tanguy, one of the paintings Eugene had passed by in silence and with disdain last week, was a bizarre landscape of amorphous, deliquescent forms that teased with an elusive meaning. The dominant image was a yellow tapered column with long stickline protrusions. Vague shapes on the point of becoming human or forever losing any resemblance to humanity were scattered and embedded in the sand around the yellow object.

On the other side of the sheet was Dalí's *The Birth of Liquid Desires*, in which the woman struggled with a naked man. Urbino and Eugene had seen the original at the Peggy Guggenheim a few minutes before Flavia's body was found floating by the terrace of the palazzo. The images were disturbing. The burst of flowers that was the young woman's head. The naked younger man reaching down into a pool of water. A pale woman in the background, her face averted from the grappling couple. The bearded older man with a woman's breast and a prominent erection.

Urbino called the Contessa.

"Are you all right, Urbino?" the Contessa was quick to ask after he said only a few words. She was one of the few people who could detect his mood—disappointment, anger, apprehension, fatigue, whatever—from just a few syllables over the phone.

"I'm fine, Barbara," Urbino answered quickly, making an effort to control his voice. "Just a little weary." He didn't want to tell the Contessa about his mugging until they were face to face. Although he had just been to Asolo, he would make a quick trip there tomorrow and fill her in on everything. He would also accompany Eugene back to Venice. "There are some things to tell you but I'll come to Asolo tomorrow. What I want to know now is if you had any luck with Corrado."

"He came through, *caro*! I've got just what you need in front of me."

She read the names and times that Corrado Scarpa had given her. Urbino copied them down.

"So Lorenzo Brollo was the last person to see Flavia alive?" he asked the Contessa.

"So it seems."

"Thank you, Barbara. I'll see you tomorrow."

"Urbino, are you sure you're all right? You seem so abrupt tonight."

Urbino assured her that he was only tired and said good night.

According to the police investigation, Ladislao Mirko had seen Flavia at seven-thirty on Thursday evening. This matched what Mirko had told Urbino. Flavia had been at the Ca' Volpi from about ten minutes before eight until eight-thirty and then had gone to see Lorenzo Brollo. Brollo said she arrived before nine and left about forty-five minutes later. It seemed that Violetta Volpi had also paid a visit to the Palazzo Brollo that same night, but she and Brollo said that Flavia had left by then. Annabella Brollo hadn't seen Flavia, but she corroborated her brother's story. No one apparently had seen Flavia alive after she left Lorenzo.

The thunderstorm had come crashing down on Venice about ten-thirty. Had Flavia been dead by then? Had she met anyone other than Mirko, Violetta, and Lorenzo that night? Were all of them—including Annabella—telling the truth about the times? It was logical to assume that the murderer would lie about having seen her that night but yet, Urbino reminded himself, just because someone might lie didn't mean he or she was the murderer. There could be other reasons for not telling the truth, and anyone could have followed Flavia after she left the Palazzo Brollo and killed her.

Urbino was happy to have the list of names. It gave him something concrete to work with. He hoped he would be able to fill in the list more.

15

BY ELEVEN THE next morning, a Wednesday, the heat and humidity were oppressive as Urbino pushed the brass bell at the Palazzo Brollo. He was looking forward to his brief trip to much cooler Asolo later that day to accompany Eugene back to Venice.

When a woman answered through the intercom, Urbino gave his name and was buzzed into the building. The woman told him to come up to the *piano nobile*. He ascended the stone staircase to the next floor. There was no sign of the woman who had just spoken.

The *sala* of the Palazzo Brollo was long and narrow, terminating in the balcony's closed doors through the chinks of which a dim, aqueous light filtered into the damp, suffocatingly hot room. Pots of ferns were arranged near the balcony doors, and throughout the room vases and urns of flowers filled the air with a heavy scent. Oriental carpets in shades of green covered the scagliola floor and the ceiling was frescoed in vaguely marine designs.

Portraits in heavy dark-wood frames ranged along the walls. With very few exceptions the portraits were in the heroic, romantic style of Hogarth, Gainsborough, Reynolds, and Romney. The Brollo family would seem to have preferred not to be shown "warts and all."

A low voice came from the shadows at the far end of the room. It startled Urbino.

"You are most punctual, Signor Macintyre," the voice said in precise British English. "San Giacomo dell'Orio is only now ringing."

As Urbino's eyes became accustomed to the darkness, the tall figure of the man to whom the low but commanding voice belonged became visible. He was standing next to a piano. The man walked up to Urbino and shook his hand firmly.

"So pleased that you could come here on short notice."

Lorenzo Brollo was a handsome man in his late fifties with pale skin, blue eyes, a deeply lined face, and sharp features. A monkish fringe of gray hair around a balding crown did nothing to detract from his aquiline good looks. He was what Urbino often thought of as an Anglicized Italian, the kind that Alvise da Capo-Zendrini had been. Urbino was sure that he was a frequent traveler to Britain and prided himself on his perfect English and knowledge of affairs in the UK. His clothes were Savile Row, not Milan, and despite the heat of the day he wore white flannel trousers, a dark blue blazer, and a cravat—a costume, in fact, not very much different from that in which Urbino had dressed for the Contessa's garden party.

"My sister Annabella will be bringing us some coffee and anisette," Brollo said, his glance lingering on Urbino's bruised eye. "Please sit down."

He indicated one of two Louis Seize armchairs flanking a matching banquette. On a small, round table was a photograph of a younger Lorenzo Brollo, a girl about ten, and a woman who bore an eerie resemblance to Flavia. Next to it were an English edition of Dickens's *Little Dorrit* and a crystal vase overflowing with crimson cattleya orchids. Brollo, who noticed Urbino taking in the photograph, eased his slim frame onto the banquette.

"My wife, Regina, Flavia, and I fifteen long years ago. That's my late wife on the wall there," Brollo added almost languidly, nodding his head to a painting across from Urbino.

Brollo's words struck a familiar chord. They were almost identical to the opening lines of Browning's *My Last Duchess*. Silvestro Occhipinti would have appreciated the similarity. And who knew? Perhaps Brollo, with his obvious Anglophilia, had intended the allusion, although he couldn't also want any comparisons drawn between his own late wife and Browning's Duchess, whose proud, jealous husband had murdered her. As Urbino gave his attention to the portrait, he caught a smile curving Brollo's thin lips.

The woman in the portrait was stunning. Regina Brollo and her daughter had shared the same auburn hair and green eyes, strong, arresting face and pale skin, and also slightly uneasy air, if one could judge by Regina's stiff, Bronzino-like pose. Urbino got up and went closer to the portrait, looking for the signature in the lower right-hand corner.

"Not by my sister-in-law Violetta, but an Englishman who used to live in Dorsoduro. He did another portrait. I have it with several others of my dear wife in a room upstairs. My sister calls the room a shrine and perhaps it is. But I've left this one out for all to see. She looks as if she were still alive." Once again the same smile as he echoed words from Browning's poem. "Amazing, isn't it, how much Flavia resembled her?" He picked up the photograph on the table. "Even as a little girl." Brollo shook his head slowly and replaced the photograph. "Time passes, Signor Macintyre. If only we could freeze it at its best moments."

When Urbino sat down again, Brollo asked in his clipped, tight speech, "Do you see anything of *me* in my daughter, Signor Macintyre?"

"She had long, thin fingers, too."

Brollo spread his hands and looked down at his well-manicured fingers. He seemed casually amused.

"You're right. The fingers of another pianist, my wife used to say. But Flavia never took to the piano—or to any other instrument. Children usually don't care to compete with their parents." His eyes flicked back in the direction of his wife's portrait. "Although if my wife had lived, it might have been she who ended up competing with Flavia as her own beauty inevitably faded. Ah! Here is Annabella."

Urbino hadn't heard the silent entrance of Annabella Brollo. She was a short woman about fifty, dressed in black. Her fair, graying hair was pulled severely back, emphasizing a sharp, pinched face. All life seemed centered in pale blue eyes that had an insolent look and rested for a few seconds on Urbino's bruised eye as she advanced, carrying a silver tray with two demitasses of coffee and a bottle of anisette. Annabella

Brollo was the woman who had slipped past him into the Casa Trieste on his first visit there to ask Ladislao Mirko about Flavia. Now, as then, he caught the odor of anisette surrounding her.

Annabella deposited the tray and, without a word, padded back across the dark *sala.*

"A remarkable woman, Annabella. I don't know what I would have done without her after Regina died. She brings color and beauty into my life in more ways than one."

Lorenzo Brollo touched the velvety petal of one of the large, flamboyant orchids. Annabella gave no indication that she had heard these words of praise. She closed the door behind her as quietly as she had opened it.

Lorenzo was now considering Urbino with a cool stare.

"I know it's a hellish day but sometimes something hot is the best remedy. Would you like your coffee corrected?"

Urbino nodded. Brollo poured a generous dollop of anisette into each cup. He handed one of them to Urbino.

"I saw no reason to wait until you contacted me, Signor Macintyre. Why put you through the embarrassment of having to impose yourself on a bereaved father? You seem to be a man of *gentilezza.* Violetta was impressed, and she isn't easily. In that respect as well as others, she's totally unlike her sister, who was much more credulous. We—*I*"—he corrected himself— "thought it best if we spoke and settled this matter of the Conte Alvise da Capo-Zendrini." Brollo crossed one long, flanneled leg over the other and contemplated the high shine on his brown wingtips. "You do appreciate directness, don't you, Signor Macintyre? You Americans are said to have that quality in abundance, whereas we Italians have acquired a completely different reputation—unjustified for many of us. Not all of us own 'a fine Italian hand'—or 'tongue,' for that matter."

"Since you mention directness, Signor Brollo, perhaps, you'll forgive me when I tell you that I'm not only here about the Conte da Capo-Zendrini but because I suspect that Flavia was murdered. It might have something to do with the Conte."

Urbino read surprise in Brollo's pale blue eyes.

"My sister-in-law said nothing about your mentioning a suspicion of murder," Brollo said, looking down at his demitasse as he stirred it with a little spoon.

"I didn't."

"Indeed?" The eyes he turned to Urbino now no longer had any surprise in them. Their blank expression seemed perfectly under Brollo's control. "But yet you drop it down on me now. Why do you think that a daughter of mine could have been murdered? The police have no suspicion of foul play."

"That's true," Urbino admitted, "but I feel differently. I—"

" 'Feel'! Surely this isn't a matter of *feeling*, Signor Macintyre. My emotions—and those of my sister and my sister-in-law—are in a terrible state of disarray. We're trying to adjust to having lost our Flavia in what must have been suicide and now you are bringing up the grim specter of murder! Think of our guilt and our pain! We feel them to the quick, I assure you! The police have said that they found medicine of some kind—something that probably disoriented her. I wasn't aware that she was taking anything, but there are many things we don't know about our children. I have to let all this go and put it behind me."

"But surely if Flavia was murdered, you would want to have the murderer found."

"Without question, my dear Signor Macintyre, but I think we should deal with some actual, verifiable accusations rather than a matter of nebulous 'feeling.' " Brollo said the word scornfully. "What I mean is this nonsensical notion my daughter had about the Conte da Capo-Zendrini, a gentleman Violetta knew many years ago. An absurdity! The last time I saw Flavia, I told her most firmly once again that there was nothing to it. She was upset when she came here and upset when she left as well, I'm afraid. Such a burden."

"What time was that?"

Brollo laughed a quiet laugh.

"I have nothing to fear along those lines, despite your 'feelings' about murder. It was about nine-thirty last Thursday."

He looked at Urbino as if he were trying to gauge his reaction to the time. Nine-thirty was the time Brollo had told the police, according to Corrado Scarpa's list.

"No one seems to have seen her after then," Urbino ventured to say.

"Indeed? And this has great import when you 'feel' that she was murdered, doesn't it? But very sadly, Signor Macintyre, there's a saying: 'Suicide runs in families.' There has already been a lot of talk. 'Like mother, like daughter.' I never thought there was much truth in such expressions but I have no doubt now. I've lost the two people I've loved the most in the same painful way."

Brollo shook his head and gave an appearance of melancholy reflection for a few silent moments. Then, as if pulling himself from far away, he said, "So you can go back to the Contessa da Capo-Zendrini—an admirable woman whose efforts on behalf of our dear city we all sincerely appreciate, I assure you—and tell her that she need be troubled no longer. That's what I wanted to tell you face-to-face. The Contessa can cast her fears off on the gentle Asolo breeze! I can imagine what it must be like to fear that the person you loved most has wronged you in some base way. I couldn't—I *wouldn't*—have endured it. So please tell your friend that her late husband was most definitely not Flavia's father and had no relationship with my dead wife whatsoever."

Brollo said this with an unemphatic air, as if the only way it was of concern to him was as an easement of the Contessa's apprehensions. His assurance, however, did not address itself to another related question, other than murder, that Urbino felt hanging in the air between them.

Brollo must have felt it as well, for he added, "Dear, dead Flavia was *my* daughter." This time there was an emphasis clearly on the possessive. He steepled his long, thin fingers by his lips and looked evenly at Urbino. "*Our* daughter."

Urbino's eyes flicked in the direction of the portrait of the beautiful Regina Brollo, so much like her daughter. When he looked back at Brollo, the pianist was staring at him with a blank, inscrutable look.

"Where my daughter got such a notion is beyond me, Signor Macintyre," Brollo said, his fingers still steepled. Brollo threw this off too casually for Urbino not to suspect the opposite of what the man was saying. "She had an extraordinary imagination, always telling tales and making up the most preposterous stories. She was quite histrionic. Some people say that all women are actresses and that we men are to blame, but I reject such theories. For my part, and in my own willing way, I have been a victim of women. It has been one of the best-kept secrets of my life that only of late do I find comfortable to admit. My Flavia was a real Sarah Bernhardt—or Eleonora Duse, I should

say, an actress she admired. Flavia created a role for herself—
how and with whose help I can only guess at. I hope this last
role gave her some pleasure, considering the pain it's brought
to a fine woman like the Contessa da Capo-Zendrini."

Urbino found it hard to believe that Brollo was quite so
unconcerned that Flavia had had what he called a "notion" that
the Conte da Capo-Zendrini was her father. Surely Lorenzo was
reining in his true reaction and feeling. Control seemed to be
very important to Brollo, a control not only over himself but
perhaps over Regina and Flavia as well.

"Could some idle talk she overheard as a child have become
magnified in her mind over the years?" Urbino asked, thinking
of the argument that Ladislao Mirko and Flavia had overheard
the summer of Regina Brollo's death. "This might have been
the start of what you call her 'notion.' "

"Idle talk? But no one had anything but the best to say
about Regina."

"Excuse me for having to bring this up, Signor Brollo,"
Urbino said, remembering what Mirko had told him about Regina, "but was it at all possible that your wife might have said
something to Flavia?"

Brollo looked at him as if Urbino had slapped his face. In
fact, two red spots appeared on his cheeks. Urbino sensed that
the man's control was being put to the test now.

"Perhaps you've heard that my beautiful wife was emotionally unstable, Signor Macintyre. There's no dispute that *she*
committed suicide. But to imply that she could have corrupted
our daughter with such a filthy lie is to strike the lowest blow at
not only me but especially at her!"

Brollo stood up. So did Urbino. Brollo held himself imperi-
ally, somehow succeeding in looking down at Urbino even
though they were about the same height.

"If you are in the habit of affronting people in such a
manner, it is no wonder that you have a bruise under your eye!
My wife barely knew the Conte da Capo-Zendrini!"

In an attempt to assuage Brollo, Urbino said, "Sometimes
a child likes to think he's a kind of changeling, dropped in the
midst of the wrong family. You say that Flavia had a great
imagination. Maybe a fantasy persisted from her childhood
and—"

"Such a child with such a thought can only be one who

is unhappy with his home. My Flavia had a perfectly happy childhood! Perfectly happy!" Brollo insisted. Urbino saw that he had in no way assuaged Brollo. Quite the opposite. "I can see that I was wrong to assume you were a man of *gentilezza*, Signor Macintyre. Perhaps you have been misled into these lapses of decorum by the lies of someone. That's it, isn't it, Signor Macintyre? Who was it who suggested that my wife would ever have told such stories to Flavia? Was it that artist fellow who doesn't care how he exploited my daughter? Or Ladislao Mirko who doesn't know what day of the week or what year it is—who wheedled money out of Flavia to put up that big nose of his and inject into his scrawny arms?"

"You mention Ladislao Mirko. What kind of relationship did your daughter have with him?"

Brollo stared at him coldly, his thin lips looking like a knife wound.

" 'Relationship'! My daughter befriended that fool, pitied him, and poured out her pocketbook to him time after time, but that was it! Flavia had no interest in him other than what a child would have for an ugly little dog found in the street. She had a good heart—too good!"

"But what about Mirko's interest in her?"

"I take it you've met that sad excuse for a man! Well, just look at him. Just smell him! I called him a dog and that's just what he is, and like a dog he—"

Brollo didn't finish expressing his thought but shook his head slowly.

"This world is full of animals, Signor Macintyre. Pleasure and sensation are all most people seem to think about. If I were a younger man—younger than you"—he added with a cold smile—"I would despair. Now that my Flavia is gone, I can face what the world will become with more equanimity, but it disturbs me to my soul. It should disturb us all." Brollo stared at Urbino silently for a few moments, several long fingers tapping the side of his cheek. "There are many kinds of animals, Signor Macintyre. And Bruno Novembrini is just as much one, despite his paint brushes and canvases, as Ladislao Mirko. Poor Flavia was as misled by him as she was by that drug addict."

"Are you aware that it was Flavia who slashed Bruno Novembrini's painting at the Biennale?"

"I suspected as much. It's the kind of thing she would do—and in the case of that painting, just the thing it deserved, and don't think it wasn't!"

"Have you ever seen the painting?"

"Certainly not! My taste inclines to more conventional portraits"—he nodded in the direction of the walls—"and most certainly not to nudes of my own daughter! I think the time has come for you to leave."

Annabella had slipped back into the room during the last few minutes and was standing tentatively in front of the open door. Brollo didn't seem to notice her. Once again he managed to master his anger. He looked over at his wife's portrait again.

"So you see, Signor Macintyre, even though I'm concerned about this story my daughter told you and the Contessa, not for a moment do I believe that she was anything but the victim of someone's malice toward her—or toward my wife and myself, or the Contessa da Capo-Zendrini—and I certainly don't give any credence to this 'feeling' of yours that she was murdered. Flavia was *my* daughter—*our* daughter. It's a cruel joke that you can prove only that a man is *not* someone's father, but where can proof be found that he *is*? I never needed any. I certainly wasn't going to have my belief and trust turned upside down by a silly notion."

It was an impassioned little speech, but Urbino found something strained and calculated breaking through it.

As Brollo turned from the portrait, he noticed his sister.

"Oh, it's you, Annabella dear. I hope we're not taking you away from your lovely flowers but Signor Macintyre was just leaving. Perhaps you could show him to the door."

"He found his way up by himself," Annabella Brollo said in Italian in a thin, whispery voice. She went over to pick up the tray, looking pointedly at the anisette bottle. A grim smile only made her face seem more pinched and sharp.

"The mother always knows," she said. Her voice was a suffocated whisper, but yet distinct enough for both Urbino and Brollo to hear. As she walked toward the open door, she added a bit more loudly, "It would be a strange mother who did not know, yes?"

She went through the door and closed it quietly.

"Words of womanly wisdom!" Brollo said with a forced

laugh. "My sister doesn't speak much but when she does she gets to the heart of things. Annabella is right. Only the mother really knows. Many men with wives different from my faithful Regina are at their mercy. Didn't Ibsen write a tragedy about just such a situation, Signor Macintyre?"

"I believe it was Strindberg," Urbino said, once again supplying the correct dramatist as he had yesterday for Violetta Volpi.

Before he left Brollo alone in the dark *sala*, Urbino asked what funeral arrangements were being planned for Flavia. Brollo gave a skeptical little smile when Urbino added that the Contessa might like to pay her respects.

"Flavia didn't believe in wakes or funerals. Only the immediate family will be present for the cremation on San Michele. Both Flavia and her mother had a horror of burial. Cremation is the sensible choice for beautiful women, don't you think? Good day, Signor Macintyre."

As Urbino walked away from the Palazzo Brollo in the enervating heat, he realized that he might not have learned anything new about Flavia, but he had certainly learned a great deal about Lorenzo Brollo. This could only be an asset as he continued to piece together Flavia's twisted and confusing life. What must it have been like for her to grow up with Brollo as her father—a man who seemed to believe that control was always a virtue? He could better understand now why Flavia had not got along with her father—had, in fact, according to both Bruno Novembrini and Ladislao Mirko, despised him.

There was another aspect to Brollo's need for control that disturbed Urbino. This was the possessive way he spoke about his dead wife—and, to a certain extent, about his dead daughter. "That's my late wife on the wall there," he had said, pointing to Regina's portrait. A perfectly normal thing to say, perhaps, but it had made Urbino feel as if Brollo were reducing his wife to an object. It was completely possible that Urbino was reading these things into Brollo's words and behavior because he didn't like the man, but he didn't think so. There was something about him that was "off," like some faint but nonetheless bad odor. That was the only way Urbino could express it. It was there when Brollo had talked about Novembrini's nude portrait of Flavia and when he had fumed against the possibility that his

wife could have been sick enough to fill Flavia's mind with the
story about the Conte da Capo-Zendrini.

And what about Annabella Brollo and her puzzling comment? Brollo had laughed it off but it had obviously bothered
him. Mirko said that Annabella had been coming up the stairs
during the argument at Lago di Garda. Had she heard anything?

Something Urbino had been thinking about yesterday
came back to trouble him now as, only a few minutes away from
where he had been mugged yesterday, he entered the almost
deserted Campo San Giacomo dell'Orio. Why had Flavia only
recently started to act on her belief that the Conte was her
father? Had something compelled her to face the truth finally?
What had happened in her life recently that might offer some
explanation?

Urbino stopped for some wine and crustless *tramezzini* sandwiches at a crowded, air-conditioned bar across from the
Church of San Giacomo dell'Orio. The patrons, most of them
workingmen, sat around discussing their upcoming Ferragosto
trips to the seaside and the country, the recent arrests in Mestre
of a counterfeiting ring, and, of course, soccer and the lottery.

Urbino found the normalcy of their conversation a needed
reminder that life has an ordinary side lived by most people. It
was the part of life he himself enjoyed at the Palazzo Uccello
and with his friends. An act like Flavia's murder turned all this
upside down and cried out for a solution so that life could
return, at least for a time, to the way it had been.

After one more glass of wine Urbino went out into the
oppressive heat, asking himself again what could have happened recently to Flavia to explain her descent on the Contessa's
garden party.

Two things stood out. One was Flavia's slashing of Bruno
Novembrini's *Nude in a Funeral Gondola* exactly a week before
her death. The other was the rape and murder of her friend
Nicolina Ricci ten days before the slashing. This had happened
in the Sant'Elena district adjacent to the Giardini Pubblici where
the Biennale modern art show was held.

Urbino realized it was time for him to learn something
about the relationship between Flavia and the fifteen-year-old
Nicolina. He hurried toward the nearest boat landing.

16

An hour later Emma Ricci, the mother of the murdered Nicolina, led Urbino into a small, airless parlor crowded with worn furniture and a television set. She was a small, dark-haired woman in her forties. Fatigue pocketed the area beneath her brown eyes.

On an old bureau a votive candle flickered in front of a black-and-white photograph. It was the same photograph of Nicolina that had appeared in the paper, showing a sweet-faced girl with dark hair and large, timid eyes.

Signora Ricci indicated a sagging armchair for Urbino to take. She sat down on the sofa. The Ricci apartment was on the top floor of a modern block of flats in the Sant'Elena quarter at the easternmost extreme of the city. Urbino, who was sweating from his long climb up the windowless, littered stairs, took out his handkerchief and wiped his forehead.

"Yes, I was acquainted with Flavia Brollo," Urbino explained again, after having given his condolences on the death of her daughter. "I'm an American living in Venice. My friend the Contessa da Capo-Zendrini, who also knew Flavia, would like to try to understand what happened to her. It's possible she was murdered like your own daughter."

Signora Ricci blessed herself.

"If that's true, it doesn't surprise me, signore, not the way the world has become." Signora Ricci had a quiet, meek voice. "But suicide is what I thought. Flavia was very upset over my Nicolina's death."

"They were good friends?"

Emma Ricci nodded sadly.

"Like sisters. Nicolina always wanted a sister. She had only a brother. Let me show you something, signore."

She got up and went to the bureau. She opened a drawer, took something out, and brought it over to Urbino. It was a broad red ribbon two feet long. In gold letters along much of its length was written LOVE, YOUR BIG SISTER FLAVIA.

"It was with the flowers Flavia gave us for Nicolina's funeral. Flavia was in a terrible state, as if she were family or someone who had known Nicolina for many years."

"How long had they known each other?"

"About a year. She met Nicolina over in Mestre where my husband works. Nicolina was bringing him his lunch. Nicolina was a wonderful girl, signore—the best of daughters. We never had any trouble from her." She took out a tissue and started to cry. "Excuse me, but to lose your child, especially like this, is the greatest pain a mother can ever have. And to think that it was Pasquale Zennaro, who ate at our table, who saw our Nicolina grow up! He was like an uncle to her! I know they say that God knows what He's doing but sometimes I feel that He's forgotten my family—and now there's poor Flavia."

She wept openly for her daughter and her daughter's friend, with deep sobs that wracked her small frame.

"I'm sorry to disturb you like this, Signora Ricci," Urbino said, getting up.

"Don't apologize, signore." Signora Ricci took the funeral ribbon from his hand and went over to put it back in the drawer. "It's good to cry. My husband doesn't like to see me crying. He says it will make me sick. I tell him he's going to get sick if he doesn't."

When she turned around, she had an envelope in her hand.

"Perhaps you can help me decide what to do with this, signore, since you knew Flavia. It is some money she gave me at Nicolina's funeral. It's a million lire," she said, naming a sum close to a thousand dollars. "She said that we could buy Nicolina the plaque to put on her stone, one with Nicolina's picture on it, but we want to buy it ourselves. Now that Flavia's dead, too, perhaps the money should go to her family. She never talked about them but I'm sure they'd appreciate a little extra at a time like this."

"Flavia wanted you to have it, Signora Ricci. Use it for memorial masses for Nicolina, or flowers for her grave—something that will help you remember Flavia's generosity."

"Maybe you're right," Signora Ricci said, returning the envelope to the drawer. "The last time I saw Flavia I promised I would do something for Nicolina with the money."

"When was this?"

"The day we buried my little girl, three weeks ago now, but my son Guido saw her after that. I'm not sure when. You could speak with him. He'll be here after seven—or you might catch him on the vaporetto. He works on the Number One Line." She glanced at a clock next to the votive candle. "His boat will be coming into the Sant'Elena landing in about ten minutes."

17

A FEW MINUTES later a breeze blowing damply off the lagoon made Urbino feel uncomfortably chilled after the heat and closeness of the Ricci apartment. He went across the strip of park to the boat landing where the Number One vaporetto was pulling in from the Lido. Urbino got on.

The young man in charge of guiding the vaporetto into the landing with ropes and opening and closing the metal gate had to be Guido Ricci. He had his mother's dark hair and his sister's large eyes.

When the boat left the landing, Urbino introduced himself, saying that he had just spoken with Guido's mother. He wanted to ask him some questions about Flavia Brollo.

"Flavia? I don't know anything about her death."

"It's her relationship to your sister that I'm interested in. As I told you, I'm trying to learn as much about Flavia as possible in order to understand her death."

Guido Ricci looked at Urbino suspiciously.

"Are you her boyfriend? I thought he was Italian."

"No, I'm not her boyfriend. Your mother said that you saw Flavia sometime after your sister's funeral."

"And what if I did?" Guido cast a quick eye over the other passengers and at the approaching landing by the Biennale grounds. Venice was spread out in a broad sweep before them. The buildings looked monochromatic in the glare of the midafternoon heat. The cloudless sky and the waters of the lagoon were both a gray leaden color.

When Guido looked back at Urbino, he had a guarded look on his face. "Is there anything wrong with that? It was right here on the boat in front of everyone. She got on at the next stop—at the Ca' di Dio—and went as far as the Accademia."

"When was this?"

"The day after that bastard Zennaro confessed to butchering my sister. It was a Friday. A week later she was dead herself. She kept saying, 'I knew he did it! Maybe it's my fault.'"

"What do you think she meant by that?"

"I'm not sure, but Flavia was supposed to stop by and see Nicolina the day she was murdered. Nicolina wasn't feeling well and didn't come with us to Lago di Garda. She had some new fashion magazines Flavia had brought her a few days before, and Flavia was coming by when she got back from Asolo. Flavia said she never came that day. I guess she thought that if she had, Zennaro wouldn't have murdered Nicolina. And maybe she was right, but that doesn't mean she was responsible. If you think that way, then my mother and father and I are, too, for having left Nicolina alone."

Guido started to prepare the rope as the vaporetto approached the landing at the Giardini Pubblici. He threw one part of it over the metal stanchion. As the boat drew closer, he looped the rope twice over the boathooks. The rope creaked as pressure was exerted on it from the boat moving against the landing.

As Guido slid the gate across to let the passengers off, he said, "Flavia had a good heart. She deserved better than to end up the way she did in the Grand Canal. My mother says the two of them are together now—if you believe things like that."

Guido bent down to lift the front edge of a baby stroller onto the boat. Urbino asked him if Flavia had known Pasquale Zennaro.

"She met him a few times at our apartment. She didn't like him. I guess she saw something that we didn't."

18

AFTER LEAVING GUIDO, Urbino called Commissario Gemelli from a café.

"Flavia Brollo and Nicolina Ricci, the girl who was raped and murdered on Sant'Elena, were good friends," he told Gemelli. "I have a hunch it might have some bearing on Flavia's death."

"A 'hunch'! Old habits die hard, don't they, Macintyre? You can't leave well enough alone, even when your Contessa seems free and clear. But I suppose she's not going to rest until she's convinced that she had a perfect marriage after all—or that her husband had a daughter he never told her about! In either case, it's no concern of the police. We get involved only in less genteel family squabbles. As for Pasquale Zennaro, he was in police custody when Flavia Brollo died. There's absolutely no sign of foul play with her as I've told you before—and even if there were, Zennaro couldn't have been involved."

"I'm not suggesting Zennaro was, not directly, but Nicolina's brother said that Flavia never liked Zennaro and seemed to be uncomfortable around him."

"Brollo and Ricci are two separate cases. We have Zennaro's confession and a knife that's got his prints all over it. Your hunches have worked out before, Macintyre, but you're way off the mark this time around. You should know that the substitute prosecutor says there's absolutely no case to answer as far as Flavia Brollo's death is concerned. I'm writing up my own report now. It was suicide."

"What about the toxicology report?"

When there was silence on the other end of the line, Urbino sensed that it was a question Gemelli wished he hadn't asked.

"No trace of the medication was found—or of any other."

Urbino made no response.

"It doesn't prove anything, Macintyre! Flavia Brollo was

robably too distraught to remember to take her pills. When
ou're considering killing yourself, you don't think about pick-
g up your laundry or taking your medicine. The fact that
ere wasn't any of the medication in her system could be con-
rued as a sign of just how emotionally disturbed she was."

"You can't have it both ways, Commissario. Have you found
ay record of Flavia Brollo being prescribed the drug? And
hat about a note? Did she leave one?"

"We haven't come across any record of the drug in her
ame—*yet*. As for a suicide note, not every suicide leaves one,
Macintyre, and when they do, the family often doesn't care to
hare it with the authorities. Her mother never left one either,
om what we know. Yes, we've gone to the trouble of looking
to Flavia's mother's death, too. The carabinieri sent us all
heir records. I suggest that you confine your inquiries to the
ontessa's personal problem. That should be enough to keep
ou busy. By the way, I hear that you were mugged in San Polo.
ith your imagination you probably think it was set up by
hoever murdered Flavia Brollo." But Gemelli's tone became
ss light when he added, "Be more careful, Macintyre. Some
f the muggers this summer are carrying knives."

After talking with Gemelli, Urbino went to catch the train
 Bassano del Grappa, where the Contessa's car would meet
im and take him into Asolo.

19

N THE TRAIN to Bassano del Grappa, Urbino turned over in
is mind everything he had learned during the past two days.
adislao Mirko, Bruno Novembrini, Lorenzo Brollo, Nicolina
icci's mother, and her brother—they had all given him infor-
ation about Flavia, but they hadn't brought him much clarifi-
ation.

Quite the opposite. On the one hand, there were Brollo's
ssurances that he was Flavia's father and Novembrini's claim

that although Flavia had apparently hated Brollo, she had never mentioned the Conte da Capo-Zendrini to him. On the other hand, there were the argument at Lago di Garda and Regina's revelation to Flavia that Alvise was her father. Ladislao Mirko, however, was the only source for these two crucial items. Flavia was no longer alive to corroborate his stories.

Gazing out at the quiet, sunbaked countryside, Urbino wondered how the rape and murder of Nicolina Ricci fit in. He had to know more about Flavia's friend, the girl she had considered her little sister. He would try to see Nicolina's father as soon as possible.

Now that the toxicology report had found no trace of the controversial drug in Flavia's system, Urbino was even more sure that Flavia hadn't committed suicide. Had she ever taken the drug at all?

As the train pulled into the Bassano station, where Urbino saw the Contessa's chauffeur, Milo, waiting on the platform, he decided not to tell the Contessa what Mirko had said about Regina Brollo. Not yet, not until he knew if Mirko was lying or innocently passing on Flavia's own lie—or her delusion.

20

EVEN IF URBINO hadn't made this decision on the train, he would have made it as soon as he saw the Contessa's face at La Muta. She looked as if she hadn't slept in the past forty-eight hours. She was trying to put a brave face on her pain—this was her way, even with Urbino, her closest friend—but he saw through it to the raw emotions beneath.

No, he couldn't tell her that Regina Brollo might have revealed to Flavia that Alvise was her father or about the argument at Lago di Garda. If there was any doubt that Mirko was lying or mistaken, he owed it to the Contessa to protect her, at least a little while longer.

The Contessa and Urbino were now sitting in the yew

embraced *giardino segreto* with its wrought-iron table and chairs and pots of flowers. In the short time he had been in Asolo, Urbino already felt refreshed. A gentle breeze blew across the hills from the Dolomites. During their light supper with Eugene, Urbino, trying to downplay the real danger he felt he might still be in, had told them how he had got the bruise beneath his eye. He hadn't shared anything else with the Contessa, however, until they were alone in the *giardino segreto*. Eugene had gone into town to see Occhipinti's Browning memorabilia. When the two men returned, Milo would drive Urbino and Eugene to Venice. The Contessa and Occhipinti would come along for the ride.

"Eugene and Silvestro have become as thick as thieves, *caro*. I really think your ex–brother-in-law—a *nom de divorce* I find myself getting fond of—is seriously considering taking a place here, maybe Villa Pippa after Lennox leaves, and the sooner she leaves the better, as far as I'm concerned. There's something that goes to the core of her that's pure unadulterated artifice—and not the kind that makes us all live our lives more smoothly."

She looked at his bruise and her face tensed. When Urbino had told her about the mugging, the Contessa hadn't seemed surprised, but she had been concerned, wanting her Asolo doctor to look at the injury.

"You think you're invincible on your walks, don't you? Oh, I refuse to believe that you were attacked because of Flavia! To think that it was anything but just another mugging would put me in a perpetual state of anxiety. To think of you wandering around in the most out-of-the-way places! I wish I could break you of the habit. Eugene has got me thinking. Why *shouldn't* I have my own gondola? If I did have one, I think you'd find yourself less interested in walking, and we could float around everywhere together, maybe even get a *felze* to hide behind! I might as well go the whole way if I'm going to have people talking about me."

She gave a deep sigh after saying this and looked off toward the entrance to the *giardino segreto*. Urbino mentioned again how upset he was to have lost the scrapbook.

"But I'm surprised you didn't tell Brollo about the scrapbook, Urbino. Legally it's his, isn't it?"

"I imagine so, but that's for him and Mirko to work out if it ever turns up."

"You know, Urbino," the Contessa said, slowly picking off some brown leaves from a zinnia plant, "I'm beginning to breathe a little more freely—about Alvise, I mean."

Urbino stirred uneasily in his chair.

"Both Violetta Volpi and Brollo consider it ridiculous that Alvise—or anyone other than Brollo himself—was Flavia's father," the Contessa went on. "And Novembrini said that Flavia never even brought up the topic with him. I agree with Lorenzo Brollo. This idea about Alvise started somehow with Ladislao Mirko," the Contessa said with an air of forced confidence, making Urbino feel increasingly uncomfortable. "Flavia trusted him. Adolescent bonds are almost impossible to break. He might have been able to get some power over her by planting that lie in her pretty little head. Drugs will drive people to do anything, and if he was in love with her—or whatever you want to call it!—it might have been his way of getting some kind of revenge when she wanted to be nothing more than his friend. Of course, there's Annabella Brollo and her strange comment about how a mother should know the father of her own child. Somehow, though, I think that if you spoke with Annabella she would say that it was Violetta who poisoned the girl's mind just as Violetta said about her."

The Contessa got up and went over to the fountain with a statue of the flutist of spring by Antonio Bonazza. She took out a lace handkerchief, dipped it in the water and, after wringing it out, applied it to her temple. When she turned back to Urbino, tears were in her eyes.

"I'm so ashamed of myself, *caro*! All I seem to care about is Alvise. You must find me a monster! It's Flavia I should be thinking about—and the person somewhere out there who killed her for whatever twisted reason! Now that we know that none of that drug was found in her system, it's become even more clear to me that she didn't commit suicide. I don't know what's the matter with the substitute prosecutor and Gemelli!"

"I don't think Gemelli is quite so sure about suicide anymore."

"What is he waiting for? Does he want you to make a fool of yourself or—or worse?" she said, glancing nervously at his eye. "He should be looking into what Lorenzo Brollo or Violetta Volpi have to gain from Flavia's death. It's obvious from what you've told me that both of them are afraid to show any guilt

even though they *say* that they believe she committed suicide. I
ask you! Is that normal? They should be ravaged with guilt. *I*
think they're afraid to show it because one—or both—of them
are guilty in a worse way."

"I agree with you, Barbara."

"So go after them!" she said, as if she were talking about
foxes on a hunt.

"That's exactly what I'm doing."

Footsteps sounded on the pebbled path. A few moments
later the Contessa's maid, Rosa, came into the *giardino segreto*.

"Milo has returned, Contessa."

With a quick glance at Urbino, the Contessa got up.

"*Grazie*, Rosa. Could we go back to the house, Urbino?"

She gave him her arm and, with Rosa hurrying ahead of
them, they walked in silence back to the house. While the
Contessa was talking to Milo, Urbino went to the balcony outside
the *salotto verde* to join Eugene and Occhipinti. The birdlike
man stared at Urbino's bruise but didn't say anything.

"I guess the time has come to drag me back to Venice!"
Eugene said. "I won't be leavin' without regret. It's not just all
the peace and quiet and fresh air. It's the Countess. She's a
mighty fine woman. We've enjoyed our confabs. Your ears were
probably burnin' back in that little palace of yours, Urbino!"

"Eugenio loves to talk, yes," Occhipinti came close to chirp-
ing. "I've learned many new English words."

"Listen to him!" Eugene said. "There's nothin' he can learn
from me! He's always spoutin' that English poet! He even taught
me some. How did it go, Sylvester? 'Dust and ashes, dead and
done with'—then something about Venice."

" 'Venice spent what Venice earned,' " Occhipinti finished
for him.

"By the way, Signor Occhipinti," Urbino said. "I thought I
saw you in Venice yesterday in the San Polo quarter."

"I don't know what you mean," Occhipinti said, eyes blink-
ing behind his round spectacles. Perspiration gleamed on his
bald head. "I haven't been in Venice since last week. You're not
trying to blame your bruise on me, are you? Ha, ha! Eugene
said they were much younger men than me. I don't even have
the energy to walk Pompilia these days."

"Come on there, Sylvester. You've got a powerful lot of
strength! By the way, Urbino, why are the two of you so formal

with each other? It didn't take Sylvester and me all that long to get on a first-name basis. What's this 'Signor Occhi' and 'Signor Macintyre' all about anyway?"

"Your cousin is a very polite man, Eugenio. He inspires me. Young people today have thrown so much to the winds."

"Urbino's only a few years younger than I am, Sylvester. Are you tryin' to tell me I was steppin' over the mark by bein' so palsy with you right away?"

Occhipinti clearly didn't follow what Eugene was saying, his answer only a shrug of his thin shoulders. The Contessa came out from the *salotto verde*, carrying a large woven-leather Bottega Veneta bag.

"We should leave. Urbino and Eugene shouldn't get back to Venice too late. Urbino, I must say you look marvelously restored in only a short time. You see how easy it is to pay me a quick visit? But let's go to the car. If we leave now, we'll have time to stop at the Ponte degli Alpini in Bassano del Grappa. Silvestro insists on buying Eugene a grappa at Nardini's," she explained with a little smile. "Terrible stuff, that grappa, but maybe it'll attack the vestiges of that cold you have, Silvestro dear. Urbino and I can take a walk while you two indulge yourselves."

The Contessa's face no longer looked as pained as it had in the *giardino segreto*, but was now softened with a little smile, as if she were in possession of a private joke.

21

ON THE DRIVE from Asolo to Bassano del Grappa for their stopover at the Ponte degli Alpini, the Contessa commented on the scene outside for Eugene's benefit, but she seemed preoccupied.

"You know, Countess Barbara," Eugene said as the Bentley turned into a narrow street off Piazza Libertà and continued toward the Alpine Bridge, the Ponte Vecchio of Bassano, "Urbino and I can just as easily take the train back to Venice. No criticism intended of your fine car, of course, or of Milo here. Besides, Milo told me he just returned from Venice. We wouldn't want him scootin' back and forth just for our convenience."

"He loves to drive," the Contessa said, as if Milo wanted nothing more than to be in perpetual motion and in someone else's service. "One of these days, Urbino," she said quickly, reaching over to touch his shoulder, "we're going to take a motoring tour of Europe in true turn-of-the-century style."

Parking was restricted in the area of the Ponte degli Alpini. The covered timber bridge itself was closed to everything except pedestrians and bicycles. Milo pulled the Bentley over on the street above the bridge.

The four of them got out and walked the short distance to the bridge designed by Palladio in the sixteenth century. Eugene and Occhipinti went into the wooden shop on the left. Nardini's was the oldest grappa distillery in Italy and carried the strong brandy in many flavors.

Urbino and the Contessa walked along the bridge that spanned the Brenta River. They went past the little houses with their fading frescoes until they reached the middle. Here, a point of vantage provided a view over the Brenta. Buildings, some with wooden balconies, lined the river, which came down from the foothills of the Alps and Monte Grappa. A strong Austrian flavor permeated the scene.

"Eugene is trying to enlist my aid in getting you to meet with Evangeline, you know. I told him that you always do exactly what you want. The worst thing was to try to pressure you, but what made your obstinacy bearable was that you usually ended up doing the right thing in the end. He was more than skeptical about that. 'Maybe for *you*, Countess,' he said. 'I can see he wants to please you.' Your ex—brother-in-law seems to think we have a much closer relationship in certain areas than we do. As he said last night, 'He always did like older women. Maybe that was one of the problems with Evangeline.'"

She stood at the rail and gazed off at the mountains for a few moments before turning back to Urbino and gently touching his bruised eye.

"The bruise should go away in a day or two. *Poverino!* You don't know how you make me worry! I know you care more about having lost the scrapbook than having been hurt like this. It's such an infuriating loss, isn't it? To think we'll probably never know what was in it."

Quite inappropriately, a shadow of a smile curved the Contessa's lips. It threw Urbino a little off balance.

"But don't feel too responsible, *caro*," the Contessa continued, her words of comfort almost like a gentle chastisement. The shadow of a smile was still there on her lips. "I hope that Brollo's not too hard on you when he finds out—or Ladislao Mirko, for that matter."

Urbino felt like a little boy squirming uncomfortably as he was being made to feel guilty.

"I'll give the police a call when I get back to Venice."

To his surprise, the Contessa shook her head slowly and said, "I wouldn't do that if I were you, *caro*."

"Why not?"

"Because of this."

She opened her Bottega Veneta bag and reached inside. She took out Flavia's scrapbook.

"But, Barbara, however do *you* come to have it?"

The Contessa was smiling now without any restraint. It made Urbino feel good, despite his puzzlement, to see her smile.

"Because Milo went to Venice to collect it," the Contessa explained.

"Milo?"

"Your housekeeper, Natalia, called La Muta a few hours ago. The police tried to get in touch with you at the Palazzo Uccello. They said they had found the scrapbook and were bringing it over. I told Natalia I would send Milo to get it from her. There was always the chance you and Eugene might stay until tomorrow, and I knew you'd want to have it. It certainly looks like the police are being accommodating. You must have impressed them with how important it might be. And I'm sure Corrado had something to do with it. He heard last night about your mugging and told me all about it when he called back with the information I asked for. He assured me that you were fine but that you were '*molto turbato*,' as he put it, to have lost a book of some kind. I had no idea what he was talking about."

Urbino now realized why the Contessa hadn't seemed surprised when he told her about the attack earlier—and why she had seemed so solicitous over the phone last night.

He took the album from her. The back cover and the edges of some of the pages were soiled. He opened it and leafed through it quickly.

"Anything missing?" the Contessa asked.

"I wouldn't know."

"I wouldn't be surprised if Mirko took something out of it himself before he gave it to you," the Contessa said. "I started to glance through it but decided to leave it for you. My fear was stronger than my curiosity. Go through it and let me know what you find, but don't spare my feelings. They're the least thing we should take into consideration. The truth above all, *caro*, but let it be a gentle one." The Contessa gazed toward the mountains again. "I've been concerned for myself during the past two weeks, but I don't want the truth for only myself now, but for Flavia, too. What about *her*? If the poor girl was murdered, who did it, and did it have anything at all to do with Alvise? And if she killed herself, did I contribute to it by how I behaved toward her? I'm afraid there's no way that I'm not going to feel a blow from all this when the truth, whatever it is, comes out. I'm going to lose in some way in the end, I just know it."

Despite the gentle warmth of the early evening, she shivered, but the next moment a smile was on her face again. She looked at Urbino and touched his arm.

"I trust you, *caro*. You can't change the truth but you'll find out what it is and be the one to tell me. Ah! there are Eugene and Silvestro." She lifted her hand to the two men who had just emerged from Nardini's, both of them more red-faced than they had been a short time ago. "Go back to Venice with your ex–brother-in-law and continue your sleuthing, but be careful," she continued, putting her arm through Urbino's. "It seems that those men who attacked you had nothing to do with Flavia since they discarded her scrapbook, but what do we really know at this point?"

Very little, Urbino answered silently, and perhaps a great deal too much as well. As he and the Contessa walked toward Eugene and Occhipinti, he hoped that Flavia's scrapbook would provide some insight into what had happened to her before her body surfaced in the Grand Canal beneath the flamboyant *Angel of the Citadel* statue with its erect penis.

"Sex and death," Urbino said involuntarily, thinking aloud. When he said this, the image of Nicolina Ricci flashed across

his eyes and he seemed to see something else flashing as well—
not a face but words, brightly lit words. What were they?

The Contessa looked up at Urbino sharply. Eugene was
calling their names and waving a Tyrolean hat he had somehow
come in possession of. As the Contessa and Urbino were about
to join the two men, the Contessa repeated what she had said
earlier, but this time much more quietly.

"I trust you, *caro*."

More than ever before, Urbino felt the weight of the
Contessa's trust. It was very heavy indeed.

PART THREE

Carnivorous Flower

1

"ARE YOU REALLY sure you won't join the fun, Urbino?" Eugene asked for what must have been the fifth time as he and Urbino had drinks on the terrace of the Danieli after returning from Asolo. "We'll just float along for a few hours. It's a lovely evening."

He indicated the cloudless early-evening sky arching over the lagoon.

"Cooled down a bit," he went on. "We'll float right up the Grand Canal there. Can you imagine just lyin' back and sailin' past that white church with the domes? And then we'll sneak into the pokey little canals and get a water rat's view of the town. How about it, Urbino?"

Once again Urbino declined, but not without a small twinge of regret. It would be the first—and possibly the last—time he would ever be part of a flotilla of six gondolas, complete with mandolins, accordions, and a serenader, plying the waters of the city. But even if he had been more tempted, he had Flavia's scrapbook to look at tonight, and he wanted to do it as soon as possible.

"Well, you're not goin' to worm out of tomorrow, I hope," Eugene said. "Remember we're goin' to that lace island. I want you here tomorrow bright and early and rarin' to go. Maybe you've forgotten how to enjoy yourself, my boy. Countess Barbara can't take any of the blame for that, I can see. The old girl had me in stitches half the time though she pretended not to know what I found so funny. So until tomorrow, Urbino—and if you're not there, I'm goin' to come to that pathetic palace of yours and drag you out by your nose! Evie always said you needed a bit of forceful encouragement. Just a pity that her and Poppa used most of it to try to push you along into Hennepin. All *I* want—all I *ever* wanted—is for you to enjoy yourself!"

On the vaporetto back to the Palazzo Uccello, Urbino resisted opening Flavia's scrapbook and instead took in the passing scene from the prow of the boat. Night was falling and he caught glimpses of ceiling frescoes, chandeliers, and golden interiors of palazzi along the Grand Canal. This was one of his favorite times to be on the water, and he envied Eugene his flotilla tonight. If only the Contessa would get a gondola. She was right. He would be in it whenever possible. What had he just read in Peggy Guggenheim's memoirs? Something about floatingness being the essential quality of life in Venice. As she had said in a letter to a friend, she adored floating around in her gondola so much that she couldn't imagine anything as enjoyable since she had given up sex—or, she had then amended, since sex had given her up.

Urbino would have liked to live in Venice in a previous era, preferably the end of the last century when Robert Browning, Henry James, John Singer Sargent, and other Anglo-Americans had been caught up in what James had called "palazzo-madness." Whistler, who had taken studios in the Ca' Rezzonico, used to be rowed all over the city in a gondola filled with prepared etching plates, boxes of pastels, and sheets of colored paper. Too much had been lost since those days. Lorenzo Brollo's lamentations over the passing of a time of greater gentility rang in Urbino's ears as the vaporetto continued up the Grand Canal.

So much of the scene reminded Urbino of Flavia. It wasn't just the Palazzo Guggenheim with Marino Marini's equestrian statue making its ecstatic statement, but also the Gothic Palazzo Barbaro where Eleonora Duse, whom Flavia had so admired, had lived. And on the opposite side of the Grand Canal was the small Casetta Rossa, once the home of Duse's lover, the writer Gabriele D'Annunzio. As if showing Urbino that the past was always alive, a pomegranate tree, planted during the First World War by the ugly writer, flourished next to the little red house.

And then there was the Ca' Volpi. Urbino looked through its iron water gates into the dark garden illuminated dimly by one lone bulb, the others apparently having burned out. Violetta Volpi's studio was dark.

As the vaporetto continued up the Grand Canal, Urbino realized that if he had the use of a gondola, he could glide silently up to the Volpi water steps right now and see what, if anything, he could learn from Violetta's husband. Only something as secretive and silent as a gondola, so often compared to a floating coffin, seemed appropriate for approaching this man apparently locked away in his own world.

Once back at the Palazzo Uccello, Urbino lost no time in giving his attention to Flavia's scrapbook. With Serena curled in his lap and a wineglass and a bottle of chilled Bianco di Custoza next to him on the table, he opened the scrapbook.

On the first page, centered carefully and in a large, confident hand in black ink, was written "Scrapbook of Flavia Maria Regina Brollo."

Urbino turned the page and started to read. He read for almost an hour and then started over again. Flavia's scrapbook was just what Madge Lennox had said it was: an odd assortment comprising autographs, newspaper clippings, entrance tickets, programs, photographs, postcards, and pages ripped from books and magazines, though among none of these ripped pages did he find the one missing from the Guggenheim catalog. It was just what you would expect of someone who wanted to preserve the too easily forgotten details of life.

In his work as a biographer Urbino had many occasions to pore through things like this, but never had he done so with such a sad and fearful feeling. When he finished going through it the second time, he poured himself another glass of wine and sat sipping it as he thought about the Contessa and Alvise, Alvise and Silvestro Occhipinti, and Flavia and Nicolina Ricci. Then he opened the scrapbook again to a sheet of paper about ten by twelve inches. It was Regina Brollo's death notice, the kind that it was customary to display throughout the deceased's parish with a photograph attached. The notice was similar to the one for Flavia that had been on the Brollo door in San Polo. Very similar.

Despite the portrait he had seen at the Palazzo Brollo, Urbino was startled by the black-and-white photograph of Regina Brollo. He felt he was looking at Flavia. The photograph showed a Regina Brollo closer to Flavia's twenty-six years than to the forty-five she must have been at the time of her own death. She gazed at the camera with a wistful smile. How many times had Flavia looked at this photograph of her mother, as well as at others and the portrait at the Palazzo Brollo, and seen the resemblance to herself? What kind of comfort had it given her? Might it also have filled her with some sense of premonition? Had she ever thought that this kind of beauty might eventually have its price?

Urbino took another look at the two items he had been particularly disturbed to find in the scrapbook and considered the ones he should have found but hadn't. He stroked the purring Serena. The Contessa was going to be upset. Once again Urbino regretted having agreed to help her. It might have been better for her to have engaged a private investigator through her Italian solicitor, someone with whom she had no relationship other than a financial one.

Regrets would get him nowhere, however. He looked at his watch. Almost eleven. Out of consideration for the Contessa he decided to wait until morning to tell her what he had learned. Let her sleep as well as she could tonight. The time had come to tell her all the bad news—or at least most of it.

2

BUT URBINO HADN'T counted on the Contessa's own anxiety. She called him fifteen minutes later, after he had poured the rest of the wine into his glass.

"Either you didn't look at the scrapbook yet, which I refuse

o believe, or you're afraid to tell me what you found," the
Contessa said angrily. "You're supposed to be helping me. Didn't
I tell you that not knowing was the worst possible punishment?"

"I'm sorry, Barbara. I was going to wait until the morning.
I figured you were asleep by now."

The Contessa drew in her breath.

"That means the absolute worst. No one with a heart delays
elling someone good news. What did you find?"

Urbino took a sip of wine.

"There's a section at the beginning of the scrapbook, Barbara. People's signatures and their good wishes, platitudes, witty
sayings—things of that kind. Flavia started keeping the scrapbook on her thirteenth birthday. There are entries over the
years by her mother, Violetta Volpi, even most recently Nicolina
Ricci and Madge Lennox. Flavia seems to have had a sentimental side even into her adulthood. After her mother's entry almost half a page has been scratched out with ink. It could be
what Lorenzo might have written, or entries by both Annabella
and Lorenzo. I held it up to the light but couldn't make out
anything."

Urbino paused and took another sip of wine.

"I can tell you're fortifying yourself with alcohol! Would
you please go on? Unless that's the extent of the damage," the
Contessa said with a note of hope in her voice.

"I'm afraid not, Barbara. There were two other entries. Let
me read the first one." He paged through the scrapbook until
he found what he was looking for. " 'I have lived indeed, and
so—(yet one more kiss)—can die!' "

"Whatever does *that* mean? It sounds like a quotation of
some kind. I've never heard it before, have you? Oh, my God,
it's Silvestro, isn't it!"

"Exactly. It's signed 'Your friend, Signor Silvestro Maurizio
Ugolini Occhipinti' and it's dated thirteen years ago this past
June."

"What else is there?"

The Contessa was trying to keep her voice under control.
Urbino wished there were some way he could prepare her but
perhaps the best thing was to be as direct as possible.

"I'm afraid there's an even more surprising signature, Barbara—Alvise's."

There was a long, stunned silence. Urbino thought he could

hear the Contessa gasping for air. When she spoke, however, her voice didn't quaver.

"What does it say? Give it to me exactly! I'll never forgive you if you don't."

Urbino read, " 'To the beautiful and charming Flavia, Il Conte Alvise da Capo-Zendrini.' There's no date but it's right after Occhipinti's entry."

"If it had been volumes longer it couldn't be worse! Can't you see that it's intended to reveal as little as possible? It doesn't look good, Urbino, does it? Not good at all," the Contessa said in a small voice. "He knew the girl and he never mentioned her to me—not once."

"There could be any number of reasons why he didn't," Urbino said half-heartedly. He didn't want to give the Contessa any false hope. He still hadn't told her what Mirko had said— that Regina Brollo told Flavia that Alvise da Capo-Zendrini was her father. Before Urbino told her this, as well as about the argument at Lago di Garda, he needed to be sure. He didn't want to take Mirko's word for these two crucial pieces of information. Only if and when he had far less reason to doubt Mirko would he tell the Contessa.

"It could have slipped Alvise's mind," Urbino said. "He might have met her only once or twice under completely innocent circumstances. Just because he signed her scrapbook doesn't mean he was her father. He probably thought it too unimportant to mention."

"Or he thought it *too* important. If Flavia started keeping her scrapbook about thirteen years ago, that means it wasn't long before Alvise died. That makes it all the more strange. We were together almost all the time then except—"

She broke off.

"Except when, Barbara?"

"Except when he stayed with Silvestro at Lago di Garda for a week the summer before he died," she said flatly. "I was in Milan. No, I don't think it looks very good at all."

"I also found newspaper clippings," Urbino hurried to say. "Most of them were about Novembrini's and Violetta Volpi' exhibits. There were also some theater and concert programs. Flavia played the role of Brighella in Goldoni's *Two Venetian Twins* in a small theater in Mestre a few years ago. I didn't recognize anyone else's name in the cast. Except for one or

Nicolina Ricci's murder, none of the clippings seems more recent than a year and a half ago. The missing page from the Guggenheim catalog wasn't there. I thought she might have torn it out to put in the scrapbook with her other memorabilia."

"Pictures like those? But one can only guess at the terrible taste passed on to her by an aunt like Violetta Volpi! But what about the clippings of Alvise and me, and the one of Alvise and Silvestro?"

It was obvious that her mind had trouble focusing on anything but Alvise.

"They weren't there."

"Weren't there? Whatever do you mean?"

"Just that. But there were several blank spaces scattered throughout the book. I can't say she kept a neat scrapbook. Some things were glued, others taped, and even retaped with the page thinned and peeling away underneath."

"Perhaps Madge Lennox made it up about those clippings. Who knows what went on between her and Flavia! She might be very pleased indeed that the poor girl is dead and can't tell any tales. She probably had no idea you would ever see the scrapbook. Didn't I tell you that you should be careful she doesn't pull the wool over your eyes? Didn't I tell you that she's absolutely brittle with artifice? I refuse to believe anything she says, and I refuse to believe that Alvise was ever unfaithful to me. Who knows? That entry in the scrapbook could be a forgery. I want to verify the signature. You'll have to give me more proof than what you've been able to come up with so far!"

Urbino desperately hoped that he wouldn't have to but he was beginning to doubt it. Proof, he feared, existed somewhere.

3

THE NEXT MORNING, a Thursday, Urbino—the bruise under his eye now hardly noticeable—called Eugene at the Danieli to postpone their trip to Burano.

"It's this business with the dead girl and the Countess Barbara, isn't it?" he said. "Maybe you should tell me all about it. You might be able to use some good common sense. I'm ready, willin', and able whenever you are. But don't feel that you're lettin' me down about the lace island. As things turn out, I was goin' to tell you we'd have to cancel. I've got some business with ole Massimo Zuin. But I still insist on seein' you today. Let's say at one o'clock at the restaurant by the modern art show. I promise it won't take long and I promise you'll be pleased—and surprised. See you then."

Urbino set out for the Guggenheim, hardly noticing the noisy crowds or registering the heat that had clamped back down on the city after the respite last night. As he walked, he kept seeing Flavia's face in front of him and thinking how much she had resembled her mother, how she had seemed to have very little of Lorenzo Brollo in her. Urbino wished he had known Alvise. If he had, would he have seen any traces of him in Flavia? Urbino had seen many photographs of Alvise but, unlike the portrait and the photograph of Regina Brollo, they didn't help him one way or another. If the Contessa had noticed any likeness, she was keeping it to herself—perhaps even *from* herself.

It was a few minutes past eleven and the Guggenheim was just opening. Urbino bought postcard reproductions of Tanguy's *The Sun in Its Casket* and Dalí's *The Birth of Liquid Desires* at the counter and asked the young man if he could see the director. While he was waiting, he went to look at the Tanguy and the Dalí, studying their bizarre and disturbing images.

Although Urbino knew the dangers of being literal-minded when it came to art, he suspected that the young Flavia Brollo—and perhaps even the mature one—might have "read" the two paintings as if they were a story. Urbino contemplated the Tanguy landscape with its peculiar forms that seemed to inhabit a shadowland between things living and things dead. What had someone once said about Tanguy? That "he painted the most tragic landscapes the mind has never seen." What interest had the painting held for Flavia?

Urbino turned his attentions to the Dalí with its naked men and white-gowned women, one of whom had her arms around the older, sinister-looking man. This was the one with a woman's breast visible as well as an erect penis, covered by a scarf.

A few minutes later the director, a tall man in his early forties wearing an Ermenegildo Zegna suit, joined him. Urbino introduced himself, saying he was considering writing a biography of Peggy Guggenheim in Venice and had some questions about the Tanguy and the Dalí.

"Ah, yes, *The Sun in Its Jewel Case* or *Le Soleil dans son écrin*. Many people like to translate *écrin* as 'casket.' It gives the painting an extra fillip, induces *un certain frisson*. But the painting is quite disturbing with any title, I'm sure you would agree. It was painted in 1937. Miss Guggenheim first saw it in 1938 at the Tanguy exhibition in London. It frightened her, but she eventually overcame her fear and bought it. There are four other Tanguys in the collection. As for *La nascita di desideri liquidi*," the director said in an Italian as faultless as his French as they moved over to the Dalí, "it's one of our two Dalí's. Gala, Dalí's wife, chose the painting for Miss Guggenheim in the winter of 1940 when Miss Guggenheim had decided to buy a 'picture a day.' Miss Guggenheim—"

The director continued with more details about the painting's provenance. When he finished, having seemed to bow his head every time he mentioned Peggy Guggenheim's name, Urbino asked if anyone had ever tried to harm them. The director stiffened.

"The Guggenheim Collection has never had any problems of that kind, sir."

"I'm glad to hear it. Have you ever seen this woman here?"

Urbino showed him the obituary photograph of Regina Brollo from the scrapbook. It wasn't Regina he was interested in knowing about, of course, but in the absence of a photograph of Flavia, this might serve the purpose.

The director frowned when he looked at the photograph and quickly handed it back.

"I can see that you have less interest in the Peggy Guggenheim Collection than in the young woman whose body was found in the Grand Canal. We have already made our statements to the police. Good-day."

The director nodded stiffly and hurried away.

"Sure I recognize her," the young man behind the counter said a few minutes later. "Beautiful red hair, right?"

Urbino would have found it amusing if so much wasn't at stake. No more than the director had, the young man didn't seem to realize that he wasn't looking at a photograph of the young woman he remembered so well, although he squinted down at it again with a puzzled frown.

"She usually comes on Saturday evenings when there's no charge—sometimes two or three Saturdays in a row. I've been on vacation for the last two weeks. Today's my first day back. Maybe she'll be in this Saturday. Do you want me to give her a message?"

"Was she interested in any school of painting or any particular artist?" Urbino asked, ignoring the question.

"Certainly was. She loved the Dalí over there—*The Birth of Liquid Desires*—one of the ones you bought a card of. She used to come in just to look at it. It isn't as strange as it sounds, though. We get a lot of people who study one or two paintings, sometimes for weeks. I tried to become friendly with her about two months ago. I was working the floor and started to talk about the painting—more or less a one-sided conversation. I said I liked it, too. She asked me why, and I started to talk about Dalí's use of collage and color and the water symbolism—all in Italian. I was proud of myself. She just laughed and said in almost perfect English, 'You read all that in a book, didn't you?' She was mocking me. I guess she's a bitch but she's a real looker."

"Was she interested in Tanguy's *The Sun in Its Casket*?"

"I can't say that she paid a whole lot of attention to it—not the way she did to the Dalí, but they're usually hung in the same room, so I might not have noticed."

4

FORTY-FIVE MINUTES LATER Urbino found Eugene waiting for him at the Caffè Paradiso outside the gates of the Biennale exhibition grounds. They had sandwiches and beer on the crowded terrace. Judgments and opinions about the art in the pavilions were thick in the air, and deals were being made at many of the tables. Hectic though it was today, it was nothing compared to the way it had been before the late-June opening. Urbino had gone to several cocktail parties at the time, all of which the Contessa had declined to attend. After her disorienting experience during the last Biennale, when she almost passed out at the United States Pavilion in the room with the electronic lines of colored text, she had steered clear of the modern art show.

Eugene stared at Urbino's face, putting down his now empty beer mug. He shook his head.

"That dead girl's heavy on your mind, Urbino. You still get that scrunched-up look when you're thinkin' hard. Evie would say, 'I can tell he's thinkin' something and he's thinkin' something bad, Genie.' Used to worry the dickens out of the poor girl with your moods, especially toward the end when she knew you were lookin' for another reason why you couldn't go into sugar cane. And you *still* worry her! I know I'm tellin' tales out of school, but what the heck! I talked to Evie this morning and told her you're pokin' your nose into other people's business— a dead girl's business, I said. Didn't breathe a word about murder. Evie of course wanted to know what the dead girl looked like. Had to tell her I *heard* she was a beauty but she was dead by the time I got to see her, and she wasn't lookin' so good then. I had to imagine real hard what she must have looked like, I told her, but I'm about to change all that now. Come on. Let's go to the Italy Pavilion."

Eugene wouldn't give any further explanation as they went into the Biennale grounds. As Urbino caught sight of the neoclassical United States Pavilion, straight ahead, something tugged at his mind. Once again, as had happened when he was with the Contessa on the Ponte degli Alpini, words of some kind were trying to intrude on his consciousness.

When Urbino and Eugene entered the Italy Pavilion, Eugene strode ahead into the room with Novembrini's paintings. Both Bruno Novembrini, dressed as usual in commanding black, and Massimo Zuin seemed to be expecting Eugene, but were surprised to see Urbino entering behind him.

"Here it is," Eugene said, throwing his arm out.

On the wall was *Nude in a Funeral Gondola*. Flavia stared directly and provocatively at Urbino, her hand nestled between her legs like Titian's naked Venus. Nothing seemed damaged about the painting—not Flavia's pearl-colored skin, her green eyes, the ebony funeral gondola, or the lion weeping into a black handkerchief.

"It's repaired already?" he asked Zuin and Novembrini.

"Certainly is," Massimo Zuin responded, rubbing his hand beneath the long gray hair at the nape of his neck. Today he wore a mauve pocket square with his light blue suit. "It wasn't all that damaged."

"So what do you think, Urbino?" Eugene said with a big smile. "I can see why you're hung up on the dead girl."

Eugene took in Flavia's exposed flesh and seductive position in the black gondola.

"She was certainly a looker, but what's that angel with a beard supposed to mean? And that lion with a handkerchief? It's almost as strange as that *Liquid* picture at the Peggy that Urbino and I took a gander at last week—the one with buck-naked men lurkin' around some rocks. Do you know the painting I'm talkin' about, fellows? Oh, yes, I have to admit I've seen some very peculiar pictures in this town. No offense to you, Mr. November. Your painting of this naked girl might be strange but I bought it, didn't I?"

"You bought it?" Urbino said.

"Yessiree! Told Mr. Zuin if he could get it fixed up quick I'd be mighty happy. He wants to keep it here until the big show's over. Seems I was biddin' against someone almost as eager to get it as me. Thought it might be you at first, Urbino. Ha, ha! Just the kind of thing you would do. But Mr. Zuin said it wasn't. Somebody who wanted to remain anonymous. Couldn't offer you a bit more, could I, Mr. Zuin, so that Urbino can take it home right now?"

Novembrini and Zuin looked stunned. Urbino wondered who the other bidder could have been. Perhaps there hadn't been one. Dealers were known to drive up the price of a painting by even more devious methods than that.

"But Mr. Hennepin, I thought you would be taking it back to the States with you," Zuin said.

"With me? Ha, ha! I'd just like to see what May-Foy would do if I brought something like that home with me! No offense, but May-Foy doesn't take to naked ladies."

"Eugene, I couldn't possibly accept it," Urbino said, turning to his ex–brother-in-law.

"Now don't tell me you don't like it. I know you do. My thinkin' is this. If you have the picture, then maybe you'll get this dead girl out of your system. After a while you won't even notice she's in the room. That happens all the time to me with our stuff back home. I'm always sayin' to May-Foy, 'Lookee here, dear, wherever did this come from?' Seems most of it's been there for years!"

Novembrini said something under his breath to Zuin, who colored and looked nervously at Urbino.

"We'll talk about it later, Eugene."

"You can talk as much as you want, Urbino, but you ain't goin' to refuse a gift given from the bottom of my heart. Don't worry. I didn't pay as much as I expected. I can see from the look on your face, Mr. Zuin, that you're surprised about that! Well, the deal's over and done with. The painting's mine, and now it's Urbino's."

Eugene started to make a circuit of the room—"My last chance to see Mr. November's paintings," he said—and left Urbino in uncomfortable silence with Novembrini and Zuin. Urbino took out the Dalí postcard.

"Does this mean anything to you, Signor Novembrini?" he asked, handing it to the artist.

Novembrini stared at it for a few seconds.

"Does it mean anything to me?" Novembrini repeated in his melodious voice, handing back the postcard. "It certainly does! The height of charlatanism! The work of a showman, not an artist. What's the anagram that Breton made of Dalí's name? 'Avida Dollars,' right? Suited him perfectly. *The Birth of Liquid Desires*, indeed! More like *The Desire for Liquid Cash*!"

"Come, come, Bruno!" Zuin said, putting a hand on Novembrini's shoulder but quickly removing it when the artist moved almost imperceptibly away. "You owe something to the Surrealists, as you well know, and a bit of showmanship in an artist isn't necessarily a bad thing. What's the good of an artist who has no sense of his own worth?"

"You won't get me to say much good about that painting or about Dalí himself," Novembrini said, irritated. "He's far from a favorite of mine."

"Was he a favorite of Flavia Brollo's?"

"She had better taste than that," Novembrini said. "I used to rant and rave against Dalí from time to time but she never said anything. She just listened. What's this all about, Macintyre?"

"It's just that Flavia used to visit the Guggenheim to see the painting. An attendant there says she liked it very much."

"It's the first I ever heard of it."

"And there's another thing. Flavia ripped out the page in her Guggenheim catalog that had the Dalí reproduction. On the other side was this Yves Tanguy."

He handed Novembrini the other card. The artist looked at it silently and gave it back with a disinterested shrug.

"Means nothing to me as far as Flavia is concerned."

"Maybe she didn't like the Tanguy and didn't want it in her book even if it was on the other side of the Dalí," Zuin suggested. "She seems to have been in the habit of stabbing at things she didn't like. I guess I shouldn't have said that, should I?" He gave Novembrini a nervous glance. "Let me see the Dalí card, Signor Macintyre."

Zuin stared down at the reproduction.

"Flavia used to rip things out of books and magazines," Novembrini said. "She would put them on the wall of my studio. She ruined a lot of books but it didn't seem to bother her. By the way, Macintyre, I told Massimo about our conversation in Campo Santa Margherita. He's just as skeptical as I am that Flavia might have been murdered. And as for the Conte da Capo-Zendrini, Massimo knows no more about that business than I do."

Zuin handed the postcard back to Urbino without comment. Urbino knew little about Zuin except that he was Novembrini's dealer. But then he remembered what Novembrini had told him about his dealer during their talk at the café on the Grand Canal—that Zuin had mixed feelings about Flavia.

Zuin's eyes suddenly lit up with a broad smile as he looked toward the entrance.

"So what are you and Papà cooking up between you for a poor defenseless girl?" said a petite dark-haired woman who had just come into the room with a bounce in her step.

She kissed Zuin on the forehead and straightened his pocket square. Then she kissed Novembrini, tugging playfully at the hair at the nape of his neck. She was the young woman who had joined Novembrini at the café on the Grand Canal.

She smiled brightly at Urbino as Zuin introduced her as his

daughter, Tina. Zuin's face shone with pride. Novembrini, with almost a challenging look at Urbino, drew her aside.

"Now don't you forget to deliver that naked girl to Urbino's little palace when this shindig is over, Mr. Zuin," Eugene said when he and Urbino were leaving a few minutes later.

On the way to the Danieli, where he would leave Eugene, Urbino was abstracted as Eugene went on about *Nude in a Funeral Gondola*. Urbino realized that he now had another piece to try to fit into the puzzle of Flavia's life—Tina Zuin, the daughter of Novembrini's dealer, who appeared to be on more than just friendly terms with the artist. Zuin obviously doted on his daughter. Urbino couldn't help but think of the contrast between Zuin and Brollo. Lorenzo had seemed, throughout his conversation with Urbino, strangely detached from Flavia, as if he hadn't cared about her at all.

Tina could be the reason why Massimo Zuin hadn't liked Flavia. Had this been the source of the "mixed feelings" that Novembrini had mentioned? Most likely, however, Zuin didn't have any mixed feelings about his daughter's friendship with his star artist.

After depositing Eugene at the Danieli, Urbino went to see Violetta Volpi.

5

DRESSED IN A lemon-colored linen tunic, Violetta Volpi was alone under the ivy-covered pergola behind her studio when Urbino was brought out to the garden by her maid. She was planing a wooden panel, her bracelets jangling. Out here in the sun and in the reflected light from the Grand Canal, her brown hair was vivid with red highlights. Her full-bosomed body, now close to sixty, gave off a wave of voluptuousness that must have been powerful in her youth. The not unpleasant pungent aroma that her perfume failed to mask was even stronger this afternoon, perhaps encouraged by the sun.

Violetta interrupted her work to look at the Dalì postcard. She gave it only a glance and then put it on the wrought-iron bench and continued her work.

"One of my niece's favorite paintings," she said in her throaty voice.

Urbino watched Violetta as she continued to plane the panel that she said she was going to use in a new series. She was a resourceful and even unpredictable woman. Not only was she planing the panels herself and filling in the knotholes with sawdust and glue, but she had even glued the various pieces of wood together. Once again, as on his last visit, Urbino felt that Violetta was using her work as a way of putting a barrier between them, of making it difficult for him to see how she was really reacting.

"Did you use pyrene for the glue?" Urbino asked her.

She shot a quick look at him from her light green eyes.

"You know something about these things, I see. No, not pyrene, but an old concoction that works very well. I've got my own recipe for it."

She laughed, as if at a private joke.

"Cheese and lime?"

"You *do* know what you're talking about. Yes, cheese and lime, but if you want the exact proportions, forget it! How do you know so much about art materials, Signor Macintyre?"

Urbino explained about his courses in art restoration. Violetta nodded her head as she bent over the panel. Urbino brought up Dalì's *The Birth of Liquid Desires* again.

"*I* introduced Flavia to Dalí," she said, putting aside the plane and inspecting the panel. "When she was about twelve. We went to the Peggy Guggenheim Collection and I gave her a tour of all the paintings. She loved the Surrealist paintings best, and was particularly fascinated by Dalí. She preferred that Dalí"—she nodded over at the postcard on the chair—"to the other one. She met Peggy Guggenheim once. Miss Guggenheim told her some anecdotes about Dalí and the painting. A most interesting woman. Did you know her?"

"Unfortunately not. I've heard that Flavia went back to the Guggenheim many times just to see that painting."

She smiled and laid the panel down on the table, rubbing her hands together.

"If you make an impression on a young mind, it lasts for-ever. That's why it's important that the impressions be the best. But perhaps you're more conservative in your tastes. Perhaps you think that something like *The Birth of Liquid Desires* isn't suited for young people."

"Is there any reason why your niece might have found that particular painting so interesting?"

Violetta Volpi laughed.

"I can see you don't know children! It's a limitation for an artistic temperament not to be around them. Thank God I had Flavia. The answer is simple. The painting is quite sexual. You've got two naked men in the painting and two fair maid-ens—and one of the men is in an obvious state of arousal."

She looked at Urbino directly when she made this latter observation. He felt she was trying once again to provoke him into a criticism of Dalí.

"I saw the copy of the Guggenheim catalog you gave Flavia. It was among her belongings at the Casa Trieste. There's an inscription from you on the inside cover."

"I gave it to her on her twenty-first birthday," Violetta said with almost palpable sadness in her hoarse voice.

"The page that the Dalí plate is on was ripped out. On the other side is a Tanguy—*The Sun in Its Jewel Case*." Since Urbino was speaking Italian, the title didn't carry any ambiguity. "Did your niece like the Tanguy as well?"

Violetta didn't answer right away.

"Not as much as Dalí." Violetta now had a worried, even slightly angry frown on her face. "Since she was a child my niece had a terrible habit of ripping pages from books. I considered it a sacrilege. I would scold her, but she liked tacking things on the wall and putting them in a scrapbook she kept. If I didn't know that Flavia had that habit, I'd almost say it was Annabella who ripped out that page. She's a bit of a prude and has proba-bly never seen a naked man in her life. Yes, Stefana?"

Violetta's maid told her that she had a phone call, and Violetta went into the studio. Urbino walked down to the low, wrought-iron gate between the garden and the semicircular water steps. Part of the terrace of the Guggenheim Palazzo could be seen on the other side farther down the Grand Canal beyond the Accademia Bridge.

The Volpis were obviously in the process of repairing the
white stone wall that separated the garden from the Grand
Canal. A pile of stones was stacked to the left of the water gate.

Urbino was about to turn away when he noticed that the
gate was broken. It looked as if it had been pushed outward
toward the Grand Canal. It could no longer be closed.

"A bit of vandalism, I'm afraid," Violetta said, startling
Urbino. "You know what high season is like here. People come
up to our water steps in boats and try to come in. It takes much
of the pleasure out of being here on the Grand Canal at this
time of the year. They seem to have parties right on the steps.
We find empty wine bottles and cigarette stubs all the time. The
garden isn't as well lit as it should be to begin with and several
of the light bulbs have blown out."

When Urbino turned around to face Violetta, he noticed
Bernardo Volpi looking down at them from a second-story
window. Violetta followed Urbino's gaze.

"I see that Bernardo is finished with his nap. I'll have to
see if he needs anything. I'll walk you to the door."

As they made their way along the narrow hall flanked with
torchères, Urbino told Violetta that Mirko had found Flavia's
scrapbook at the Casa Trieste and had given it to him temporarily for safekeeping. This seemed the best way to explain the
delicate situation. He said nothing about the mugging.

Violetta seemed stunned.

"*You* have the scrapbook? Lorenzo has been wondering
where it is. You must give it to him at once! He'll be furious."

"Of course I'll give it to him. I thought it might be safer
with me than with Mirko," Urbino added, feeling guilty as he
said this, considering the mugging. "I confess that I looked
through it."

"I have no doubt that you did," Violetta said coldly.

"There's a section of autographs. One of them is Alvise da
Capo-Zendrini's. Do you have any idea how it got there?"

Violetta stopped and turned to him, breathing heavily.

"I am not the repository of all knowledge about my niece,
Signor Macintyre—and neither is her father. I haven't the
slightest idea how the Conte da Capo-Zendrini's autograph
came to be in Flavia's scrapbook—if indeed it is there."

"I haven't shown it to the Contessa yet to authenticate it
but—"

"Return the scrapbook to my brother-in-law immediately, Signor Macintyre! You are trying our patience in this as in other things. Lorenzo has told me about your insinuations about Regina saying something to my niece about the Conte da Capo-Zendrini. My sister was emotionally ill. Sometimes she could hardly remember details from the day before. Someone is misleading you—someone you may be too eager to believe instead of Lorenzo and me. And as for my niece having been murdered! Well, both my brother-in-law and I find that unthinkable! Whoever would have wanted to murder her?"

"I'm trying to find out, Signora Volpi. That's why I need your help—and your brother-in-law's. I know that Flavia was here on the Thursday evening before her body was found. Did she say anything about the Conte or her mother then?"

"I don't know how you found out that she was here, Signor Macintyre!" Violetta glared at him with burning eyes. "Neither my brother-in-law nor I would be pleased to discover that the police are sharing information with you. It is none of your business what occurred between my niece and me, I assure you. It was the last time we saw each other. I would prefer to keep it private."

Urbino thought it best to drop the topic for now, and not to bring up how Violetta had gone to the Palazzo Brollo after she had seen Flavia.

They went up the staircase in silence. When they reached the upper hall, Urbino decided to risk one more question, wanting to bring up the argument that Mirko said he and Flavia had overheard.

"You were at Lago di Garda at the time your sister Regina drowned, weren't you?"

"Yes, I was," Violetta answered, stiffening. "Why do you mention that sad occasion?"

"Ladislao Mirko said that he overheard an argument between you and your brother-in-law."

Violetta turned to him, her light green eyes burning and her face flushed.

"Ladislao Mirko!" She came close to spitting out the name as if it were poison. It was in her anger that she reminded Urbino most of her niece—especially the Flavia who had stormed out of Caffè Florian. In animation Violetta's coarse features assumed almost an attractiveness that was a ghost of

Flavia's beauty. "I wouldn't believe anything Mirko has to tell you. Surely you know he's on drugs! He can't tell day from night. If he has your ear, then you're being led astray. Goodday, Signor Macintyre."

After leaving the Ca' Volpi, Urbino rang the bells of the people who lived on both sides of the Volpis. Most refused to answer his questions, but those who did said that they had heard and seen nothing unusual on the last night Flavia was known to be alive, although they remembered the violent thunderstorm and the shouts of carousing tourists.

And yet, as Urbino stood at one of the neighbors' windows and looked down into the Volpis' garden, he felt that he was looking at the site of Flavia's death. The water gate was broken. Violetta's explanation hadn't completely satisfied him. And Bernardo Volpi's bedroom had an even better view of the garden than Urbino did now.

There was also the pile of stones. Flavia's murderer could have picked one up and hit her in the head with it, stunning her, pushed her into the Grand Canal, and left her to drown. The stone could then have been tossed after her into the Grand Canal.

According to the chronology of Flavia's last night, she had left the Ca' Volpi to go to see Lorenzo. How could she have been murdered back at the Ca' Volpi? Violetta had gone to see her brother-in-law and arrived at the Palazzo Brollo after Flavia had left.

Where had Flavia gone *after* the Palazzo Brollo? What had led her to her death?

6

URBINO NEXT WENT to the archives of *Il Gazzettino* across from Caffè Florian to read through newspaper articles on Nicolina Ricci's murder. Something might be in them that had meant nothing to him before Flavia Brollo entered his and the Contessa's lives.

Flavia Brollo's name wasn't mentioned in any of the articles, but Urbino hadn't expected it to be. He pored over all the details of the blood-soaked sheets and the chaos of Nicolina's bedroom, the multiple knife wounds and the T-shirt stuffed into her mouth. He read the neighbors' testimonials about what a "good girl" Nicolina had been and the descriptions of how distraught her family was. Not until Urbino came upon two details, however, did he feel that he had finally found something. One was the way Pasquale Zennaro, who eventually confessed to the murder, was described as a "close friend of the family" and "almost an uncle to the slain girl," a man who "at first seemed as disturbed as if it had been his own child." Signora Ricci had said similar things about Zennaro.

Urbino remembered what Nicolina's brother Luigi had told him—that Flavia had never taken to Pasquale Zennaro. Urbino had passed this information on to Commissario Gemelli but Gemelli apparently found it of no interest.

The other piece of information that jumped out at Urbino was this:

> Carlo Ricci, the father of the murdered girl, has returned to his job at the Volpi Import-Export Company in Mestre.

Could this be what Urbino was in search of, something that would explain the possible relationship between Nicolina Ricci's murder and Flavia's? If it was, it seemed to put Bernardo Volpi, the owner of the Volpi Import-Export Company, in an entirely different light—and perhaps his wife as well.

Urbino was about to leave when he thought of something else. It took him a long time to find the article on the death of Vladimir Mirko, the father of Ladislao. It was in an issue of *Il Gazzettino* from ten years ago.

Vladimir Mirko, forty-two, had died in an explosion in his apartment in the Castello quarter caused by his freebasing cocaine. It obviously hadn't deterred his son from living just as dangerously.

7

FROM CAFFÈ FLORIAN Urbino called Oriana Borelli, the Contessa's friend. She gave him the address of Graziella Gnocato, the old nurse who had taken care of Oriana's husband, Filippo, and Regina Brollo.

An hour later Urbino was in one of the most dismal quarters of Venice, the housing estate of Santa Marta with its dreary, uniform rows of low tenements, lines of washing, and wilted geraniums in window boxes. Cranes, warehouses, and even cars—an anomaly in Venice—were visible beyond the wall that cut the area off from its former source of spiritual comfort, the Church of Santa Marta, now just one more warehouse on the waterfront. In an unshaded basketball court, children in torn shorts and dirty T-shirts were kicking around the metal screw-top from a jar.

The sickening odors of motor oil, frying fish, and cigarette smoke formed a pall over the quarter, emanating from its dark row houses and the nearby warehouses, railway docks, and maritime buildings. This was an area that never found its way onto a postcard or into the heart of a tourist.

Urbino found the building where Graziella Gnocato lived with her niece. It was on a corner within sight of a railroad siding where a man was hosing down a line of railway cars. The fresh coat of salmon paint on the building didn't succeed in hiding its shabbiness. A stout, gray-haired woman about sixty answered the bell, wiping her hands on her apron. When Urbino explained who he was and that he was there to see Graziella Gnocato, the woman frowned.

"I'm sorry, signore, but my aunt is expecting the priest from San Nicolò dei Mendicoli. He comes every week to confess her. She can't see you now."

"It's important, signora. You can call Oriana Borelli. She'll assure you that I'm not here to disturb your aunt."

"Francesca?" a woman's voice called from within the apartment. "Is that Padre Ferrucci? You know I like to see him right away."

"It's not Padre Ferrucci, Zia Graziella."

"Who is it then? I might not have my sight but I can hear as sharp as I ever did. I can hear you talking with someone. Bring our visitor in."

With obvious reluctance Francesca escorted Urbino to a small, stuffy bedroom crowded with pictures and statues of saints. Urbino made out the Infant of Prague, Saint Anthony, the Blessed Virgin, and assorted other saints, mostly female. Over the bed hung a blown-up photograph of the preserved body of Saint Lucy, a virgin saint invoked against afflictions of the sight. Saint Lucy was shown laid out in her crystal coffin in the Church of San Geremia on the Grand Canal. Not so much laid out as propped up with pillows in her own bed was a small, wrinkled, white-haired woman in a blue bed jacket. Half a dozen pill bottles and a glass of water were on the bedside table.

"Leave us alone, Francesca," the woman said in a surprisingly strong voice. "Wait for Padre Ferrucci."

With a glance at Urbino, Francesca complied, closing the door quietly behind her. Urbino explained that he was a friend of Oriana Borelli.

"You have a young voice, signore. You are English? Ah, yes, American. So, you are a friend of Signora Borelli. She called me a few days ago. Please tell her that we are very grateful for all her help."

Urbino explained how Oriana Borelli had said that Graziella might be able to tell him some things about Flavia Brollo. Graziella had already told Oriana that Violetta and Regina were sisters.

"I'm concerned about how Flavia died," Urbino said. "She visited a friend and me several times before her death. You see, Signora Gnocato, I suspect that Flavia didn't kill herself but might have been murdered."

"Murdered? My poor Flavia murdered?" Fear threaded the old nurse's voice. She crossed herself and two tears rolled down her withered cheeks. "Flavia was as good as she was beautiful, signore," she said after several moments of staring sightlessly ahead with tear-filled eyes. "She never forgot me. Never! I could always count on her for a visit. We would play guessing games, and years ago she would bring her sweet friend Tina, and we would all have such a good time. Oh, everyone loved Flavia, even the dogs and the cats in the street."

"When was the last time you saw Flavia, Signora Gnocato?"

"The Thursday before they—they found her poor drowned body. About six o'clock."

This was one and a half hours before she had been at the Casa Trieste with Ladislao Mirko and more than an hour after she had stormed out of Florian's.

"Why did she visit you?"

"She came for information. I told her and now I regret it. You say she might have been murdered. Maybe it was because of what I told her."

Graziella shifted uneasily under the worn sheet.

"What did she want to know?"

"About her mother. I looked after Signora Brollo and Flavia from the time they came back to Venice from the clinic outside Milan where Flavia was born. That was for about three years. Then I worked for them again almost ten years later until Signora Brollo drowned herself at Lago di Garda, God have mercy on her soul."

"Do you remember the name of the clinic?"

"Oh, yes, it's well-known."

She gave Urbino the name.

"What was it about her mother that Flavia wanted to know?"

"I heard Signora Brollo tell her daughter many times that a prominent man named Alvise da Capo-Zendrini was her father. She said he was a count. I've told myself over and over again that Signora Brollo was just hallucinating—that it was her illness speaking—but she seemed to know exactly what she was saying. She had the schizophrenia. She had it since she was an adolescent, I understand, but it became much worse after she married."

Graziella sighed.

"She was afraid of so much. The pigeons at the windows. The church bells. Even Flavia's dog. Flavia had to get rid of it. Signora Brollo was afraid that her husband would tell her and Flavia to leave the house and never come back. It was her illness that made her so afraid. Signor Brollo was always very good to her and to Flavia. He never raised his voice once. But that didn't make any difference to Signora Brollo. She would say, 'We'll have to live in a gondola or in one of those little huts in the lagoon where the hunters hide to shoot the birds.' Such a pity! She even thought at times that I was her mother! But she had her lucid moments. She knew what she was saying some of the time, you can be sure, and maybe that's the way it was when she talked about this count. She had a large envelope filled with newspaper clippings with this man's picture. Do you know who he is?"

"I never met him. He's dead now. But why did Flavia want this information from you if she already knew it?"

"She said that she needed someone besides herself—someone people would believe—to say the name, to tell others what her mother had said. You see, signore," Graziella continued, "Signora Brollo would say this many times to Flavia when she was a little girl. It was like a game between them. Signor Brollo would get upset, but never in a mean or loud way, and would tell his wife that she didn't know what she was saying, that she was hallucinating. Would you give me some water, please, signore?"

Urbino held the glass of water to Graziella's mouth as she took a sip.

"Sometimes her mother would mention this man's name," Graziella went on, "and other times Signora Brollo wouldn't know who he was when Flavia would talk about him, especially in the last years of her life."

"Did Flavia want you to meet someone and tell them about all this?"

"Oh, no, signore, my Flavia had more regard for me than that. I can't leave my apartment. Flavia had a little recording machine and I spoke into it. I didn't think it was a good idea. I thought that Signor Brollo—and Signora Brollo's sister Signora Volpi—would have it in for me, but I was only telling the truth, and Flavia begged and pleaded."

Was this, then, the proof that Flavia had stormed off from Florian's in search of? The confidence of an old nurse that Flavia had recorded? Someone whom the Contessa was sure to believe?

"I never thought of what could happen to Flavia," the nurse said sadly. "I only thought that I was making her happy. She kissed and hugged me and left. That was the last time I saw her. I did her no good, signore. I'm responsible for a grievous sin if someone murdered her!"

"But who, Signora Gnocato?"

"Probably someone who doesn't want anyone to know that this Alvise da Capo-Zendrini was her father! Oh, I can tell who you're thinking about, but it wasn't Signor Brollo! That's impossible! He's a gentle, quiet man. You don't have to be afraid of him. He never raised his voice to me or anyone else. He always wanted things as smooth as glass. No matter how bad things would get he always was as calm as anything and could make things better." She screwed up her face. "Maybe Annabella Brollo, his sister. She's a strange one with all her flowers! She never had anything good to say about Flavia. She wanted her brother only for herself. She probably danced the day Signora Brollo died."

"What happened to Signora Brollo?"

"Drowned herself. She insisted on taking the boat to Gardone by herself. Flavia wanted to go, too, because the villa of some famous man is there"—it was Gabriele D'Annunzio's villa Il Vittoriale—"but Signora Brollo said that she wanted to be alone. Flavia threw a tantrum and went to her room to pout. Forty-five minutes later Signora Brollo jumped into the lake from the boat—and that was it. Yes," she sighed, shaking her head, "that was it."

"Did the police ask you any questions about Flavia?"

"The police? I haven't seen a policeman or a carabiniere in years!"

"What about your niece?"

"Francesca minds her own business. Besides, I never told her why Flavia came that last time."

"Would you know if Flavia was on any medication?"

"Medication? I wouldn't know, signore, but I don't think so. I remember having to force her to take aspirin and she didn't like to see all the pills I have to take." She waved her hand toward the bedside table. "She said I would be better off without them."

Graziella didn't know anything about an argument at Lago di Garda in Regina Brollo's bedroom and she had never heard of Salvador Dalí or *The Birth of Liquid Desires*. She did, however, have some choice words to say about Violetta Volpi, who, as

Oriana Borelli had told Urbino, had once hired her to look after Bernardo.

"I never took to her—or to any of those godless paintings she does!"

"Did you work for her before or after Signora Brollo's death?"

"A couple of years before. She used to make me sick the way she would pretend to care about her husband when all she ever seemed to think about were her paintings. If you meet her on the street, you might think she was a fine woman, but she was always stabbing people in the back."

"Like who?"

"Like her own sister! Telling Signor Volpi that she had a crazy woman for a sister who didn't know anything about raising a child, who was going to make her own daughter as *pazza* as she was. The poor man never would say anything. He's a saint. I would have to listen to Signora Volpi many times as she was painting away like a demon! She kept talking about some Englishwoman who had ruined her life, how I don't know."

Leaving the old nurse, with a promise to visit her again soon, Urbino walked past the gates of the Venice Port Authority to the boat landing.

The most important thing he had learned from Graziella Gnocato was that Regina Brollo *had* told Flavia that Alvise da Capo-Zendrini was her father. Ladislao Mirko hadn't been lying. And according to Graziella, Regina Brollo seemed to be the source of the clippings about Alvise that Flavia had put in her scrapbook. Graziella had also confirmed some of his suspicions about Violetta Volpi.

There was no question about it. Urbino had learned a lot from the old nurse, and none of it made him feel easy. He decided to go back to the Palazzo Uccello and get Flavia's scrapbook, and then go to Asolo. Two weeks ago, the Contessa had literally had to drag him off to her country retreat, and here he was going back and forth so often—both yesterday and today. But he needed to speak with Madge Lennox and Silvestro Occhipinti face-to-face, and he wanted to show the Contessa Alvise's signature. Also, on the way to Asolo he could get off the train at Mestre on the other side of the lagoon to talk with Carlo Ricci at the Volpi Import-Export Company.

8

ALL TRAINS TO and from Venice stopped in Mestre, a sprawling city of concrete that continued to woo Venetians with its promise of high, dry, and modern apartments. Urbino considered it a blight and avoided it, unless, like now, he had business there.

He took a taxi to the Volpi Import-Export Company. A blond receptionist smiled brightly at him when he came in the front office, but the smile disappeared when he told her he would like to speak with Carlo Ricci. She seemed more suspicious than relieved when he said he had nothing to do with the police. After eyeing his Caraceni suit, she picked up the telephone and had Ricci paged.

Carlo Ricci was a brawny, good-looking man in his forties with gray-flecked black hair and dark eyes that turned down at the corners. He was dressed in a blue jumpsuit with "Volpi" embroidered over the breast pocket.

"My wife told me about your visit yesterday, signore," Ricci said when they had sat down on a sofa against the wall. "She said you were a friend of Flavia."

"Yes, Signor Ricci. First of all, let me extend my condolences over the death of your daughter."

"*Murder*, signore! A slaughter! I have forbidden even my wife to call it only a 'death.'"

Ricci's raised voice drew the attention of the receptionist.

"I understand, Signor Ricci. I'm not here to upset you any more than you have already been, believe me. I'm here about Flavia. A close friend and I who came to know Flavia near the end of her life are concerned about exactly how she died. We're trying to settle things in our own minds. You know how important that is—to know what happened to someone you care about and to find out who might be responsible."

"You're right, but what help can I be? I hardly knew Flavia.

She was my daughter's friend. At first I thought Nicolina shouldn't hang around with someone ten years older, but I soon saw I was wrong. Flavia was good for her."

"In what way?"

"She encouraged her in her studies—told her how important it was to do something with herself. Nicolina wanted to design clothes. She used to sew gifts for us for our birthdays and Christmas."

"She was obviously a good girl, Signor Ricci."

"The best. She missed having a sister. She has an older brother, and he always looked out for her, but it wasn't the same. My wife is very understanding, but sometimes mothers and daughters find it difficult to talk with each other, especially at the age that Nicolina was. Not that we ever had any trouble with Nicolina—never! But there are problems young girls have in growing up. Flavia was there to help her. My wife told you about the funeral garland Flavia sent my daughter, didn't she?"

"She did. She also told me that the funeral was the last time she saw Flavia. What about you?"

"That's the last I saw her, too."

"Your son Guido says that he saw her about a week later."

"On the vaporetto, yes. She told him she felt guilty about Nicolina's murder—that if she had been there, it wouldn't have happened. Flavia never seemed to take to that bastard, Pasquale Zennaro. He ate at our table like one of the family! I noticed he would look Flavia up and down whenever he saw her."

Ricci stood up abruptly.

"But you'll have to excuse me, signore. I have to get back to work. Volpi's the best boss a worker can have and I wouldn't want to take advantage of him just because he's too sick to keep his eye on the business."

"You know that Flavia was Volpi's niece, don't you?"

"By marriage."

"Did Flavia ever say anything about him?"

"Lots of times. Only good things. He was very generous with her, she said, always giving her money. It's hard for a man not to have any children of his own. He treated her like his own daughter from the time he got back from a business trip and married Signora Volpi. Oh, he's a good man! Always asking after my Nicolina and Luigi. He would have made a good father if he had been blessed. If there's any other way I can help you, signore, please stop by our apartment on Sant'Elena. Guido and I are usually home by seven."

On the train to Bassano del Grappa, Urbino studied the reproduction of *The Birth of Liquid Desires*. As Violetta Volpi had said, Dalì was just the kind of artist to appeal to an adolescent mind.

But why had Flavia ripped the page from the catalog? Had she ripped it out and then put it in her scrapbook? If so, then she had taken it out at a later date—or someone else had removed it.

Urbino took one last look at the Dalí, at the naked man with one sock bending over a pool of water, at the woman in the background with her face averted pouring some kind of liquid from a jug, at the ambiguous embrace between the woman with flowers for hair and the older man with a woman's breasts, an erection, and one foot in a bowl of water.

Urbino shook his head in exasperation and shoved the postcard back in his pocket. "Avida Dollars," he said under his breath, repeating André Breton's anagram. Urbino had never had much patience with Dalí under the best of circumstances, and that minimal patience was being strained to the limit now.

The train was pulling into Bassano del Grappa. Urbino hurried off the train, hoping he would have time for a drink before the bus left for Asolo. He needed one.

9

As SOON AS Urbino got to Asolo, he went to Villa Pippa to ask Madge Lennox about the scrapbook. She might be able to help him piece things together. As he listened to her and watched her practiced features, however, he couldn't help but hear the Contessa's warning that the actress was "brittle with artifice."

"I remember perfectly well, Urbino," Madge Lennox said with a nervous little laugh in the front parlor of La Pippa. She was wearing a vermilion turban and harem pants in a lighter shade of red. "I have an excellent memory. I can still remember lines from characters I played a long time ago. Would you like some more ice?"

Urbino declined. She went to the liquor cabinet, poured more gin into her glass, and added another ice cube.

"There's no reason to change my story from what I told you on Sunday," she went on in her low, controlled voice. "If I hadn't wanted you to know about the clippings, I wouldn't have said anything then."

She turned a bright smile on Urbino, looking at him unfalteringly with her bold, dark eyes. Once again Urbino found himself wondering how many artless gestures she had. Was this ingenuous smile one of them, or was it something that had proved its usefulness under the lights and for audiences larger than just one?

"Why is it that you remember those particular clippings?"

"It's not that I remember *only* them. I remember some other things in the scrapbook—even if I had only a quick glimpse. The clippings with the photographs caught my attention because I recognized Signor Occhipinti and the Contessa da Capo-Zendrini."

"And the Conte?"

"I didn't *recognize* him, no. How could I?" she asked with a little smile. "I never met him, but he *was* one of the men in the pictures. It said so."

Madge Lennox seemed to have had more than just a brief glimpse of the scrapbook.

"And you recognized no one else?"

"No one."

"Did you tell anyone else about the scrapbook?"

"Yes. Signor Occhipinti. I told him he hadn't changed in what must be more than ten years. The clippings had to be at least that old since the Conte da Capo-Zendrini has been dead for longer than that."

"When did you tell Occhipinti about the clippings?"

"A few weeks ago, not long after I saw the scrapbook. I said it belonged to a young woman I knew. I didn't mention her name," Madge Lennox said, anticipating his next question. "Did I do something wrong? I have nothing to do with the missing clippings, believe me. What business were they of mine?"

Urbino handed her the Tanguy postcard.

"Do you recognize this?"

She looked at it a few moments, then turned it over to read the back. She returned it with a shake of her head.

"What about this?" Urbino asked, giving her the Dalí card.

"It looks like a Dalí painting. I don't like Dalí."

She handed the card back to Urbino with distaste.

"They're part of the Peggy Guggenheim Collection in Venice," Urbino explained. "A page with reproductions of both paintings was torn from Flavia's copy of the Guggenheim catalog. Did you notice if it was in the scrapbook?"

"You mean the page? No."

Madge Lennox was staring down at the Dalí postcard in Urbino's hand. A strange, nervous unease seemed to possess her. She went to the window, moving aside the curtain and gazing out at the front yard for a few moments. When she turned around, a hand was at her throat and her head was slightly to one side. She looked bewildered and on the point of saying something. She searched Urbino's face as if for some sign that she should—could—go on. When she did, however, it was to say, with an inappropriateness that at first puzzled Urbino, " 'Carnivorous flower.' " She smiled weakly. "That's what someone called Dalí. 'The carnivorous flower of the Surrealist sun.' I forgot who it was. *Carnivorous Flower* was the title of an experimental play in New York in the sixties. I played Gala."

Madge Lennox began to reminisce about the play, growing more animated as she moved farther and farther from the topic Urbino had come to Villa Pippa to ask her about. He sensed that she was stalling for time, trying to absorb something he had said, just as she had done in the cemetery when he mentioned murder.

Urbino let her go on with her reminiscence. He was certain that Madge Lennox knew something important about Flavia that she wasn't telling him. She might be an actress—and might be doing the best she could to conceal her thoughts and feelings—but he felt that she was uncertain, off balance, even afraid—and it had something to do with Dalí's *The Birth of Liquid Desires*.

Urbino waited until Madge Lennox finished.

"Flavia didn't commit suicide," he said. "I have hopes that the police will realize it, too. They're not quite ready yet."

"You know so much more than they do?"

Madge Lennox seemed to intend the question as a joke, but it came off with an edge of sarcasm. She was smiling but she didn't seem amused. She seemed a little afraid.

"The Commissario told me yesterday that no traces of a medication that they believed Flavia was taking were found in her system," Urbino said. "The drug's been linked to suicidal tendencies. And there were the wounds on her head which haven't been conclusively established to have occurred after she fell in the Grand Canal."

"But surely poor Flavia didn't need to be influenced by a drug of some kind to kill herself. Many people do it with quite clear minds."

"I don't think suicide rings true for Flavia."

"On the contrary! I'm afraid it rings only too true!"

Fear, rather than anger, was the unmistakable thread in her voice.

"If there's anything that you know—or even vaguely suspect—I need to know it too."

"Flavia couldn't have been murdered."

She looked down at the Dalí postcard that Urbino still held in his hand.

"Flavia seems to have cared for you, Madge."

It was the first time Urbino had used the actress's first name. She smiled at him. There were tears in her eyes.

"She trusted you," Urbino added. "And you said she felt safe and secure with you."

"Yes," Madge said quietly. "She did."

"If there's anything that you remember, Madge—anything that you want to tell me—don't hesitate. It could be very important."

"A matter of life and death, you mean?"

Madge Lennox tried to toss this off lightly, but her voice had a dark thread of fear in it.

"Yes."

Urbino gave her his card and told her she could call him at any time.

Walking up the hill from Villa Pippa into Asolo itself, Urbino considered what Lennox had told him. Before Flavia's death the actress had seen clippings of the Conte, the Contessa, and Silvestro Occhipinti in Flavia's scrapbook, but the clippings weren't in the scrapbook now. Lennox had told Occhipinti about them—Occhipinti, a man who Urbino believed would want to protect the Contessa and his old friend however he could.

As Urbino followed the road through the wall of the city, passing Eleonora Duse's house, he asked himself what it was about the Dalì painting that disturbed Madge Lennox so much. She had appeared to be on the point of saying something after looking at the postcard a second time.

Did Madge Lennox have something to hide—not for Flavia's sake, perhaps, but for her own? If she did, then Urbino was afraid that she would remain an actress until the very end, just as the Contessa said she would.

Urbino had to talk with Occhipinti again. He quickened his stride in the direction of the Via Browning.

10

OCCHIPINTI, WITH POMPILIA on a leash, was just coming out of the door of his apartment building under the arcade. The little man, without his jaunty straw hat this afternoon, was blowing his nose vigorously. He still hadn't shaken his summer cold. Urbino remembered how quick Occhipinti had been to say that he must have caught it from a neighbor, yet he might just as easily have caught it by getting soaked and chilled during the thunderstorm in Venice the night Flavia had died. As the Contessa had mentioned to Urbino, he had been in Venice for some business at the Ca' Rezzonico.

"Why not join us on our walk, Signor Macintyre?" Occhipinti said brightly in his high-pitched voice. "So lovely out. Nothing like what it must be back in Venice. I'm happy I've been able to stay cool up here in Asolo."

Occhipinti had made his point and Urbino let it pass without any comment. The man had already denied being in Venice two days ago. This latest comment made Urbino even more certain that it had been Occhipinti he had seen crossing the bridge in the San Polo quarter.

Urbino and Occhipinti walked under the arcades toward the main square. Occhipinti's brisk pace slackened when Urbino mentioned the scrapbook. Urbino was carrying it in a small satchel, but he had no intention of showing it to Occhipinti unless it was absolutely necessary.

"Yes, Signora Lennox said she saw my picture in that girl's book. I don't deny it. 'Truth ever, truth only the excellent!' I guess I didn't think it was important."

"Did you see the young woman's scrapbook yourself?"

"See it? Of course I didn't see it! Did *you?*" the bald-headed man was quick to ask.

"I saw it yesterday."

Once again, without any hesitation, Alvise da Capo-Zendrini's old friend asked, "Is it true what Signora Lennox said, then? That I haven't changed since that picture was taken?"

Occhipinti stared at Urbino with his round, birdlike eyes. Urbino didn't quite trust this pose of innocence.

"Neither the picture nor the clipping that went along with it was in the scrapbook," Urbino said, staring down at Occhipinti.

"But Signora Lennox said the picture was. *She* saw it."

"She did, but it wasn't there by the time I looked through the scrapbook."

Occhipinti shrugged.

"Nothing to do with me. 'Innocent am I, innocent as a babe, as Mary's own'!"

The old man's look, however, didn't match his words. He looked as guilty as a child with his hand in a cookie jar.

"Could you describe the photograph, Signor Occhipinti?"

"It must be the one of me and Alvise at Browning's Ca' Rezzonico with some municipal officials and a man from London—a relative of Browning. It was taken about fifteen years ago when I lent the Ca' Rezzonico some of my things for an exhibit."

A young girl on a bicycle came flying down the alleyway

next to the Hotel Duse. Pompilia started barking loudly, and
Occhipinti pulled back on her leash with more force than was
necessary.

As they approached the real estate office, Urbino decided
to risk shaking the man up slightly.

"Perhaps you've forgotten that you *have* seen Flavia Brollo's
scrapbook, Signor Occhipinti," he said.

"Are you trying to upset me? I know you have to ask a lot
of questions about this girl, but don't treat me like Barbara's
enemy."

"How does your signature come to be in the scrapbook? I
didn't even know 'Ugolini' was one of your names."

Occhipinti seemed genuinely puzzled, and even more so
when Urbino added, hoping his memory wasn't too inaccurate,
" 'I have lived, and now, with one more kiss, can die!' "

"Some of the words are wrong," Occhipinti said, "but that's
from *In a Gondola*. I don't understand."

"It's what you wrote in the scrapbook."

The old man seemed to take several moments to think.

"I remember now," he said in a barely audible voice. "I *did*
write in her scrapbook, but it was a long time ago."

Occhipinti seemed surprised by his own memory.

"So you did know Flavia Brollo?"

"Know her? She was just a young girl at the time! I didn't
see her from that time until she turned up in Asolo."

"But why didn't you tell me you knew her?"

Occhipinti had a defeated look on his little face.

"Because of Alvise—and because of Barbara! It was at Lago
di Garda the summer before Alvise died. He was staying at my
villa there. Barbara thought that a change of scene would be
good for him, and she had to be in Milan. That's when I met
Flavia Brollo. We *both* met her, you see—Alvise and I." Occhipinti looked down at his hands. His chest was heaving quickly like
a frightened bird's. "And we also met her mother."

Occhipinti halted next to the Caffè Centrale, where the
Contessa had told Urbino about her life with Alvise the day
after her garden party. Urbino had come a long way in his
understanding of Flavia Brollo since then, but he still had a
good distance to go.

Occhipinti looked at Urbino.

"Signora Brollo was beautiful," he said. "She had 'great

eyes, deep with dreams of Paradise'! Even then you could see that her daughter would grow up to look just like her, but beauty like that is a curse. Both mother and daughter, dead in their prime, and the same way!"

"So you know that Regina Brollo drowned?"

"Oh, yes, I read about it. My sister and I had sold the villa on Lago di Garda by then or else we might have been there when it happened. I was here at Villa Pippa." He paused before adding, "And Alvise had died that winter."

"You said that Alvise also met Regina Brollo."

"Yes, on the garden terrace of the Grand Hotel. I had gone inside to make some telephone calls and when I came out young Flavia was there with Alvise. Alvise introduced us, and Flavia asked me to sign her book. She had just got it for her birthday. I did, and then Alvise did, too. Signora Brollo came out and Flavia introduced her. We chatted about the weather and the Grand Hotel, and that was it. I never saw Signora Brollo again— and as for her daughter, not until she showed up at the Contessa's party."

"But you soon realized who she must be because she looked so much like her mother? And you must have remembered that you and Alvise had met her—as well as her mother?"

Occhipinti nodded almost reluctantly.

"But it was the only time we ever saw her!"

"Violetta Volpi says that you met her sister on several occasions years ago when you were seeing each other. She says that Alvise might even have been with you."

Occhipinti let out a long, audible breath.

"She's lying," he said.

"Signor Occhipinti, you know how much Barbara wants to get to the bottom of this. She wants the truth, no matter what it is."

Occhipinti gave a high-pitched laugh.

"Don't be so sure of that, my friend! People might say that but they usually don't mean it. Maybe she thinks she can deal with the truth but it would break her." He paused. "You wouldn't want to be the one responsible for that, would you? But what am I saying, Signor Macintyre? 'How each loved each, he her god, she his idol'! Never doubt it!"

Occhipinti hurried off in the direction of the civic museum. As he was going past the winged-lion fountain, he started to gesticulate with his free hand, and a few indistinguishable words were carried to Urbino on the gentle breeze.

11

AN HOUR LATER when Urbino went in search of the Contessa along the pebbled path above the maze at La Muta, he was taken aback to find her dressed in a stunning pair of white silk palazzo pants. It was the first time he had seen the Contessa in pants. They became her, giving her less a contemporary look than one reminiscent of Marlene Dietrich and the 1930s.

"And what are *you* looking at, may I ask?" the Contessa challenged him, lifting her well-defined little chin. "If a woman can't wear what she wants in the privacy of her own home, what would you suggest she do? Oh, I know what you're thinking, but your dear Madge Lennox's pants are distinctly along the harem line—to go with those turbans she wears, I assume. At any rate, I don't intend to parade around in these," she added, looking down at what she considered her own much more suitable version of Madge Lennox's preferred attire.

Just how little intention the Contessa had of parading she immediately showed when she took Urbino's arm and started to stroll with him down the pebbled path.

"So tell me, *caro*," the Contessa said, glancing at his satchel. "Have you run away so abruptly from the heat and crowds of Venice or from your charming ex–brother-in-law? You'll notice that I'm not vain enough to assume you might quite simply have run *to* me for no other reason than my company. You—"

The Contessa stopped suddenly and looked at him. Her gray eyes were touched with fear.

"You have bad news. You had to tell me in person. Oh, *caro*, I've had a premonition all day."

It was true, of course. Urbino did have bad news. The time had come to tell the Contessa everything that he had held back from her so far about Alvise. Earlier, as long as he had had only

Mirko's word to go on, he could justify not saying anything to
her, but now he could spare her no longer. She had to know.
He couldn't allow her to keep thinking that Alvise had had
nothing at all to do with the Brollos, that Alvise's entry in Flavia's
scrapbook might have been forged. Although Urbino had
brought the scrapbook with him so that she could authenticate
Alvise's signature, it no longer seemed necessary in light of what
Occhipinti had just told him.

The Contessa must have seen the hesitation in his eyes, for
she rushed on to say, with a touch of pique, "Do you know what
it's like for me? Do you know what I think about every single
minute of every single day and night? I can't lose Alvise in this
way—no, not after he's already gone. I can't! I refuse!" she
added, as if it were up to her.

The Contessa put a hand to her face. For one of the few
times since he had known her, she was crying. A sob escaped,
and her shoulders heaved. Urbino put his arm around her.

"Is it something else in the scrapbook—some letter, some
document? What is it, Urbino? You have to tell me the truth."

Still with his arm around her, Urbino first described how
Graziella Gnocato had heard Regina Brollo tell Flavia that Alvise was her father. Flavia had confided the same thing in Mirko,
Urbino said. Then he recounted the argument that Mirko
claimed he and Flavia had overheard at Lago di Garda the
summer of Regina Brollo's suicide.

"Violetta Volpi shouted to Lorenzo that Flavia wasn't his
daughter and asked him why he didn't admit it. Mirko and
Flavia heard Alvise's name mentioned and then there was a
slap. Violetta started to cry and then so did Regina. Lorenzo
warned Violetta to leave Regina and him alone."

The Contessa was stunned.

"Regina Brollo herself? She was the one to tell Flavia?" The
Contessa gave a hollow, humorless laugh. "I suppose she would
know, wouldn't she? What did Annabella say? 'It would be a
strange mother who doesn't know her child's father'!"

She eased herself from Urbino's arm and went over to lean
against the trunk of a palmetto, her back to him. She seemed
to be taking deep breaths. When she turned around, she said,
"Don't be angry with me, Urbino, but I refuse to believe it. The
memory of an old woman? The ramblings of a drug addict?
And we only have *his* word for the argument at Lago di Garda!

Remember that we're dealing with what we think is murder here. No, I'm sorry, Urbino," she repeated. "All this isn't enough and don't try to convince me it is."

"I understand—and I agree with you."

"You do, *caro*?"

She came over to him and slipped her arm through his. They continued along the pebbled path toward the maze.

"Yes. But there's another thing. It's Silvestro. He's hiding something."

"Then I'll see him right away! I'll tell him he *must* tell me. I don't want to be protected by him—or you—or anyone else! He's in a position to put me out of my misery. I won't believe a senile old woman or a drug addict, but I'd believe Silvestro."

"Please, Barbara. Let's sit down." He guided her to the marble bench near the opening of the maze. "I may be wrong. He might be hiding something that has nothing to do with Alvise—or with Alvise and Regina Brollo."

"What did he say?" the Contessa asked in a resigned voice.

Urbino told her about Occhipinti and Alvise's meeting with Flavia and Regina at Lago di Garda shortly before Alvise had died and about how Occhipinti denied that he and Alvise had ever met Regina before—or after—that day. It was best to get everything out in the open at the same time. The Contessa had a handkerchief pressed to her mouth as Urbino continued.

"Silvestro is holding something back. He was in Venice at the time Flavia was murdered and I'm sure I saw him on Tuesday evening in the San Polo quarter, but he denies it. He's hiding something, Barbara, but I don't know what his reason might be, not yet, anyway."

"His reason? To protect me and Alvise! Don't be a fool!"

Urbino stared at the Contessa until she turned away and looked at the opening of the maze.

"I'm sorry, *caro*. It's just that everything is turning so ghastly for me. My heart is in a thousand pieces."

"If there were any way I could make all this just disappear, I would do it, Barbara."

"Oh, I know you would! There's no reason to feel guilty. Since I have to know the truth, I don't want to know it from anyone but you. Thank God you're here for me."

Urbino felt a surge of love and admiration for the Contessa. He suspected that she was stronger than he was. He hadn't acted at all as well when he discovered Evangeline's infidelity. But Urbino reminded himself that the Contessa and he still didn't know for sure about Alvise and Regina. Would they ever? He hoped for the Contessa's sake that they would. She would be able to take anything except having to live the rest of her life with doubt.

He took the scrapbook from his satchel and showed the Contessa Alvise's signature. She nodded her head slowly in assent, saying quietly, "Yes, it's his."

Urbino now told the Contessa about Flavia's visits to the Guggenheim to see the Dalí painting and about his conversations with Novembrini, with Violetta and her neighbors, with Nicolina Ricci's father, and—just a short time ago—with Madge Lennox. He finished with Tina Zuin and her apparent relationship with Novembrini.

The Contessa shook her head slowly. It was a lot to take in. She sat there thinking for several minutes. Urbino didn't interrupt her.

"But Flavia's death could have absolutely nothing to do with my Alvise, even if he *was* her father," the Contessa said eventually. "Regina Brollo killed herself. Flavia was obviously troubled, and her friend Nicolina Ricci was viciously raped and murdered—there's enough to explain the poor girl being driven to suicide."

She stopped speaking suddenly and shook her head.

"Oh, it's no use, Urbino! Even if I *am* right, I'm not going to feel any better unless I *know* I am—about Alvise or about Flavia. Which just brings us back to the beginning, doesn't it? I'm afraid that our hands aren't on all the ropes, not yet, if ever! Listen, Urbino. It might be more convenient if you just borrowed the Cinquecento so that you can use it to go back and forth between here and Venice. You can put it in the garage at the Piazzale Roma. I hardly ever use it. That way you can pick up and come here whenever you want."

"I'll think about it, Barbara, but you know I'm not fond of driving."

Footsteps along the pebble path revealed themselves to be those of the maid, Rosa, who appeared around the corner of a Japanese boxwood hedge. The Contessa had a phone call.

The Contessa excused herself. While Urbino was waiting for her to return, he went a few turnings into the maze. Many minutes passed as he thought about Occhipinti and how far the man might go to protect Alvise and the Contessa. He had already lied and concealed information, and Urbino was convinced that this wasn't the end of it.

Urbino wondered, however, if what he was learning about Flavia's family and Alvise's probable relationship to it was bringing him closer to an understanding of how and why Flavia had been murdered, as he still believed she had been. Was it possible, as the Contessa had just said, that Flavia's death didn't have anything to do with Alvise, even if he was her father? Not very long ago Urbino had assumed that, in trying to find out whether Alvise had actually been Flavia's father, he would be led to the reason why Flavia had been killed. He wasn't so sure of this anymore.

The Venetians like to say that "there's no north or south in Venice." Urbino was beginning to feel the same way about this case, which was very much like the labyrinth of the city or, for that matter, the Contessa's maze that he didn't want to venture too far into this evening. As Urbino stopped at a junction, another Venetian saying came to mind: *"sempre diritto."* "Straight ahead" was what you were often told when you asked for directions to your destination. The irony, of course, was that there was no "straight ahead" or direct route to your destination in the twists and turns of Venice. There didn't seem to be in this case either, and all Urbino could do was continue to seek a solution in the Venetian way of *"sempre diritto."*

"Urbino, where are you?" the Contessa called, pulling him out of his thoughts. Her voice held a rasp of excitement. "Are you going to come out from hiding or are you afraid to hear what I've just learned?"

Urbino emerged from the maze. The Contessa was smiling, and Urbino knew that Occhipinti was dead wrong. The Contessa wouldn't break.

The call had been from Corrado Scarpa.

"I called him again yesterday to see if he could get some more information for us."

Corrado had said that Flavia, not surprisingly, hadn't made a will, and whatever she had would go to Lorenzo Brollo. Corrado had also looked into Ladislao Mirko's affairs. As Urbino already knew and had told the Contessa, Mirko's father had been a drug addict and had been killed in an explosion while freebasing cocaine in his apartment in the Castello quarter. This hadn't discouraged Mirko from his own drug taking or—it was suspected—from occasionally dealing in drugs to supplement his income. It seemed that Mirko was often pressed for money and had come close to losing the pensione several times.

"I couldn't agree with Lorenzo Brollo more," the Contessa said as they made their way back to the house. "Mirko's a bad lot. He was accused of attacking some girl in Verona several years ago. She was high on drugs at the time and no one believed her. You yourself have said that he acts suspiciously, and I know you didn't like that scratch on his cheek. How convenient for him that he has a cat! You can't believe a word he says."

"But it would be a mistake to assume that Mirko isn't telling the truth about some things. Don't forget that Graziella Gnocato backs him up on what Regina Brollo told Flavia," Urbino reminded her.

"As far as I'm concerned, the jury is still out on all that, caro."

For a few minutes Urbino and the Contessa walked in silence along the path with its rose bushes, oleanders, and edges of lavender.

"And about Regina Brollo's death," the Contessa went on with what Scarpa had told her, breaking off a sprig of oleander. "There's absolutely no question that she killed herself. Thirteen years ago the poor thing filled the pockets of her skirt with stones, took the steamer out into the lake, and jumped off. None of her family was with her. Before anyone could get to her she was gone. She had a history of emotional illness, as Graziella Gnocato told you. Corrado thinks Flavia wanted to get money out of me and that we're wasting our time trying to find out if there's any truth to her story. He says to let it go, but how can we? Especially when we think Flavia was murdered. Let me continue to do what I can, Urbino. I'll contact the clinic outside Milan that Graziella Gnocato mentioned. We're going straight ahead with all this, and I tell you from the bottom of my heart and soul that I don't care where it leads."

She gripped his arm, dropping the oleander blossoms.

"I don't! I don't! I don't!"

PART FOUR

Open My Heart and You Will See

1

BACK AT THE Palazzo Uccello later that night Urbino called
Bruno Novembrini.

"I thought you might contact me, Macintyre—but Tina
isn't here."

"You're right. I would like to talk with her."

"Well, Tina doesn't live at home with Massimo any longer
and I'm not about to give you her address or phone number.
I'll tell her you'd like to talk with her."

Novembrini hung up before Urbino could ask him anything else.

Urbino went down to his workshop on the *piano terreno* to
work on the Bartolomeo Veneto portrait of a lady. He had
finished her corkscrew curl and was now working on her drop
pearl earring. The work soothed him after his busy day, and
part of his mind was free to try to get a clearer, truer picture
of the other young woman who had also once been flesh and
blood.

He ran through what he was coming to think of as something not unlike his own special portrait gallery. There was
Lorenzo Brollo, the man who swore he was Flavia's father and
professed a devotion to his dead wife. Violetta Volpi didn't

disagree with any of this. In fact, Regina's husband and Flavia's aunt were very much together in their stories. The two of them seemed to be closing ranks, understandable enough when it came to a controversial death in the family. Urbino wondered what had taken place when Violetta visited the Palazzo Brollo on the night Flavia died—and when Flavia had come to see her at the Ca' Volpi earlier.

Violetta's husband, Bernardo, might be able to tell him a great deal. Carlo Ricci said that Bernardo had cared a lot about Flavia, but had Bernardo felt this way up until the end—an end that Urbino believed had possibly taken place in the garden of the Ca' Volpi where someone struck Flavia over the head and pushed her into the Grand Canal?

"Up until the end." Urbino repeated it to himself as he continued to work on the drop pearl earring. Had Ladislao Mirko been Flavia's faithful friend—the brother she had never had—up until that end? Novembrini had sarcastically called Flavia and Mirko "Beauty and the Beast," but Flavia's relationship with the homely little man could very well have been the closest and most important of her life. After all, she had confided things in him that she hadn't told Novembrini, hadn't she? And Mirko, abandoned by his mother and completely misguided by his father, might have found in Flavia the one true friend in whom he could confide all his own secrets and insecurities. The Contessa might suspect, perhaps with good reason, that Mirko was lying, but Graziella Gnocato, like Mirko, said that Regina had named Alvise as Flavia's father.

Urbino considered Novembrini and Tina Zuin, wondering if Flavia's slashing of *Nude in a Funeral Gondola* had been provoked by the artist's betrayal of her. Novembrini had seemed to be afraid of Flavia when he and Urbino had had their first talk beside the Grand Canal, but perhaps it was she who should have been afraid of Novembrini.

As for Massimo Zuin, what might he have done if he had suspected that his most lucrative client's career was being endangered by Flavia?

That left Madge Lennox and Alvise's old friend Occhipinti both back in Asolo and both, Urbino had no doubt, hiding something.

Was there anyone else? Urbino asked himself as he began to work on another of the earring's pearls.

Yes, there was. Annabella Brollo, who had struck Urbino very much like a wraith in the way she had appeared silently in the Brollo *sala*, in how she had slipped past him into the Casa Trieste on his own first visit there, looking at him from the corners of her pale blue, bloodshot eyes and leaving behind the odor of anisette. Had Lorenzo's sister seen or heard anything of the encounters between Brollo and Flavia and Brollo and Violetta on the night Flavia was murdered? She impressed him as the kind of person who frequently listened from the other side of a closed door, who might appear on the scene when you least expected her. And Mirko said that she had been coming up the stairs of the villa in Lago di Garda during the argument.

The doorbell sounded. It was almost eleven o'clock. Looking through the peephole and seeing Novembrini's handsome, insolent face, Urbino opened the door. Tina Zuin was standing nervously next to Novembrini.

2

"As soon as Bruno told me you wanted to talk with me, I realized I should come right away. I know it's late but I wanted to get it over with, Signor Macintyre," Tina said in her wisp of a voice when they were all seated with cool drinks in the parlor. "I don't want you to have the wrong idea about me—or about Bruno. I had nothing to do with Flavia and Bruno's problems."

"Flavia was your friend," Urbino said.

The dark-haired young woman nodded. Tears formed in her round brown eyes.

"I never thought she would end up just like her mother."

"You knew Flavia's mother?"

"Oh, yes. Flavia and I were very close until her mother died. I spent a lot of time at her house. My own mother had died a couple of years before. Signora Brollo was beautiful, and she loved Flavia so much. She would cling to Flavia, as if she were life and health themselves. I suppose it had a lot to do with her illness, and with her miscarriage before Flavia was born. She was a lot of fun for young girls to be around, always telling romantic stories, reading us poems, acting out characters with us. That's when she was well. At other times I wouldn't see her for months."

As Tina talked quietly, Novembrini looked around the room, paying particular attention to the Bronzino of a Florentine lady that the Contessa had given Urbino. He reached into the breast pocket of his sport jacket and took out a packet of cigarettes.

"Did Regina Brollo ever mention the Conte Alvise da Capo-Zendrini? Or a man named Silvestro Occhipinti?"

"Never," Tina said without any hesitation. "And she never said that Lorenzo Brollo wasn't her father. Yes, Bruno told me." She looked at Novembrini, who was searching for a place to put his spent match. "Perhaps you shouldn't be smoking. I don't see any ashtrays around."

She gave Urbino an embarrassed smile.

Novembrini shrugged and dropped his cigarette and match into his glass. Tina turned red.

"I didn't say anything about Tina, Macintyre, because I didn't want to get her involved. I didn't think she should come here tonight or even see you at all."

"But I told Bruno that you would think the worst of us both after seeing us together this afternoon. Bruno has told you about his relationship with Flavia. It had a lot of ups and downs, but not because of me. I admit that I've always been half in love with him," Tina said with a blush coloring her cheeks, "but I would never have done anything to come between Flavia and him. Maybe Flavia and I hadn't been close in the last ten years but I still cared about her, and I knew how vulnerable she was. But now, with her gone, it's—it's different. Bruno and I have gotten to know each other better."

Her blush deepened. It was obvious that Tina was in love with Novembrini and felt especially guilty about their relationship, now that Flavia was dead. But Urbino wanted to know more about Flavia's childhood and adolescence.

"How did Flavia feel about Lorenzo Brollo?" he asked.

"She adored him, at least when we were kids. She tried so hard to please him, but he was cold to her, never giving her a kiss—completely different from the way my father was with me.

After Flavia's mother died, her feelings for her father seemed to change completely. It was as if she made all her love turn to hate. We were drifting apart by then, and she kept to herself a lot. She didn't have many friends, mainly me and Ladislao Mirko. I know Ladislao has a bad reputation, but he was always good to her."

"Did you ever meet his father?"

"Oh, no, he kept his father far away from Flavia and me. He was ashamed of him. Mirko used to have black eyes and bruises a lot, and I figured it must be his father, but he would just say that he had a fight with someone. I always thought that Flavia knew what was happening between Mirko and his father, but if she did she never told me. She was a faithful friend. There were things I told her and asked her to swear she'd never tell, and she never did." A wistful look came over Tina's gamin face. "When we were kids, Flavia and me, we used to play the 'secret sharing' game. I would tell her something she didn't know about me and she would tell me something about herself. We used to have a lot of fun with it. Sometimes Mirko played with us."

"Did Flavia ever tell you any secrets about Lorenzo or Mirko, or her mother or any of her aunts?"

Tina shook her head.

"We just exchanged silly little secrets. We were only kids. Really, Signor Macintyre, I don't know anything that could help you and your friend the Contessa."

"How did she feel about her aunt Annabella?"

Tina screwed up her face.

"She didn't like her. Neither did I. Her father would make her go to visit Annabella. This was before her mother died. Flavia always wanted me to come with her. Her aunt Annabella's apartment was spooky. It was filled with plants and flowers and was always dirty. We used to joke that her aunt was a witch and made poisons from her flowers. When Annabella wasn't looking, we would pour the drinks she gave us into the plants. She gave us the creeps. She was completely different from the other aunt. We would love to visit her."

"And Ladislao Mirko? Did you like him, Tina?"

The question seemed to take her by surprise.

"Like him?" She looked quickly at Novembrini and then away. "Why I—I never disliked him. I suppose I felt sorry for him, considering the hard life he had. He's trying to turn over

a new leaf now with his pensione. He has a good side. I went
out with him for a while when I was sixteen. It was so strange.
It made Flavia jealous even though she didn't want him as a
boyfriend."

"I can't imagine you going out with that creep," Novembrini interjected, an edge to his smooth voice.

"Well, I did," Tina responded almost defiantly. "He's not
attractive, that's for sure, but he could be charming in his own
way, and he was an older guy and all. But he tried to pressure
me to go too fast. I wasn't ready. In any case I wouldn't have
wanted anything to come between me and Flavia. Even though
we weren't as close as before, she still considered me as her best
girlfriend. Why, just a few weeks before she died, right before
she got some crazy idea and slashed Bruno's painting, she gave
me a whole lot of money. I decided to move into a place of my
own. My father was against it, and I needed money. Flavia gave
me two million lire," Tina said, naming a sum close to two
thousand dollars. "She said it was mine, and she laughed in
such a strange way that it frightened me. I didn't want to take
it but she said she had more from where it came from."

This was the first Urbino had heard about Flavia having
had a lot of money. What became of it? Was it possible that he
was dealing with a case of a mugging gone wrong? Could she
have left the money somewhere for safekeeping?

"Tina, would you tell him about the Dalí painting so we can
leave? I need a cigarette."

"Oh, yes, the Dalí. Flavia loved that painting. Her aunt
Violetta introduced her to it. We used to go to the Guggenheim
every couple of weeks. I'm afraid we were silly, running around
giggling at the crazy paintings, especially the ones with nude
men and women. We got a big charge out of the nude man on
the horse on the terrace next to the Grand Canal and—"

This obviously awakened an unpleasant association and
Tina Zuin stopped short.

"But the Dalí was Flavia's favorite," she went on. "We
laughed over it even more than we did any of the other paintings. We were just kids. All we saw in the painting was sex! Two
naked men, and the older one even had a woman's breast and
a very large—" Tina blushed and didn't finish the sentence. "I
think she eventually outgrew the painting, though. She hardly
mentioned it after her mother died. When I brought it up

recently to cheer her up and remind her of old times, it seemed to do the opposite, so I let it drop. You see, Signor Macintyre, there's not that much that I can tell you, but I want you to know that Flavia was a good girl. I never would have done anything to hurt her and neither would Bruno."

Urbino asked Tina if Flavia had been taking any medication. To her knowledge she hadn't. One of the last things Tina said was that Flavia had been very careful about taking even aspirin and that she seldom, if ever, drank.

After they left, Urbino took out the postcard of Dalí's *The Birth of Liquid Desires*. Aside from what the painting might "mean" or what it had "meant" to Dalí, it had obviously fascinated Flavia with its sexuality. This Urbino could understand.

But was it true that Flavia had "outgrown" it, as Tina Zuin had suggested? If she had, then why did she tear the page with the Dalí color plate out of the catalog? Violetta had given her the catalog only five years ago for her twenty-first birthday. Had she torn out the page to put on her wall or in her scrapbook, or had she done something else with it?

When Tina had brought up the Dalí painting with Flavia recently, Flavia didn't seem to find it a pleasant reminder. If Urbino could only find out why Flavia had reacted this way, he might be closer to understanding what had happened to her the night she had been murdered.

Tina Zuin had ended up telling him much more than she seemed to realize. Arranging it with everything he already knew, Urbino was trying to see a pattern. He believed that he was close to seeing one, but there was still too much getting in the way. He needed more time and more information to clear away the debris.

3

AT TEN THE next morning, a Friday, the air was heavy and damp when Urbino left the Palazzo Uccello. He had been kept up almost all night, tormented by his speculations and by a squadron of the *laguna morta*'s most persistent mosquitoes. Urbino was on his way to the Palazzo Brollo on the other side of the Grand Canal to return Flavia's scrapbook and to ask Lorenzo Brollo some more questions.

As Urbino was ferried across the Grand Canal in a gondola that had given its best years to the tourist trade, he was more oppressed than relieved by the fetid breeze that stirred the slightly oily waters of the canal. Even the sea gulls and pigeons seemed to be in a torpor. The thunderstorm on the night Flavia was murdered hadn't broken the heat wave, but perhaps another one would. Only something violent could make a change. The city might then enjoy a few days of comfort before it once again became trapped under a glass bell of heat and humidity.

Urbino got off the gondola and walked slowly through San Polo toward the Palazzo Brollo. The canals were low, exposing the understructures of the buildings and giving glimpses of debris embedded in the sludge of the canal beds. Only flat-bottomed boats like gondolas and sandolos could negotiate these canals at low tide.

Several years ago the canal by the Palazzo Uccello had been drained, revealing all the refuse on the bottom. The odor had been unbearable, and Urbino had stayed at the Ca' da Capo-Zendrini until the work was finished. His housekeeper Natalia had covered her nose and mouth almost constantly with a scented handkerchief.

Annabella Brollo, smelling of stale sweat and anisette and with purple rings of fatigue beneath her eyes, showed Urbino up to the dark *sala* with its Oriental carpets, portraits in heavy wooden frames, and profusion of plants and flowers. This morning the long, narrow room seemed even more like an aqueous tomb than it had two days ago. The air, heavy with the scent of flowers, was even staler, as if the balcony doors hadn't been opened since then. Brollo must have finished *Little Dorrit,* for on the small, round table next to a fresh arrangement of crimson Cattleya orchids and the photograph of Brollo, Regina, and ten-year-old Flavia was *The Old Curiosity Shop.*

"I believe you have something that belongs to me, Signor Macintyre," Brollo said without preliminary. Dressed in his English blazer, cravat, and flannel slacks, he was seated on the

Louis Seize banquette near his wife's portrait. Urbino handed him the scrapbook and sat down in one of the armchairs.

"More than a little belated," Brollo said in his precise British English, running a palm over his bald crown. "I wonder what pleasure you get invading my daughter's privacy like that. Well, you might be relieved to know that I blame mainly Ladislao Mirko for this impropriety. It wasn't his business to give the scrapbook to you. He hasn't made a clear-minded decision in decades." Brollo tossed the scrapbook on the low table in front of the sofa. "I've also heard that you've been showing around some kind of postcard. Yes, Violetta told me. She might be only a sister-in-law but she has a devotion to the Brollos. And we Brollos still *are* a family—Annabella and I, sadly reduced though we are."

As delicately as possible, Urbino mentioned what Graziella Gnocato had said in reference to Regina Brollo's confidences to Flavia about Alvise da Capo-Zendrini.

"Mirko said that Flavia told him the same thing."

An effort at control was visible along Brollo's jawline.

"So this is what you were getting at the other day! I don't believe for a second that my wife said such a thing! You shouldn't trust the memory of an old woman, Signor Macintyre. She should be more careful than to malign a dead woman, a woman who, I might add, was always good to her and even provided for her in her will. As for that poor excuse for a man, Ladislao Mirko, it is beneath me to speculate about the possible motives of someone who is always high on one substance or another! He's ruined every business he's turned his hand to! He'll lose that pensione sooner or later and end up just like his father. As the French say, '*Tel père, tel*—'" Brollo declined to complete the adage, so similar to the one he had used two days ago about Flavia and her mother. He frowned. "Let me assure you of something, Signor Macintyre," he said, raising his voice slightly. "If you bother me anymore with questions such as these, I will inform the police. This is harassment. You are meddling in affairs that are no concern of yours. This is an affront, an invasion of our privacy!"

"The Contessa da Capo-Zendrini—"

"I don't care a fig for the Contessa da Capo-Zendrini and any crazy notions my poor daughter might have passed on to her or any fantasies either of you have about my daughter having been murdered! Now Violetta tells me that the two of you think that you've got proof of some kind just because none of that medication was found in my Flavia's body! You aren't seeing things clearly because you don't *want* to! Tell your friend that she will be much happier if she just accepts the truth—that my daughter was a disturbed young woman who ended up hurting people who loved her."

Brollo shook his head sadly.

"My daughter said many things that weren't true. I hesitate to call them lies only out of respect for her now that she's gone. Children can be very cruel to their parents. You are trying to find some silly intrigue here, Signor Macintyre. I tell you there is none. All this talk about Salvador Dalí and Yves Tanguy and tape recordings and pages ripped out of books! What do they have to do with me? Nothing! I'm not interested in looking for answers to every question that might trouble me in any one day. I'm not a stranger to grief and I know that—at least for *me*— when someone dies you have to let go of a great deal." His eyes flicked in the direction of his wife's portrait. "Guilt, the baggage of the past, suspicions, unanswered questions—they all have to go when you lose someone you love. Best to close the door on everything but the good memories and the things you know for sure. Regina was a good wife to me, the best she could be. If she ever hurt me, it was because of her illness—but she never hurt me in *that* way!"

Brollo sat back. But his eyes were softer now and, with his neat gray fringe of hair, for a moment he struck Urbino as a lapsed monk, as someone who remembered and regretted a better life. Involuntarily, Urbino's heart went out to this man who had lost his wife and his daughter—if Flavia had been, in fact, any flesh of his.

Brollo sighed deeply.

"I'll satisfy you on one score, Signor Macintyre. I'll tell you what I think of this Dalí painting. Violetta described it for me in more detail than I cared to hear. I've never seen it. My tastes are more traditional," he said, turning down his mouth in almost a parody of distaste. "My sister-in-law is an intelligent and talented woman, but perhaps she made a mistake in exposing my daughter to that kind of art at a vulnerable age. I would have preferred that Violetta had encouraged her along different lines. The Accademia Gallery is where she should have brought her. Why not give her a catalog of their Tintorettos and Giorgiones and Veroneses! The mind and the soul are inspired by great art!"

Urbino, who couldn't have agreed with Brollo more, once again felt a surge of understanding for the man, but it didn't deter him from posing another question that was bound to disturb him.

"Did your sister-in-law also tell you that I asked her about Lago di Garda—about an argument Mirko says he heard between you and Violetta in your wife's bedroom?"

Urbino asked the question just as Annabella entered the *sala* without a sound. He was happy to see that her tray didn't hold coffee and anisette on this sweltering day, but just two *spremute di limone*.

Brollo stiffened, but Annabella showed no response. She moved Flavia's scrapbook aside to make room for the tray and left as soundlessly as she had entered.

"Yes, Violetta told me, but no such argument ever took place, at Lago di Garda or anywhere else. Ladislao Mirko is always hearing voices, and when he isn't, he's spreading lies for his own advantage. Just ask yourself this question, Signor Macintyre: If you had a lovely, intelligent daughter with her life all before her, would you want her hanging around the likes of a Ladislao Mirko, someone just waiting to pull her down to his level, just waiting for his chance to do with her as he wanted? No!"

Beads of perspiration stood out on Brollo's slightly quivering upper lip. Urbino had just been given another example of the anger that Brollo was able to keep in check most of the time. Brollo took out a handkerchief and patted his lip.

"Your inquiries are an insult to me and my wife—and to our daughter," Brollo said, his voice now back under control.

Urbino expected to be asked to leave, without even having a chance to touch his lemonade, but Brollo, perhaps wanting him to go away only with the best impression of him, pulled his mouth into a thin-lipped smile.

"There's no need for all this quibbling," Brollo said in his clipped voice, with a transparent effort at downplaying the hostility that he obviously felt for Urbino. "Why don't we just sit here and drink our lemonades in a civilized manner, Signor Macintyre? Then I'll play something on the piano for you."

Brollo, with no attempt at transition, then began a quietly controlled tirade against the Biennale, making conversation unnecessary. He passed from this year's Biennale to the one two years ago, reserving most of his scorn for that exhibit's United States Pavilion.

"All those lights flashing those absolutely ridiculous statements. So pathetically American, excuse me, Signor Macintyre. I can still remember some of them. 'Romantic love was invented to manipulate women' and 'An elite is inevitable' and 'Expiring for love is beautiful but stupid'! I ask you, Signor Macintyre, are such things art?"

Brollo, pleased when Urbino made no effort to defend the exhibit, went to the piano and started to play a Mozart sonata. Under the spell of the sonata the discomforts of the hot dim room began to recede, and Urbino almost forgot the urgent questions that only Brollo might be able to answer.

Whatever kind of man Brollo was, he was a masterly pianist. The *sala* seemed magically transformed by wonderful waves of sound that were also somehow a bath of light flooding the room's darkest corners. Like some aged dryad charmed from a wood, Annabella emerged from the deeper recesses of the house and stood in the doorway listening, her arms crossed and an expression on her sharp face that was as much a sneer as a smile.

As Urbino continued to listen, however, something started to intrude on his enjoyment of the sonata. He was carried back to the Ponte degli Alpini in Bassano del Grappa, when the Contessa had pulled Flavia's scrapbook out of her Bottega Veneta bag like a rabbit out of a hat. Something had tugged at his memory then, and he was close now to knowing what it was. It had to do with Brollo's tirade against the electronic lines of text at the United States Pavilion at the last Biennale.

Urbino didn't trust Brollo. He was convinced that the man was lying about Flavia, but exactly how and why Urbino didn't know. It had something to do with Flavia's last meeting with this man who claimed she was his daughter. Once again, Urbino tried to imagine what had taken place that Thursday night between Lorenzo and Flavia and, a little later, between Lorenzo and Violetta—and also what Annabella's role might be in everything. These three might individually or together or in some combination, one with the other, have spun a web of intrigue that Flavia had become caught up in during her short life.

It was time for Urbino to leave. Annabella started to walk toward the staircase.

"Signor Macintyre can find his own way out, Annabella dear. You have to get ready for your doctor's appointment."

"I'll only be a minute, Lorenzo," she said quietly.

The other time Urbino had been at the Palazzo Brollo Lorenzo had urged the reluctant Annabella to accompany him to the door. This morning their roles seemed reversed.

Annabella didn't look at her brother as he stood uneasily in front of his wife's portrait. She went down the stairs silently with Urbino, casting a quick glance over her shoulder back up at the *sala*. She still said nothing as she opened the door for him.

When Urbino stepped out into the *calle*, however, she leaned toward him and whispered in a stifled voice, "He's lying to you! That's all he's ever done, lie! lie! lie!"

The smell of anisette hung between them in the hot, humid air.

"What do you mean? Lying about what?" Urbino asked in a low voice, sensing Brollo's presence at the top of the staircase.

Annabella stared at him through narrowed eyes. Urbino thought she was about to answer but she just kept on staring. He decided to try a different tack.

"Did you ever hear an argument at Lago di Garda the summer your sister-in-law died? An argument between Violetta Volpi and your brother?"

"I've heard many arguments in my life, signore," she said slyly. "Flavia was usually the one who made the most noise." She found this amusing and started to laugh. "Maybe you should be asking about arguments Flavia herself had not too long before she died."

"What do you mean?"

"I mean the one she had with her boyfriend's art dealer, the same dealer that Violetta has. What's his name? Massimo Zuin?"

"When did this happen?"

"Three weeks ago. I was on my way to see a friend near the Casa Trieste, the pensione of Flavia's friend. Flavia was standing at the open door with Zuin. She was very upset."

"What did she say?"

"Something like 'You'll have to kill me to keep me away from him, but thanks for the money anyway. I'll put it to good use.' Massimo Zuin cursed her and stormed past me. Neither of them saw me. I haven't mentioned it to anyone before, even though I knew it must be important, what with Flavia dead and all." She smiled mischievously. "I know I should have. I've been naughty."

"You should have told the police."

There was more amusement than fear or guilt in Annabella's blue, bloodshot eyes.

"Perhaps," she answered.

"Is there anything else you know or might have overheard that could be important? Like an argument at Lago di Garda?"

Urbino thought he heard the click of the intercom above the bell push. Annabella held up a thin finger against her lips, reminding Urbino of the woman in Odilon Redon's painting *Silence*. Then, with a cold smile, Annabella put her thumb and forefinger together and twisted them against her lips. She closed the door quietly and firmly behind her.

Urbino stood there in the deserted little square for a few minutes, looking up at the wicker basket tied to the balcony and the closed shutters of the Palazzo Brollo. It was difficult to imagine Lorenzo Brollo ever leaving his domain, although surely he must. The Palazzo Brollo was very much a world closed in on itself, now inhabited by only an unmarried sister and her widowed brother who had just lost the young woman who might or might not have been his daughter. Flavia had been determined to escape from her father's house—from the profusion of plants and flowers tended by her aunt, from the icy control exercised by the man who insisted he was her father. Urbino could understand why Flavia had preferred to live in a room at the Casa Trieste, why she had felt more at home at Villa Pippa with Madge Lennox.

Something about the Palazzo Brollo reminded Urbino of the Hennepin residence in the Garden District in New Orleans. The Hennepin mansion, despite its high, wide porches and annual coat of fresh white paint, had always seemed turned in on itself, too—a closed, hothouse world. Urbino had been admitted, obligingly if not warmly, but the Hennepins—mainly Evangeline's father, Emile, the so-called "Sugar Cane King"— had wanted Urbino to close the door behind him and to leave much of his own world on the other side. Evangeline herself, out of weakness, had ultimately wanted him to do the same.

As Urbino left the little square and walked in the direction of the Casa Trieste, he replayed his visit to Lorenzo Brollo. The pianist had denied any knowledge of the Dalí, his wife Regina's confidences to Flavia, or the Lago di Garda argument, but had Urbino really expected anything different? Urbino had come to understand that denials and silences and giving answers un- related to questions asked could often be more revealing than an hour of tearful confession.

How was Urbino to interpret Annabella Brollo? He could understand why Flavia and Tina had joked about her being a witch when they were girls. There was something out of focus about her, and he suspected it wasn't just the anisette she seemed to drink like baby's milk. How much could he believe her? Not only had she accused her brother of being a liar, but she had also pointed a finger at Massimo Zuin. Urbino thought he knew what the argument between Flavia and Zuin had been about—Zuin's star artist, Bruno Novembrini. It was fairly clear that money had changed hands, perhaps a very large sum. Urbino would have to speak with Massimo Zuin.

When Urbino reached the *calli* on the other side of Campo Giacomo dell'Orio, the crowds thickened. Usually he preferred to be solitary, but this late morning, with the experience of the Palazzo Brollo so disturbingly fresh in his mind, he was happy to be among people who seemed troubled by nothing more than where they would go for lunch. He stopped in a bustling trattoria and had a plate of risotto and half a carafe of wine. He wasn't all that hungry, but he felt that he wanted to do something that affirmed life. What better way than eating?

No sooner did he think this than he thought of another way: sex. But because of Urbino's obsession with Flavia Brollo's murder, his mind didn't rest there but inevitably flowed on to the final destination in this world of stone and water, dreams and desires—death.

It was as if he saw the two words embracing there in front of his eyes as he looked through the windows of the trattoria.

Sex and death. Those had been the words he had spoken out loud on the Ponte degli Alpini, taking the Contessa by surprise.

Now, here in the trattoria, surrounded by the boisterous diners around him, Urbino realized what had been teasing his mind since that moment on the Ponte degli Alpini. It was as neon-bright as the sign in the trattoria window. It was a phrase that had flashed in electronic text before his eyes at the last Biennale, part of the disorienting barrage that had driven the Contessa from the exhibit room like Mrs. Moore from the Marabar Caves.

FATHERS OFTEN USE TOO MUCH FORCE

Lorenzo Brollo hadn't mentioned this particular phrase from the exhibit he had despised. And neither had he mentioned two others that also burned their way into Urbino's mind now in the busy trattoria:

MURDER HAS ITS SEXUAL SIDE
EVEN YOUR FAMILY CAN BETRAY YOU

4

"BROLLO TOOK FLAVIA'S stuff," Mirko said as he sprawled on the threadbare sofa at the Casa Trieste. He was wearing his woolen skullcap and a green kimonolike robe, and he kept jiggling his foot. In the hall outside, a small, dark woman about forty was sweeping the floor. "He came a few hours after you left with a big brute of a guy. I kept some things for myself, though. This is hers"—Mirko indicated the robe—"but I always wore it more than she did."

The robe must have made him feel close to Flavia.

"What else? Did Flavia leave any money here? Did you give it to Brollo?"

Mirko shot him a quick look. The scratch was still faintly visible on his cheek.

"Money? What money did she ever have? She lived mainly on handouts from Violetta and Bernardo. And didn't I already tell you I never took any money for her room! Listen! Are you spying for Lorenzo or something? He gave me hell about the scrapbook. Swore up and down, said that he could get me in trouble with my license. All I kept was this robe and that book over there."

He indicated the biography of Eleonora Duse on the table.

"About the scrapbook," Urbino said. "Things were missing. Some clippings with photographs—photographs of the Conte and Contessa da Capo-Zendrini—maybe some other items as well."

Mirko seemed genuinely surprised.

"I remember a lot of clippings with photographs," Mirko said, running a finger under his nose. "Flavia pointed out some of the Conte once. There was one with his wife and another with several men. The Conte had his arm around the shoulders of a little man with round glasses. So those clippings were missing? I guess Flavia took them out."

"But you don't know for sure?"

"Of course not, but who else would have done it? You don't think I did, do you? There are plenty of people who come in and out of here."

"Didn't you put it in the safe?"

Mirko's foot stopped jiggling and a veiled look came into his eyes.

"Maybe I should have, but I didn't think it was anything valuable."

The cleaning woman peeked around the door. She looked nervous.

"Excuse me for interrupting, Signor Mirko, but I couldn't help hearing what you said. There was a strange old man in the parlor here on Tuesday afternoon when you were out. As old as Methuselah, he was. Must have been let in by one of the guests. Said he was looking for a room but that he didn't think this was the kind of place for him. I don't know how long he was here. I was cleaning one of the rooms upstairs. He left right after I came down."

"Why didn't you tell me, Agata?"

Mirko was obviously angry with her.

"I—I'm sorry, Signor Mirko. You were at the Questura with the registration slips and I left before you got back. I forgot all about it till now. I hope I haven't done anything wrong."

"It's all right, Agata," Urbino said. Mirko looked at him sharply, as if it wasn't his place to excuse the woman for her laxness. "Exactly what did this man look like?"

"Very small and thin—and old, as I said—maybe as old as eighty, but he had a lot of energy. I hope I have his energy if I get to be his age."

It sounded like Silvestro Occhipinti. Agata said the man had come to the Casa Trieste on Tuesday, the day Urbino was sure he had seen Occhipinti crossing the bridge in San Polo. Tuesday was also the day he had been mugged.

After Agata left, Mirko remained silent for a few moments. Then, barely able to control his irritation, he said, "Does this old man sound like someone you know?"

"No," Urbino lied.

"Well, do you think he could have taken those clippings from Flavia's scrapbook?"

"It's possible. Did you notice a reproduction of a painting by Salvador Dalí in the scrapbook? It was on a page torn from the Guggenheim catalog."

Mirko got up and went behind the table that stood in front of the curtain drawn across his private quarters. He opened a drawer and took something out.

"*This* page?" He handed Urbino the missing catalog page. "Flavia gave it to me two or three years ago."

After examining the page and seeing that there were no marks or writing on it, Urbino handed it back to Mirko.

"Why?"

"Because she knew I liked it. I don't mean the painting you're talking about—but the one on the other side. The one by Yves Tanguy. Ever since I was a teenager I liked his stuff. It looks like things I used to see in my own head when I was—was 'expanding my consciousness,' as we used to say back then! Before Flavia's mother died we used to go to the Guggenheim, sometimes with Tina Zuin. They would go to look at the Dalí. I would look at this one here"—he pointed to Tanguy's *The Sun in Its Casket*—"and the three or four other ones they have by

Tanguy. I felt as if I were on a trip! He was probably on some-thing when he painted them!"

"I'm surprised that you didn't tell me about it when I was looking at the catalog."

"Don't try to make anything of it, Macintyre!" Mirko slapped the page down on the cluttered desk. "I didn't even think about it at the time."

"That's hard to believe."

"Hard to believe or not, it's the truth!"

It was completely possible, Urbino supposed, that a mind clouded by drugs could have forgotten about the missing page. What had Brollo said? That Mirko had probably not made a clear-minded decision in decades?

"Do you still have the catalog?"

"I told you that Brollo took just about everything."

Mirko gave Urbino a resentful glare, furtive and sullen.

"Is there anything else you haven't told me?" Urbino asked. "It's in your best interests to tell me everything you know."

"What the hell do you mean by that? I've got nothing to hide! I've been up-front with you. My God! Brollo comes here like he owns the place and throws all this money at me. I took it. I'm no fool. Brollo says the money's for Flavia, but I could tell he wanted me to keep my mouth shut. Even if I hadn't already told you what I know, I would tell you everything now no matter if Brollo likes it or not! Listen, Macintyre. All this hasn't been easy on me, you know. I cared for Flavia. I loved her."

Tears seldom make a person more attractive and Mirko, homely to begin with, was no exception. He took out a handker-chief.

"She was the only person who really cared for me. The only one! Do you know what that means to someone like me?"

Mirko wiped his face. He shrugged and gave an embar-rassed smile.

"I know what I look like, Macintyre. And I know what people think of me. When you're not attractive, they treat you differently. It's as if you're living on a separate planet. But Flavia made me feel special. Now all I have is this."

He threw out his thin arms, indicating the walls of his pensione. His face clouded, and he lowered his arms. What schemes had Mirko been involved in to keep his pensione solvent and to keep himself supplied with drugs? Urbino thought of Flavia and the money she had got from Massimo Zuin.

"Is Annabella Brollo a frequent visitor here?" Urbino asked suddenly.

"Annabella Brollo? Why should she come here? Flavia never got along with her."

"Not to see Flavia. To see you. She was slipping into the pensione when I was leaving the first time I came here."

"Well, maybe she did come that day, but it was the first and only time."

"I don't think so. I think she comes very often. She just told me that she overheard an argument between Flavia and Massimo Zuin at the door of the pensione. Do you know anything about it?"

Mirko seemed genuinely puzzled, screwing up his thin, ugly face. He dabbed at the end of his nose with the handkerchief.

"The only argument I ever overheard that had to do with Flavia was the one at Lago di Garda, and I've already told you about it. If Flavia and Massimo Zuin had some words together, I never heard them. Maybe I was at the Questura with the registration slips. Flavia never mentioned it to me."

"Why does Annabella Brollo come here?"

"She—she wants things from me. Something to help her sleep. She has insomnia. I give her some of my sleeping pills. Don't get me in trouble, please," the man pleaded. "It's nothing more than that."

"I'm not interested in what pills you might have given Annabella Brollo. But speaking of pills, what about the ones the police found here among Flavia's things?"

"What about them? I've already told you that I don't know where she got them."

"Didn't she get them from you?"

"From me? You're crazy! It must have been some doctor."

"Perhaps. Did you ever see her take any of those pills?"

"See her?" Mirko looked confused. "People don't always take their medication in front of other people."

"True enough."

In the silence that followed, Mirko seemed pensive, as if he were weighing various possibilities.

"You're trying to get me into trouble," Mirko eventually

said with a sniffle. "Even the suspicion that I could have had anything to do with those pills Flavia was taking could make things rough for me. I can't get into any trouble about drugs. You understand that, don't you?"

"I would think that you'd be more careful, Signor Mirko, especially after what happened to your father. Yes, I know how he died. Drugs can be dangerous."

The fear in Mirko's face seemed more genuine now than it had a few moments before. Urbino stared at him. Gradually, the fear was replaced by a lopsided smile, exposing his yellowed teeth. Despite the smile, however, there was still a guarded look to Mirko's face.

"I'm as careful as I can be, Signor Macintyre. We all have our little vices, no?"

For a few brief seconds Mirko looked like a mischievous urchin. Tina Zuin had said that Mirko could be charming in his own way, and perhaps he had been ten years ago when she had dated him.

When Urbino asked Mirko if he knew that Tina Zuin and Bruno Novembrini were having a relationship, Mirko seemed relieved at the change of topic.

"Sure," Mirko said. "It just goes to show you what a bastard that Novembrini is. They were probably even carrying on when Flavia and Novembrini were together."

"Did you give Flavia advice about her relationships?"

Again Mirko gave his crooked smile.

"Like brotherly advice? I suppose I couldn't help it."

Urbino tried to detect something other than fraternal affection in Mirko's face before Mirko took his handkerchief from the pocket of Flavia's robe again and wiped his nose.

5

AFTER LEAVING THE Casa Trieste, Urbino set out for the Danieli Hotel. He had promised to help Eugene move to the seclusion

of the Cipriani Hotel on the Island of Giudecca for the last few
days of his stay.

On his walk through the thronged *calli,* Urbino thought
about Ladislao Mirko, Occhipinti, and the Lago di Garda argument.

Mirko's fear could almost be smelled like the rancid odor
the man threw off, but was it fear of getting into trouble
with the police because of drugs? If that happened, he could lose
the Casa Trieste. Who knew? Maybe his drug habit had already
seriously endangered his pensione and he was hanging on by
only his dirty fingernails. Brollo had said that Flavia had given
Mirko money. Could Mirko be feeling the pinch more now that
Flavia was dead—and, with her, her generosity? There was still
the question of the money that Zuin had given Flavia. Had
Flavia given it all to Tina and the Riccis? Brollo had given Mirko
a large sum, ostensibly for Flavia's expenses, but Mirko said he
had been trying to buy his silence. If Brollo had, were there
other things Mirko could tell him about Brollo that he hadn't
told him yet?

Then there was Silvestro Occhipinti. He wasn't a complete
innocent in this matter of Flavia's murder. Urbino now knew
one of the things Alvise's old friend was hiding—a visit to the
Casa Trieste after Flavia's death. Agata had described a man
who was either Occhipinti or someone who looked and acted
very much like him.

Had Occhipinti taken the clippings of himself and Alvise
from Flavia's scrapbook? Perhaps he had gone to the pensione
more than once. Occhipinti had been in Venice at the time of
Flavia's death and, considering his cold, he might very well have
been out in the storm on the last night she had been seen alive.

It would be a double blow to the Contessa to have to face
both Occhipinti's villainy, no matter what the motive, and Alvise's betrayal. Although the argument at Lago di Garda and
Graziella Gnocato's revelation of what Regina Brollo had told
Flavia about Alvise in no way came close to proving that the
Conte was Flavia's father, they didn't disprove it either. How
far would Occhipinti go in protecting Barbara and Alvise's reputation?

As Urbino waited for Eugene in the Danieli bar with its
smell of leather and its air of expensive comfort, he went over
the argument that Mirko said he and Flavia had overheard at

Lago di Garda: Violetta's challenge to Brollo to face reality and admit that Flavia wasn't his daughter. The mention of Alvise's name. Regina's cry of despair. Brollo's rejection of Violetta. The slap.

Yes, the slap. But who had slapped whom? Mirko had assumed that Brollo slapped Violetta, but perhaps Regina had slapped her, or one of the women had slapped Brollo. Or Brollo had slapped his wife. Mirko could be telling the truth but only the truth as he had *heard* it, not as he had seen it. There could be a big difference.

Not long after the Lago di Garda argument, Regina had killed herself. More than ten years later her daughter was murdered.

It made sense that Regina would have confided in her sister about Alvise, especially since Violetta had once gone out with him. Regina might even have taunted her sister with it, making Violetta furious enough to reveal everything to Lorenzo. According to Graziella Gnocato, Violetta often used to rave against the Contessa. Now, however, Violetta was keeping her silence. Perhaps her desire to have revenge upon the Contessa was weaker than her fear of Lorenzo.

Urbino could understand fearing Brollo. The man was in control, yes, but once he let himself go, it could be violent. "Fathers often use too much force," Urbino repeated to himself.

He had to talk with Annabella. She had been living in the Palazzo Brollo since Regina had killed herself. Surely she could tell him about Flavia's life behind those forbidding walls. Hadn't she already said, at the door of the Palazzo Brollo, that her brother was lying—that, in fact, he always lied? If he could unlock her lips, what could they tell him?

6

EUGENE HAD SAID he would be satisfied with nothing less than a gondola to the Cipriani, so here they were being rowed across the stretch of water between the Doge's Palace and the Island of Giudecca. For part of the distance they were accompanied, almost stroke for stroke, by another gondola with a reclining couple being serenaded by a dark little man with a mandolin.

But for the rest of the trip their gondola was like a black swan among Leviathans as it made its way to the Cipriani at the tip of the Island of Giudecca. Eugene's face became tense whenever they were washed by the wake of a boat, but he said nothing and pretended to be enjoying every minute of it.

Urbino felt a little like a pasha against plump Oriental cushions and fantasized about being rowed to a remote part of the lagoon, far away from the madness of high-season Venice and the swirl of questions surrounding Flavia's life and death. Perhaps when this business about Flavia and Alvise was all over, in whatever way it might happen, he could redeem the summer in Asolo with the Contessa, who might need his companionship more than ever. They could take day trips throughout the Veneto in her Bentley, haunt the Caffè Centrale, and seclude themselves in her gardens for long, restorative afternoons.

"Summer afternoon," "summer afternoon," this phrase echoed in Urbino's mind as the gondola slid through the water toward the Cipriani. These were the words that Henry James had said were among the most lovely in the English language, and they floated Urbino back to the long, sultry summer afternoons of his life back in New Orleans when so much had seemed right with the world.

Evangeline and he had had some of their best days together during summer—outings to Lake Pontchartrain, a riverboat cruise up to St. Louis, languorous weeks at the plantation house of Evangeline's *marraine*, or godmother, in the hills near Baton Rouge. Yes, summers had been the happy times, all too soon replaced by the less than idyllic and much more protracted ones of the tug-of-war over whether Urbino would join the Hennepin family business. Evangeline wanted him to prove to her father that he wasn't the dilettante that the Sugar Cane King feared he was. He should leave his position as an editor at Louisiana State University Press. Emile could find a place for him in whatever part of the Hennepin business Urbino wanted to turn his hand to—perhaps public relations or personnel.

Urbino had known, however, that, whatever the position,

it wouldn't have been the place he wanted for himself. Not only would he have been more bound to the Hennepins, but Evangeline would never have had a chance of separating herself from their somewhat baleful influence. Eugene had escaped it, or maybe it was more exact to say that he had comfortably adapted to it. But Evangeline, even if she hadn't quite realized it herself, needed a different life apart from them, and Urbino had hoped to provide it for them both.

But why think of the difficult times, he told himself now, as he sank more deeply into the gondola chair? Why not remember days very much like this one when problems had seemed far, far away even if they were only around the next turning?

Eugene broke into Urbino's thoughts with startling appropriateness.

"We haven't talked about Evangeline for a while, Urbino," he said. "I hope you've been givin' her some thought. She's not a bad sort. She's kept a picture of you all these years and goes kind of soft in the face when she looks at it. I know you're in a fret about this dead woman but time is gettin' short. Evangeline and I will have to be movin' on. I was just talkin' to her in Florence and she said that she was dyin' to come to Venice but won't lay a foot in the city unless you give her the go-ahead."

"She doesn't need my permission to come, Eugene."

"Now you know very well what she meant, so don't go pretendin' you don't! She just wants to know that you welcome her. What's wrong with that, I ask you? She's said good-bye to bein' pushy. She's my own flesh-and-blood sister but I know how she used to be. She's a changed woman these days, Urbino. She looks as good as ever but she's got a changed heart. I'd like nothin' better than for you to see for yourself. I'm just tryin' to be an enablin' factor. So what do you say? Give old Evie the word and she'll be here lickety-split. Even Countess Barbara thinks you're bein' kind of mopey about the whole thing. Her advice was not to push you. I don't agree. From what I remember, half the time you would never have budged but for a little push. Do you remember the time up in Natchez when you, me, and Evie—" Eugene said, beginning a long reminiscence that took them the rest of the distance across the Basin of San Marco to the Cipriani landing.

When Eugene had finished and they were getting out of

the boat, however, he hadn't forgotten what had set him off in the first place. He asked Urbino again to decide if and when Evangeline could come to Venice for a quiet little get-together for old times' sake.

"No strings attached, Urbino."

Urbino didn't believe this, but surprised himself by saying, without having made any decision that he could consciously remember, "All right, Eugene. Why not have Evangeline join you in a day or two?"

Urbino suspected that all the apparently unresolved history and unanswered questions of the Brollos and the Contessa and Alvise were lurking behind his decision.

"Yes," Urbino said again as they went into the Cipriani lobby. "Tell her to come. We can make a reservation for her at the Cipriani right now."

"Of course, Urbino! You didn't think Evie or I presumed she'd be stayin' with you, did you? Not yet anyway," Eugene said with a laugh, leaving Urbino with the feeling that he very well might have made the wrong decision after all.

7

WHEN URBINO LEFT Eugene at the Cipriani Hotel at two, he knew that Zuin's gallery would be closed for a few more hours. He went back to the Palazzo Uccello and called the Contessa to give her his suspicions about Occhipinti.

"I insist that you let me talk to Silvestro," the Contessa said. "I might be able to find out what he's hiding. There are things you can do there. Besides, you have Eugene."

Ah yes, Eugene, Urbino thought—and also Evangeline within the next few days. He had yet to tell the Contessa about that.

"But, Barbara, Silvestro might be withholding information not because of you and Alvise but because of himself."

"You mean the poor little man might be immobilized between wanting to give me proof that Alvise *wasn't* Flavia's father and not wanting to incriminate himself? But that would mean that—that *he* was Flavia's father! Or that *he* had pushed her into the Grand Canal! How ridiculous!"

"Ridiculous or not, Barbara, be careful. He'd never do anything to hurt you, I'm sure, but don't forget that one of the clippings contained *his* picture as well as Alvise's. And I'm pretty sure I saw him in Venice on Tuesday and that he was at the Casa Trieste.

"I can depend on Silvestro's honesty more than I can your eyes, *caro*! At any rate, do you really believe that silliness about criminals revisiting the scene of the crime? If you do, then what about Madge Lennox?" she asked sharply, revealing once again her antipathy to the retired actress. "Maybe you should be looking into *her* affairs instead of Silvestro's. She says she was in Milan when Flavia died, but how do we know she traveled on to Milan when she got to Venice with Flavia? She could have waited until the girl left the station and stalked her!"

Urbino's mind started to wander as he thought about Madge Lennox. He was pulled back into what the Contessa was saying, however, when she mentioned the clinic outside Milan that Graziella Gnocato had named—where Regina Brollo had gone to give birth to Flavia twenty-six years ago.

"I did what I could, *caro*, just as I promised. Dear Corrado helped me again, bless the man, but there's no record of Regina Brollo having been at the clinic. The woman that Corrado put me in touch with has been there since the early sixties. She said they lost some records and drugs from a break-in a few years after she started to work there, but she does vaguely remember the Brollo name. I tried my best, but that's all I came up with."

Urbino commended her on her sleuthing. If this case hadn't so directly involved her, he would have liked both of them to have interviewed some of the suspects together. Her perspective was one that he valued above anyone else's.

"As I've told you before, Urbino, I just don't feel easy about putting so much faith in the words of a possibly senile old woman and a man who's probably always in an opium trance or something! Maybe Mirko *thinks* he heard that argument at Lago di Garda and convinced Flavia that she did, too. They might have taken opium together! Friendship is a fine and beautiful thing—look at Alvise and Silvestro! look at you and me!—But when you put a beautiful girl like Flavia together with someone like Mirko, you're bound to find the Mirkos of this world yearning for more than friendship."

"Couldn't it also be the other way around, Barbara?" Urbino asked, disagreeing with her so as to get her reaction. "Maybe it was Flavia who yearned for more."

The Contessa's response was a healthy laugh.

"I think I know where that idea comes from, *caro*! I mean Evangeline Hennepin Macintyre and whatever her name is now. *I've* seen the sweet girl's photograph. Not exactly a Flavia Brollo, no—but very attractive *and* very determined-looking. You're thinking of *her* yearnings, aren't you?"

So far was it from what he *had* been thinking about Flavia and Ladislao Mirko—and yet so close to what he hadn't yet told her—that for a few moments he didn't know what to say.

"Not that I think you might share anything with the drug-crazed and homely Mirko except the possibility of his having been pursued. He, too, might have wanted to run as far in the opposite direction as he could, although I doubt it."

With not a little satisfaction, Urbino finally broke his silence to tell the Contessa that she was, in the matter of Evangeline, completely wrong—at least as of that afternoon. He wasn't running any longer.

"I told Eugene that I'd like to see her. She'll be here soon."

"By whatever twisted logic or guilt did you come to that decision, *caro*? I don't know whether to be proud or appalled that you decided all by yourself—without *me*, I mean. I think your decision has something to do with Flavia Brollo."

"And in what way would that be?" Urbino asked. Hadn't he been thinking something similar in the gondola across the lagoon to the Cipriani Hotel?

"I wouldn't embarrass either of us by daring to bring it to my lips. Good-bye!"

8

AFTER SEVERAL CUPS OF COFFEE, a shower, and a change of clothes, Urbino went to Zuin's gallery. Urbino ignored Zuin's look of surprised annoyance and immediately brought up the argument Zuin had had with Flavia at the Casa Trieste before her death. When something seemed to collapse in Zuin, Urbino realized that Annabella Brollo had told him the truth.

"Sit down," Zuin said in an unnaturally low voice. He sat across from Urbino. "How did you find out?"

"That's not important. You went to see Flavia to convince her to stay away from Novembrini, didn't you? You even gave her a large sum of money. Did you know that she gave some of it back to your daughter Tina to help her set up her apartment?"

"Tina?" A pained look passed over his lined face. "I don't deny I went there to talk with Flavia—and yes, I gave her money—a lot of it. Ten million lire." About eight thousand dollars. "It was my commission from the sale of some of Bruno's paintings. I know it was a lot of money but I thought that if I could get rid of Flavia—I mean, if I could get her to stop being a thorn in Bruno's side—then he'd be a lot happier and productive and make that amount for me ten times over. Bruno didn't know about anything. He still doesn't. I wouldn't want him to know—or Tina either. I know it wasn't the right thing to do."

"When did you realize that? Before or after Flavia was found dead? I advise you to go to the Questura and tell them about this whole thing."

"Listen here, Macintyre," Zuin said, standing up. "I had nothing to do with Flavia's death! I just told her it would be best if she stayed away from Bruno—and best for Bruno, too! She just took it as a big joke, made me feel like a fool, said she'd keep the money and decide what she wanted to do with it and with herself. Everyone's made a mistake about her. She was strong and could take care of herself."

"But she *was* murdered."

Fear crossed the man's face, and he ran his hand through the long gray hair at the nape of his neck. He sat down heavily.

"But who would want to murder Flavia?"

Any number of people, Urbino answered him silently. Zuin looked at him. Urbino still said nothing as he waited to see whom the art dealer would defend first—his daughter Tina or Novembrini.

When he had finished, Urbino was fairly certain that, despite the lies and maneuverings of Zuin, Novembrini, and perhaps even Tina, none of them was Flavia's murderer. This wasn't the same thing as saying, however, that they hadn't unwittingly played a role in her death.

Before Urbino left Zuin, he asked him one more question.

"Eugene said that someone else was bidding against Novembrini's painting of Flavia. Who was it?"

When Zuin named the person, Urbino nodded his head. It made perfect sense. Who else, indeed?

9

ON SATURDAY MORNING Urbino and Eugene took their postponed outing to Burano. It was a full week since Flavia's body had surfaced at the Palazzo Guggenheim. Urbino thought that a change of scene away from Venice and Asolo, both of them associated as they were with Flavia and his investigations, might do him some good. It might help clear his mind and perhaps bring him closer to seeing the pattern he knew was there in Flavia's death.

Burano, with its pastel houses and little canals, its decorated boats and draped fishing nets, never failed to lift Urbino's spirits. Eugene wasn't immune to its attractions either, having said several times within the first hour of their arrival that it was "as pretty as a picture." He had already bought a fistful of postcards and a pile of decorative place mats, but the purchases had in no way taken the edge off his appetite for things more expensive.

"Oh, look, there's another little old lady sewin' away or tattin' or whatever you call lacemakin'. See if *she* has some."

By "some," Eugene meant four matching lace fans that "*looked* old." He didn't want any real antique fans—not, he emphasized, because he was unwilling to pay the price but because they might fall apart when May-Foy, his two daughters, and Evangeline used them. Urbino and Eugene had already approached half a dozen women and looked at a large assortment of fans, but Eugene hadn't found any to suit him.

The woman Eugene had drawn Urbino's attention to was sitting in a chair in front of a lemon-yellow house. She could have been any one of the other lacemakers they had already tried to do business with. It wasn't only that she was typical of the rest. It was something more—something that struck to the heart of what Urbino considered the essential inbred quality of this lagoon island. He suspected that families had a long tradition of intermarrying with not-too-distant cousins. He saw it in the faces as well as the infirmities—there was a considerable percentage of cripples, for one thing. It was only his little theory, however, one which he had never tried to verify.

This particular Buranella lacemaker was in her seventies, with pure white hair pulled completely back from a round face. She wore a black dress, small pearl earrings and, of course, glasses, for none of the women seemed to escape years at their skill without damaging their eyesight. A *tombolo* cushion was on her lap to help her with the lacemaking. Another cushion supported the small of her back. Her feet, shod in low black shoes, were propped on a stool.

Unlike the other lacemakers they had met today, she spoke English. Eugene was happy to be able to speak with her directly rather than through Urbino, whom he somehow blamed for not having yet found the fans. Urbino left Eugene to his negotiations while he wandered a short distance on his own, telling Eugene to call him if he needed any help or wanted his opinion.

Urbino ducked under a line of laundry strung across the little square on the canal. White lace curtains billowed from the windows of a fuchsia house and gave glimpses of a woman, almost a replica of the others, bent over her work.

Although Urbino had hoped for a respite from thoughts about Flavia here on Burano, he now found himself plunged into them once again. His thoughts were not unlike the forms in *The Sun in Its Casket*, the Tanguy at the Guggenheim— amorphous, deliquescent, fluid, teasing him with an elusive meaning. So much seemed at the point of coming together, but not quite yet.

Perhaps what was making things difficult, Urbino thought, was that Flavia's murder could have resulted from not just one strand in her life but from the disastrous knitting together of several on that crucial last night she was seen alive. Urbino's intuition, something he trusted almost as much as his intellect, was sounding the alarm almost as loudly as a fire bell. He had been going mainly under the assumption that a variation of the cliché *"Cherchez la femme"*—in this case, *"Cherchez le père"*—would lead him to Flavia's murderer. He wasn't so sure about this now, but he did believe that the more he continued to learn about Flavia, the more tightly he would close in on the person who had seen no choice but to murder her. He hoped he would be able to identify who it was before the person might strike again.

"Urbino, where have you disappeared to? What do you think of this?"

Urbino rejoined Eugene and the old lacemaker. Eugene was examining a pink lace parasol.

"She don't have any fans but maybe this will be nice for May-Foy. Don't know if it'll do much good in the hot Louisiana sun but May-Foy will get a kick out of just carryin' it around. Maybe she can use it for Mardi Gras. I think I'll take it."

After Eugene bought the parasol, they sat at an outside table at a restaurant on Via Baldassare Galuppi. It was perhaps inevitable that Urbino's thoughts now took the turn they did as he watched the crowds pass on this main thoroughfare, only half listening to Eugene run on about the leaning campanile. Because the street was named after the Buranello composer who was the subject of Robert Browning's *Toccata of Galuppi's*, Urbino started thinking of Occhipinti. The verses from the poem that Occhipinti had perplexed Madge Lennox with last week at the Contessa's garden party came back to Urbino. The verses had him thinking of not only Occhipinti and Lennox but especially the two dead Brollo women, Regina and Flavia, mother and daughter. How did they go?

> Dear dead women, with such hair too—what's become
>   of all the gold.
> Used to hang and brush their bosoms? I feel chilly
>   and grown old.

Eugene turned to stare at Urbino.

"Hold on there, boy!" Eugene said loudly. "Talkin' to your-self again, are you? That's what comes of livin' alone. If you only had someone besides that pussycat of yours—"

And Eugene now launched into a diatribe against Urbino's solitary existence, the point of which was that Urbino was going to have a wonderful reunion with the long-lost Evangeline.

10

URBINO SPENT THE next morning under an umbrella on the Cipriani terrace gazing off at the Church of San Giorgio Mag-giore and watching Eugene disporting in the pool. Every ten or fifteen minutes Eugene burst into a stream of raillery to induce Urbino to get out of his street clothes, put on a bathing suit, and join him in the pool. Urbino remained where he was, sipping his Bellinis. Although the exercise would be good for him, he was too distracted by thoughts about Flavia to want to do anything but stay where he was for a while longer.

After a buffet lunch Urbino took Eugene to the Scuola Grande di San Teodoro near the Rialto Bridge where there was an exhibit of Dalí's sculptures and illustrations. Urbino vaguely hoped that the exhibit might provide some insight into Flavia. Near the entrance was a sculpture of a huge flesh-colored tongue, a woman's lips, and a nose that was also a painted clock forever telling the hour of five to one.

Eugene pointed to a fire extinguisher nearby.

"Good idea that," he said. "Must be quite a few people who end up settin' these kind of things on fire."

Shaking his head, Eugene went over to a bronze sculpture of an extremely long-necked Venus with a small, pullout drawer for her bosom and a deeper drawer for her stomach, all resting on a U-shaped stand.

"I ask you, Urbino—what's the point? You're supposed to know about these things. I liked the *Liquid* picture at that Guggenheim gal's place—or I *think* I did—but these just leave me feelin' they're a joke I'll never understand even if I live as long as Sylvester!"

Fortunately Eugene didn't wait for Urbino to try to comment on the Venus but went over to a group of paintings.

"My God, Urbino, look at *this* one," Eugene almost shouted. "Just listen to this here title: *My Nude Wife Contemplatin' Her Own Flesh Becomin' Stairs, Three Vertebrae of a Column, Sky and Architecture*. Now ain't *that* a mouthful!"

Several people turned in Eugene's direction. A woman's raspy voice said in Italian, "Why do people like that even bother to come to a Dalí exhibit?"

Urbino was surprised to find that the speaker was Violetta Volpi—and the recipient of her comment Bernardo, who was sitting in a wheelchair. Violetta must have brought her husband on an outing—one, Urbino assumed, of her own choosing.

Violetta and Bernardo were in front of Dalí's *Lady with Head of Roses*, a silk screen that reproduced an original 1935 painting. The woman with the flowers covering her head was immediately suggestive of the young woman in the white dress in *The Birth of Liquid Desires*, which had been painted several years before.

"Signor Macintyre," Violetta Volpi said when she saw Urbino. Bernardo didn't even look in his direction. "What a surprise! Are you here to refine your appreciation for Dalí?" She nodded toward Eugene, who was bending over to get a better view of the painting he had just described so loudly. "Can you imagine such people!" She shook her head.

"Actually, Signora Volpi, the gentleman is with me," Urbino said, feeling strangely gratified to admit his association with Eugene.

"I see. It seems that he has something in common with Bernardo. He's not enjoying the Dalís as much as we expected, are you, dear?" Bernardo made no response but continued to stare blankly at the *Lady with Head of Roses*.

Eugene came up and Urbino made the introductions.

"I don't take to any of these paintings here," Eugene explained to Violetta, "but I kind of like the *Liquid* picture at the palazzo with the top chopped off. Do you know it, ma'am?"

"Yes, I do," Violetta said, speaking in almost accentless English. "It's one of my favorites."

"Wanted to buy it, but Urbino here said it wasn't for sale. Had to settle for a measly little postcard."

"How interesting," Violetta said.

Eugene started to talk to Bernardo about Dalí's "cockeyed view of things," finding Bernardo the best audience possible since the man, as usual, made no response. Violetta drew Urbino to one side.

"My brother-in-law tells me that you've returned the scrapbook, Signor Macintyre. He said that you parted on fairly good terms."

"With the strains of his Mozart sonata still in my ears."

Violetta looked at Urbino sharply, as if to detect any irony in his response.

"He is a master, isn't he?" she said.

"Most definitely, Signora Volpi—just as you are."

Once again Violetta looked at him as if in search of something beyond his words.

"A master, however, of a different art, of course," Urbino went on. "But all the arts—whatever they are—are one."

"Yes, they do say that. Well, we must be on our way, Signor Macintyre. Pleased to meet you, Mr. Hennepin," she added in English. "I hope you continue to enjoy the exhibit."

Urbino and Eugene watched Violetta Volpi wheel her husband to the exit where an attendant helped her.

"Maybe the woman was hopin' for a miracle cure, Urbino, her poor old husband bein' all crippled up the way he is. Maybe she thought he'd get up and start walkin' out on his own steam just to put some distance between himself and all this stuff. That's what I intend to do. Come on. Let's go have one of those beers that cost an arm and a leg."

11

IN EARLY EVENING, after he had returned to the Palazzo Uccello for a rest, Urbino went to the dilapidated building in the Castello quarter where Ladislao Mirko had lived with his father, Vladimir. He had to ring only two doorbells in the building before he found someone who could tell him something. Venetians seldom moved. When they did, it was usually completely away from Venice.

"Oh, yes, signore, I remember the family very well," the stout, elderly woman said as they stood in her front hallway. "More Yugoslavian than Italian, they were. My husband and I were friendly to them when they first arrived. That must be more than twenty years ago. How time flies! I could see right away that the mother had her eye on other men, always smiling at my Giovanni, and it was no surprise to me when she just up and ran away with some man or other. Never came back. Left her son and her husband just like that." She snapped her fingers. "A husband needs a good woman and a son needs a good mother. The father ended up taking everything out on his son. The arguments we would hear!" She shook her head at the memory. "That poor boy was beat up real regular every week, it seemed. Alcohol and drugs were the devils. Well, they finally did the father in. He nearly burned down the whole building about ten or so years ago with his drug-taking. A noise as loud as anything, it was, in the dead of night. His apartment went up like a tinderbox. The firemen had a hard time saving our building."

"Was his son home at the time?"

"He wasn't or he would have ended just as burned up! No, he went off hours before, after one of their arguments. Didn't even know what happened to his father until the next day when he came by with this real good-looking girl I saw him with from

time to time. Didn't seem at all upset, and I didn't blame him.
I took pity on him and let him stay in our spare room until he
found a place of his own. Haven't seen him in years. From what
I hear, he'll end up the same way. Not much better than his
father and twice as ugly, though that's not any of his fault.
Opened a pensione somewhere in Dorsoduro."

The woman's telephone started to ring.

"Excuse me, signore, but that's all I know. Good-day."

After talking with the woman, Urbino stopped at a nearby
café for several soggy *tramezzini* sandwiches left over from
lunch, trying to fit what he had just learned into the pattern of
events swirling around the life and death of Flavia Brollo. Before leaving the café, he called the Questura, but was told that
Commissario Gemelli had left for the day.

Urbino walked slowly back to the Palazzo Uccello, choosing
a less frequented route. The temperature had dropped, and
fog had started to creep into these relatively quiet alleys and
empty squares. The fog transformed the few people he met
into mysterious figures who might have been ghosts from a
former era. Whatever sounds occasionally intruded seemed to
come from far away even though they might be emanating from
the building he was passing or the *campo* he had just left. It was
one of the tricks of the city, this distortion of sound, and was
as characteristic—and as disorienting—as the twinning of the
stones in the waters below and the signs that pointed in two
different directions for the same destination.

Urbino entered a dark passageway beneath a building.
Above him were the wooden beams supporting someone's parlor or bedroom, but the *sottoportego* itself was a public passageway that connected the *campo* he had just left with the
embankment of a canal twenty meters ahead. Fog curled up
from the water of the canal and was drifting into the covered
passageway in stealthy waves.

Occasionally Urbino would step into one of these passage-
ways to find someone doing the same at the opposite end. It
was as if he were looking into a mirror. For a few confusing
moments, the details of the other person became his own. He
was looking at himself, walking toward himself and wanting to
turn around and flee. These moments were always brief but
they were unsettling, leaving their ghostly imprint on his nerves

long after he had passed the other person and had given what he suspected was an embarrassed smile.

And now it was all about to happen again. Turning into the other end of the *sottoportego* was a tall, slim figure. Whether a man or a woman, Urbino couldn't tell from the darkness and fog. Instead of continuing on through the passageway toward Urbino, the figure halted, stood still for several moments, and then turned quickly and disappeared around the corner it had just come from.

Urbino stopped. Because the other person's behavior had departed so drastically from what he had been expecting, he was taken aback. And there was something else. The figure had seemed vaguely familiar to him, and he couldn't shake the feeling that the other person had recognized him.

Urbino considered retracing his steps, as he couldn't help but remember what had happened in the deserted *calle* last week when he had been mugged by the two men in caps. But he advanced under the *sottoportego*, his step perhaps just a little less assured than it had been a few moments before. When he reached the canal end of the covered passageway beneath the building, he walked even more slowly and peered around the corner in the direction the figure had gone.

The fog was much thicker here, but Urbino could make out the tall, slim form standing next to a street shrine of the Virgin. Should he go ahead or turn around? He decided to continue along the canal embankment, but not without a feeling of apprehension. Lighted windows were open, but how long would it take for someone to respond to the sound of a scuffle or a cry for help?

As he drew nearer to the figure, it seemed to become more and more familiar until recognition came a few seconds before a pleasant, well-modulated voice said, "Urbino, it *is* you! I don't know whether I was hoping or dreading that it was."

Madge Lennox's androgynous face gleamed whitely through the fog.

12

FIFTEEN MINUTES LATER Urbino and Madge Lennox were sitting in the parlor of the Palazzo Uccello. She had said little on the walk back from the canal embankment, telling him she would explain everything in the safety and comfort of his place.

"I was searching around for your little palazzo for an hour! I was afraid someone was following me," Madge was now saying in her low, controlled voice as she sat in the Venetian baroque chair with a gin and tonic. She was wearing yet another turban, this one in tones of lavender and lilac. Urbino realized that he had never seen the retired actress's hair except, of course, in her films. And then it had seemed to vary from light brown to a deep auburn not unlike Flavia's. "With the dark and the fog I got completely lost and then when I saw you at the end of the passage I suddenly didn't think it was a good idea anymore and turned around. Maybe I should leave well enough alone, I thought. I might be putting myself in danger. I was trying to make up my mind when you came after me." She took a sip of her drink. "You said that Flavia trusted me. You were right, but at first I thought that was why I shouldn't tell you anything more. Now I realize it's exactly why I should tell you what I know."

Remembering her reaction when she had seen the Dalí reproduction, Urbino said, "It's about the Dalí, isn't it?"

She seemed almost offended, as if an actress shouldn't have been able to give anything away.

"Yes," she said, looking at him unblinkingly with her dark eyes. "It's about the Dalí."

Before Madge started to tell him exactly what it was, Urbino knew. What else could it be? Everything had been there, ready to fall into place: Flavia's fascination with the Dalí painting, her subsequent uneasiness when Tina Zuin even mentioned it, Nicolina Ricci's rape by a close friend of the family, Lorenzo's

reaction to hearing that Flavia had torn Dalí's sexual tableau
from her copy of the Guggenheim catalog, and what Urbino
had learned from Zuin—that it was Lorenzo who had been
bidding against Eugene for Flavia's nude portrait. Lorenzo
would have had the painting for his own delectation in his
private collection at the Palazzo Brollo. Once again the words
from the Biennale flashed across his mind, "Fathers often use
too much force."

He waited for Madge Lennox to go on. She looked down
at the coffee table as if in search of something.

"I hope you won't mind if I smoke." She didn't wait for an
answer, but took out a gold cigarette case from her purse and
extracted a cigarette. Before Urbino could light it for her, she
did it herself with a small gold lighter. She inhaled, but quickly
blew out the smoke. Urbino got her a small ceramic dish he
used for burning incense.

"Why Flavia told me, I still don't understand," the actress
began. "It was a few weeks after we met at Eleonora Duse's
grave. I was telling her about my own life, confiding in her,
woman to woman. I felt a strange compulsion to tell her things
only a few other people know, but many suspect. I may as well
be completely frank with you, Urbino. I was attracted to Flavia.
I'm not ashamed to admit it. Years ago there were rumors about
me and we all tried to keep them down. It wasn't too difficult—
especially since there were also rumors that I had had a child
out of wedlock. Those *were* rumors."

She gave a distant smile and put the cigarette to her mouth,
inhaling, but once again quickly blowing out the smoke.

"Flavia was a modern-thinking young woman. She wasn't
judgmental and—I have to emphasize—neither did she need
to be afraid I might force my attentions on her. I never have
with anyone, and I certainly wouldn't have with her. She was
fragile beneath all her bravado. I knew she couldn't easily bear
being taken advantage of in any way. That evening, confidences
encouraged confidences, as they so often do, and by the end of
the evening I had learned everything about 'Lorenzo il Magnifico'—how he stifled her mother, controlled her every move,
every thought, how he had done the same to her, being scornful
of her friends, especially a boy several years older than she was.
She tried to get her mother to stand up for her, but Regina was
afraid and wasn't emotionally or physically strong. Flavia had

endure everything alone. She was in Lorenzo's control both
before her mother killed herself and afterward. Very *much* in
is control."

Madge stared down at her cigarette.

"You wonder what happens in a family," she said, shaking
her turbaned head slowly. "How love can become all twisted
round and become hate or something even worse! I think
ou know what I mean, Urbino. An ailing, bedridden wife, a
eautiful young daughter who looked like her, and a father
who expected compliance from everyone! Lorenzo at first just
nade her feel uncomfortable and uneasy, opening her bed-
oom door when she had closed it behind her, sitting on the
dge of her bed and consoling her when she cried over her
mother's illness, sometimes lying next to her most of the night.
as you probably realize now, it eventually went beyond such
nnocent things—if they were so innocent—when she was
leven or twelve. She endured it. She told no one at the time,
specially not her mother. Lorenzo said it would make her
nother sicker and they would have to institutionalize her."

As Madge Lennox spoke with nervous energy, Urbino saw
he closed shutters of the Palazzo Brollo with its wicker basket
ied to the balcony to draw up provisions. A world turned in on
self, as Urbino had thought, looking up at the building after
his last meeting with Lorenzo Brollo. Now Madge Lennox was
evealing what had gone on behind its walls, where Lorenzo
Brollo—the man who had never shown any affection for his
daughter in front of Tina Zuin, who had seemed cold and
detached—could do what he wanted within his domain. Over
he years Lorenzo must have lived in fear of being exposed as
he man he really was. How much closer was Urbino now to
eroing in on Flavia's murderer? Was this the crucial strand—
Lorenzo's sexual abuse of Flavia? Was this the break that he
needed, or did he still have a long way to go?

Urbino didn't want to interrupt the actress to ask her ques-
ions or to make any comments. He just continued to listen.
Madge seemed to have almost as much a need to get all this out
s Urbino had to hear it.

"Then Flavia's mother drowned herself. Flavia blamed Lo-
enzo and, in part, herself. She thought that maybe her mother
id know what Lorenzo was doing to her and might even have
eld Flavia responsible. And yes, Urbino, she did say that her

mother told her about Alvise da Capo-Zendrini—that he was
her father—and Flavia threw it in Lorenzo's face. It was one of
her ways of coping with what Lorenzo was doing to her, of
pretending it wasn't as terrible as it actually was. Can you understand why I didn't want to get involved? To betray Flavia's
confidences when she had been betrayed so horrendously in
her life? And I was sure that she had killed herself. When you
first mentioned murder, I didn't give it much thought, but the
second time we talked, you seemed so much more positive that
it—it frightened me. I began to think that Flavia *could* have
been murdered, like that girl she was friends with. I was afraid
to say anything."

Madge stubbed out her cigarette and immediately lit another.

"What changed your mind?" Urbino asked gently.

"Seeing that horrible Dalí painting! It made me realize how
it must have affected her. It was like a distorted mirror of what
she had gone through. It must have haunted her. She must
have seen Lorenzo's face on that naked older man's. Who
knows? Maybe she even associated her poor mother with the
woman whose face is turned away! I felt her pain all over again
when you showed me the painting. And the whole idea of murder kept going around and around in my mind. If Lorenzo had
done such a beastly thing to her—and I never had any doubt
that she was telling the truth—then what might he have done
to keep her quiet once she started talking about it? What might
he do to *me*? Or *you*? Would it be better to tell you or to keep
quiet? I was afraid. I still am."

She took a deep breath.

"But I couldn't keep my secret any longer. I knew I had to
tell you. But it doesn't mean I'm any less afraid."

Madge shivered involuntarily, snuffing out the cigarette
that had never touched her lips.

"Do you know someone named Ladislao Mirko?" Urbino
asked her.

Madge appeared to think for a few moments.

"The name is vaguely familiar. Should I know who it is?"

"He was a friend of Flavia's—short, thin, not particularly
attractive."

"Very *un*attractive, right? Yes, I saw him with her once

They came to Asolo together one day about a month ago. I'm afraid I got her upset by what I said about him."

"What was that?"

Madge seemed embarrassed.

"It was stupid, really. I said that he looked like her D'Annunzio. I meant Gabriele D'Annunzio, you know, the homely writer who was Eleonora Duse's lover. You remember how I told you in the Sant'Anna cemetery that Duse was Flavia's heroine."

"What was Flavia's reaction?"

"She became very upset, as I said. I felt terrible. She said that this man was only her friend, nothing else, and that she wished people would stop thinking anything else and would also stop saying that he was ugly. What difference should that make? she asked. Needless to say, I never brought the topic up again. I shouldn't have in the first place."

Madge Lennox looked at her watch and got up.

"I should be getting back to Asolo. I don't want to spend a night in this city. I'm going to be nervous until I get on that train."

Helping her with her light jacket, Urbino said that he would see her to the train station. She was clearly relieved.

"Poor Flavia," she said, understandably not able to let the topic go now that she had finally told Urbino the story. "She carried around a photograph of herself as a young girl. She used to take it out, look at it, and show it to me from time to time. It reminded her of when her life used to be different—before Lorenzo started to bother her."

Flavia had shown the photograph to Urbino and the Contessa in the *salotto verde* of La Muta. He remembered how sadness had permeated her voice when she had explained that the photograph had been taken a long time ago.

"I'll say whatever you want me to—and to whomever you want—as long as it's the truth. Be careful! And please give my apologies to the Contessa—my apologies for not having spoken when I should have and, now, for having such a sad story to tell about her husband's daughter."

13

THE TELEPHONE WAS ringing when Urbino returned from escorting the fearful Madge Lennox to the train station. It was the Contessa.

"I'm at sixes and sevens, *caro*! Silvestro confesses."

"Confesses?"

"Not to killing Flavia, you silly boy, if that's what you're thinking, but to taking the clippings from the scrapbook! Oh, he's such a dear man. How you could ever think he would harm anyone even in his thoughts! He said he wanted to help me. I held his hand most of the time and Pompilia was getting so upset. You know she hardly ever makes any noise and there she was yapping away and—"

"Barbara," Urbino interrupted, "are you trying to avoid telling me what he said?"

"Of course not! I've already told you, haven't I? Silvestro took those things on Tuesday just as you thought, but don't be upset with the poor little man, Urbino. I told him I forgave him. It's to his credit that he didn't try to conceal it."

But he did, Urbino thought, up until now—and what else was he still hiding? Occhipinti had given very little information to either Urbino or the Contessa without being pressed.

"And he did it for me and Alvise, just as I thought. After Flavia died he found out where she had been staying and went there to see if he could find out anything about her. He said he thought he might be able to learn something and help you in your sleuthing. He went into Ladislao Mirko's pensione, found the scrapbook, saw the clippings with the pictures of him, Alvise, and me, and pulled them from the scrapbook. The cleaning woman interrupted him and he left. He thought he was doing the right thing."

Much of Occhipinti's story didn't add up. How had he known where Flavia was staying and where to find the scrap-

book? And although Occhipinti had told the Contessa that he
had just wanted to see what he could learn about Flavia so he
could pass it on to Urbino, he had done just the opposite:
removed potentially important information and concealed it
until now. Had he been to the Casa Trieste on another occasion,
perhaps when Flavia was alive? He had been in Venice on the
Thursday Flavia was killed. No, Urbino said to himself, there
was more to Occhipinti's story than this, and the Contessa was
too sharp a woman not to realize it herself.

As if to illustrate this very thing, she said, "I failed, didn't
I, *caro*? I let him get away with something. Oh, I realized it at
the time, but I couldn't press him. He looked so ravaged."

Urbino allowed the Contessa to ring off without telling
her what he had learned from Madge Lennox. His reason, he
convinced himself, was that he wanted to wait until he could
present her with a more neatly wrapped package. He had her
peace of mind at stake.

After the Contessa's call Urbino considered the major suspects.

Lorenzo Brollo would seem to have had the strongest motive to murder the woman who might have been his daughter.
With Flavia out of the way he no longer had to live in fear that
she would reveal his sexual abuse. His world would remain
closed, private, and inviolable. His sister Annabella, who had
lived in the Palazzo Brollo from the time of Regina's death,
might have desired the same end and done what she could to
bring it about—or she might have been driven by jealousy and
resentment.

As for Violetta Volpi, what motive might she have had to
murder her niece? How much had she known about Flavia's
life behind the walls of the Palazzo Brollo? If she had discovered
the truth, however, she wouldn't have struck out against Flavia,
would she, but against her brother-in-law? But the emotional
life of the Brollos and of Violetta and her sister Regina was far
from conventional. Urbino realized that little, if anything, about
them could end up surprising him.

Urbino's mind now turned to Silvestro Occhipinti and to
Ladislao Mirko, both of whose love and loyalty might have
ended up being as twisted as that of the others. Urbino believed
that a person's virtues, whatever they were, had their shadow
sides, which could be even more powerful. How dark and de-

structive were the shadows of Occhipinti's devotion to Alvise and the Contessa, and of Mirko's devotion to Flavia? And what would happen if self-interest was thrown into the picture?

Lorenzo Brollo, Annabella Brollo, Violetta Volpi, Silvestro Occhipinti, and Ladislao Mirko—a rogues' gallery unlike any Urbino had come across before. During the hours he tossed and turned in bed that night, he couldn't shake the feeling that whichever one of these had murdered Flavia, the others were also, in their own dark fashion, responsible.

Madge Lennox's masklike face then gleamed in front of Urbino's closed eyes as it had earlier tonight in the fog. Despite whatever truths she had told him, he couldn't yet exclude her from his gallery. Perhaps it was this realization, carrying with it as it did the Contessa's benediction, that finally helped him drift off to sleep.

14

EARLY THE NEXT morning Urbino went to the cemetery island of San Michele. The new day was already stifling and the sky was as gray as it had been yesterday, but from the wind blowing damply across the water Urbino could tell that a change would come soon.

He had little trouble finding Nicolina Ricci's grave, with its bouquet of fresh flowers and a porcelain photograph of the dead girl. It was like a wound in the stretch of green grass at the eastern end of the cemetery island. Salamanders darted across it.

Not far from Nicolina's grave was a field in the process of disinterment. The requisite twelve years had passed, and the dead were now being interrupted from their brief rest to be brought to a common grave or to one of the ossuaries in the cemetery walls. Space for the dead was limited on San Michele.

After leaving Nicolina's grave, Urbino wandered into the Russian Orthodox section. Yet another ballet slipper was on

Diaghilev's memorial stone. Farther along the wall a bouquet of fresh red roses rested in the arms of the stone effigy of a woman named Sonia. There was no last name. Dead at twenty-two, not much younger than Flavia and—if one could judge by the recumbent statue—just as beautiful.

And just as beautiful as Regina Brollo, whose beauty her daughter Flavia had eerily inherited. If only he could also see in the dead Flavia Alvise's patrician nose, or Lorenzo's musical talent, or—

Urbino stopped himself. This was ridiculous. A person wasn't a neat genetic pie to be sliced up. What did it really mean, for example, that he, Urbino, was half Italian, half Scotch-Irish? He looked a lot less like his own father than he did his great-uncle on his mother's side, a man who had lived not far from Venice.

Urbino made his way to a section of wall devoted to the Brollo dead. It wasn't far from the crematorium, and the sickeningly sweet scent of its smoke hung on the heavy air.

About twenty feet away he saw a man and a woman of late middle age, dressed in black and surrounded by sorrow. They were staring blankly up at the wall. The woman was sobbing, so passionate in her grief that Urbino could read into it a world of other passions, especially in her youth. The man had his arm around her waist. The woman took a black lace handkerchief from her dress and pressed it to her nose.

The man was Lorenzo Brollo and the woman, Violetta Volpi. Brollo kept his arm around his sister-in-law as she wept unrestrainedly on his shoulder. They could let themselves go, since they didn't think there was anyone around to see.

Urbino halted, concealing himself behind the wall of a mausoleum, not wanting to intrude. He could have turned around and left them alone, but of course he didn't.

Uncomfortable but unable to look away, he observed the intimacy of their grief—an intimacy that seemed, in fact, more than that of grief. It went on for long, painful moments until the two of them withdrew as if under a dark cloud.

Urbino stood there, still concealed behind the wall of the mausoleum. He remembered another scene, also not sought out but impossible to turn his eyes from. This was the scene behind the door he had opened during Mardi Gras in New Orleans, surprising Evangeline in the arms of her second cousin, Reid Delisle. When the shock and the pain had dimmed somewhat in the weeks that followed, what surfaced was the grim yet also sad appropriateness in Evangeline's turning to her cousin. Reid was someone who she believed could understand her better—someone who already understood her and her family because he *was* the family, even if the Delisles were on her mother's side. It had been far less a matter of sex than of the family bond. And here in Italy the family bond was even stronger. Flavia Brollo had devoted much of her short life to escaping from it—and might even have died because of it.

Lorenzo and Violetta were now out of sight. Urbino went up to the wall of the Brollo tomb, where there were half a dozen *loculi,* or burial niches. A plaque, with a fresh red rose in a vase next to it, commemorated Regina Brollo. Beside it was another plaque with Flavia's name and dates on it and a rose like the one left for Regina.

Urbino, with the intuitive understanding that often visited him after periods of puzzlement and was usually triggered by some fortuitous contact or observation of others, was almost certain now, with no proof yet, that Mirko had been wrong about the argument at Lago di Garda. Yet he hadn't lied about it either. Standing there in front of the Brollo tomb, after his observation of Lorenzo and Violetta during their unguarded moments of grief, Urbino went over the argument again, with the assumption this time that Flavia *had* been Lorenzo's daughter and that Violetta knew it. This opened a whole new world of speculation for him.

Lorenzo's obviously unfeigned grief helped convince Urbino more than all Brollo's affirmations ever could. Lorenzo was Flavia's father, and Lorenzo had abused his own daughter. But had he also murdered her?

If the presence of Lorenzo and Violetta at Flavia's grave told Urbino so much, the absence of Annabella spoke its own silent volumes. Annabella wasn't there because she didn't want to be there. Annabella wasn't there because she had hated Flavia just as she had hated Regina. Her hatred was like a black, smothering blanket that also covered Violetta, perhaps even Lorenzo, and probably even herself.

Twenty minutes later from the church doorway, Urbino watched Lorenzo and Violetta get into a waiting motorboat. He then took the next vaporetto to the Fondamenta Nuove. From there he went by water taxi to the Palazzo Brollo. If he had some luck, Lorenzo and Violetta weren't going directly back to the Palazzo Brollo.

Urbino got out of the water taxi on the canal embankment behind the building and told the *motoscafista* he could go. He didn't want Lorenzo and Violetta to come up in their own boat and find his waiting.

Urbino went into the little square and looked up at the Brollo windows with their pots of flowers. The windows were shuttered as usual, but the house seemed less forbidding now that he knew some of its secrets. He pushed the bell. There was no answer. Footsteps approached in a *calle*, and Urbino waited apprehensively for someone to appear around the corner. The footsteps continued but no one appeared. A door opened and closed. Then there was silence.

Urbino pushed the bell again. He thought he heard a click in the intercom above the brass bells.

"Signorina Brollo? It's Urbino Macintyre. I was wondering if I could speak with you."

Silence.

Urbino rang again, but still there was no response. When a motorboat throbbed in the canal behind the Palazzo Brollo, Urbino hurried away, taking back alleys that would lead him circuitously out of the quarter.

He called the Questura from a bar in Campo San Giacomo dell'Orio, first telling Commissario Gemelli what he had learned from Madge Lennox about Lorenzo Brollo's abuse of Flavia.

"Even if it's true, Macintyre, it doesn't mean that he killed her. There's no evidence to support that at all. In fact, there's not even a scrap of evidence that there *was* foul play involved in Flavia Brollo's death."

Urbino brought up again the wounds on Flavia's head and the fact that no traces of the medication had been found in her system. He then mentioned the argument between Massimo Zuin and Flavia. Gemelli said that Zuin hadn't come to the Questura yet with his story.

"What about the money Zuin gave her?" Urbino asked. "She still had a lot left over even after what she gave to Tina Zuin and the Ricci family. Where is it now?"

"Probably sweeping out to sea or washed up somewhere for some lucky people. It wasn't in her room at the Casa Trieste."

Urbino told him how Mirko had kept some of Flavia's things for himself.

"And maybe he kept the money, too?" Gemelli asked. "But we don't know if there *was* any money left over. She could have given the rest of it away to some other people. She seemed to be in that kind of a mood. Spreading the wealth she no longer had any use for once she decided to kill herself. I'll call Massimo Zuin in, though. I'll even send someone up to Asolo to talk with the American actress again. But even if Lennox had told us about Brollo and his daughter the first time around, it would only have lent more weight to death by suicide. Surely you can see that, Macintyre."

Not inclined to concede anything, Urbino didn't respond but instead told Gemelli about the death of Mirko's father ten years ago and pointed out that it could be related to Flavia Brollo's murder.

"Flavia Brollo's *death*," Gemelli corrected him. "You seem to be riding quite a few hobbyhorses these days. The money Flavia Brollo got from Zuin, her possible sexual abuse by Brollo, and now this connection to Ladislao Mirko's father. You're doing more than your usual snooping and legwork, Macintyre. I'm almost inclined to be impressed—but only almost! Of course we looked into the business of Ladislao Mirko's father! That all happened before I came here from Verona, but the police did a thorough job back then. Mirko's father died while he was freebasing cocaine. What is it with you? Don't go around trying to smell out a conspiracy everywhere, making connections to satisfy some perverse need for order! You're so American, Macintyre."

And with this intended insult, Gemelli hung up. Urbino was left holding the phone, wondering if he should call Gemelli back and tell him about Silvestro Occhipinti's visit to the Casa Trieste after Flavia's death and possibly before. Loyalty to the Contessa, almost second nature to him, held him back.

15

HALF AN HOUR later Agata, Mirko's cleaning woman, let Urbino into the Casa Trieste. Although it was past eleven, Mirko was still asleep. Urbino pushed aside the curtain behind the parlor and, to the right of the kitchen area, found Mirko's small bedroom.

It reminded Urbino of van Gogh's painting of his bedroom at Arles. Mirko's room contained a similar sturdy bed, washstand, and two chairs. There were several small framed pictures over the bed, one of them a color photograph of Mirko and Flavia at the wintertime Luna Park along the Riva degli Schiavoni and the other, a simple painting of the bay of Trieste, where Mirko had lived as a boy.

Whereas van Gogh's painting conveyed a calculated brightness and normalcy, however, Mirko's bedroom was dark and oppressive. The bare floor slanted alarmingly toward the lone window and paint was peeling from the ceiling in long, sharp-looking pieces. A sour odor permeated the room. Mirko lay supine on the bed in Flavia's kimono, his mouth open. His cat was curled up at his feet. Grateful to be able to take the homely man by surprise, Urbino shook him.

"Wake up, Mirko! You've been holding back."

"What the hell is going on? Macintyre!" Mirko sat up and rubbed a hand across his face. His breath was foul. The cat jumped from the bed and ran out of the room. "What are you talking about?"

Urbino stared at Mirko and saw a shadow of alarm cross his face. Mirko reached for a glass of water on the table beside the bed and took a drink. Although the scratch on his face had almost healed, there were fresh ones on his hand. When Mirko looked back at Urbino, wariness lurked in his eyes. He seemed to be weighing possibilities, deciding exactly the best way to respond. Drugs might have dulled his mind but they hadn't destroyed it. It might still come to his aid in an extreme situation.

"You know, don't you, Macintyre?" Mirko said, running a finger under his large nose. Still Urbino said nothing. Let Mirko tell him what he thought he knew. Let him take his pick and maybe give himself away. "You—you know about Flavia and Lorenzo, don't you?"

Mirko was holding his foul breath, waiting to see what Urbino's response would be. Urbino hoped his face was noncommittal as Mirko now fully corroborated what Urbino already knew from Madge Lennox about Lorenzo's sexual abuse of Flavia.

"But I promised her I'd never tell anyone, and I didn't! She said I was the only one she had ever told," Mirko whined. He reached out to grab Urbino's arm. Despite his size, his grip was surprisingly strong. "She told me about ten years ago and I never told anyone, I swear! I hated him every time I would see him. I wanted to spit at him, to—to—"

"To do what? Blackmail him? Tell him that you'd let his sister and Violetta Volpi and the whole community know? Is that why Brollo gave you that money? What else do you know about him that you're not telling me?"

"You're wrong, Macintyre!" Mirko was gleeful and Urbino saw that he had been mistaken. Mirko wasn't blackmailing Brollo—not yet, anyway.

"When were you planning to put your claws into him, Mirko? Were you trying to persuade Flavia to let you do it? Now that's she's dead, I don't think your chances of getting money out of Brollo are as good as they were before."

"You don't know what you're talking about!" Mirko pressed the heels of his hands into his eyes. "I was always Flavia's friend. Always! Yes, even now that she—she's gone. That's why I didn't tell you. It was our secret."

"And what secret did you tell her about yourself? Didn't the two of you—and Tina Zuin, too—have a game, an understanding that you would exchange secrets between you?"

"That was just kid stuff!" Mirko said, but Urbino could see that he was frightened.

"Wasn't it only logical to tell her something about yourself when she told you about Brollo? Maybe to make her feel better, to show her that she had been right to trust you? You would have done just about anything to have her care for you, wouldn't you?"

"She *did* care about me. We cared about each other."

"You know what I mean."

"No, I don't!"

"Did you tell her about your father?"

Mirko seemed stunned. Something close to hatred flashed in his eyes. Urbino was afraid that Mirko was going to attack him, but then Mirko relaxed and seemed to collapse. He put his face in his hands. Urbino wished he knew what was going on in Mirko's mind. How intelligent and crafty was he?

"You're right, Macintyre. Yes, I told Flavia about my father." He paused, his face still in his hands. "I told her how he used to beat me, how he used to take the little money I had. I wanted to show her that—that we had something in common and that I would always be her friend. I told her I'd never tell anyone what she had told me."

"Are you sure that's all you had to tell her about your father? Did she promise she'd never tell anyone what you confided in her?"

"Of course she promised!"

Mirko, however, didn't answer the first part of the question. He leaped from the bed and went to the window, moving the shutter to see down into the little square.

"And did she keep her promise?"

"You're trying to mess up my head, Macintyre! Flavia and I were true to each other. Let her rest in peace!" He turned from the window and looked at Urbino with a cold gleam in his eye. "Don't you think I've thought over and over that I should have told someone about what Lorenzo did to her? Maybe then she wouldn't have killed herself! That's what I have to live with!"

"And there were the pills, too. You feel guilty about them, too, don't you?"

"The—the pills? But I had nothing to do with them!"

"Don't worry, Mirko. I have no intention of turning you over to the police because of drugs of any kind. You gave Flavia those pills."

Something seemed to collapse in the homely little man. He nodded his head.

"You're right. She came to me and gave me the name of these pills she had heard about. She thought they would help her with her depression over Lorenzo. It was getting so bad right before she killed herself. I told her to go to a doctor but she didn't want to, so I—I got them for her."

"Where?"

"I have my contacts, but please, Macintyre, don't say anything to the police!"

"As I've said, I'm not interested in getting you into trouble about your dealings in drugs."

" 'Dealings'! I—"

"At any rate," Urbino interrupted, "no traces of the drug were found in Flavia's system."

"They weren't? But I know she was taking them."

"You do? But you said that you never saw her take any."

"I didn't! But I noticed that some of the pills were missing from the bottle."

"When did you notice that?"

Mirko didn't answer right away.

"I don't remember."

When Urbino left a few minutes later, he was convinced that Mirko was already running for his syringe or his powder or his pills—whatever made him feel better for a time. Soon he might be drifting into a world that resembled the Tanguy landscapes he said he liked so much.

As he walked to the nearest café to use the phone, Urbino quickly reviewed the last hours of Flavia's life. Her visit to Graziella Gnocato to get the old nurse to speak on the tape recorder, her visit to Mirko at the Casa Trieste, then to Violetta Volpi and to Lorenzo Brollo. Flavia had been desperately driven that night to confront some of the most important relationships in her life. But where had she gone after leaving Lorenzo? Annabella said that Flavia had left the Palazzo Brollo and Violetta said that Flavia hadn't been there when she herself arrived. Could the two women be lying to protect Lorenzo? Maybe Flavia had stayed at the Palazzo Brollo—or maybe Brollo had followed her. How far would he have gone to protect his deep, dark secret?

From the café Urbino called the Questura, but Gemelli was out. He gave his name and said he would call again in an hour, asking the officer to tell the Commissario that it was very important.

16

AFTER CALLING THE Questura, Urbino went to the Zattere embankment and sat down at the outdoor terrace of Da Gianni where he and Eugene had lunched on the latter's first day in Venice. Dark, menacing clouds were piling up from the northwest in the direction of Asolo. Urbino ordered a quarter liter of white wine and watched several boats of the Bucintoro rowing club hurrying back to their quarters. Gazing absently off at the Island of Giudecca, he began to consider the pieces of the puzzle.

Urbino kept coming back to Flavia's visits the last night of her life. Had she sought out anyone in addition to the people he already knew about? Or had she returned to see someone she visited earlier? Not the nurse Graziella, but Brollo, Violetta, or Mirko? If she had, that person could be her murderer—or could know or suspect who her murderer was. Lies were being told about that night, lies about what had actually happened and when it had happened. Perhaps more than one person knew how and why Flavia had been attacked and then thrown or pushed into the stormy waters of the Grand Canal.

Urbino went over the various possibilities and combinations several times, not sure if he was getting a clearer or a more distorted perspective on things. He left the café and struck out along the Zattere toward the Punta della Dogana da Mar at the mouth of the Grand Canal. Venetians, who had a seaman's sense of changing weather, had long ago started to secure their kiosks, outdoor tables, shutters, and boats. An artist was chasing one of the aquatints that had blown out of the kit he was folding up. It blew into the canal and was lost.

Usually this was one of Urbino's favorite walks—past the Church of Santo Spirito, the Magazzini del Sale, or salt warehouses, where Biennale exhibitions were mounted, and the villas of Milanese industrialists and foreigners—but this afternoon it was little more than an accompaniment for his thoughts which were as turbulent as the gusts of wind.

He soon reached the isolated Punta della Dogana, where the Giudecca Canal, the Grand Canal, and the lagoon met. He sat on a bench. A cold, damp wind blew across the waters, whirling around the weathervane statue of Fortune positioned atop the golden globe on the Customhouse Building. On a nearby bench a young couple was embracing, completely oblivious to Urbino or the changing weather. Urbino was reminded of how the Contessa, inspired by Yeats, had disdained the lovers out in the Piazza on the afternoon they saw Flavia at Florian's— "the young in one another's arms," she had said. But even more vivid to Urbino than these words was the embrace between the naked older man and the young woman with flowers for hair in Dalí's *The Birth of Liquid Desires*.

Urbino gazed out at the broad expanse of gray water beneath the lowering sky, with the Doge's Palace and the Piazzetta on the left and San Giorgio Maggiore on the right. Here, with the wind whipping in his face, it was easy to imagine that he was at the prow of a ship, sailing into Venice. Unbidden, the last scene from *Queen Christina* came into his mind—Greta Garbo standing at the prow of the ship carrying her away from her homeland, the ship that was also carrying the body of her murdered lover. Garbo's expression was unforgettable—a mask, completely blank and vacant, into which everything and nothing could be read. It was very much Madge Lennox's face.

Urbino tried to concentrate his thoughts and considered Lorenzo Brollo's abominable guilt and the intimacy of grief he had observed between him and Violetta at the cemetery that morning, and what he believed it revealed. Brollo's abuse of Flavia and the scene at San Michele were proving to be the most intractable pieces of the puzzle. Although he thought he knew how they fit into the puzzle that was Alvise and Regina, he still didn't know how they fit into the greater puzzle of Flavia's death. Brollo's pride and desire for control could easily have led him to commit murder—or to have found someone willing, for whatever reason, to do his bidding.

Urbino, however, kept coming back to Ladislao Mirko and his father and the rest of the money that Flavia had gotten from Zuin. He felt himself being pulled away from what he originally believed was the crucial question of Flavia's paternity—the question which, if answered, he had thought would lead to her murderer.

While Urbino sensed that he was close to seeing the pattern that he knew was there hiding behind so much, something still eluded him.

Urbino believed in benevolent deception—the kind of lies, tacit or spoken, that protected others as well as oneself from painful truths. As a biographer he often had to bring these lies to light, but when it came to his other line of work, he often left the lies where he found them. What had Occhipinti said last week in Asolo, quoting as usual from Browning, "Let who lied be left lie"? Good advice for many situations, certainly, but not for murder.

Abandoning the bench and the enamored couple, Urbino walked along the Grand Canal, past the Customhouse Building and beneath the snowy cupolas and towers of the Baroque Church of the Salute. He crossed a wood-and-stone bridge and passed the studios where many of Venice's paintings were restored, wondering when he would be able to return with an unclouded mind to his own work on the Cremonese lady waiting for him at the Palazzo Uccello.

Urbino's brisk pace soon found him standing in front of the welded-iron-and-Murano-glass gates of the Palazzo Guggenheim. The museum hadn't closed yet and Urbino was tempted to take another look at the Dalì painting that had played such an apparently changeable role in the life and death of Flavia.

But he decided against it and continued on to the Accademia Bridge, his own thoughts much more real to him than the frantic activity in the alleys and canals. He climbed the wooden steps of the bridge and stopped for a few moments in the middle, looking down at the sweep of the Grand Canal. The upper decks of a ship were visible behind the buildings on the right as the ship made its slow way through the Giudecca Canal to the Maritime Station.

Urbino took a detour and entered the Palazzo Pisani, where the young and hopeful Contessa had studied music more than thirty years ago. He went into the courtyard and stood by the covered wellhead. Above him was an increasingly darkening sky and around him a myriad of sounds—sea gulls, a piano, a

trumpet, a flute, a soprano, several overlapping conversations,
laughter. Urbino, reminded by all these sounds of the confusing
facts and speculations surrounding Flavia, succeeded in picking
out some of the individual harmonies underlying the cacophony
before leaving the courtyard.

In Piazza San Marco Urbino found a swarm of tourists.
The arcades were packed, and people were sitting on the steps
or leaning against the columns, having already found spots to
ride out the coming storm.

Florian's combined Babel and pandemonium, but it was
good enough for a drink at the bar. As he perched on a stool
drinking his Campari soda fortified with wine, Urbino considered his alternatives. He felt an urgent need for action.

Downing the remainder of his pleasantly bitter drink, he
paid his bill and hurried out to the Molo for a water taxi,
determined, first of all, to get Bernardo Volpi to tell him what
he might know.

17

THE STORM BROKE when the water taxi entered the Grand Canal.
Jagged pieces of lightning split the sky above the Lido. The
gale-force wind peaked the waters of the lagoon and threw rain
against the windows of the tossing water taxi. Urbino felt as if
he had passed into Violetta Volpi's picture of the storm-tossed
Grand Canal with dark-gowned, featureless women standing
on the Accademia Bridge, their hands clapped over their ears.

In the interval between two blasts of thunder, the sound of
breaking glass, followed by a woman's screams, drew Urbino's
attention to the right bank. A woman was lying on the ground,
her hand to her face. A man was bending over her. Pieces of
shattered glass littered the ground around them. Urbino looked
up at the top story of the building above the man and the
woman. He thought he could make out a broken windowpane.

It wasn't a good time to be out in the open—or even in the

closed cabin of a motorboat. Venice was in the grip of the kind
of evil storm that threatened its fragile existence more than any
barbarian horde or rival empire ever had.

Urbino told the driver to pull up to the Volpi water steps
and to wait. Buffeted by the wind and rain, Urbino made his
way carefully up the slippery steps. The iron gate hadn't been
repaired yet. Opening it without any trouble, he was in the
Volpi garden. The storm and the coming night made it difficult
to see except when lightning seared the scene. The door to
Violetta's studio was agape. Urbino approached the open door
carefully, searching the pergola and the area along the walls for
a sign of someone. He saw no one. The studio was dark except
for a small lamp in a far corner. Urbino moved slowly into the
room.

A heavy blow fell on his shoulder.

18

URBINO TURNED QUICKLY. Violetta held a hammer. Fury con-
torted her coarse-featured face. She raised the hammer again
to deliver another blow. Urbino grabbed her arm. She looked
at him in surprise and dropped the hammer.

"It's you!" Violetta's voice was more throaty than usual. "I
thought you were Annabella. She just attacked Bernardo."

Violetta rushed to a dark corner where Bernardo lay on
the floor, ashen and his eyes wide. Urbino touched his hand. It
was cold and clammy. Vomit stained his shirt.

"Tell Signor Macintyre it was Annabella," Violetta said. "It
was Annabella, wasn't it, Bernardo?"

The man said nothing.

"He looks as if he's had a heart attack," Urbino said. "Have
you called for an ambulance?" Violetta nodded. "We should
put something under his head."

Violetta took a cushion from the sofa and placed it under
Bernardo's head.

"Why do you think Annabella did something to him?" Urbino asked Violetta.

"Because she must have! She was here! I talked with her upstairs. She was vile! I told her to leave. I went to my bedroom for ten minutes to compose myself. When I came down here, I found Bernardo like this. It had to be Annabella!"

Violetta gripped his arm and brought him to the other side of the studio, away from Bernardo.

"I don't know what to do now. I try to be a strong woman but I'm at the end of my strength. I thought everything would be all right if you just left us alone! I saw you this morning on San Michele. Lorenzo didn't."

"I wasn't spying on you and Brollo."

"It doesn't matter anymore! What matters is that Annabella tried to kill Bernardo the way she killed Flavia! Why she did it, I don't know! It has to end."

Violetta stared out through the door at the water gate and began to cry.

"Now I know why Flavia killed herself!"

"But you just said that Annabella killed her."

"I don't know, I tell you! If it's not her fault, it's Lorenzo's— or both of them! Not mine! You've been asking a lot of questions. I don't know what answers you've been getting and what you've figured out. But Lorenzo hasn't told you the truth! He's been lying!" she screamed. "He's been lying to everyone! His whole life's a lie!"

This was just what Annabella had said.

"Lorenzo *is* Flavia's father, isn't he?"

"I've told you that from the beginning!" she rasped. "I wish to God he weren't! I see now why Flavia was so desperate to believe he wasn't!"

"But that's not all of it, is it, Signora Volpi? Flavia looked just like your sister, didn't she? The same hair, the same color of eyes, almost the same face? But she had a lot of you in her, too. Your eyes aren't as green as hers but I've seen very much the same look in them as I have in Flavia's—when they weren't dull with all the pain she went through. And Flavia had your spirit, even some of your artistic sensibility." He paused. Violetta Volpi looked afraid. She was waiting for his next words. "Flavia wasn't Regina's daughter. She was yours."

Violetta drew in her breath sharply and cast a quick glance at Bernardo. But Urbino had been speaking very quietly.

"But how do you know?" she whispered, not even bothering to deny it.

"I really didn't know for certain until right now." Urbino kept his voice low. "But a lot of things started to come together today at San Michele when I saw you and Lorenzo. You were very much together in your grief. You had both lost the same thing—a child—your child together. Right before I saw you together, I was thinking about how genes had worked out in my own family, actually chastising myself for trying to search out traits in Flavia that she might have inherited from Alvise or Lorenzo. It all eventually started to fall into place."

Violetta wasn't looking at Urbino any longer but at her husband. He had regained a little color.

"But I don't understand," Urbino went on, "why you were shouting at Lorenzo at Lago di Garda that Flavia wasn't his daughter. You both knew that she was, and Regina—"

Urbino stopped. His mind was whirling. What about Regina? He started to make some more connections.

Violetta's smile was chilling.

"Ah, Regina!" she repeated throatily. "My beautiful, disturbed sister Regina!" Violetta nodded her head slowly. "You think you know so much," she said scornfully, "but you can't even begin to imagine the way it was!"

Violetta delivered this as if it were a boast.

"I knew Lorenzo before he met my sister. I hoped we would get married."

Bruno Novembrini had said that Violetta had known Lorenzo before Regina, Urbino remembered, but he had said nothing about any possible future marriage.

"But once Lorenzo saw Regina—when she came back to the land of the living after one of her relapses!—he fell straightaway in love with her. He married *her*, not me," she said bitterly, "just the way Alvise married your friend! It all happened so fast I was almost in shock! Bernardo, who knew that Lorenzo and I had been seeing each other, stepped in to console me. He had been interested in me for a long time. Several months after Lorenzo and Regina were married, Bernardo proposed and I accepted. He took me by surprise, asking me the night before he had to leave for almost half a year to put his business in order in the States, South America, and Asia. But what Bernardo didn't know—what *no* one knew—was that Lorenzo and I were still very much together. Not long after her marriage, Regina fell back into her pit again, and there I was, you see, still in love and seething with resentment against Regina. Everything was the way it had been before, you might say." She gave a harsh laugh. "Except for a few things here and there—my sister was married to Lorenzo, I was engaged to marry a saint of a man, and I was also pregnant!"

Violetta suddenly remembered her husband and went over to him. She bent down and whispered something in his ear. Urbino filled a glass of water from the sink and brought it over but Violetta waved it away.

"He'll be all right, won't you, darling? Just rest until the ambulance comes. Whatever is taking it so long!"

Violetta looked impatiently out the door into the driving storm where lightning was still searing the scene, periodically illuminating the studio. Cracks of thunder reverberated beneath their feet.

Violetta led Urbino to the other side of the room and continued her story, her face occasionally bleached out by flashes of lightning. Whenever the thunder came, she paused for a few moments, obviously impatient to continue. Urbino had often seen people act the way Violetta was acting now, eager to reveal what they had concealed for years. Actually it was not unlike those many occasions when he himself had sat in a dark confessional and bared his soul to a silent priest on the other side of a screen.

"Yes, I was pregnant," Violetta went on, "but Lorenzo forbade me to get an abortion, said he would tell Bernardo all about us when he returned from his business trip. Lorenzo has always liked being in control, and it suited him for me to have this child. He had a plan, and to my shame I went along with it. I had the baby five months later, and from then on she was Regina's, and only Regina's! I told her Alvise da Capo-Zendrini was the father. Lorenzo was afraid that you were on to us. It was because of something you said to him when you saw him last."

Urbino remembered what it was—his guileless comment, meant to pacify Lorenzo, that sometimes children liked to fantasize that they had been dropped in the middle of the wrong family. Lorenzo's reaction had seemed to be anger, but it must have also been fear.

"But believe me, Signor Macintyre, everything was much easier than you might think. It amazed even us. Lorenzo arranged for Regina and me to go to a private clinic outside Milan, telling everyone Regina was pregnant. He let it be known that none of our family and friends should intrude. Regina needed this rest, he said, for both her pregnancy and her nerves, and I was there to help her. He reminded them that Regina had had a miscarriage the year before, which was true. You'd be surprised how far away people stay when there's illness—especially emotional illness. That—and the fact that everyone knew how much Lorenzo liked to be in control and wouldn't brook being crossed—kept everyone at a distance. Of course there were telephone conversations and letters, but no visits. Eventually Regina came back with 'her' baby. Even Annabella believed it. She was the only one in a position to suspect anything, but Lorenzo kept Regina away from her and from everyone else for a long time. We—Lorenzo and I—were Regina's only keepers."

"But surely it's impossible!" Urbino said. "However could you and Lorenzo have made Regina think that Flavia was her own daughter? My God, she couldn't have been so ill that she didn't know she hadn't given birth!"

"You're right, Signor Macintyre," Violetta said with a smile of satisfaction. "Of course she knew! It would be preposterous to assume anything else, even given her illness. Regina was more than willing to go along with it, all the more so because Lorenzo convinced her how they'd be able to make the child their own. After the miscarriage the doctors didn't think she would ever be able to carry a baby full-term. She yearned for a child to take care of. She thought it would heal her to have someone who needed her so much."

Tina Zuin, who had known Regina Brollo, had said something very similar during her late-night visit to the Palazzo Uccello.

"And here was Regina's own niece with the Grespi blood running in her veins," Violetta continued. "Maybe Regina thought she was making up to me for all the times she had been the center of attention because of her beauty and her illness. At the time I didn't see any way out—the excuse everyone has who does something they shouldn't. I'm ashamed to say that I also saw it as a double revenge—against your friend the Contessa and my sister. They had both taken men from me."

There was a twisted, almost diabolical logic in it that appalled Urbino as everything was laid out before him. Only a woman as emotionally disturbed as Regina Brollo would ever have agreed to raise her sister's child as her own. Yet he had heard of cases in which a mother raised her daughter's child as her own. What made the Brollo and Volpi situation so different was all the deceptions that had begun even before the birth of Flavia. Regina had believed she was helping her sister, her husband, and herself, while in reality she was just Violetta's and Lorenzo's pawn.

In the distance a siren wailed.

"What about the argument at Lago di Garda?" Urbino asked, trying to work out what had been going on in Regina's bedroom as Flavia and Mirko eavesdropped in the hallway outside. "That argument took place, didn't it?"

"Oh, yes, it took place all right, but not exactly the way Flavia and Ladislao Mirko heard it. Regina's periods of lucidity became fewer and farther between over the years. Eventually she became confused about the events of her own life. There were times when she didn't know who Lorenzo was, or me, and times when she thought her nurse was our mother. She began to think that Flavia *was* her daughter, but not by Lorenzo but by Alvise. Rather a fitting punishment for us, wasn't it?" Violetta added wryly. "To think we had always feared the opposite— that she would tell the truth to someone! Well, it all ended up making things easier for Lorenzo and me, of course, but I felt that I had lost my child twice over. The argument that Flavia and Mirko overheard wasn't what it seemed, as I said. I wasn't shouting at Lorenzo! I was shouting at Regina—trying to break through her wall, to make her realize—remember—that she *wasn't* Flavia's mother. I was going to bring her the birth certificate. I must have been in a strange state myself if I thought that would mean anything to her, but I was desperate. Lorenzo slapped *me,* to keep me quiet. Fourteen years of seeing Flavia grow up as Regina's daughter—when Bernardo and I couldn't have children of our own—had become more than I could bear. Thank God I had my painting."

Violetta looked around her studio, at all the evidence of

her art, with a blank expression. She seemed exhausted. Almost as an afterthought, she looked at what should have been another source of comfort to her, Bernardo. Urbino wondered how much Bernardo had known or suspected over the past twenty-six years.

"What happened when Flavia came to see you here on that Thursday evening?" Urbino asked as the siren continued to wail, drawing closer to the Ca' Volpi.

"I finally told her the truth," she said in a low, defeated voice. "Can you see now why I didn't want to tell you anything about that visit, why I lied to the police? Lorenzo isn't the only one who has lived with lies. All those years I lied to Flavia— told her that this story about Alvise da Capo-Zendrini was a figment of her mother's disturbed imagination. But I couldn't take it anymore. I saw what was happening to Flavia, and hoped that the truth would help her, even if it threatened to destroy the love she had for me. So I told her. She wouldn't believe me until I showed her the birth certificate. I've never seen such pain and—and hatred in a person's face before."

"Then she rushed off to see Lorenzo, didn't she?"

"Yes, to see if he would tell her the same thing—that she was *our* daughter and that Lorenzo and I had allowed her mother to believe that Alvise was her father. I went to Lorenzo an hour later, to deal with what I knew would be his fury, but Flavia had already left in a rage. The truth was too much for her. She rushed off and killed herself. Don't you see? We're both responsible—Lorenzo and I!"

Earlier Violetta had said that Annabella had murdered Flavia and now she was saying that she and Lorenzo were responsible for her suicide. Urbino was reminded of what he had suspected earlier—that more than one person had contributed to Flavia's death. When Urbino mentioned Annabella, Violetta's response was immediate.

"An evil-minded woman! She has always been filled with hatred—for me, for Regina, for Flavia, maybe even for Lorenzo!"

"And you saw how much she hated you all because of what she told you tonight, didn't you?"

Violetta had a dazed look on her face. She seemed even more depleted of energy than she had been a few minutes ago.

"Now you know how Flavia *really* felt about the Dalì painting, don't you, Signora Volpi?" Urbino asked. "Annabella told you all about Flavia and Lorenzo, didn't she?"

Violetta drew in her breath sharply.

"You know! But—" Surprise soon gave way to anger. "You tricked me! You knew all along. There must have been some way you could have let me know instead of leaving it to Annabella. Did you put her up to it?"

Her hands were trembling. She cast a quick, apprehensive glance at Bernardo.

"I had nothing to do with Annabella coming here to see you, Signora Volpi. I think you had better tell me as quickly as possible what happened here tonight. Lives could depend on it. Look at what almost happened to Bernardo."

The ambulance boat was pulling up to the water steps.

"Her mouth was all twisted up when she said that Lorenzo had—had done terrible things to Flavia. How could I believe such a thing? How! But you're right. Suddenly I thought of how Flavia had torn out the Dalí picture from her catalog, and then I knew it was true. I remembered comments Flavia had made, hints she had dropped that I hadn't quite understood—and I knew! Maybe there were even things I saw myself but dismissed! It was as if I had known all along. I've read about these things in the newspapers—Italian fathers and their daughters, the closeness of the family."

"But what made Annabella come to see you after all this time?"

"She said she had just found out about Lorenzo and me. She must have wanted to strike back at both of us—and this was her way of doing it! She kept this—this abomination to herself all these years just to drop it like a bomb when it would give her the most satisfaction. Well, she got her satisfaction tonight, damn her! And damn Lorenzo, too!"

The medics hurried across the garden to the studio and started to tend to Bernardo. Violetta and Urbino went over to see if they could be of any help but were told to move aside. When one of the medics said that Bernardo was out of immediate danger, Violetta smiled weakly at Urbino and seemed about to reach out to touch his arm, but drew her hand back. As Urbino watched the medics lifting Bernardo onto the stretcher, he went over the convoluted emotions and behavior of the Brollos and the Volpis, trying to fit into the picture the person who had ended up murdering Flavia, for he was now convinced more than ever that she had been murdered.

Violetta, with one eye on Bernardo as he was being secured in the stretcher, continued her explanation.

"Annabella knew I would despise Lorenzo for what he did to Flavia, for the way he had deceived us both! And I do!" Tears streamed down her face. "And I despise myself most of all! Can you imagine how I feel? Poor Flavia! My poor daughter! We're as guilty of her death as if we had pushed her into the Grand Canal. I hope you and the Contessa are satisfied! I can imagine how she'll gloat—along with her lackey, Silvestro Occhipinti."

"Occhipinti?"

"Of course! He's been poking around just the way you have. He came to see me. He wanted to know where he could find Flavia—other than at her own house, that is. But I refused to tell him. He said he would find out."

"When was this?"

"The morning of Flavia's last visit here."

19

WHILE THE MEDICS were taking Bernardo out to the ambulance with Violetta following anxiously behind, Urbino called the Palazzo Brollo. There was no answer.

He went out into the garden. Bernardo was now in the ambulance, and Violetta was standing on the water steps in the wind and rain as the boat prepared to leave.

When the ambulance went into the choppy waters of the Grand Canal, Urbino's water taxi eased back to the landing and he got in. Urbino told the *motoscafista* to take him to the Palazzo Brollo. As the motorboat pulled away, he had a distorted glimpse of Violetta standing in the rain.

The storm had passed its worst point, and the sky was starting to lighten slightly, even with the coming of night. In less than ten minutes the water taxi arrived in the canal behind

the Palazzo Brollo. Urbino rang the bell, praying that Annabella
was there. Even if Lorenzo was home too, he would insist on
talking to Annabella.

The door opened and a pale Annabella stood there against
the dark hallway. She seemed to be in a daze.

"Your work is finished, signore," she said, her voice unchar-
acteristically thick, as if she had a bad taste in her mouth. It was
also higher, no longer the suffocated whisper it had been before. "Everybody is miserable. Miserable or dead—or miserable
and dying!"

"Is your brother here?"

She ignored the question and said, "You want to know
about Violetta, don't you? Yes, I went to see that bitch. I told
her all about her precious little daughter and my brother. Oh,
yes, I know everything! I know what Lorenzo did to Flavia! I
knew it back then!" She seemed proud of it. "But it took that
whore of a Flavia to make me realize that Lorenzo had carried
on even with Violetta! Flavia wasn't trying to keep her voice
down that night, screaming at Lorenzo, accusing him of everything under the sun! Every time I told him what I'd heard Flavia
say, he would deny it—until tonight! He must have known he
couldn't lie forever! Not with me! Not with me!" The unre-
strained emotion behind Annabella's words struck Urbino as
almost orgasmic. "Ah," she said, drawing the word out as if it
had more than one syllable, "I've been a fool all these years!
Both sisters!"

A perverse jealousy throbbed in Annabella's bloodshot blue
eyes.

"Did you attack Bernardo Volpi an hour ago?"

"Attack Bernardo? I want him to live to a hundred so that
Violetta will have to take care of him. She's probably waiting
for him to die so that she can marry Lorenzo." She leaned
against the doorframe and laughed. "No, I didn't attack Bernardo, but I didn't spare any words telling him what kind of a
woman he had married. Much better it would have been for
Violetta if I *had* attacked and killed him instead of telling him
the truth."

There was one more thing Urbino wanted to know. It was
about Silvestro Occhipinti.

"That silly little man from Asolo?" Annabella answered.
"The one who's always mumbling nonsense? I heard that Vio-

letta had hopes he would marry her in the old days, but he must have seen through her."

"Have you seen him recently?"

"Yes. The day Flavia drowned like Regina. In the morning. I told him where Flavia was staying. I called up Ladislao Mirko to tell him that an old man might be coming by the pensione. He didn't think it was important until two days ago—Friday. He wanted to know who 'the skinny old man' was. I told him. Ha! Do you think an old codger like that would believe he had a chance with Flavia? But who knows? Maybe she ended up liking older men after Lorenzo!"

Annabella laughed hysterically until tears rolled down her sallow cheeks. Urbino couldn't imagine flowers or anything else blooming under her baleful touch.

He was about to turn away when he was startled to see Lorenzo Brollo's face staring at him from within a cracked mirror in a far corner of the dark hall. The face was immobile, the eyes sharp and glaring. In the few moments before Annabella closed the door, Urbino couldn't decide whether he was looking at Brollo's actual reflection or the reflection of a portrait that had gone unnoticed on his other visits. Whichever it was, the eyes stared unblinkingly into Urbino's, as haughty as ever.

Turning his back on the dark and twisted emotions of the Palazzo Brollo, Urbino told the *motoscafista* to take him as quickly as possible to the Casa Trieste. The puzzle pieces were all finally coming together.

20

"MIRKO'S NOT HERE," Agata said when Urbino got to the Casa Trieste fifteen minutes later. "He left about two hours ago, not long after you were here."

"Do you know where he went?"

The woman shook her head and was about to close the door.

"By the way, Agata, did you ever notice a bottle of pills anywhere in Flavia Brollo's room when you were cleaning it?"

"Pills? I don't think so."

Urbino asked if he could use the pensione phone and waited until he heard Agata sweeping before he dialed. He first called the Contessa and, in a low voice, asked her to have Milo wait with the car in Bassano for the next train from Venice, which was leaving in an hour. Then he asked if she had seen Occhipinti that day.

"No, but he called a few hours ago. I've been trying to contact you. He said that he hadn't told me everything. He was at the Casa Trieste before Tuesday."

"Just what I thought."

"He said he didn't like lying to me, that he was ready to tell the whole truth, but that he wanted to tell you and me together. What's going on, Urbino? I'm frightened. Are you coming here because of Silvestro? Or is it Madge Lennox? She went by in a taxi a little while ago in the direction of La Pippa."

"I'll explain everything later, Barbara, but you can stop worrying about Alvise. He wasn't Flavia's father. No, that's all I have time to tell you now, but please stay at La Muta."

Urbino next called Occhipinti, letting the phone ring a long time. When no one picked up, he called the Questura.

Commissario Gemelli hadn't returned. Urbino, speaking softly so that Agata wouldn't hear, told the duty officer what had happened at the Ca' Volpi, what he had learned from Violetta Volpi and Annabella Brollo, and what he knew about Silvestro Occhipinti in relation to Flavia Brollo and her death. He said that he was going to Asolo to Occhipinti's apartment and gave the exact address on the Via Browning. The Questura should alert the carabinieri in Asolo and try to locate Ladislao Mirko. Praying that when Gemelli got all this information he would realize, as Urbino himself did, how urgent the situation was, Urbino went through everything again with the duty officer as the minutes flew by.

Urbino went out into the little square. As he hurried into the *calle* that would eventually take him back to where the boat was waiting, he realized how much danger he was in. He felt it much more keenly now than ever before.

The *calle* was deserted, filled with puddles from the recent storm. Urbino quickened his step, as much out of apprehensiveness as urgency. He was reminded of how he had been mugged not far from here, and he still wasn't sure whether it had been a random attack or not. Quick footsteps came from what he thought was ahead of him. When he turned the corner, however, no one was there. Water dripped from the eaves of the buildings onto the pavement.

Suddenly Urbino heard a shout and a dark object came crashing down in front of him, within inches of hitting him in the head. It smashed on the pavement. Pieces of earthenware, soil, and the leaves and flowers of a geranium were scattered on the stones.

"*Mi dispiace*, signore." A woman looked down from an open window. Two pots of geraniums remained on her sill. "I'm planning to put up wires to keep the pots from falling," she went on nervously. "Are you all right?"

Urbino said he was fine and ran to the waiting boat. Ten minutes later, thanks to the Rio Nuovo shortcut, Urbino was walking up the steps of the Santa Lucia train station. As he looked at the sky above the modern white building, it was as if some visual residue of the recent lightning were flashing "Fathers often use too much force." Urbino had come full circle since more than two weeks ago when, sitting on the veranda of the Grand Hotel des Bains, he had remembered those words from a previous Biennale d'Arte. They meant something very much different to him now than they had then. From now on they would be associated with a cycle of violence that he feared might not yet be over.

"Urbino!" It was Eugene. "I thought you'd never get here! I called Countess Barbara and she said you were takin' the next train up to see her. Thought I'd join you if you don't mind. I've got something to tell you. It's goin' to disappoint the hell out of you though. Ha, ha!"

"I'm in a hurry, Eugene. The train leaves in a few minutes."

"Let's get goin' then! I want to see Countess Barbara once more before I leave. I'm off to Rome tomorrow morning."

Urbino and Eugene made their way up the steps of the station, where groups of youths, many with backpacks, were lounging.

"Tomorrow?"

"Afraid so. Got to catch up with Evie. Don't look like the two of you are goin' to get together here in Venice. Who would've

thought that spunky little sister of mine would be the one to get
cold feet? She went to Rome today. But you ain't free and clear
entirely—not by a long shot! There's a method in the girl's
madness."

Urbino forged ahead of Eugene through the open doors of
the station. The odors of sweat and wet clothing assaulted him.

"What do you mean?" Urbino called back over his shoulder.

Eugene was trying to keep up with him and was short of
breath.

"Slow down, Urbino! What do I mean? I mean that Evie
wants you to come to Rome. Neutral territory, she calls it. I said
she should meet you in Switzerland then! The problem is she
didn't think she should come here, seein' it's your home now
and all. But Rome's different. I think she's a mite suspicious of
Venice. Could be because of some of the things I've been tellin'
her about what's been goin' on here. She didn't take to the story
of that girl who ended up dead. Bawled me out, too, about
buyin' you that picture of her. Anyway, Evie said something
about a promise you made to her back in the good old days—
something about a cemetery!"

Urbino remembered. In the early months of their marriage
he had promised to take Evangeline to Keats' and Shelley's
graves at the Protestant Cemetery in Rome. Evangeline loved
the Romantic poets and had read about pilgrimages to this
particular cemetery by devotees. The trip to Rome had been
postponed, however, from their first anniversary to their second, until it was beyond all possibility as their marriage soured,
failed, and then quickly ended after Urbino had discovered
Evangeline and her cousin Reid together.

"Evie's just as strange as you are when it comes to cemeteries! You know how much she loves St. Louis Cemetery. Anyway,
I said I'd tell you, and now you can do as you see fit. We're
stayin' at the Boston Hotel for a week. I'd be happy to see you
down there but don't think I'm pressin' you anymore. To be
honest, Urbino, maybe my little sister is givin' you the kind of
test you can't win. She's a crafty one."

Urbino checked the announcement board to see if the Bassano train was leaving from the usual track.

"I don't know if I can get down to Rome, Eugene. I don't
know if I *should*. It might be better to leave things the way they
are, but I'll think about it."

On his way to Asolo like this, with his mind filled with
speculation and uneasiness, was no time to consider the possibility of a reunion with Evangeline and what it might mean. Reflection about that would have to come later.

"Well, you just think about it then. Meanwhile I guess I can
make my good-byes tonight to Sylvester," Eugene said. "I just
might rent his villa next year. How would you like that, Urbino?
Me and your Countess hobnobbing it up in Asolo."

As they hurried to the Bassano del Grappa train, Eugene
painted a detailed, rosy picture of what life might be like for
him and Countess Barbara in the hills of Asolo.

21

WHEN URBINO AND Eugene arrived at Bassano, the Contessa's
Bentley was waiting. The Contessa hadn't listened to Urbino.
She hadn't stayed at La Muta but had come to meet him.

"What a delightful surprise, caro!" the Contessa said.
"You've brought our dear Eugene with you."

On the way to Asolo, the Contessa and Eugene dominated
the conversation while Urbino withdrew into himself, looking
out the window and making only obligatory responses. The
Contessa's eyes slid in his direction many times, but Urbino was
sure that Eugene detected nothing amiss in her attention. All
the while, Urbino knew that she was agonizing over what might
happen next, although she was certainly relieved to know that
Alvise hadn't been Flavia's father after all.

At one point, hurrying to speak in a convenient interval in
Eugene's monologue, she said, "I must say that you've been in a
brown study since Bassano, Urbino."

"A brown study, Countess?" Eugene asked, screwing up his
face.

"Your former brother-in-law is thinking very deeply, Eugene. He's lost to us. Can't you see it as plain as day?"

"Oh, that funny look on his face! I know what you mean.

Well, he's always been a thinker, Countess Barbara. Let's jus
hope he ain't thinkin' anything bad about *us*!"

The Contessa queried Urbino silently with her eyes.

"Why don't you have Milo drop you and Eugene off at La
Muta," Urbino suggested. "Rosa can have a nice light suppe
ready and we—"

"A 'repast'!" Eugene broke in with a laugh. "That's th
ticket. But forget about droppin' me off! I want to see Sylvester
too."

"Silvestro?" the Contessa said in a choked voice, putting
hand to her throat.

"Yes, Countess Barbara, good old Sylvester! I want to sa
good-bye. Poor fellow wasn't lookin' all that good the last time
I saw him."

The Contessa gave Urbino a pleading look. She clearl
feared that Urbino was about to pull down her secure littl
world of Asolo.

"Maybe I'll make some arrangements with Sylvester fo
next year," Eugene said with a wink at the Contessa. "You migh
have more than one boy from New Orleans on your hand
before you know it, Countess Barbara—but I promise you I'l
be a lot more rambunctious than Urbino!"

The Contessa told Milo to go to Occhipinti's directly, de
spite Urbino's repeated suggestion that she be dropped off a
La Muta. When the Bentley pulled up beside the arcade of th
Via Browning, Urbino got out quickly.

"Hold on there, Urbino," Eugene said. "Don't forget m
and Countess Barbara."

"I think Barbara will be more comfortable staying here."

Urbino looked pointedly at the Contessa. She collapse
against the seat as if she no longer had any energy.

"You can go back to La Muta, Barbara."

"I certainly will not. I'm staying right where I am."

Despite her determined words, the Contessa's eyes wer
painfully vulnerable. Urbino didn't like to leave her like this bu
he had little choice. As it was, he had to deal with Eugene, wh
was probably thinking only of a fond, apparently temporar
farewell to Occhipinti.

They came to Asolo together one day about a month ago. I'm

22

As URBINO AND Eugene went under the arcade and up to the door of Occhipinti's building, an elderly woman was coming out. She glared at them suspiciously but let them go in. A dog was barking sharply.

Urbino hurried up the stairway to the third floor, Eugene right behind him. The dog's barking became louder and sharper, then was followed by a yelp of pain. There was no doubt that the dog's cries were coming from behind Occhipinti's door.

Urbino knocked as hard as he could.

"Sylvester!" Eugene called from behind Urbino. "It's Eugene and Urbino. Is your little dog all right?"

Eugene went up to the door and pounded on it. Urbino tried the doorknob. The door was locked.

"Let's see if we can break the door down," Urbino said.

Without waiting for an explanation, Eugene pushed his shoulder against the door. It hardly budged.

"Let's get a good runnin' start," Eugene said.

Urbino and Eugene went to the banister and then ran together toward the door. They both hit it with their shoulders at the same time. The lock gave way and they were carried by their own momentum into the room.

"What the hell!" Eugene said as he took in the scene.

Pompilia had resumed yapping and was circling the sofa. Sprawled on the sofa, flat on his back, was Silvestro Occhipinti. At least Urbino assumed it was Alvise's old friend, for the still, small figure's face wasn't visible. How could it be beneath its burden?

As he and Eugene ran to the sofa, Urbino wondered if the last words poor Occhipinti might have seen in his long life—if in fact it were now truly over—were,

Open my heart and you will see,
'Graved inside of it "Italy."

For these were the words embroidered on the silk pillow that
Ladislao Mirko was holding over the face of the birdlike little man.

Footsteps clattered up the stairs. Three carabinieri in blue
uniforms rushed into the room. Behind them, out of breath,
was the Contessa, her eyes wide with worry.

Death over Gelato

THE CONTESSA INSISTED.

Five minutes later a matching *Coppa Duse* was placed in front of Urbino on the plant-screened terrace of the Caffè Centrale in Asolo. The Contessa, in a silk chiffon tea gown in an antique rose print, sat across from him in the filtered sunlight. The only sounds were the soft conversations at the other tables, the playing of the winged-lion fountain in the piazza, and *La Traviata* spilling out of an open window.

"It will help soothe you, *caro*, as you give me the rest of the grim and grisly details."

It was Wednesday afternoon, two days after Urbino and Eugene had burst in on Ladislao Mirko holding the Browning pillow over Occhipinti's face. Alvise's old friend was recuperating at La Muta with his faithful Pompilia, and both should soon be walking up and down the streets of Asolo together again.

"You know the worst of the details now," Urbino said, his spoon poised over the whipped cream soaked with blue syrup. He had already told her on Sunday about Lorenzo and Violetta's affair, their plot against Regina, and Lorenzo's sexual abuse of Flavia—his own daughter, as they now knew.

He had never seen the Contessa so stunned—so stunned,

in fact, that she hadn't immediately registered that she could stop worrying about Alvise.

"I feel abominably guilty," the Contessa said now, already well beyond her whipped cream. She was looking considerably better than she had. The deep rose of her print dress was complemented by a gentle glow in her cheeks. "I've gained so much"—Urbino's eyes couldn't help but flick in the direction of her *coppa* as she said this, which wasn't lost on her—"and it's all been at poor Flavia's expense."

Urbino knew what she meant. It was the turmoil and ghastly events of Flavia's life, ending in her death at Ladislao Mirko's hands, that revealed the young woman's accusation for what it actually was—a desperate attempt at denial and evasion, at remaking her life.

"Of course, Barbara, Brollo denies that he ever was anything but the perfect father to her—denies that she ever broke down the last night of her life and accused him, once she no longer had the illusion that he actually *wasn't* her father, of all the terrible things he had done to her."

"Oh, we've turned over a rock, haven't we? Such repulsive white squirming things under it! I definitely feel more revolted than enlightened."

"There are things we'll never know for sure." Seeing an apprehensive look come into her gray eyes, he quickly added, "But I don't mean about Alvise."

"You're sure?"

He reached out and touched her hand.

"Absolutely. Brollo and Violetta admit that Flavia was their daughter but Brollo denies that he ever touched her in any but a fatherly way. Although he admits that she made those accusations—he can hardly deny them since Annabella heard them—he says that they're one more indication of how disturbed she was."

"And disturbed she well might have been, being brought up in that atmosphere! She couldn't trust anyone, could she? Not the schizophrenic Regina whom she loved as her mother, not Annabella who hated her, and certainly not Lorenzo! And not even her real mother, Violetta. Flavia *thought* she could trust her, but Violetta didn't tell her the truth until the night of her death. And then there was Ladislao Mirko."

Yes, Ladislao Mirko had ended up confessing everything

to the police, admitting that Flavia had made not one but two
visits to the Casa Trieste on the fateful Thursday evening. She
had come back to the pensione after leaving the Palazzo Brollo,
distraught over Lorenzo's corroboration that she was definitely
his daughter and that Violetta was her mother. She told Mirko
everything she had learned since leaving him two hours earlier.

It was then that Mirko betrayed Flavia the first time that
night by getting carried away as he tried to console her in the
manner he had always wanted to. All the years of holding back,
of pretending to have only a brotherly feeling for her, had
become too much for him. What had been smoldering for so
long finally burst out into flame. His attack on Flavia was also
consistent with his earlier attack on the drugged-out girl from
Verona that Corrado Scarpa had mentioned to the Contessa.

The second time that night that Mirko betrayed Flavia's
love and trust—this time irrevocably—had been near the water
steps of the Ca' Volpi. He had pursued her there after she
left the Casa Trieste, revolted by his advances. There he had
murdered her.

"When Flavia ran out of the pensione into the thunderstorm and he went after her," the Contessa said, continuing her
decorous demolition of the *Coppa Duse* and leaving Urbino far
behind in his own efforts, "Silvestro saw them, right? Part of
his recuperation seems to be to tell me over and over again
about his first visit to the Casa Trieste. He feels terribly guilty
about it."

"And he should, although I doubt he could have prevented
Flavia's death. Even if he could have kept up with them that
night, he wouldn't have been able to follow them into the Ca'
Volpi. But he should have mentioned it to the police or to me.
By comparing the times we would have known that Flavia had
been to the pensione twice that night."

"But Silvestro says he never thought that Mirko had killed
Flavia. He thought that Mirko was going after her to calm
her down and that she killed herself later," the Contessa said.
"Otherwise he would have been too frightened to go back to
the pensione afterward and take those clippings from the scrapbook. He never would have let Mirko into his apartment. Mirko
told him that he was looking for me. Silvestro only wanted to
help me—and Alvise. That's all he ever wanted to do."

"And all Mirko wanted to do was to get him out of the

way—once he realized that Silvestro was the man he had rushed past outside the Casa Trieste the night he murdered Flavia."

The Contessa shivered and put down her spoon, eyeing Urbino's own rapidly melting *Coppa Duse*.

"Did you ever suspect that Silvestro might have killed Flavia?"

"The finger certainly seemed to be pointing at him on various occasions. He was in Venice at the time of the murder, he knew where Flavia was staying, he had a motive—to protect Alvise and you—and he was not being completely honest. He says he didn't mention being outside the pensione the first time—the night Mirko murdered Flavia—because he didn't want us to think that he could have done her any harm. Silvestro wasn't thinking very clearly, was he? And he was acting very suspiciously because of it. But he became less and less of a suspect as facts about Mirko started to fall in place. There was the scratch on his face that Mirko said he got from his cat. There were the pills that Flavia apparently never took, pills that we now know Mirko planted in her room, knowing their reputation and hoping that they would make suicide seem more probable. Then Mirko, starting to run scared as I got closer to the truth, asked Annabella the name of the man she had sent to the Casa Trieste. And the biggest thing of all was the death of Mirko's father. I had no way to prove it, but I had a hunch that something wasn't right there. Vladimir Mirko had physically abused his son, and his son decided not to take it anymore. Gemelli says that Mirko is now whining and telling them the whole sordid story. He killed his father and made it seem like an accident from freebasing cocaine."

"Obviously Mirko could see murder as the only solution to his problems. He would probably have eventually gone after you!"

"Yes, and maybe even Bernardo Volpi for fear of what he might have seen."

"Did Bernardo see anything?"

"I thought he might have, but apparently not."

"But why did Flavia go back to the Ca' Volpi after her second encounter with Mirko?"

"Maybe she wanted to have it out with Violetta—or be consoled by Bernardo whose affection was untainted with anything suspect. Mirko was right behind her. He says he passed

an old man at the end of the *calle* by the Casa Trieste when he
rushed out after Flavia, but he didn't pay him much mind until
later, as I've said. Flavia went to the Ca' Volpi where she used
her own key to get in. Violetta wasn't there. She had gone to
see Lorenzo."

"Leaving Bernardo all alone?"

"Yes, but he was asleep. Flavia went to the studio, telling
Mirko to stay away from her. When she didn't find Violetta, she
tried to get away from Mirko by going into the garden. They
argued. Flavia was shattered. You can imagine how she must
have felt about what she learned that night! Mirko still couldn't
seem to understand how his sexual advances back at the pensione had almost pushed her over the edge. He tried to put his
arm around her, this time in the kind of closeness they used to
share, and she shoved him against the water gate. He almost
crashed through it into the Grand Canal. It was either then or
earlier that she scratched his face. He doesn't remember. The
thunder was very loud, and there wasn't much water traffic
because of the storm. Some lights had recently burned out by
the water steps. I noticed that the gates had been forced out
toward the Grand Canal from the garden, not the other way as
might have happened if someone had broken in from the water
side as Violetta thought.

"Flavia let Mirko know in a big rush what she thought of
him now—how much she despised him—how he had left her
with nothing to believe in, not even friendship—how she had
stood by him when everyone had said he was bad and made fun
of him because he was ugly—how he should understand her
feelings more than anyone else because of the way his own
father had treated him—how she had always understood why
he had killed his father, but that now she saw him for what he
really was and maybe she would tell someone else if he didn't
leave her alone. In a rage he picked up one of the stones from
the pile near the water steps. He hit her several times and
pushed her into the Grand Canal. Then he ran from the Ca'
Volpi."

"How horrible!"

"And off he went back to the pensione to start covering his
tracks and to take possession of the money Flavia had put in his
safe, the large sum left over from what Massimo Zuin had
bribed her with. It was a financial windfall—something Mirko

got out of Flavia's death in addition to not ever having to worry that sometime in the future she might let it out that he had killed his father."

"Maybe it was Mirko's idea all along to kill Flavia for the money," the Contessa suggested. "How much was there?"

"Enough. Zuin had given her ten million lire—almost eight thousand dollars. Flavia had given Tina about a third of it, saying, if you remember, that it was hers anyway, although she didn't mention that it had come from Tina's father. She gave the Riccis another million. I wondered what became of the rest of it. Was it lost in the water? Was Flavia robbed and then murdered? Or had she left the money somewhere for security? Mirko's safe, I thought. The money had to be very tempting for someone with a drug habit but I don't think he would have killed Flavia for the money. In his own way, he did love her"— the Contessa started to protest but Urbino raised his hand and continued—"but in the end his fear that she might reveal that he had murdered his father was stronger than his love. He probably regretted many times that he had confided in Flavia but—"

"When did he confide in her?" the Contessa asked, this time succeeding in interrupting him. "And why would he?"

"He did it about ten years ago after Flavia moved out of the Palazzo Brollo and trusted him enough to tell him what Lorenzo had been doing to her. Wanting to show her how much he, for his part, trusted her, Mirko told her that his father's death hadn't been an accident as everyone thought. Mirko was in love with her. He would have done anything for her, maybe even have killed Lorenzo. When Tina Zuin told me about the 'secret sharing' game that the three of them used to play, I started to ask myself what kinds of secrets might have passed between Flavia and Mirko. Once I knew about Lorenzo's sexual abuse and had my hunch about Mirko's father, the two fit perfectly. I admit that I was misled for a time because Mirko was a help to us, up to a point, in looking into the business of Alvise. He gave me the scrapbook—although only after looking through it again to be sure that Flavia hadn't said anything about his father, Vladimir."

"Whatever 'help' Mirko seemed to give was all for his own devious ends!"

"True, and like any person trying to conceal murder, Mirko had a lot he had to be careful about revealing," Urbino went on. "And drugs were complicating matters for him, confusing his mind. Should he remain completely silent or dole out some information? And how much would be too much? How much would be too little? Mirko never really knew what he should tell and what he shouldn't. Yet he did know that if he could incriminate Lorenzo while giving me the impression that he didn't intend to, it would look better for him. And he was right. He always had to be careful not to show any knowledge of what had happened to Flavia after she left his pensione the first time."

"Did he?"

"Almost. When I awakened him suddenly from his stupor late Sunday morning and told him he hadn't been honest with me, he was frightened. He thought I knew about Violetta being Flavia's mother and had found out somehow that *he* knew about it because Flavia visited the pensione a second time that night. He was frightened, but he recovered quickly enough when he recalled the other big secret of Flavia's life—Lorenzo's sexual abuse. Later I remembered his reaction and started to speculate and—"

"And eventually pulled out a plum that's left us all gaping! You realized he was close to the breaking point and that Silvestro, Bernardo, and you might be in danger! I think I understand, but why didn't Mirko mention the sexual abuse earlier?"

"He was crafty, always looking out for himself when his mind was clear. My guess is that he didn't want to seem *too* eager to make Lorenzo look bad. After all, almost everyone said Flavia's death was suicide, and he was better off leaving it that way. Maybe he realized that Lorenzo's sexual abuse was too close to what he had done to Flavia himself. And who knows? He might have been afraid of giving himself away, of pointing me in one of the worst directions if he was to continue to avoid detection."

"But he did show you that horrible Dalí that Flavia ripped from the catalog. The painting almost shouted about Lorenzo's sexual abuse to anyone with even a suspicion of what might have gone on between Lorenzo and Flavia."

"I'm not so sure Mirko understood its significance. He

might have believed that she had ripped it out to give him because of the Yves Tanguy on the other side."

"I'll never—absolutely never!—be able to look at that Dalí painting again. *The Birth of Liquid Desires* indeed!"

Urbino smiled to himself. The threat and self-denial in the Contessa's statement were minimal considering how she had always felt about Dalí and how infrequently she even went to the Guggenheim Collection.

"I've never cared particularly for anything by Dalí," Urbino said. "Flavia was at an impressionable age when Violetta introduced her to him, and she was fascinated with *The Birth of Liquid Desires*. But it's obvious why she started to feel differently about it later when Lorenzo's sexual attentions became so aggressive. She might even have associated Regina, Violetta, or Annabella with the other woman in the painting whose face is averted, thinking they might have known or *should* have known. After all, Annabella *had* known what was going on. As for Violetta, she now realizes that Flavia was trying to tell her about Lorenzo's sexual abuse in indirect ways. I'm surprised Flavia didn't try to slash the Dalí as well as Novembrini's portrait."

"Such a sad young woman—and definitely emotionally unbalanced. But how could she help it? Look at the way she had to live! And she had the Grespi blood running in her veins. Genes have a strange way of asserting themselves. She ended up looking more like Regina—her aunt—than her real mother, Violetta. Just think of it. One Grespi sister emotionally disturbed for most of her life—and then the other one! Violetta!" The Contessa said the woman's name with quiet contempt. "She and Lorenzo are almost as responsible for their daughter's death as Mirko. They put everything in motion over twenty-five years ago for their own selfish—yes, even *fiendish* reasons! I'm not throwing the word out lightly, *caro*. I don't care if Regina agreed to the whole thing either. She was in no position to be allowed to. Her sister and her husband should have protected her. The whole thing was diabolical, I tell you! Violetta ended up protecting herself and having her revenge against both Regina *and* me at one blow. As for Lorenzo himself, he's beneath contempt. To think that nothing can be done to him! He murdered Flavia in his own way. He murdered her soul!"

The Contessa seemed to contemplate this final statement

for a few silent moments, as Urbino recalled what Flavia had said to him in the *salotto verde* at La Muta: that a person's soul shrivels up when someone he loves and trusts betrays him. Then, rousing herself, the Contessa asked why Lorenzo hadn't let the truth about Violetta and him come out after Regina died.

"Maybe he was afraid of what Flavia might do to herself or to him if she knew the truth. He was caught up in the lies for so long that he was probably comfortable with them. Maybe it assuaged his conscience to have his daughter believe that he wasn't her father. Lorenzo seems to have been convinced that she committed suicide because of what he had done to her and how he and Violetta had deceived her. He must have been afraid my treating her death as murder would bring everything to light—as it eventually did. He gave Mirko money, ostensibly to cover Flavia's bills at the pensione, but he must have been hoping he could buy Mirko's silence if he knew about the sexual abuse."

The Contessa watched as Urbino desultorily attacked his *coppa*.

"What about Nicolina Ricci?" she asked.

"Her death could have triggered much of Flavia's subsequent actions. What had happened to Nicolina—being raped by a trusted family friend, someone like an uncle, someone around whom Flavia had never felt comfortable, seeing in him what she had seen in Lorenzo—was too close to what had happened to her years ago. That must have been the significance in Flavia's inscription on Nicolina's funeral wreath: 'From your older sister'—not sisters by blood, of course, but because of similar experiences. Nicolina's murder reopened all the wounds. And don't forget that Lorenzo was showing an interest in Novembrini's nude portrait of her. We don't have Flavia here to tell us what was going on in her mind. She was very careful in whom she confided—apparently only Madge Lennox and Mirko, possibly Nicolina. There must have been something about Bruno Novembrini that she didn't quite trust despite their intimacy."

"You don't think that Madge Lennox and Flavia—"

"I don't know," Urbino cut her off. "It's not important, is it? You wouldn't want to begrudge the poor girl whatever consolation she found as long as she wasn't deceived or taken advantage of." The Contessa looked rebuffed. "What is important is that Flavia trusted Lennox—that she felt safe and secure in Asolo with her. There's no suggestion that Lennox let her down. You can imagine how important trust was for a woman who had been betrayed the way Flavia was."

"Yes—and how vile silence and secrets are!" The Contessa's face was shadowed with sadness. "What do you think that poor girl really wanted from me, Urbino?"

"To accept her as Alvise's daughter. If you had done that, it would have been more real for her, and she would have been even more distanced from Lorenzo. I have a feeling that Mirko wanted her to try to extort money from you, but money isn't what she wanted."

"So it was my peace for her own. Oh, Urbino, I would have done what I could for her! I keep seeing that old photograph of her she showed us at La Muta. If there had continued to be the slightest bit of doubt, I would have accepted her. I would have mothered the poor thing."

"I know you would have, Barbara. You would have made a big difference, but it wasn't meant to be."

"'Wasn't meant to be'—I suppose that's less disturbing than saying something could have been different, that there was a choice we failed to make. I'm not thinking of you and me—of what we did or didn't do for Flavia—but of Alvise and me. It wasn't meant for us to have children. If Flavia had been given to me in the painful way I was almost beginning to accept, I would have considered her as something from Alvise after all these years. It's madness to say it—especially since I wasn't put to the test, was I?—but I would have. I would! I've always tried to convert the bad things that come my way into something good. I'm far from believing that every cloud has a silver lining—I leave that philosophy to you Americans!—but sometimes we have to refashion our pain."

Urbino thought the Contessa was going to end on this somewhat philosophical and perhaps even puzzling note, when, after taking a quick sip of mineral water, she went on.

"And you know, Urbino, even though all we've gone through has made me only too aware of the sadness that can befall the Flavias and the Nicolinas of this sorry world—and the Mirkos, too, I suppose—I wish that Alvise and I had had our chance for that kind of happiness. I regret that Flavia was

natched from me. I could have made a difference in her life."
She paused. "She could have made one in mine."

Urbino could add nothing to her heartfelt admission. He
finished his gelato. When the waiter came over to take the empty
goblets, the Contessa ordered another *coppa*.

"I don't care what anyone thinks today. I need to be
soothed. It has absolutely nothing to do with appetite!"

Together they looked out at the placid scene. The jitney
bus had just pulled in from the bottom of the hill and three
young women descended. A boy on a bicycle waved to the
women as he flew across the square and down the Via Browning.
An old woman was watering geraniums at a window above the
opposite arcade. When she finished, she stood at the window
smiling and listening to the music of *La Traviata* still filling the
afternoon air.

The Contessa broke the spell by bringing up Flavia's tape
recording of the nurse Graziella Gnocato's statement.

"It must be somewhere at the bottom of the Grand Canal
or sucked into the mouth of a trash boat," Urbino said. "But it
doesn't matter now. It never really did. It had nothing to do
with the truth."

"And the attack on you in San Polo?"

"It wasn't connected with the scrapbook—or with Flavia. It
was just one of those things."

"Listen to you! 'Just one of those things'! You're aiming for
a blasé note but it falls flat, *caro*. I know you were terrified, as
well you should have been!"

The Contessa looked at Urbino with a bemused expression
for a few moments. Urbino sensed that she wanted to say something but wasn't quite sure how to bring it up. When she spoke,
he realized she was taking the direct approach.

"Tell me, *caro*, what are you going to do with Novembrini's
painting of Flavia when Massimo Zuin delivers it to you after
the Biennale?"

"Keep it. Will that bother you?" Urbino said, being as direct
in his answer as she had been in her question.

"I'm not a Philistine, Urbino. I think you know that, even
if I can't bear Dalì and his ilk. It's just that it makes me sad to
think of that painting. Poor Flavia! To think that Lorenzo
wanted it for his private collection. But maybe you're right
about it, Urbino. Keep it as a grim memento. Who knows whose

hands it might get into otherwise? At least we're sympathetic to its history. As time goes by we might be able to look at it without a pang although I know I'll never be able to like it."

The waiter brought over the Contessa's second *Coppa Duse*.

"Could we put aside this whole sad story for a while, *caro*?" the Contessa said with a sigh as she picked up her spoon. "Let's put the rock back down in place."

The Contessa dipped her spoon into the blue-drenched whipped cream. A yellow and black butterfly landed momentarily on her shoulder, perhaps mistaking her floral print for the real thing, and then fluttered off toward the geranium plants across the square.

"Tell me, wasn't Evangeline supposed to have come to Venice?" she said teasingly. "Don't tell me you've left the poor girl languishing, albeit in luxury, at the Cipriani while you stay cool and aloof here in Asolo!"

Urbino told her that Evangeline had decided against coming to Venice and had gone to Rome instead. When he explained about Keats, Shelley, and the Protestant Cemetery, the Contessa's well-arched eyebrows rose fractionally.

She finished another spoonful of the *coppa* before saying, "My! Two graveyard romantics! How could such a marriage of true minds ever have foundered? Tell me, then. Will this meeting in thunder and lightning take place?"

Urbino had had little time to think about Evangeline during the past few days. Since Monday when Eugene told him about her move to Rome, he had been busy with the authorities in Asolo and Venice. Last night at the Palazzo Uccello he had tried to think things through, but hadn't been able to get far before Flavia inevitably intruded. Only toward the end of his solitary hours, with Serena in his lap and Mahler's Fifth Symphony on the player, had he made a decision.

"I'm going to Rome for a few days," he now told the Contessa, "but there won't be any trip to the cemetery."

"Should I be relieved? Why aren't you making a ghoulish visit?"

"Because I know Evangeline. I know how she thinks. If were to go to the cemetery, it would be an acknowledgment that I wanted to begin something with her again or that I might be considering it—and neither is true."

"I see! You don't want to keep your ghoulish appointment because you loathe being manipulated."

The Contessa nodded her head, as if she had found the skeleton key to all her friend's peculiarities.

"But I've decided to go to Rome, haven't I? She's manipulated me into that."

"So that's how you *do* see it! In that case, you should stay right in Asolo and not budge an inch. Summer is absolutely marvelous here, you have to agree. We'll 'do the social' together, take walks, hide away in the *giardino segreto* where I'll tell you over and over again how much I appreciate what you've done for me and how I'd never do anything to hurt you. Maybe we can even plan another *fête champêtre* together to make up for my garden party."

"I *have* to go, Barbara," Urbino said, surprised at his apologetic tone. "If I don't, Evangeline will misinterpret it. She'll think I still have some romantic feelings for her that I would rather not deal with. Besides, I have no ill will toward her. She might have hurt me at the time by taking up with Reid and I wish she had been honest with me instead of having me find out the way I did, but I take a lot of the responsibility. I wanted to protect her more than I loved her. I see that more clearly now than I ever have."

"It's amazing what even an intelligent man won't allow himself to see until he has to!" the Contessa interjected.

"And now I finally want to put it all behind me," Urbino persisted, "and the best way is to see her. I'll take the train to Rome tomorrow with Eugene. Evangeline and I will go to dinner, spend some civilized hours with each other, maybe go to the Borghese Gardens or the Villa Farnesina, and talk about the good times. She'll see that I care about her and wish her well, but nothing more. Perhaps I *am* being presumptuous to assume that she has something else in mind now that her marriage to Reid seems to be over, but if I stay up here it won't do either of us any good. Things would be unresolved between us. I don't want her to wonder why I didn't come to Rome. And *I* don't want to wonder why either!"

Urbino and the Contessa remained silent for several moments. Then, under his breath so that the Contessa only heard an indistinguishable mumble, Urbino whispered, "*Colla fami-*

glia—the family glue." Urbino had long been fascinated by this play on words which also meant *con la famiglia* or "with the family." The expression had more resonance for Urbino now than it ever had.

In Italy so much was done *with* the family, so much was done *for* the family and, most decidedly, *because* of it. The family was, indeed, like a glue that held its members together, but not always for their own emotional health. One of the light-emitting diode signs from the previous Biennale came back to Urbino again: "Even Your Family Can Betray You." The history of Flavia Brollo's family revealed this clearly and tragically—as did Ladislao Mirko's relationship with his abusive father in which both father and son had betrayed each other.

And the family glue was there also in the Hennepin family, although admittedly to a lesser extent, where it was as thick as the molasses made at the Hennepin sugar houses.

Yes, the family glue. Urbino had resisted it, and he didn't regret that he had.

"I'll have Milo drive you and Eugene down, *caro*," the Contessa said, apparently accepting his decision to go to see Evangeline in Rome. "Perhaps I can come along, too. August is an atrocious time for Rome, but I haven't seen Alvise's cousin Nerina in ages."

"It would be better if I went alone, Barbara."

"Believe me! I have no wish to intrude on 'auld lang syne'! But remember, it can be a somewhat bitter brew. As you wish, *caro*, but my squadron of Roman spies will tell me if you slip off to the cemetery," she added with a smile, apparently having recovered from her brief high dudgeon.

The waiter came to their table for the empty goblets.

"*Un'altra Coppa Duse per il signore*," the Contessa told the waiter.

"But, Barbara, I don't want another one."

"Wanting has nothing to do with it! You need a lot of soothing this afternoon, *caro*. I'm concerned that you make your descent on Rome cool, calm, and collected. If you don't, who knows what will happen?" The Contessa looked at him earnestly, as if to show him how much it would pain her if certain things were to happen in the Eternal City. Then her gray eyes became mischievous. "And if by chance you can't quite finish your *coppa*, I'll help you. Don't you know that's one of the things I want most in the world to do?"

Perhaps seeing the confusion he felt, she quickly added, "I mean, of course, my desire to *help* you. Poor, muddled, well-meaning men like you bring that out in a woman."

"If you really mean that, Barbara, would you tell me something?"

Urbino made a long pause.

"Well, what is it, *caro*?" the Contessa asked with a touch of impatience.

"Would you tell me why I'm *really* going to Rome?"

The Contessa laughed, seeming to take his question less seriously than he had intended it.

"I thought you'd never ask, but let's wait for the *coppa*," the Contessa said, reaching across the table and touching his hand.

When the *coppa* came, however, the Contessa delayed giving Urbino the benefit of her opinion until he turned the whole concoction over to her, permitting himself only an initial spoonful. Then, with a smile on her attractive face that made Urbino wonder whether it was in anticipatory relish of the gelato or of her imminent illumination of him, the Contessa launched into just why *she* thought he was going to Rome to meet Evangeline—and a long, involved explanation it proved to be.